Joanne,
Thank you for
Loving my boys!
♡

RECKLESS & RUINED

The Chicago War, Book Two

BETHANY-KRIS

Bethany-Kris

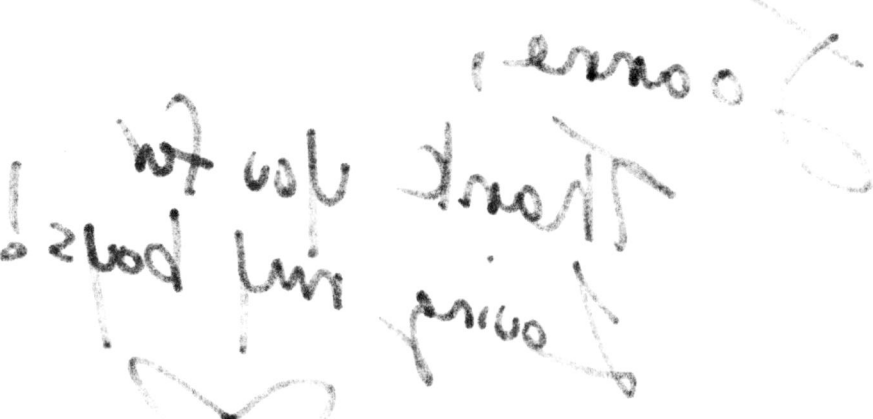

Copyright © 2015 by Bethany-Kris. All rights reserved.

WARNING: The unauthorized distribution or reproduction of this copyrighted work is illegal. No parts of this work may be used, reproduced, or printed without expressed written consent by the author/publisher. Exceptions are made for small excerpts used in reviews.

Published by Bethany-Kris

www.bethanykris.com

eISBN: 0-9947909-8-9
eISBN 13: 978-0-9947909-8-9
Print ISBN: 0-9947909-9-6
Print ISBN 13: 978-0-9947909-9-6

Cover Art © Jay Aheer
Editor: Dominique S.

This is work of fiction. Characters, names, places, corporations, organizations, institutions, locales, and so forth are all the product of the author's imagination, or if real, used fictitiously. Any resemblance to a person, living or dead, is entirely coincidental.

For Tracy.
One of the best people I've met in this writing journey of mine.
Thank you.

CONTENTS

PROLOGUE

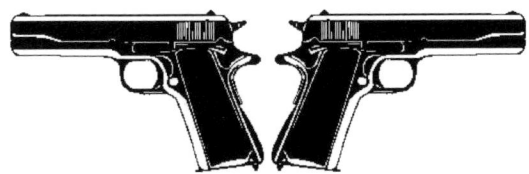

"You're only young and stupid once."

Alessa thought that had to be the dumbest thing she'd ever heard. "Exactly. You're only stupid once, Dean. In my family, that means you only get one chance not to mess it up. Because if you do, you're screwed."

Dean laughed, taking another step toward Alessa. She backed further under the willow tree, keeping a safe distance between her and Dean. The guy was cute, as far as that went. It was just about the only thing he had going for him and cute didn't add up to a whole hell of a lot when your personality was seriously lacking. Dean didn't seem to understand the word 'no' when Alessa said it.

It was just too damn bad his father was a Capo in *la famiglia*. For Alessa, that put her in a bad situation whenever Dean showed up. Terrance, Alessa's grandfather and the boss of the Outfit, didn't mind Dean or the guy's father.

Dean screamed bad news in the worst way.

She didn't care that he was affiliated with the Chicago mob at only eighteen-years-old or that he was as arrogant as they came. No, that wasn't it at all. Alessa's biggest issue with Dean was that his interest in her only went as far as her position as Terrance Trentini's granddaughter. Dean didn't like Alessa because of who she was as a person, but rather, he liked the people she came from. The guy just wanted to situate himself with a pretty face, a good last name, and a piece of ass to get him higher in the mob.

Alessa wasn't going to be that girl.

"Come on, Alessa," Dean said, grinning as he took another step toward her. "Go out with me and have some fun tonight."

"Like how you took my sister out last month?" Alessa asked.

Dean's jaw tightened. "We're just friends."

Right.

Alessa loved her sister Abriella, as far as that went. But Abriella was a little on the wild side and didn't know how to follow the rules. If she went out with Dean, it wasn't because the two were friends. And if Abriella didn't take Dean out again, he definitely wasn't worth Alessa's time.

"I didn't realize I had the word idiot stamped on my forehead," Alessa said, smiling as sweetly as she could manage. "Let me go wash that off for you so there's no confusion the next time we meet."

Using her sarcasm as an easy and obvious way out of the conversation, Alessa ducked under the low lying branch of the willow tree and headed back toward the Trentini mansion. She didn't make it very far. Dean caught up to her before she could get out of the privacy of the tree, grabbed her around the waist, and pulled her back into his chest.

"Hey, let me go," Alessa barked, jerking away from Dean.

Dean held tight. "Come on, Alessa. Don't be like that. We both know—"

"—That you're a fucking tool," Alessa interrupted hatefully.

Dean grabbed even harder, squeezing the air right out of her lungs. Panic saturated Alessa's insides, freezing her in place as Dean grabbed the ends of her wavy brown hair and tugged firmly enough for it to really hurt. All of the air in Alessa's lungs rushed out in a whoosh.

"Be nice and stop acting like such a spoiled little bitch," Dean said in her ear.

Alessa shivered, the disgust rolling thick. "Let me go, Dean."

"No, I think we're good here. First time I've actually been able to get you alone. I think you're one of those girls that likes to tease and fuck around with a guy until he can't take it anymore and just snaps. Then you get it rough just like you like, right?"

"No," Alessa whispered.

She didn't know what he was talking about, but she didn't like it. Fear compounded in her heart. She was too far away from the back of Trentini mansion to be heard even if she yelled at the top of her lungs for help.

Alessa felt stupid for having left the afternoon party without taking someone with her, but everyone else was busy doing their own thing. She had just wanted to get the hell away from Dean and his constant badgering. When she thought Dean wouldn't notice her missing, Alessa took the chance to slip out of the back of the house and take a walk on the large property. She needed the breather. Dean followed her like the creep he was.

Dean's hand drove down Alessa's back to her ass where he grabbed her through her summer dress. When he tried to stick his hand under her dress, Alessa yelped and pulled away from him fast enough to take him off guard. Spinning in her ballet flats, she struck him on the cheek with her open palm. The sound of the slap reverberated through the quiet hush of the wind whistling through the tree leaves.

"You bastard," Alessa hissed, readying to hit him again if he came near her. "I am not some piece of ass for you to handle however you want. Don't you understand that I don't want you? I have never wanted you, Dean! You're a self-righteous, entitled, disgusting little prick. And you'll be lucky if I don't tell my father and grandfather what you just tried to do to me!"

Dean laughed a dark sound. "Your father? You mean the guy who isn't even good enough to be in with the Outfit, but just a used up lawyer for your grandfather? Get real, Alessa. What is he going to do to me, huh?"

"Terrance—"

"Your grandfather thinks I'm made of gold," Dean interrupted with a cruel smile. "Go on ahead and whine to him all you want, but he isn't going to believe you. In fact, if my father gets his way, I'll be standing there to meet you at the end of an aisle while you wear a white dress. Keep holding onto your skirt like that's going to protect you, Alessa. I'll get it one way or the other."

Alessa felt sick. "Fuck you."

Like hell and over her dead body. She would never marry this man.

"That's the plan, babe," Dean said, smirking wickedly. "Even if it takes me a little while to get you there. You're sixteen now, but eighteen is just around the corner. How long do you think you'll last after that before your grandfather marries you off to the best man he can find in the Outfit? Right now, I'm looking mighty fucking good to him."

Alessa barely held back the vomit. She trembled from her head to her toes as her hands balled into tight fists at her sides. "I'd slit my throat first."

"So dramatic. I like a crazy girl. They're always fun."

What was wrong with this guy?

"Plus, you know Ben will make it happen," Dean added with a wink. "He's best friends with your grandfather and all. My uncle wouldn't mind getting me a little closer to the top. You have to admit, we'd make a damn good pair."

At Ben DeLuca's name, Alessa barely managed to supress her shudder. Ben happened to be the right-hand man to Alessa's grandfather and Dean's uncle. Dean, being the son of Walter and Patricia Artino who were both thoroughly integrated with the DeLuca side of the Outfit, had a great deal of power behind him. Maybe even as much as Alessa had behind her. Patricia, Ben DeLuca's younger sister, was also close to Alessa's mother.

A marriage between her and Dean would put the Artino family front row and center for once. They were usually overshadowed by the DeLuca side of their family when it came to the mob. Alessa would not be that family's way to the top, regardless of whatever plans Dean and his father might have for her.

"Keep dreaming," Alessa said, refusing to show Dean how his words affected her. Trentinis didn't show fear, ever. Her grandfather wouldn't marry her off to a man like Dean, right? "Because that's all you're ever going to get from me."

Her words didn't seem to faze Dean a bit. As he spoke, he moved toward her again. Slowly, one step after another, he came closer to Alessa like she was a mouse and he was a snake ready to swallow her whole. She felt cemented to the ground, unable to move or run.

"Think about it, Alessa. Your grandfather needs to set something up for when he's good and done running the Outfit. Your father isn't in with the family."

"My brother—"

Dean barked out a laugh that chilled Alessa to the core. "Joel? He's such a fuck up. Get your pretty little head out of the clouds, girl. He's not going anywhere. Terrance is going to go for the next best thing—marrying his granddaughters off to the strongest and best families he can find. Look no further, Alessa. I'm exactly where you're heading in the foreseeable future."

Dean was close enough to reach out and grab her again if he wanted. She refused to give him that chance. Alessa's legs finally decided to catch up with her screaming mind and pounding heart. She turned to bolt out of the cover the willow tree provided and ran straight into something hard.

The strong arms of Adriano Conti caught Alessa before she hit the ground. Something akin to a sob caught in her chest as Adriano righted her without a word and moved her slightly behind him. Alessa fisted her hands into the back of Adriano's T-shirt like it was the only lifeline she had left.

"You all right?" Adriano asked, never taking his glare off Dean for a second.

"Yeah," Alessa mumbled. "I'm okay, Adriano."

"Good."

Alessa felt Adriano's hand reach back and cover hers. He squeezed her hand and then let it go. Adriano Conti was the same age as Alessa. They even went to the same private school. His father was heavily involved with her grandfather and the Chicago mob, seeing as how Riley Conti was the Outfit's front boss.

What Adriano had never done, was pay Alessa very much attention. He stuck to his side of the Outfit, and Alessa stuck to hers. They passed one another by from time to time at family dinners and parties, but they didn't make an effort to be friends. Adriano was the high school football star, a mob *principe* for the Outfit, and a player on and off the field. Every single girl Alessa knew had tried to get a piece of this guy—her not included.

That didn't mean she never wanted to, though. Alessa would be a damned liar if she ever said Adriano wasn't gorgeous and interesting to her.

The contrast between Dean and Adriano under the willow tree as they had a stare down was visible to Alessa. Adriano might have been two years younger than Dean, but he towered over the man by at least six inches. Dean was tall and lean, but Adriano was built like the linebacker he was. He had broad shoulders, thick arms, and a stance that screamed for someone to back off.

Alessa could feel the muscles in Adriano's back tighten like coils ready to spring. He practically vibrated under her touch. His teeth bared as he sneered in Dean's direction like the guy was nothing more than a worm to be crushed under his shoe.

"Artino," Adriano said, tipping his chin in Dean's direction. "I thought that was you I saw following Alessa out here earlier."

Dean scowled. "What about it?"

Adriano shrugged. "Nothing. But when a girl says back off, it means get the fuck away before she decides to hand you over your balls."

"We were just having some innocent fun. Right, Alessa?" Dean asked.

Alessa glowered at him. "Sticking your hand up my dress is supposed to be fun for me?"

At that admission, Adriano lurched forward, going straight for Dean with a fist raised. Because Alessa was still holding onto Adriano's shirt, she went with him. Luckily, Alessa managed to catch herself and let go of Adriano. Dean flew backward, his hands raised high in the air.

"Whoa, careful there, Adriano," Dean said, grinning like an idiot. "You wouldn't want to piss your father off by messing with someone affiliated."

"Not made," Adriano said through clenched teeth.

"What is that?"

Adriano flicked his hand in Dean's direction like he was dismissing him and his warning. "You're not made which means, you're not important. I don't give a fuck about you or your father."

Dean scoffed. "We both know that isn't true."

"Wrong. Your first mistake was fucking around with a Trentini, but your second was assuming you know a goddamn thing about me." Adriano looked like he was ready and revving for a fight with Dean. Alessa didn't want to get Adriano in trouble, but she didn't think speaking up would stop him from kicking Dean's ass. "I suggest you make your way back to the house before you end up eating your teeth and you're stuck with sucking your food through a straw for the rest of your life."

"I—"

"Fuck with someone else," Adriano interrupted coolly. "She's not your toy."

Alessa watched in fascination and confusion as Dean turned around and stalked off. Once she knew he was out of hearing range, Alessa finally relaxed enough to step away from the safety Adriano had provided her.

"Thank you," Alessa said.

Adriano sighed, crossing his arms as he stared in the direction Dean had disappeared. "He's something else."

"A jerk."

"I was going to say something worse, but that works, too," Adriano muttered. "Don't thank me for getting you out of that, but where in the hell is your brother?"

"Joel?"

Adriano nodded. "He's the only brother you've got, right?"

"Somewhere. I just wanted to get away from the party."

Adriano didn't look like he believed a word coming out of her mouth. "Actually, you were trying to get away from that fucking piece of shit. I saw how he was following you around and pestering you. Speak the hell up, Alessa. Nobody will stand for his bullshit if you say something about it."

"He's never done anything like this before," Alessa said.

She wasn't trying to defend Dean. His actions were beyond contempt. But he had never once gone as far as he had today.

"Right, whatever," Adriano said, shaking his head. "What was he going on about before I stepped in, anyway?"

Alessa cringed, not wanting to go into that. Knowing Adriano, he probably wouldn't care about Alessa's fears of being married off. "Nothing."

"Hey."

"Yeah?" Alessa asked.

Adriano took a step closer to Alessa. Unlike before with Dean, she wasn't bothered by his close proximity. He reached out and tipped her chin up by using two of his fingers. She was at least a foot shorter than him and looking up made her feel incredibly small.

"Speak up, Alessa," Adriano repeated softly.

"Nobody around here cares what a girl has to say, Adriano. You know that."

"I care."

Did he?

Alessa blinked, surprised. She didn't know what else to say, but she wanted to get as far away from the topic of the Outfit as she could. "How's football?"

Adriano cocked a brow, smirking. He watched her with his green eyes like she was the most important thing to grace his presence for the moment. The guy had skills. Alessa had to give him that.

"Boring," he finally replied. "Football is boring."

"Really? You seem to like it a lot."

"I like a lot of things."

"I noticed," Alessa said before she could stop herself.

"Did you?"

Alessa's cheeks heated under his heavy regard. She dropped his stare.

"I just … never mind."

"Hey, don't do that," he said, ticking his fingers under her chin again. Alessa couldn't help but look at him. "Never do that, Alessa."

"I'm not doing anything."

Adriano laughed deeply. "Sure you're not. Don't be embarrassed, Lissa."

No one called her that except her close friends at school and her family.

"I notice a lot of things about you, too," Adriano added.

Oh.

"Did you?" Alessa asked.

"Mmhmm. You don't like football all that much, do you? I never see you hanging around the team spots or showing up at games and whatever."

Alessa wondered why he had looked for her at all.

"No, I don't like it all that much," she replied. "The football players at our school have big heads and little brains."

"All of us?"

Alessa smiled at his question. "Some of you. Maybe you could convince me otherwise."

"Maybe," he echoed.

"Are you interested in trying?"

Adriano flashed his white teeth in a sensual grin. "Very."

CHAPTER ONE

Ruined.

That was exactly how the Outfit felt to Adriano Conti.

The Chicago mob had always been the one thing Adriano trusted to never let him down. The Outfit—*la famiglia*—was supposed to be based on a strong foundation of beliefs, loyalty, and unity between men. It was supposed to be home.

It didn't feel anything like home to Adriano anymore.

"My condolences," one person said, squeezing Adriano's hands.

"You're in our prayers, son," said another.

Adriano said nothing.

He had nothing to say.

The people kept their voices low and their eyes down. Someone had killed Adriano's mother. As she stood at a table, defending her nephew against her own sister, Mia was shot in the side of the head by a drive-by shooter.

No one knew why. No one had any answers.

Instead, Adriano's father Riley was going after the next best thing for revenge, which was someone to blame. The boss didn't need to apologize for his non-involvement in the shooting. Terrance had been sitting at the table when the shooting happened. He could have just as easily been shot and killed, too. Riley needed to feed his anger and his grief. He needed to feel better. Adriano was sure his father would end up ruining the Outfit in the process.

Mia Conti's casket lowered into the ground. Adriano had already said goodbye to his mother. Her blood had coated his hands when he tried to save her life. Those visuals plagued him day and night. Whenever things got too quiet or his grief caught up with him, Mia's memories took him to a calmer place.

Mia had always been like that. For a woman involved with the Outfit, a woman who had married a made man in the mafia simply because her father told her to, Mia Conti had been a gentle soul. Adriano remembered

14

his father adoring his mother. Their marriage had been a close one, but one with struggles, like Riley's infidelity. Adriano wondered how his father could be so in love with his mother, but still have women on the side.

He wasn't angry like his father was. He was heartbroken. He didn't blame the Outfit, but he did hurt.

"To the car, son," Riley said gruffly.

Adriano jolted from his thoughts at his father's order. "What?"

"The car, let's go."

The final moments of the funeral and burial had passed him by. Most of the guests were slowly making their way out of the cemetery. Adriano's sister, Evelina, tossed a single white rose into the grave before she blew a kiss at her mother's casket and then turned away from the grave. Evelina was taking their mother's death hard. She didn't know how to deal. Adriano didn't know how to help.

A splinter of pain settled in his chest. Two men, groundskeepers for the cemetery, picked up shovels and uncovered the mound of dirt. Adriano thought his mother was far too good to be covered with mud.

Adriano still wasn't ready to leave. "Give me a few. I'll meet you at the car, Dad."

"All right."

Adriano watched the men begin to fill in his mother's grave. By the time he turned to leave the gravesite, the rest of the mourners had all gone. The overcast, windy Chicago day felt appropriate for the July funeral. Adriano walked along the pathway in silence, making his way toward the road where his father had parked the Mercedes.

"Adriano ..."

The whisper of his name made Adriano come to an abrupt stop on the path. He looked around but saw nothing.

"Over here," came the familiar voice.

Adriano couldn't help but smile as he caught sight of Alessa Trentini under the birch trees lining the edge of the cemetery. She wore the same black dress from earlier in the day when her family arrived at the funeral, ready to give their condolences for Mia's death. Riley kicked them out, demanding Alessa's grandfather leave immediately.

The Outfit's boss barely blinked at Riley's show of rage. Terrance gave his front boss what he wanted without question and left.

Adriano hadn't gotten the chance to speak to Alessa. He'd been more concerned with getting his father calmed down so the funeral could start and finish peacefully. By that time, Alessa had left with her family.

Just seeing her standing under the trees made Adriano feel better for the moment.

Regardless, Alessa still showed up at the burial after the church fiasco. That made all the difference to Adriano. She'd probably defied her grandfather's wishes and somehow snuck out to get to the burial site. It gave Adriano a little bit of hope that maybe, despite the fact that everyone around them seemed to hate one another, there was still a chance some didn't. There was a chance that she didn't hate him.

Adriano didn't want Alessa to get in shit for coming to him. If his father noticed her there, he would probably give Terrance another warning about keeping his family far the fuck away from the Contis.

Every inch of Adriano screamed to go—to move—to Alessa's side.

He'd felt like that about her for as long as he could remember. Their friendship had started when they were teens, but it didn't stay innocent for long. Adriano knew every inch of Alessa Trentini. He knew what she felt like, her tastes and all her sounds.

Alessa was kept in a bubble wrap of protection by her family. The boss made his granddaughters seem like they were above all reproach, like they were some kind of fucking angels. Adriano knew the risks he took messing around with Alessa at times, but he couldn't find it in himself to give a goddamn.

She always kept him at a safe distance. He figured she did that for her heart.

Fuck.

She didn't realize that he didn't know how to hurt her even if he tried.

Adriano stayed frozen on the walk, not wanting his father to notice their unwanted guest. Well, she was only unwanted to Riley.

Raising his hand high enough for her to see, Adriano mouthed, "Hey."

Alessa flashed him a small smile. "Hey."

Her hand raised up and she touched her lips with two fingers, as if to tell him to be quiet.

"I'll see you soon," Alessa said quietly, her words traveling with the breeze.

He hoped so.

"What should we do about it?"

"We wait it out, of course," Riley replied.

"Wait it out?" Kolin asked.

"Absolutely." Riley sipped from his rum and coke. He waved at the server as the young woman walked by and said, "Get me another one of these, honey."

Adriano rolled his eyes, frustrated with the entire meeting. His father had gathered his most trusted men in the Conti family and crew together to discuss the recent shooting. Someone driving Serena Rossi's car—they all suspected it was Laurent—had shot up Riley's new bar. The shooting of the Conti business by the Rossi family had been a troublesome thing to wake up to. Riley was pissed, but he brushed it off.

Adriano did, too.

Laurent Rossi's alcoholism was seriously starting to show if his rationale was so gone that he couldn't understand what it would mean to shoot up a fellow family's bar. Laurent was struggling to keep Terrance Trentini's respect and friendship. In his failed attempt to show where his loyalties truly were, he had done nothing more than dig his own hole deeper.

"It's like this, I have no issue to take with the Rossi family," Riley said, waving at the ten men sitting around the booths. "Laurent has had his problems for years. His wife likely pushed him to do it—the idiot always did pant after her ass like a dog in heat. The statement he made by shooting up my business does not reflect on the rest of his family. Believe that."

"Can you be sure?" Adriano asked his father.

"I'm inclined to side with the men who have reached out to me with an apology."

"Who?" Kolin asked.

Kolin Bastoni was a close Capo and friend to the Conti family. He also happened to be Riley's first cousin. He ran a good portion of the Conti territory under Riley's watch. Adriano had worked under the man for a long time—since his sixteenth birthday, actually.

Loyalty was everything to a man like Kolin. And he was incredibly loyal to the Conti family. His first reaction was to retaliate on anyone who hurt Riley or the man's family. A lot like the rest of the men in the Conti crew.

"DeLuca," Riley finally replied.

"Ha, which one?" Kolin asked.

Riley smiled a cold sight. "That's the million dollar question, isn't it?"

"As long as it isn't Theo," another one of Adriano's father's men put in. "You know how close he is to the Trentini crew, boss."

Riley didn't even blink at that title. In fact, he acted like the man hadn't even graced him with it. Adriano didn't like his father's reaction to being called the boss at all. There was only one boss in the Outfit— Terrance Trentini. Adriano's father might be the front boss to the public, the men on the streets, and to the FBI, but everyone who was anyone in the Chicago mob knew who the real boss was.

Claiming a title that wasn't reserved for you only spoke of two things. One, you either had a big enough ego that you believed you were eligible to fit the title. Or two, you were ready to go after the position to wear the title properly.

Adriano didn't know which one his father fell under. Neither would lead to anything good.

"Well, we can safely say one of the men who reached out isn't Ben DeLuca, anyway," Riley said, shrugging. "Being Terrance's underboss, old Ben wouldn't wipe his own ass without his boss's approval."

"That only leaves one with any worth behind his name," Kolin noted.

"It does," Johnnie, another close friend to Adriano's father, agreed. "Dino DeLuca. What'd he say?"

"That he understands and sympathizes with my frustrations," Riley said as he accepted a glass of rum and coke from the server. "Thank you, honey."

Adriano didn't bother to hide his glare. Just like how his father didn't bother to hide the way he watched the server's ass sway back and forth as she walked away. Adriano didn't understand Riley for a minute. One day, he was entirely overtaken with his grief over the loss of his wife, and the next, he was acting like an asshole.

It wasn't unusual behavior for his father, as far as that went. Riley never hid his interest in women other than his wife as Adriano grew up, but it was still a dick move. They just buried Mia a week before.

"Dad," Adriano snapped.

Riley cleared his throat, waving off the warning in his son's tone. His attention was back on the conversation at hand in a blink. "Dino is a good ally to have, as are his men."

"Dino's looking at prison time soon," Adriano said.

"Still, his men are of a similar opinion."

Adriano sighed. "*Some.*"

"Some are better than none, son. You will do well to learn that. And we have more than you think."

"So, we wait this out," Kolin said.

"Wait it out," Riley echoed. "Terrance has more than enough issues to deal with right now with all of his men divided between the families. Laurent's actions against me only pushed some along further in that. This is good. We can use this to our advantage."

"What, we just let them fight amongst themselves for a while?" Adriano asked.

"Yes," Riley replied.

Why would his father want to do that? If a reconciliation was what Riley might be looking at, letting the feud continue wouldn't lead to anything good.

"In a way," Riley said. "I'd prefer to hit him when he is weak, you know."

"Good plan," Kolin replied.

That had to be the most ridiculous thing Adriano ever heard. Adriano was not in agreement with his father about whatever plans he might have had for the Outfit's boss. It was dangerous and the feud was getting more volatile every day. Riley was obviously taking some kind of joy in that.

In fact, Adriano was starting to wonder if his father even gave a damn about Mia's death. Riley acted like his retaliation was for his wife, but his actions spoke of something different. Like maybe Adriano's father was more interested in the boss's seat but was using his wife's death as a reason to get there.

It was fucking sickening.

"No, it isn't a good idea," Adriano snapped, never taking his eyes off his father. "You're planning to go after—"

"Enough, Adriano," Riley said, cutting his son off. "Your opinion is not important."

Adriano felt like he was being torn in two different directions. One was his father, the other, the Outfit. If Riley kept feeding the issues until they were big problems that nobody could fix, that would only mean one thing: War.

"What are you trying to do here, Dad?" Adriano asked, ignoring the curious gazes of the other men in the restaurant.

"Exactly what I set out to do, son."

Which was what?

Adriano couldn't figure that out. How long had his father been thinking about taking control of the Outfit? How many people were going to be divided and torn apart because Riley was greedy?

Without a doubt, Adriano understood loyalty. He was devout to his family, but his family had always been more than just his mother and father. Riley raised him that way. He raised Adriano to trust and protect the Outfit. His father's plans wouldn't protect anything if revenge was what it was all about. No, there was no protection here, not for the Outfit. It would downright *ruin* it.

A pretty brunette with blue eyes filled Adriano's mind. He'd always protected Alessa Trentini, too. He couldn't do that when his own father could be the one to hurt her.

Riley smiled, setting his drink to the table. "Everything will work out. To our favor, that is."

Adriano didn't believe his father for a second. "What if this blows out of control?"

"Feed the flames, of course," Riley replied.

"Mom wouldn't want that," Adriano pointed out.

"Women and children are supposed to be untouchable," Riley murmured.

Adriano frowned. "I'm aware."

"Your mother wasn't included, Adriano. You will do well to remember that, son."

"I—"

"You will do well to remember that, son," Riley repeated firmly, his tone offering no room for argument. "And because you are my son, I don't have to tell you again how important blood is to us. I have repeated these things to you ever since you were a young boy. It has always been an eye for an eye. You need to learn how to curb what you want from the things that are more important. *We* are more important than your wants, Adriano."

Adriano's gaze narrowed. "Stop dancing around whatever you want to say and spit it out."

"You know what I'm saying, Adriano. You're thinking with the wrong head again, aren't you?"

Alessa.

Adriano didn't even blink. "No."

"You always were a terrible liar, son."

"Take a walk with me, Adriano." Riley tipped his head in the direction he wanted to go. "How does a cup of something sweet sound to you?"

Adriano nodded, not wanting to aggravate his father any more than he already had that morning. Despite not agreeing with his father on a lot of things, he did love his father. They had always been close and even now, just a few months shy of his twenty-first birthday, Adriano looked up to his father.

"Sure, Dad."

Riley waved down the street. "There's a little sidewalk vendor right down the street with the best chocolate gelato."

Ice-cream.

Adriano chuckled. "What am I, five?"

"You always liked gelato," Riley said quietly. "Do you want the gelato or not? Because I'm going to get myself some whether you do or don't, but you will be following me either way. We're due for a good talk without others listening in."

"I don't like chocolate." Adriano was more likely to enjoy a cold beer on a hot day than eat a bowl of chocolate flavored ice-cream. "But if you're paying, I'll have some."

Riley smirked. "Figures. The have that strawberry flavor you like, too.

Let's go."

Adriano followed alongside his father. The quiet street was devoid of traffic for the most part, but it was still early. After a good ten-minute trek, Riley stopped at the vendor with the brightly colored sign advertising gelato and the favors offered. Once his father had ordered the two cups and the creamy treat had been paid for, Adriano let Riley find them a bench to sit on further down the street.

"Eat," Riley demanded.

Adriano glanced down at the cup of strawberry gelato. He wasn't interested in food, but clearly his father had a motive behind this little ... whatever it was. Sticking the tiny spoon into the gelato, Adriano took a decent sized bite and waited his father out.

Sometimes, with Riley Conti, it was all about the wait.

"Three cars down across the street, left side," Riley said.

Adriano followed his father's gaze to find a cobalt blue Porsche with windows tinted dark. "I know that car."

"You should. It belongs to Damian Rossi."

Ah.

Tommas Rossi's cousin and right-hand man for his portion of the Rossi crew.

Everyone suspected Damian's role in the Chicago mob had everything to do with helping to run a crew, but Adriano knew better. Damian was nobody's man except for the boss's. Terrance never outright said it; he didn't have to. Damian did all the dirty work that Terrance didn't want to, like the killing.

Quiet men were dangerous men, after all.

Damian was certainly a quiet man.

"What is he doing around here?" Adriano asked.

"Business, probably," Riley replied. "He might be marrying a DeLuca, but he's got no allies to speak of. Damian never was any good at picking sides in a fight. He only ever picks his side, but that's a good way to be, too. You see, that way, he doesn't lose."

Point taken.

"Aren't you worried that Terrance might have sent him around to spy on you?"

Riley laughed. "No. Believe me, if that were the case, I wouldn't have seen Damian at all. There is a reason why we call him Ghost, Adriano."

"I'm aware of his skills, Dad." Adriano stuck another spoonful of gelato in his mouth before saying, "You know, stuffing my mouth full of food won't stop me from arguing with you."

Riley eyed his son, smiling. "You're too perceptive for your own good, Adriano."

"No, I just know you."

"Truth. We're very much alike, son."

"And entirely different," Adriano muttered.

"That we are," Riley agreed quietly. "You're angry with me."

"Figured that out, did you?"

"There's no need for your mouth to make an appearance, son. But yes, I'm very aware of your feelings. You've made them clear more than once." Riley made a disapproving sound under his breath, adding, "And you know better than to do that, Adriano. Challenging me like you have been, it's ridiculous. I won't stand for it. Family is most important. You know that. I expect you to be loyal to me at all times, son."

"I thought the Outfit was the family. That's what you always said."

"It is," Riley replied.

"Family forgives, Dad."

"Not this one, Adriano."

"Mom's body isn't even cold yet," Adriano said.

"Your point?"

"You're already looking for the next hole to fill, Dad."

Riley scowled. "Adriano—"

"I can't help but wonder if you're just using her death as an excuse to get something else that you want. And if that's the case, you're just an asshole."

"Watch yourself, son. You're treading a very thin line." Riley stood from the bench and dropped his full cup of gelato into the trash can. "I think we've talked enough."

"I think we haven't said nearly enough," Adriano replied, unfazed at his father's anger. "The least you could do is tell me the truth. Is this about Mom's death or is it about what you can gain from it, Dad?"

"It's about the family—*la famiglia.*"

Adriano wasn't sure his father knew what that was anymore.

"Your mother would understand," Riley added.

"I doubt it."

Adriano rushed through the office door leading into his father's private space without even knocking. He knew better, but he just didn't give a damn. The phone in his hand buzzed with yet another text, someone else confirming what he already knew.

Riley glanced up at his son's entrance, but continued on with the conversation he was having on the phone. "Yes, well, sad thing … I'm aware. Let him believe that, I don't care."

"Dad," Adriano growled.

"I absolutely did not!" Riley blew out a heavy breath, rubbing at his temples. "As I said, let him believe that. When I make my move on behalf of my wife, Terrance will damn well know it. Trust that."

Riley slammed the phone down without another word.

Adriano clenched his hand around the cell phone he held, a pressure growing in his chest. "Tell me you didn't do that."

"Ah, you know about the shooting," Riley murmured.

Another shooting.

More people were killed.

This time, the attack had happened at the Trentini mansion. From the information Adriano had been able to gather, a drive-by shooting after one of Terrance's usual dinners had taken the life of one Rossi and nearly killed the Outfit's underboss, Ben DeLuca. The man would be lucky to make it through the night with his life, actually.

Adriano hadn't expected to get that frantic, frightened call from Alessa Trentini. He'd missed her call because he'd been collecting payments from guys on the streets for his father. But the voicemail from Alessa … it'd *scared* him. He tried calling her back, but Alessa wasn't answering his attempts.

"Things had calmed down," Adriano said, his hands shaking in his rage.

"Not entirely." Riley shrugged like it didn't make a difference. "And regardless of what I say, you have clearly settled yourself on the idea that this shooting was ordered by me."

"Wasn't it?"

Adriano wouldn't be surprised.

"No," Riley replied. "I don't know who did it. It wasn't me or my men."

"I want to believe you."

"But you don't."

"No," Adriano said.

Adriano didn't take his eyes off his father for a second. Without knowing it, Riley had hurt Adriano in the worst way. Not with the act itself, but because of who had been the one to call and tell Adriano it happened.

Alessa.

She was *there.*

There might as well have been a giant, invisible wall building higher and higher between Adriano and his father. Riley was doing it all. Adriano's growing resentment was nothing more than a by-product.

"You're taking this too far," Adriano told his father.

Riley frowned. "I didn't do the shooting."

"You don't have to pull the trigger, remember? That's what you said about Mom."

"I didn't order it, either," Riley said shortly.

Adriano scoffed. "I still don't believe you."

"How dare you?" Riley shouted.

Adriano stepped into the living room of his family home just in enough time to see his father grab his sister by the arm. Riley shook Evelina fiercely.

"Stop," Evelina whimpered. "I'm sorry!"

Pain and fear washed over her features as tears streaked down her cheeks. Adriano's anger bubbled up to the surface fast and harsh. Never had he witnessed his father use any kind of violence against Evelina.

Evelina wasn't perfect, as far as that went. She liked to push against the rules their father set out for her, but Adriano didn't blame her.

"Hey, back off," Adriano warned, stepping closer to his father and sister.

He hoped his presence was enough to force his father to let go of Evelina without Adriano actually needing to step in. Adriano had a good four inches of height and fifty pounds of muscle on Riley. When that didn't work, Adriano jumped in between his father and sister. He shoved his sister back before giving his father one hard push. Riley smacked the wall with a thud but bounced right back like he was going to come at Evelina again.

Evelina, like the smart girl she was, stayed behind Adriano's large form.

"Back off, Dad."

"I'm sorry," Evelina repeated in a whisper.

Riley glared at his son, waving at Evelina. "Do you know what she did? Do you know?"

"I just got here to have dinner like you wanted, Dad," Adriano said through clenched teeth. "I've been running around for you all fucking day. No, I don't know what she did."

But with the way Riley had been going on lately, like he was five seconds away from losing his shit, Evelina could have breathed wrong and she'd be in crap.

"She went there," Riley barked.

"I just wanted to see—"

"You shut up, you little bitch."

Adriano took a step toward his father, zoning in on the man like he was prey. "That's enough, Dad."

Riley scoffed. "Oh, Adriano. You have not yet reached an age where you scare me, son."

"Do you want to test that theory out?" Adriano asked.

Adriano didn't move a muscle. Neither did Riley.

"I'm sorry," Evelina repeated softly.

"What happened?" Adriano asked.

"She went to that fucking wedding," Riley muttered, his voice full of hate and disgust. "After I told her not to, she still went. She, like you, clearly doesn't understand what loyalty means."

"I do!" Evelina cried. "But Lily is—"

"Nothing to us," Riley interjected cruelly. "A Rossi now—*nothing*."

Adriano felt for his sister. Evelina and Lily DeLuca—although she'd married a Rossi today—had been friends ever since they were just kids. Evelina was supposed to be in the wedding but the war between the families forced her to drop out of the party. Or rather, Riley demanded it of her.

"And who took you?" Riley asked.

Eve glanced away. "I went myself."

"You're lying."

"I am not!"

"You are," Riley ground out. "I will find out who took you, Eve."

"What does it matter?" Adriano asked. "She went and she's home. Nothing happened."

"I don't expect you to understand, Adriano," Riley spat.

"What is that supposed to mean?"

"Don't act stupid. You couldn't even follow through with the one thing I asked of you to do, son."

Adriano sighed, more frustrated than ever. Two weeks earlier, after the mess of the Trentini shooting had calmed down, Riley went after the Rossi crew. Despite acting like Laurent's attack on a Conti business hadn't mattered to him, Riley still went after the men of the Rossi crew. Adriano was starting to get whiplash with the games his father was playing.

"You retaliated like you wanted to. I didn't have to be a part of it. Have you got what you wanted yet, Dad?"

Riley smirked. "Not even close."

"Keep spilling blood and you'll eventually drown in it," Adriano bit out.

"Then I'll die a happy man," Riley said unaffected. His attention turned back on Evelina in a blink. It spoke volumes about how Riley felt toward his only son in that moment—an afterthought and entirely unimportant. "If you can't follow my rules, Evelina, I will not give you another chance to break them. Your dorm is gone. I will have two enforcers follow you to your dorm tomorrow. I want it emptied and your keys handed over. Welcome home, sweetheart."

Eve nodded. "Okay."

With another dismissive wave of his hand, Riley left his children. Adriano turned on his sister, wondering why she had defied their father when Riley was in the state he was.

"Why would you do that, Eve?"

Eve sniffed, wiping at her tears. "I wanted to wish her luck before she walked down the aisle. That was all."

Shit.

Adriano hated it when his sister cried. "Why didn't you tell Dad who took you?"

"That would have just set him off even more," Evelina said.

"Because it was someone from another family."

"Yeah."

"Who?" Adriano asked.

"Theo," Evelina whispered.

"DeLuca?"

"Yes."

Fucking *hell*.

CHAPTER TWO

Someone was always watching Alessa Trentini. Even the walls had eyes.

"Alessa, that had better not be something with alcohol in it," Terrance said, sneaking the glass from his granddaughter's hand before she could protest. He sniffed it, and then handed it back. "Smells clean."

"Because it is."

Terrance believed his granddaughters didn't lie to him. That was one of his biggest mistakes. Being raised in a family that was front row and center in the Outfit meant Abriella and Alessa needed to be above reproach. It didn't matter that their father wasn't a made man in the family, because their grandfather was the boss and he made all the goddamn calls.

"I never know with you two," Terrance said, smiling slyly at Abriella who stood beside Alessa. "I don't mind you girls drinking occasionally but tonight is not that night. Stay sober and smile for the guests. It is the least Damian and Lily deserve after the last couple of weeks. We don't need any issues at this wedding. They would surely like a quiet, happy night to start their lives off with."

Alessa couldn't help but agree with her grandfather.

The Outfit had been in the midst of a feud for a couple of months that only seemed to grow with every passing day. It started with a shooting at a restaurant and spiraled wildly out of control. Mia Conti died at the restaurant shooting. Her husband Riley blamed Terrance for reasons that were tied up with another family that wasn't even involved with the Outfit. The four major families involved with the Outfit had either taken sides with Riley or Terrance while the ones who hadn't were left struggling to keep the peace. Another shooting happened right in her grandfather's driveway during a party.

Alessa shuddered but hid it well enough. She had been present for both shootings and lucky enough not to be hurt. Watching Mia Conti die while Adriano tried to save his mother's life was something Alessa couldn't forget. And then again in the driveway of her grandfather's home, a place that was supposed to be safe, she watched two more people struggle for life because of someone's choices.

Someone no one knew.

They all had their suspicions. Riley blamed Terrance for Mia. Terrance blamed Riley for the retaliation. The DeLuca's were staying quiet but with the marriage between the Rossi family and theirs, that wasn't a surprise. The Rossi family had retaliated on the Conti family, but refused to admit their involvement even with video proof.

Alessa knew more than she was supposed to about the feud. Blissful ignorance wasn't safe. Being involved with the Chicago mob was a dangerous thing. Now, it was more dangerous than ever.

"We're being good," Alessa told her grandfather.

Terrance laughed. "Good is a relative term that rarely applies to you Trentini girls. Just keep your noses clean, *capisce*?"

"Yeah, we got it," Abriella said.

"I'm going to find your brother and parents before calling it a night. I'll see you both at my home *before* morning, yes? We're having breakfast tomorrow, you both promised."

Alessa had to force herself not to roll her eyes. "Of course."

The two Trentini sisters wouldn't want to anger their grandfather, after all. The best way to get what they wanted from Terrance was to bat their eyelashes, follow along with whatever schemes he had, and dazzle the crowd just the way he liked.

Alessa and Abriella had played these games for longer than they knew how to count.

"Joel will drag us home at an appropriate time," Abriella assured their grandfather.

"Good." Terrance waved a finger in the air, smiling. "Remember, there are a lot of eyes in here on you two tonight. Do not shame me, girls."

When Terrance was gone, Alessa shot Abriella a look. "Is he serious?"

"As a heart attack," her sister muttered. "I need a fucking drink."

Turning, Alessa scanned the crowd of guests at the DeLuca-Rossi wedding. Abriella had been the bride's maid of honor. Alessa spotted the bride dancing with one of her older brothers. Lily Rossi looked happy as Theo DeLuca spun her around and around. The groom was nowhere to be seen.

"Where's Damian?" Alessa asked.

Abriella shrugged. "Maybe he's off with Tommas somewhere."

Alessa eyed her unusually quiet sister. Abriella seemed withdrawn, which was odd. She liked a good party and tonight was a prime opportunity to let loose a little, even with the watchers.

"What is up?" Alessa asked.

"I'm twenty-one," Abriella murmured.

"So?"

Alessa was twenty. What difference did their age make to the conversation at hand?

Abriella nodded out toward Lily. "She's happy, you know."

"Seems like it." Alessa was happy the arranged marriage worked out to Lily's favor. A lot didn't where a woman was concerned. Men of the families made all the calls and the women were just expected to follow along with no questions asked. "Damian is an okay guy."

"He is," Abriella agreed sadly.

"Seriously, what is up with you?"

Abriella shrugged. "I'm twenty-one, Alessa. How much longer before that's me?"

Oh.

Alessa frowned. She didn't want to dwell on it or have her sister worrying about it, either. "With all the crap going on in the Outfit, that's probably the last thing on Terrance's mind."

Abriella scoffed. "Where in the hell have you been living for the last twenty years, Lissa?"

"With you."

"Exactly. You know better. Feuds are the perfect time for arranged marriages, and we're both aware of what that shit means."

Abriella was right. More often than not, scores and wars were settled by spilled blood and joining families. Marriages wiped slates clean and made apologies that a man wouldn't say otherwise. Alessa and Abriella were fresh meat for the market.

Goddammit.

Alessa sighed. "Sorry, you're right. I just wanted to get your mind off it. We're supposed to be having fun tonight."

Abriella said nothing as she gazed across the dance floor. Alessa followed her sister's stare to find Tommas Rossi leaning against a far wall in the shadows. The family Capo didn't seem to have much interest in the crowd, but instead, he was watching Abriella, too.

Alessa wasn't surprised.

"I guess Damian isn't with his cousin," Alessa said.

"Apparently not."

Alessa knew what her sister was going to ask before the words could even leave Abriella mouth. "Go, Ella."

Abriella chewed on her bottom lip, her gaze flitting over the people before darting back to Tommas. "Should I? Here?"

"If you don't, he looks like he's about to make his way over to you."

The smallest smile tugged at the corners of Abriella's mouth. Alessa's older sister had a way about her. Ella was quiet and fierce. She had a stubbornness that could rival a mule and a crazy side that Alessa was a little jealous of.

Because the two sisters were only a year apart in age, they were close. Alessa knew her sister's secrets, including the biggest one of them all. Tommas Rossi. The family Capo had been messing around with Abriella since she was eighteen. Alessa covered for her sister since they shared an apartment together and went to the same college.

Alessa didn't mind.

"Be careful," Alessa said.

Abriella nodded quickly. "I will."

"Say hi for me and watch out for Joel," Alessa warned.

"Will do."

Abriella handed her empty drink off to a server as the man walked by. Without another word, she disappeared into the crowd, walking the opposite way from Tommas Rossi. Alessa watched with a smile growing as Tommas waited, watched the direction where Abriella went, and then made a beeline straight for the same spot.

The two played their game well.

Sighing, Alessa gaged the crowd again. While Damian and Lily Rossi weren't exactly big time in the Chicago mob, the two had certainly given quite a show for the guests tonight. Lily's brothers were both rival Capos and since her uncle had been the underboss in the Outfit before his death, merging in marriage to another family was a huge deal. Guests of the Outfit's syndicates from all over the States had been invited to the wedding. Even a couple of the Guzzi family members from Canada had shown up to celebrate.

Alessa found her brother in the crowd, completely oblivious to the fact his sister had just disappeared with Tommas on her heels. Joel only gave a damn about Abriella and Alessa if they could do something for him. Otherwise, he was a lot like their grandfather in a way.

Don't shame me.

Right.

Joel could be an entitled, cocky asshole. Just seeing him chatting with someone affiliated with the Vegas Cosa Nostra family made a chill run down Alessa's spine. Joel Trentini only talked to syndicates when he was looking to set something up. Alessa tried to keep up to date with most of the important events in the Outfit. That way, little came as a surprise to her.

Nothing was happening other than the feud between the four major families and tonight, three of those families were sharing a space for the sake of a wedding. Maybe if it kept on this way, the Conti family would eventually be pacified into reconciling. Alessa hoped so.

She didn't like the fact that her brother was making small talk with a syndicate like he didn't want anyone else to hear. Little problems had a way of growing much bigger and Joel was sneaky sometimes. He thrived on drama when he figured he had something to win from it all.

The only thing her brother could possibly do was force the divide between the families wider. Alessa didn't want to see the Conti family pushed further away than they already were. The DeLucas would surely follow the Conti side now that Ben DeLuca was dead after being shot at the Trentini home weeks ago. Theo and Dino DeLuca were much closer to the Conti family than the Trentinis.

The Rossi family was still a toss-up.

Where did that leave Adriano Conti?

Where did that leave Alessa?

Thinking about Adriano made a dull pain settle into Alessa's heart. Adriano, Riley Conti's only son, was another casualty in the Outfit's mess. Because his father was fighting with Alessa's grandfather, their families had been pushed apart. The two had never put any titles on one another that would get them into trouble with the Outfit. Adriano had been the one person who got close enough for her to let in besides her sister. She kept her heart protected, because her availability was never guaranteed as the granddaughter of the boss, but Adriano had a way of breaking through her walls.

Nothing was ever easy.

Alessa cleared her throat and downed the rest of her drink, not wanting to stay on those thoughts for long. A form crept in beside Alessa, making her tense. Dean Artino said nothing as he watched the guests mingle. Alessa wondered what game the guy was trying to play with her today.

Dean backed off on Alessa a lot over the years, but he still managed to insert his nasty self into her life every once in a while. Mostly, Adriano's presence kept Dean at a safe distance. Her grandfather and brother had always considered Adriano a chaperone of sorts for Alessa, one that wouldn't cross any lines and knew the rules.

They didn't know a damn thing. Alessa and Adriano broke those rules in the back seat of his 1969 Camaro SS just after her seventeenth birthday.

But with the Conti and Trentini families fighting, Alessa was left without her *chaperone*. Dean had apparently taken notice as he'd been around a lot more lately, leaving Alessa feeling ickier than ever.

"Evening, Alessa."

"Dean," Alessa greeted politely.

She figured there was no reason to be rude to the man. Not yet, anyway.

"I didn't see you at Ben DeLuca's funeral," Dean said, giving her a look from the side.

Alessa shrugged. "I was there."

In the back, far away from Dean.

"Sad day," Dean murmured.

"It was."

Dean laughed. "No, I meant today."

Alessa's brow furrowed. "Why is today a sad day? The wedding was beautiful and the couple is happy. You can't ask for much more than that."

"DeLucas shouldn't marry lower than their status," Dean said in explanation. "That would be like Abriella running off to marry whoever she wanted. Lily married into the Rossi family. That's a goddamn shame."

"You forget your last name isn't DeLuca, Dean."

"My mother's was."

Alessa fought the urge to roll her eyes. "Just because Ben was my grandfather's underboss—"

"Soon to be my father," Dean interjected lowly.

"What?"

Dean grinned. The sight was almost predatory in nature. "With Ben gone, a seat needs filled in the family. Terrance might have looked to Riley as an underboss for a while but with the whole mess going on right now, that isn't going to happen."

"Dino DeLuca," Alessa said instantly, referring to the bride's oldest brother. "He'll be considered the head of the DeLuca family with Ben dead."

Dino was a Capo in good standing, and for the most part, ran a great portion of the DeLuca crew alongside his now deceased uncle, his brother Theo, and Dean's father.

"He could easily step into Ben's spot," Alessa added.

"Sure he could," Dean agreed. "Except that nasty trial he's got coming up. Everybody knows Dino is going to spend the next twenty years behind bars, doing hard time. And before you toss out Theo DeLuca's name, let me stop you. The guy is too young."

Adriano was young, too, Alessa thought, *but he had a great deal of control with the Conti crew.*

"Like you're any better?" Alessa snorted indelicately. Her politeness had run its course where Dean was concerned. "You're only twenty-two."

"I said my father, not me."

Alessa shivered, hating the very thought of Dean getting any higher in the mob than he was. As far as she knew, Dean wasn't made, yet. His father, Walter, didn't have a high enough standing to give his son the button just because he wanted to. Dean didn't have the family clout behind him that others in the Outfit had.

But if his father was being considered for Terrance's new underboss ...

Christ.

That would all change.

"Such a shame," Dean repeated quietly, shaking his head as he continued watching Lily Rossi dance with her brother. "I don't know why Ben stood for that. She married down, Alessa. Ask anyone."

Alessa didn't have to. "She didn't marry down. You're just being a snob."

Dean smirked. "You're not any different. Besides, with my father higher, he'll want to align me with someone of a strong name. How do you think you'll feel about being an Artino?"

Oh, God.

"Not going to happen," Alessa said shortly.

"You say that now …"

"I'll say that forever."

Alessa practically spat the words at him.

She hated this man.

Dean shrugged like it didn't make a difference. "They'll want to strengthen the families, Alessa. The war between the Conti and Trentini families has divided all of us in one way or another. Even if the DeLucas aren't fighting with your family, we're fighting with someone else's family. Think about it. Your grandfather is mad at the Rossi family for retaliating on Riley Conti without his permission. Laurent Rossi is digging his heels in on the fact he didn't do a thing, even though we all know he did.

"Somehow, they're going to need to reinforce the bonds to make sure something like this doesn't happen again," Dean said with a cold smile as he turned to stare Alessa down. "The best way to do that is to connect the families together again. Marriage sounds like a good plan, doesn't it?"

"Do you want a wife who despises you?" Alessa asked.

Dean reached out and stroked Alessa's cheek. She refrained from jerking away from him, but only because people would see. "I don't mind a wife in need of training, Alessa. The good ones always need to be broken in first."

"What, like a horse?"

"As long as she's not dead, there's no reason not to beat her," he quipped.

Alessa couldn't believe the gull of him. "You're disgusting."

Where did he learn this kind of behavior?

And what was even more awful, why did her grandfather like Dean so damned much?

This was a terrible situation for Alessa to be in. The more she considered Dean's promises about a marriage between him and her, the worse she felt. It was as if a spike of dread had been driven straight into her spine, holding her in place.

Alessa had stopped worrying about being married off, especially to a man like Dean. Her grandfather never mentioned much about the issue, but her brother Joel occasionally dropped hints. Alessa had brushed Joel's comments off as the bullshit it was. Terrance never let his grandson make those kinds of calls.

But her grandfather … Terrance liked Dean. He liked the man's father, too.

Dean sighed, drawing Alessa from her thoughts. "Tell me …"

Alessa swallowed back the bile rising in her throat. "Tell you what?"

"Did that Conti prick—Adriano—ever get the chance to fuck you like he wanted?"

Ouch.

Alessa did lurch away from Dean that time. His words were as good as a slap. "I beg your pardon?"

Dean's expression didn't change a bit as he said, "Just curious, Alessa."

"That's none of your business."

"Ah, you don't have to say a thing," Dean said, chuckling. "Your face says it all. That's fine—virgins always cry, anyway. Less fight, you know."

Jesus Christ.

This man was a vile pig.

"Get away from me," Alessa snapped.

Dean grinned but didn't move. "You should get used to the fact that I have a cock hanging between my legs and you don't. Having that extra appendage means I make all the calls, Alessa. The quicker you realize that, the easier it'll all be."

"Eat shit," Alessa muttered.

"So crass," Dean scolded, clicking his tongue almost mockingly.

"You haven't seen anything yet."

Dean leered. "I plan on seeing everything, remember?"

"I promise that would be the last thing you ever got to see."

With those words, Alessa left Dean stunned and looking stupid.

Just like he always did.

Alessa needed a breather. The venue picked for the Rossi-DeLuca wedding was more than big enough to handle the amount of guests, but she still felt suffocated by all the people. Italian families didn't know how to be quiet when it came to a celebration. Hell, the word quiet didn't even exist.

Stepping outside into the parking lot, Alessa took a deep breath of air. It didn't seem to matter what time of year it was, Chicago always had a chill and a little bit of wind. August in the city was known to be a rainy month, but the wetness had held off, thankfully. The cool breeze was just what Alessa needed.

Raised voices echoing from around the side of the building caught Alessa's attention before she could even fully relax. She knew better than to eavesdrop or insert herself into a conversation between men in the Outfit, but those familiar voices drew her in like a moth to the flame.

Alessa peeked around the corner of the building where more cars had been parked. She froze at the sight of Adriano Conti leaning against his familiar 1969 Camaro with his arms crossed and a scowl marring his handsome features. Theo DeLuca stood only feet away from Adriano, looking unruffled and calm as the young man across from him only raged.

"You're un-fucking-believable," Adriano said, sneering. "And you're selfish as hell."

"Me?" Theo asked, scoffing. "Come on, Adriano. I did my sister a favor; that was all."

"And you got my sister in trouble in the process!"

Alessa frowned, confused.

Evelina Conti, Adriano's sister, was supposed to be Lily's maid of honor. The shootings and murders had pushed Evelina's father to cull her from the wedding party. Alessa's sister took Evelina's place while one of the groom's cousins acted as the stand-in for a bride's maid. Nonetheless, Evelina hadn't shown up at the wedding or reception. At least, not that Alessa knew.

"I'm sorry your father is a fucking asshole right now, but Eve is Lily's best friend," Theo said, unaffected. "I figured they would both like to see each other today. It was only for a few minutes. I sent Eve home with someone from a neutral family."

"You sent her home with one of your cousins," Adriano growled.

"So?" Theo tossed his hands high, saying, "I could have sent her home with Joel! Would that have been any better? Fuck no. Right now, sending her home with a DeLuca relative was better than sending her home with someone else."

Adriano's gaze narrowed. "Now you're just being an asshole. Nobody is neutral in this, Theo. My father is in a fit and Eve is taking shit for it. Thanks for trying to be nice, but next time, don't bother at all. She doesn't need your kind of nice and I don't want to run around cleaning up any more messes because of your family."

Theo didn't even blink at those words. "What is that supposed to mean, Adriano?"

"You know what it fucking means. Leave my sister alone."

Theo DeLuca was a loyal, happy guy. He could be pretty loud when he wanted to be and he knew how to charm a lady with just a smile. His brother Dino, on the other hand, was quiet, reserved, and sometimes a little intimidating. Lily, the youngest of the three DeLuca siblings, was a mixture of both quiet and good-natured.

Alessa had seen both Theo and Evelina interact over the years, but she hadn't once seen anything romantic between the two. Then again, Alessa never saw anything intimate between her sister and Tommas Rossi, either, but those two were … yeah.

"Whatever, kid," Theo said. "I'm over this shit. Here's the thing, it's not me who needs to drop it. Let your sister know she can lose my number. I'm done trying with your family. You just lost another ally."

With those words, Theo turned on his heel and headed back toward the front of the building. Alessa barely managed to slip around the side out of view. Theo didn't seem to notice Alessa against the wall as he took the stairs two at a time, yanked open the glass door, and disappeared inside the building.

Alessa let out another breath, happy she hadn't been caught eavesdropping. Turning to peek around the corner of the building again, she came face to face with Adriano. Her heart kick-started at the sight of his grin. He could be playful and sweet when he wanted.

"Adriano," Alessa whispered.

"Where have you been?" Adriano asked her.

"Here and there. You?"

"Staying out of trouble. Unlike you." Adriano winked. "You thought I didn't see you there, huh?"

"I wasn't listening," Alessa said.

"That's your story?"

"Yes. And I'm sticking to it."

"Smart girl," Adriano said, chuckling.

"I learned from the best."

The sound of Adriano's laughter was dark, rich, and deep. It rolled over Alessa's senses like liquid sugar, promising to make her high and wake her up at the same time. His green eyes surveyed her, looking over the dress she wore and the black pumps on her feet. Adriano had always been able to make the rest of the world disappear when he had Alessa in his sights.

She didn't have the first clue how to feel about this man. Their closeness over the years had been explained away to everyone around them as nothing more than friendship, but Alessa knew it was more than that.

They had always been more than just friends.

"Cute," Adriano noted, fingering the capped sleeve of her dress.

Alessa cocked a brow, mocking offense. "Cute? That's not exactly the look I'm going for tonight."

Womanly. Grown up. Sexy. Beautiful.

Anything but *cute*.

"It's pink," he said simply.

"So?"

Adriano's smirk could make a woman wet. Alessa was no exception. "You know I like you best in blue, *bella*."

Alessa laughed. "I do. But you're not here."

"And you're not dressing for me, huh?"

Alessa's heart sank as she considered his words. "You haven't called me in weeks."

"I'm trying to keep you out of trouble, Alessa."

"Oh?" she asked.

"Of course. You know how much I care about you."

Did he?

"And my father is being an asshole," Adriano added quieter. "Better if I don't urge him on."

"I guess."

Adriano ticked his fingers gently under Alessa's chin, making her look up at him. The action was so tender, so familiar to them, that it made her heart stutter. "I miss you, though."

She didn't have to ask if he meant that. His eyes said it all.

"I miss you, too. It sucks when you're not around to chase all the jerks off."

Adriano laughed loudly. "I agree."

Alessa chose not to mention Dean. Adriano probably had enough crap to deal with and worry about. She didn't need to add her stupid issues onto him.

A sadness lingered in Adriano's gaze. Alessa couldn't have missed it if she tried.

"How are you doing?" Alessa asked.

Adriano smiled briefly, the darkness in his gaze leaving as quickly as it'd come. "With what?"

"Your mom."

"Oh." Adriano cleared his throat and stepped around the side of the building, straightening to his full height. That forced Alessa to look up at him. "It's been a month and a half since she was killed."

"I know," Alessa said.

"And it's not much better," Adriano admitted.

"I'm sorry."

Adriano shrugged. "Don't be. Right now, I'm just waiting this whole mess out and then I can focus on what happened to my mother."

"What is that supposed to mean?" Alessa asked.

"Don't worry about it, pretty girl."

Alessa grinned, unable to help herself. "You know I can't do that."

"Learn to. How much am I missing in there?" he asked, nodding toward the front doors of the venue.

"The usual," Alessa replied. "Lots of talk, not much else."

"Talk leads to gossip and gossip leads to issues. The Outfit has enough of that without adding to it. The talk is what I'm worried about, Alessa."

Alessa was, too.

She was also incredibly worried about Adriano. He was made in the family, even at his young twenty years. Being the son of the front boss for the Outfit gave Adriano a lot of clout and respect just based on his last name alone. Alessa couldn't remember a time when Adriano hadn't been involved in the Outfit in some way. His father had groomed him for this life. A lot like Alessa and her siblings had been groomed for their roles.

But at the end of the day, Adriano was still a made man. The Outfit was still his family and it would always hold his loyalties. The problem was, where should his loyalties go when everyone was divided like they were?

"They'll work it out," she said instead of voicing her thoughts. "Your dad and my grandfather, I mean. This is just ..."

"A mess," Adriano finished for her, his voice uncharacteristically soft. "Hopefully, Dad will take Terrance up on his offer to have a sit-down next week."

"Granddaddy offered that?"

"Sure. Terrance doesn't want to fight with Riley," Adriano said. "He wants to get everything settled."

"You don't sound like you want to fight, either," Alessa pointed out.

"I don't. I also don't blame him for what happened to my mom. Nobody was pointing the gun right at her, Alessa. It hurts, but Terrance didn't pull the trigger."

"Yeah. I get that."

She wished it could be that simple but it rarely ever was.

"Be careful, Lissa."

Alessa blinked up at him, confused. "Huh?"

"I need you to be careful, because I might not be able to look out for you."

Laughing, Alessa said, "Adriano, I'm twenty-years-old. You don't need to keep looking out for me, all right."

"Yeah, I kind of do."

CHAPTER THREE

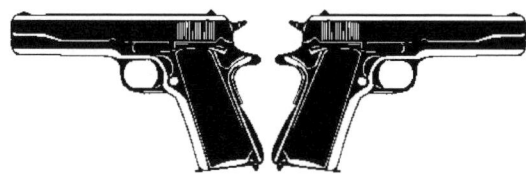

Alessa frowned. "Don't worry about me, Adriano."

Adriano didn't know how to tell Alessa, but the fact was simple: he didn't know how to *not* worry about her. He'd been half in love with this girl ever since he caught her from falling to the ground underneath a willow tree four years ago.

Well, if Adriano was honest, he'd liked Alessa for a lot longer than that. But being the son of Riley Conti meant Adriano had to follow the goddamn rules. Like the fact Riley had never approved of Adriano's interest in the boss's youngest granddaughter.

Adriano's father wanted to situate his only son in a marriage of Riley's making to a family outside of the Outfit. One that would either strengthen the Outfit in allegiance with another organized crime affiliate, or put Adriano front row and center as a prospective future boss. Adriano wanted to do his own thing—Riley didn't agree.

Regardless, Alessa was a no-go.

Adriano didn't know how to stay away from the girl. He blamed Alessa for that entirely. She didn't even have to do a fucking thing, either.

Adriano caught Alessa's plump bottom lip under the pad of his thumb. "Stop that."

Alessa's brow furrowed. "Hmm, what?"

"That," Adriano said, pointing at Alessa's frown. "I hate that. You know I do. You shouldn't frown, ever."

"Prettier when I smile, huh?" she asked sweetly.

Adriano laughed under his breath. "Beautiful when you smile, Lissa."

"Smooth, Adriano."

"I try."

The sounds of voices and laughter drew Adriano's attention to the front doors of the venue where the Rossi-DeLuca wedding was being held. A few people stumbled outside, clearly drunk and happy. With the issues in the Outfit, he didn't want to be seen and cause a problem. Adriano slipped around the side of the building and took Alessa with him.

Her breathless laughter filled the air as he pressed her to the brick wall, keeping them both hidden from view. Alessa didn't seem to mind being pinned under Adriano's weight.

He sure as fuck didn't mind.

Alessa had to be the sexiest girl he'd ever had the pleasure of laying his eyes on. Her brown hair, highlighted with reds and blonde, fell just above the small of her back in waves. It was the perfect length to wrap his hands in and pull, which he knew she adored. Adriano would be a goddamn liar if he tried to say he didn't like the way her tiny frame fit his hands when she was wearing nothing but her skin. She was pixie-like in appearance with wide blue eyes that spoke of innocence.

The girl wasn't innocent at all.

Adriano knew that first hand.

"Oh, my God," Alessa said, still laughing. "Why did you do that?"

"I wasn't finished talking with you," Adriano replied.

Adriano leaned down and kissed Alessa. She hadn't been expecting the sudden move if her gasp was any indication. He loved all the sounds she made for him.

Alessa's lips parted just enough to allow Adriano inside. He took in the heat and taste of her mouth with his tongue, kissing her hard enough for his teeth to scrape along her bottom lip. Alessa's hands fisted into his shirt and pulled him into her tight little body.

Too soon for Adriano's liking, Alessa pulled away. Her cheeks were flushed with a pink he knew traveled all the way down her chest when she was turned on. Through the silk of her dress, he could see she wasn't wearing a bra. He cupped her tits in his hands, rolling his thumbs over her nipples through the fabric.

"Christ, yeah," Adriano mumbled. "I've missed you."

Alessa sighed, arching into his hands. Adriano's cock ached under his jeans. The zipper bit into his erection through his boxer-briefs.

"You're shaking," Alessa said as he wrapped her hair in his hands.

"No, that's you, pretty girl. Don't worry. No one has seen me."

"You and your pet names."

Adriano grinned. "You're the only girl who gets the pleasure of hearing them."

Alessa watched him under her thick, dark lashes. The sight reminded Adriano of when Alessa was on her knees with his cock in her mouth, looking up at him.

Fucking *hell*.

No, not innocent.

Not at all.

"I better be the only one," Alessa said.

The warning in her tone was as clear as day.

Adriano chuckled. "Someone's territorial for not wanting me to put a label on her."

Alessa shrugged, a sly smile curving her pretty pink lips. "No, of course not. But there was this sexy guy from the Vegas crew that—"

Adriano pushed Alessa against the wall roughly, quieting her instantly. She giggled, flashing her teeth at him as she grinned.

"Alessa," he warned.

"Hmm?"

"No one else." Adriano tilted her chin up higher to catch her mouth in another kiss. The force of his lips pressing down to hers was punishingly hard. This girl was his—no matter what. She just was. Dotting kisses over the apple of her cheek, he said, "Ever, Alessa."

Alessa's smile faded. "You know—"

"We can't be that," Adriano interjected. "I'm getting really fucking sick of hearing those words coming out of your mouth. The only things you should be saying right now are *yes, Adriano* and *steal me away for the night, Adriano.*"

Her laughter was light and airless. "You can't be serious."

"I've missed you," he repeated.

Nobody got Adriano like Alessa did. They could be quiet in a room together and that was enough. She looked damn good in his shirts come morning.

She was supposed to be his, for fuck's sake.

"You know I lo—"

"Don't," Alessa muttered.

Adriano scowled. Whenever the feelings came out, Alessa ran.

"We've been doing this shit for years, Alessa," Adriano said, trying to keep his cool.

"And sometime, it's going to have to end," Alessa replied. "Can't we just leave it like it is and then the rest will be easier on us?"

"That's never going to be easy."

Letting go couldn't be easy. Not if that meant letting go of her.

"Well, that's how I need it to be," she said.

Adriano wasn't giving up like that. "Remember the last time I had you pinned against a brick wall?"

Alessa's cheeks turned pink as her mouth popped open. Yeah, she remembered.

"Short skirt, white cotton underneath, and you had just aced that final exam," Adriano continued, unfazed. "I was the first person you called to celebrate that accomplishment. You wanted me there, but I already was. Right? I was outside waiting for you, just like I always am."

"Stop playing games," Alessa said, glancing away from him.

"You're not a game to me. Years, Lissa. I'm not just going to go away."

"It's not a good time, Adriano."

Adriano laughed darkly. "It's never going to be a good time. We'll figure it out. Something, anyway."

"But—"

"No buts. We're good, we always have been. This crap with the Outfit, it'll end eventually. I'll still be here."

Alessa blew out a heavy breath. "You're going to get me in trouble someday."

"Maybe." Adriano cupped her face in his hands, forcing her to look at him. "I bet it'll be a hell of a lot of fun."

Her smile faded fast. "We don't have a chance, do we?"

"Why the hell not?"

"Too many reasons to name," Alessa said softly.

This somber, moody crap wasn't Alessa Trentini's style. Adriano didn't have the first clue what was up with her tonight.

"What happened?" Adriano asked.

Alessa wouldn't meet his stare. "I don't know what you're talking about."

"I think you do."

"Please just leave it alone. There's enough going on with my grandfather and your father. I can handle myself, Adriano. You know this."

"Make this easy on us both and spit whatever it is out so that I can fix it."

Alessa glowered. "It's not about fixing it. The problem can't be fixed."

Adriano didn't believe that for a second. Anything could be fixed with a few words, a bullet, or an action. If more men in the Outfit realized that, things would go a hell of a lot smoother.

"Tell me," Adriano demanded.

Quietly, Alessa said, "Dean."

Oh, hell.

"Again?"

Alessa flinched, likely from the venom in Adriano's voice.

"Shit, you know I hate that fool," Adriano said quickly. "It's not about you."

"Yeah, I got it."

"What did he say?"

"Same old," Alessa said, sighing. "Except now he's implying that his father is moving in on Ben DeLuca's old position."

Really?

Huh.

Adriano filed that info away for later.

"He's a prick," Adriano said. "He's useless, Lissa."

"And if this crap keeps up between the families in the Outfit, he's a damn good candidate for my grandfather to look at as a husband for me," Alessa said.

That wouldn't happen.

Ever.

"What did he put inside your head that makes you think—"

"He doesn't have to put anything in there that I don't already know, Adriano. There's only two ways to end a war. A marriage or a lot of death. Terrance never liked to kill just for the sake of killing and marrying Abriella and I off is a much easier way to go about it."

"Alessa, stop," he said, holding her trim waist tighter in his grip. "I'd never let that happen. Not if you don't want it. You know that."

"Your father won't forgive Terrance," Alessa said. "Tell me that's not the truth."

"I don't know that, Lissa."

"He won't."

Adriano hated that she might be right. Riley was very angry about Adriano's mother's death and the possibility that it had been caused by his best friend's choices. Add on that Riley was using Mia's death as a way to move himself higher in the Outfit, and it all screamed bad news.

"And we're both aware of what that means," Alessa continued, frowning again. "Terrance is going to have to strengthen what allies in the family he has. Dino aligned his side of the DeLuca family with the Rossi family. Who does that leave?"

"The Artino side of the DeLuca family," Adriano said, though he didn't want to admit it.

"Yeah." Alessa sighed, turning her head to the side. "I should get back in there before someone notices me gone."

"I'd rather you stay out here with me."

Alessa's lips curved with a wicked smile. "There was no Vegas guy, by the way."

"Better not be." Adriano punctuated those words by pushing his body into Alessa's. There was no hiding the hard ridge of his erection as it drove into her toned stomach. She pushed right back into him, driving him insane. "I'd fucking *kill*, Lissa."

She hummed a soft sound. "Don't say that."

"Too bad. This is mine," Adriano said, running his hands down Alessa's sides. "All of you is mine, pretty girl. And I will gladly cut the hands off anyone who even thinks they have the right to touch you."

Adriano was always honest with Alessa. He didn't fuck around on her, regardless of if she wanted to put titles on them or not. He was a one-woman kind of man. Seeing his mother hurt every time she had to turn her cheek to Riley's affairs had been enough for Adriano to know he didn't want to be that man.

But Alessa … she was *his*. Just the thought of someone else being near her drove him fucking crazy.

"There was no Vegas guy," she repeated, laughing. "You know that."

"Mmm."

"What, Adriano?"

"Nothing. You already know," he said.

"Do I?" she asked.

"Yes."

Alessa bit her bottom lip. "You would kill."

"You know it."

"Alessa!"

Alessa's eyes widened as her head flew to the side. Adriano stepped away from Alessa at the familiar voice. Damian Rossi stood at the corner of the building with crossed arms and a blank expression. Adriano put another couple of steps between him and Alessa.

"Damian," Adriano greeted.

"Conti." Nodding at Alessa, Damian said, "Your brother is probably looking for you, Alessa. I suggest you head back inside before he comes out here searching."

Alessa nodded quickly and left Adriano behind.

"What are you doing, looking for some kind of trouble?" Damian asked once Alessa was gone.

Adriano shrugged. "No."

"You're going to find it if you keep messing with that girl."

"I've done okay so far," Adriano replied.

"Oh, a smart mouth. Funny. I'm sure that'll keep your dumb ass from getting shot when someone else catches you dry fucking against a wall with a Trentini girl."

Adriano refused to grace that with a response.

"Shouldn't you be inside with your new wife?" Adriano asked.

Damian cocked a brow. "Shouldn't you be at home with your father?"

"Point taken." Adriano shifted on his feet, uncomfortable. "Listen, I—"

"I am so fucking sick and tired of hiding everybody else's secrets in this goddamn family." Damian pointed at Adriano's Camaro and said, "You get in that damn thing and go, Adriano. And if you're a smart man, like I think you are, you'll stay the hell away from Alessa Trentini until this whole mess with the Outfit blows over. You're twenty-years-old, kid, but I can bet you won't see your twenty-first birthday if you keep this nonsense up. You've got a lot of learning yet to do where the Outfit is concerned and let this be your first lesson from someone who isn't your father."

"What is that?" Adriano asked.

"I'll keep my mouth shut about what I just saw."

"Thanks."

Damian smirked. "But you fucking owe me."

Shit.

"Is that all?" Adriano asked.

"For now. Get gone."

Adriano's fingernails bit into his palms as the newscast kept playing. The pain of clenching his fists so hard only served to keep Adriano from speaking. He wanted to demand answers from his father, but Riley didn't look like he was in the mood to give any.

On the screen of the television, Adriano watched as a stretcher was rolled out of the entrance of a familiar mansion. Two EMTs stepped back from the lump on the stretcher as men wearing blue windbreakers moved closer. With their shoulders touching, the view of the stretcher was obscured on the camera, but the three letters on the backs of the officials' coats were as clear as day: FBI.

After a few seconds, the officials stepped away from the stretcher. The EMTs took their place again. One fixed the top of the body bag before they resumed moving the stretcher down the large steps of the home. Police tape barricaded the front entrance and several vehicles swarmed with people, clearly investigators, stood chatting in groups.

The reporter on the left of the screen touched the ear piece on the side of her head and nodded.

"Officials have confirmed the identity of the deceased," the woman stated, her voice monotone. "Terrance Trentini, aged sixty-nine with one living son and a daughter who is deceased, has been found dead in his home office early this morning. Mr. Trentini had a long running affiliation to the Chicago mob. In fact, many believe he was the purported leader of the family although others have argued that Riley Corrado Conti runs the main operation.

"Regardless of who is controlling the infamous Outfit, everyone agrees there has been a great deal of trouble within the crime empire. Several recent shootings and deaths have been linked back to the mob and all signs point to an inside war that is raging with no reason to name. This death could very well be yet another incident in this growing feud."

Riley barked out a bitter laugh. "Sweetheart, you have no idea."

The reporter touched her ear piece once more and said, "The officials will not release the name of the family member who found the body, but they did say the alleged mob boss had been celebrating at a wedding last night before returning home early without his family. As of now, they're calling the death suspicious but no other information, including cause of death, has been given. The FBI is scheduled to give a public statement alongside the commissioner of the Chicago Police Department later in the afternoon. We will keep you updated on this story. Parker, back to you."

"Yes, thank you, Delilah," a new reporter said as the screen flashed back to the station.

Riley turned off the television.

"Of course," Riley muttered. "It couldn't be just a regular investigation. It has to be those fucking pigs. They just keep digging no matter what kind of mud they have to crawl through."

Eve said nothing beside her father, but she shot Adriano a questioning look. Adriano shrugged his shoulders in response. He didn't know what, if anything, to tell his sister about what they saw played out on the broadcast.

"I should call my lawyer and give him a heads-up," Riley said.

"Why?" Adriano asked.

Riley waved at the television. "Didn't you see that?"

Yes.

"So?"

Riley blew out his frustration in a breath. "Chances are, I'll be called in for questioning. Not that I'd talk, but if I can help it, I don't want to be dragged downtown at all."

"Did you do it?" Adriano asked.

"Adriano!"

He didn't even flinch at the heat in his father's tone. "Did you?"

Riley passed a glance at Evelina. "This isn't the time, son."

"She isn't stupid. She knows what goes on around here," Adriano said.

"I'm uh … going to go get the breakfast started," Evelina muttered, pushing up from the couch. "You're staying for breakfast, Adriano?"

"Yeah," he confirmed quietly.

Once Evelina was gone from the space, Riley stood from the chair. "You are unbelievable, Adriano."

"You didn't answer my question, Dad."

"I am not required to, son."

Adriano's jaw clenched so hard, his molars ached. "You could have settled this without killing the boss."

"I never said I did," Riley murmured, appearing completely

unbothered. "But it'll all come out in the wash. Everything usually does, my boy."

A small smile played at the corners of Riley's mouth, proof of his joy over the news. It made Adriano sick.

"You had no reason to kill Terrance," Adriano said.

"Assuming things only makes an ass out of you and me, Adriano. I had nothing to do with Terrance's death." Riley shrugged, asking, "But where were you last night, son?"

Adriano stilled. "I beg your pardon?"

"You didn't stay for dinner like you were supposed to. I had guests after you left that asked after you. I need an excuse to pass off your absence if questioned. Give me one."

"Are you suggesting I might have killed—"

"I suggested nothing. Give me an excuse."

Adriano didn't like liars and he wasn't one, but he also didn't want to get his sister in more trouble by telling on her for hanging around with Theo DeLuca. Adriano went with the next best thing—he didn't mind taking his father's bullshit.

"I went to see Alessa."

Riley's lips drew thin. "Well then. Why?"

"I wanted to check up on her."

"This … little interest you have in that girl needs to stop, Adriano. I've never agreed with your fancy," Riley said.

"I just look out for her, Dad."

"Right. I didn't realize my middle name was idiot."

Adriano cleared his throat. "I didn't say it was."

"You are both beyond the age where people will believe you're simply *looking out for her*, son. Right now, with the Outfit in an uproar, it is even more important that my children be open and available for a marriage if the need arises."

Like fuck.

"I'm not going to marry someone just because you tell me to."

"You will do as I say," Riley replied.

"I have done everything you wanted me to. I quit college to work under your men fulltime. I look out for Eve like you ask. You've marked out every second of my future without my input, but I didn't mind. I will not let you force me into a marriage with someone I don't know or give a shit about."

Riley's expression remained passive and cool as he said, "I married a woman I barely knew and didn't care much for. Look at how we turned out."

"Yeah, look at how you turned out," Adriano said, scoffing. "You fucked around on Mom every chance you had and now that she's dead, you're acting like the vengeful, grieving husband to propel yourself higher. Oh, I fucking see, Dad. Don't worry."

"Watch your mouth, Adriano."

"I'll refuse to marry if you push me into it."

"You won't have a choice. You're more than aware that in this life, love has very little say, Adriano. You chose the button and the family, now you live with what it means. Do I have someone in mind for you yet? No. That doesn't mean something might not come up in the near future. Make it easy on us all and cut whatever ties you have to Terrance's granddaughter."

Adriano's spine straightened. "Alessa—"

"I don't want to hear her name coming out of your mouth again."

"Are you telling me to stay the fuck away from her entirely?" Adriano asked. "That even if this all blows over, I can't have anything to do with her?"

Adriano didn't think he could do that.

Riley just laughed. "Oh, Adriano. I won't have to. After today, that girl won't want a damn thing to do with you. Who do you think that family is going to blame for Terrance's death? It doesn't matter if I didn't do it, they just need a proper scapegoat. We're the perfect one to use."

"You're wrong," Adriano said.

He had to be wrong.

"You know I'm not."

"Christ, haven't you heard of a dishwasher?" Evelina dropped the dishrag into the sink, splattering bubbles everywhere. "You have at least a few days' worth of dishes to wash, Adriano."

Adriano resisted the urge to bark at his sister. His irritation was beginning to manifest into annoyance at every little thing. Evelina didn't deserve his anger. "I've been busy the last couple of days."

"Doing what?"

"Nothing," Adriano said quickly.

Eve eyed her brother over her shoulder. "You can talk to me. You know that, right?"

"Sure."

"So talk, little brother."

"You realize I tower over you, right?" Adriano asked.

Eve shrugged. "So? I was born almost two years before you. Size matters very little. I'm still the older one."

"Whatever. I could pick you up and jog around the block and still not be out of breath. Little my fucking ass."

"Keep thinking that," his sister teased in a sing-song manner.

Adriano watched his sister begin washing the dishes in his sink again. "I can do those dishes, Eve."

"I know."

"So stop. I don't need a damn maid."

Eve sighed. "Yeah, but then I'd have to go back to Dad's. At least when I'm at your apartment, he leaves me the hell alone."

True enough.

Adriano dropped it and decided to move onto something different. He wanted to test the waters with Evelina and how she felt about their father's actions and Terrance Trentini's murder. Sometimes, with Adriano's family, it was good to know who was thinking what before he blurted out his own thoughts.

"The funeral for Terrance is next week. Monday, actually."

"I've heard," Evelina said quietly. "How long did they hold the body before releasing it?"

"Not long," Adriano answered. "But they had the cause of death. Bullet wound to the face. It's probably going to be a closed casket."

"Why wait so long for the funeral?"

"It's not that long, Eve," Adriano said. "They were lucky to get the body released after just four days with all the crap from the FBI."

"Long enough, Adriano. They're waiting another four days for the funeral."

"I imagine they're just getting everything sorted. Plus, they're probably waiting for the happy couple to be done with their honeymoon so they can be at the funeral, too. We weren't invited."

"Heard that, too," Evelina replied.

"Dad is going," Adriano said.

Eve's stance turned rigid. "Seriously?"

"Yeah."

"He's got some balls," Evelina said, shaking her head.

"Well, it's either that, or he wants to really piss someone off."

"Considering how he kicked Terrance out at Mom's funeral, does he really think the Trentini family is just going to welcome him in with open arms?" Evelina asked.

Adriano stayed silent, not knowing how to answer that question.

Evelina must have noticed his reluctance, because she turned to face him with a raised eyebrow. "Adriano?"

"I don't think his point is to try and make up with them, Eve," Adriano said slowly, hoping his sister would get the point.

"Oh?"

"No."

Evelina chewed on her inner cheek before asking, "What, then?"

"I think he's looking to make a point without saying anything at all."

"Stop being a little shit and tell me whatever it is that you're dancing around, Adriano."

"Dad wants to show how powerful he is without Terrance's influence on the other families," Adriano explained. "Like, he's the one making the calls. He's the one who can make the calls. The boss is dead, you know."

"And another one is ready to step up," Evelina whispered.

"Basically."

Eve frowned. "What about us? Are we going to have to go to the funeral, too?"

"Yeah," Adriano confirmed.

"That seems really ... asshole-ish."

"I get it, Eve." Adriano noted his sister's long sleeved shirt. For it nearing the last weeks of August, it was a little muggy outside for her to be wearing that. "Bruises still there?"

Eve turned back to the sink quickly. "Don't worry about it."

"You know I'm going to."

Especially now that Riley had ordered Evelina to live back at home. Adriano briefly considered moving back as well, just to keep an eye on his father and sister, but he had enough on his own plate and that would just mean extra travel. He didn't think Riley would go after Evelina in a physical way again, not after Adriano stepped in the last time.

"He's not being a fucking jackass, right?" Adriano asked.

"Dad isn't talking to me at all," Evelina replied.

"That's not what I asked, Evelina."

"I know."

"So tell me."

"He's been okay, but sometimes he's just off," Evelina said. "Weird, you know."

"My place is open," Adriano told her.

Eve nodded, continuing her work at the sink. "I'll keep that in mind if anything happens again."

"Do that."

"And what about you?" Evelina asked quietly.

"What about me?"

"You've been staring at your phone all afternoon, Adriano."

Adriano winced, shoving his phone under the table as his sister turned to face him again with curiosity coloring up her green gaze. "I have not."

"Liar. Thinking about calling someone?"

"No," Adriano said honestly.

Eve pursed her lips. "No?"

"Nope."

"Waiting for someone to call you?" she asked.

Yes.

Alessa hadn't tried to contact Adriano since the night of the wedding. He'd sent her a couple of vague texts, just trying to get a response. But he got nothing back. He didn't like that at all.

Adriano sighed. "You're goddamn nosy."

Eve shrugged. "Keeps me out of trouble."

"Actually, it gets you in trouble."

"Is it Alessa again?" his sister asked.

"I never should have told you about us."

Eve grinned. "You didn't. I caught you that time after one of your football games, remember?"

Adriano laughed, wishing he could forget that memory. The backseat of his beloved Camaro had seen more of Alessa and Adriano than anyone else ever had. Evelina had come to one of his final games in high school before graduation without letting him know she'd be there. Evidently, she'd stumbled upon more than she bargained for when she found her brother and Alessa in the parking lot.

"You're such a bitch, Eve," Adriano said. "You're never going to let me live that down."

"The parking lot was lit up like Fort Knox! It was your own damn fault." Evelina's smile faded as she asked, "It's her, yeah?"

"According to some people, nothing is about her," Adriano replied, his frustration growing again. "And I'm just ..."

"What?"

"Trying to keep her out of trouble by staying away."

Eve gave her brother an apologetic smile. "I don't know how you ever ended up in the Outfit, little brother."

"Quit it with that fucking shit."

Eve laughed his warning off. "Seriously, I don't know how. You've got a soft heart."

"I do not."

His sister didn't have the first clue about Adriano or what he was capable of.

"I think you do," Evelina murmured. "Even if it is just for one person. There's nothing wrong with that. At least you know you're not going to end up like Dad. Whoever you end up with, you'll care about her. Beyond the surface, you'll actually give a damn."

There was only one person Adriano wanted to end up with.

Alessa.

"Do you want to talk about it?" Evelina asked.

"No, I'm good. Thanks, though."

"Boo, you suck."

Adriano laughed. "Why, because I don't want to talk about my feelings? You need to get some friends."

Eve frowned. "I had friends. Dad took them away."

Shit.

"Sorry," Adriano muttered. "I just meant—"

"I know what you meant," she interrupted. "And I didn't mean talk about your feelings, you asshole. I meant, talk about her or whatever you plan on doing."

"You don't know that I'm planning anything."

Eve didn't bat a lash. "I don't have to, Adriano."

"Why?"

"Because I know you."

"Run over to Burton's place and grab me a fucking sub, would you?"

Adriano rolled his eyes. "Seriously?"

"Yeah," his Capo said, "I'm hungry and busy. Drop it off at my restaurant."

"You're at your own restaurant, and you want me to get you a sub from another place?"

How in the hell did that make any sense?

Sometimes, Kolin's demands were just insane.

Adriano knew the rules, though. No arguing with a Capo. You did what they said and got what they wanted, no questions asked.

Maybe he bent those rules every once in a while.

He had a dozen other things to do today, including trying to get a hold of Alessa somehow, or even get her away from her family for an hour, but the way things were going, it didn't look good.

"Where's Con?" Adriano asked, referring to the Capo's little middle man who did most of the guy's errands. "Get him to grab you food."

"I'm asking you, Adriano," Kolin said. "You're coming over here anyway. Besides, Con is busy. I sent him out for something. Bring me a sub—thirty minutes. Don't be late."

"Burton's?"

"Yeah."

"Fine," Adriano said as he unlocked the rental car.

He missed his Camaro. He'd taken it in for an oil change and then ended up having a dozen other things that needed work on. The classic muscle car was in good shape, and by the way his garage worked, he'd have back in a week, but sometimes it still needed a little work every now and then.

"And another thing ..."

"What is that?"

Adriano moved to get inside the rented Lexus, but before he could close the door, glass sprayed his face. The glass was accompanied by loud pops, loud enough to hurt his ear drums. Adriano's phone flew from his hand as he ducked down in the seat and covered his head.

More glass shattered.

More bangs followed.

Gun shots.

Lots of gun shots.

"Jesus Christ," Adriano mumbled.

His heart was in his fucking throat. With the boss of the Outfit murdered, everyone expected there would be some issues to follow. Retaliation, for sure. Adriano's father had warned him to keep an eye out, but apparently he was off his game today if he hadn't noticed a car tailing him when he was doing his rounds.

He didn't bother reaching for his gun in the glove compartment. What good would it do?

Not ten seconds after the first gun shot, tires screeched. Adriano peeked his head up just far enough to look over the steering wheel. He only saw the flash of taillights turning a corner as people started to flood the streets.

Shit.

Adriano did not need this today.

"Kid!"

Kolin's shout reminded Adriano of his phone. He found it on the passenger seat and picked it up with a shaky hand. Willing away the shock, he put it to his ear.

"Yeah," Adriano said, his tone hoarse.

"Dammit," Kolin muttered, "you worried me there for a second."

"You should be me right now," Adriano replied, scanning the street for another car to come down with guns blazing.

"What just happened?"

"I think we both know."

Kolin cursed severely. "Joel retaliated."

"I think we can safely assume so, yes."

"No blood?" the Capo asked.

"Not a drop."

"You always were a lucky little shit."

Despite the situation, Adriano laughed.

CHAPTER FOUR

"Let me explain this to you again," Joel growled. "This arrangement is decided. It might not be official, but once things are calmed down enough for me to see it through, I will. There is a solid promise of an engagement in the near future. You're going to marry Dean Artino when I give the okay regardless of if I have to force you down the aisle on your hands and knees, begging and bleeding, Alessa. Your opinions are not important to me. I don't give a single fuck what you want."

Alessa tried to catch her breath, but she couldn't. It was like someone had wrapped a wire around her throat and was pulling it with all their might.

"Joel, please," Abriella pleaded softly. "Just give her a second to process all of this."

"There's nothing to fucking process, Ella," Joel replied, his words cold and cruel.

Alessa just wished her lungs would take in air.

"I don't want to," Alessa finally said.

"You don't make the decision," Joel snapped.

Abriella flinched. "Joel, she's only twenty. She hasn't even finished school."

"My God. She isn't even going to need her education, Ella. Don't you get that? Dean isn't looking for an intelligent wife. He doesn't want someone who will work outside of the home. What he wants and needs is a woman who will know her place, birth him a few kids …"

Alessa didn't hear what her brother said after that. Her mind tuned him out.

Birth him a few kids …

Fucking hell.

No.

"Anyone else," Alessa said, her voice pitching high.

Joel didn't flicker with emotion. "I've made my choice."

"Anyone else, Joel. I will marry any other man but that one, please."

Abriella crossed the apartment's small living room and caught her sister's hand in hers. She squeezed tight, giving Alessa silent support.

"I need to get things in order," Joel said. "This is just one way to do that. I want to align myself with the best families so that we don't have to be concerned with whatever Riley Conti might have planned for us. This is about keeping control of the Outfit with Terrance dead. Understand that, Alessa. It has nothing to do with what you want or don't, for that matter. It's business, nothing more."

Great. Alessa was business. The only good thing about this was that the engagement wasn't an official thing. Alessa wasn't Dean's fiancée just yet. But Joel was promising she would be—*soon.*

"Daddy won't let you do this to me," Alessa said. "He won't, Joel."

Joel barked out a laugh. "You think?"

"Alessa, don't," Abriella whispered in warning.

She knew Abriella's words had nothing to do with Alessa fighting with Joel. No, Alessa knew Abriella was telling her not to beg, not to fight.

Alessa didn't relent. "Daddy won't let you do this to me. Granddaddy is dead, Joel. Daddy might have let him make all the calls where the Outfit and we were concerned, but you don't have the fucking power. You don't have anything. I won't do it. I won't marry him. I won't ever marry him."

Joel shrugged like Alessa's words were nothing but water rolling off his back. "You're wrong."

"I am not and you know it."

Abriella kept holding onto Alessa's hand, refusing to let go. "Alessa, stop."

"No," Alessa barked. "He should realize he's just a fucking made man without Terrance backing him. And that means nothing. You're not the boss. There is no boss, Joel! Nothing, Joel, you're fucking noth—"

"Haven't you ever thought about why I'm so much older than you?" Joel asked, unaffected.

Alessa blinked, confused. "What does that have to do with any of this?"

"A lot."

"Joel!" Abriella hissed.

"No, let's tell her, Ella," Joel said.

Abriella straightened beside her sister. "It's not important. Just give her a few days to calm down."

"Tell me what?" Alessa asked.

Joel grinned a wicked sight. "The bastard I really am. The whore our mother is."

"*What?*"

Abriella winced. "Joel, that's a bit … harsh. Have a little respect. She's still your fucking mother."

"Maybe so, but call a whore a whore." Joel pulled his wallet out from the back of his slacks, opened it up, and pulled out a folded piece of paper. As he smoothed out the creases of the paper, he said, "You see, Terrance would have forced Peter to join the Outfit one way or the other. Peter is just … weak. He's too fucking weak. He doesn't have it in him."

"But our mother?" Joel asked, smiling coldly. "She came from good stock—a proper *Mafioso famiglia*. When her father demanded she marry, that's exactly what she did. Sara didn't say a thing, she just picked out a dress and walked down the aisle."

Alessa knew all of this. She didn't know why her brother was rehashing events of the past that meant nothing. Their mother Sara had been the youngest daughter of the former Outfit boss before Terrance had taken over. Sara's father died shortly before his sixty-sixth birthday after a fight with lung cancer.

"There was a little more to it than that, Joel," Abriella said.

"Well, I'm getting to that," Joel replied.

Alessa wet her dry lips, still feeling like she couldn't breathe. "Like what?"

Joel laughed. "Like the fact she chose a yellow dress that would hide the bump underneath it."

"She was pregnant when she got married?" Alessa asked.

"Yes," Abriella confirmed quietly. "Not very far along."

"With Joel."

"Yes."

Joel waved the paper high. "Didn't you ever wonder why there were eight years between Sara's first child and her second?"

"No," Alessa admitted.

She just figured her mother and father didn't want more children until later in life.

"Peter hated her," Joel said. "Despised her. But she was his … out, so to speak."

Alessa's brow furrowed. "His out?"

"To the Outfit. Peter didn't want an *in* to the family, Alessa, he wanted out."

Alessa glowered at her brother. "Stop being an asshole and say whatever it is, Joel."

"Peter married Sara so Terrance would give him what he wanted," Joel said.

"Which was to keep him out of the Outfit," Abriella added softer.

"If he hated her so much, how did she end up pregnant with you before they were even married?" Alessa asked, her brow burrowing.

Joel tossed the paper to the coffee table. "My birth certificate. Notice the empty space where the father's name should be."

Alessa didn't want to look at the paper, but she did. It confirmed what her brother said. "Peter isn't your father."

"Nope." Joel looked far too pleased with that fact. "Terrance knew better, I think. He was fucking sneaky about it, but she ended up pregnant, anyway. He already had a wife, and he'd shamed his boss and Sara by knocking her up. She was young, only seventeen. She might as well have been a baby to him. Her father didn't have any boys and Terrance was his favorite. They were close with Terrance being his underboss and all."

Alessa's stomach might as well have turned in on itself. How did she not know any of this? Why hadn't her mother or grandfather sat her down and explained it?

"Oh, my God," Alessa mumbled.

"So, he fixed it the only way he knew how," Joel continued. "Married Sara off to his only son, promised her father that his grandson would have a place in the Outfit and in the Trentini family."

"My mother ..." Alessa couldn't speak.

"Was a whore," Joel finished with a shrug.

"Joel!" Abriella shouted. "Stop that."

"What? She was."

"She was not. She was young," Abriella argued. "She was caught up in a mess. She made a fucking mistake. Stop acting like she's worth less than any other woman because she is still your goddamn mother!"

"Maybe so, but she was still another man's whore," Joel replied quietly. "Don't you get it, yet, Alessa?"

She did ... maybe. That didn't mean she wanted to admit it.

"Peter doesn't have any control. He never has. I have all of it. Terrance didn't have a damned choice, even with my grandfather dead. Terrance didn't want people knowing what he'd done, he didn't want people knowing he might as well have been fucking a child and that he knocked her up."

Joel smirked, saying, "And all the wealth Terrance had? That wasn't his. That was my grandfather's—Sara's father's. Terrance gained his own wealth over the years, to be sure, but the house, the properties and the trusts? Those came from my grandfather and they were always meant for me. Anything Terrance had was to go to me if he wanted to keep what he was given."

Alessa was thunderstruck. "All of it?"

"Essentially," Joel said. "Peter would get very little but that was his agreement. Raise me as his son, marry the whore, keep her quiet, and Terrance would forget about his little affliction to the mafia. So you see, Peter won't help you, either. He doesn't give a damn."

That couldn't be true.

"You're such an asshole," Abriella told their brother.

"I'm aware," Joel replied, unbothered.

"Terrance treated you well, Joel."

Joel sneered. "Yes, Ella. As well as a bastard could be treated, you mean."

"He never treated you like a bastard. He gave you his last name and a father that raised you." Abriella openly glared at their brother as she added, "And you never let him live down his mistakes, you wouldn't let him forget, Joel. You wonder why he never trusted you, why he kept you at arm's length. You wonder, really? Look at yourself and what you're doing to *his* family. This is exactly why he did that! Because he couldn't trust you, Joel!"

"But the fact remains, I'm still here. Terrance tried to keep me out of a lot of things, but he doesn't get a choice anymore. I'm the only son that man had with a foot in the Outfit. Peter doesn't get a say. I refuse to let my birthright as the next boss of this family slip through my fingers simply because Alessa isn't *happy*."

Alessa flinched. "No, I wouldn't expect you to give a damn about me at all."

"I'm glad you're finally realizing this," Joel said, clapping his hands together. "The next few months should go a hell of a lot smoother if you understand what I expect from you."

Alessa scoffed, loud and rude. "You're a fool, Joel. If you think just because I understand how much of an asshole you are means I'll follow along with your demands, you're stupider than I thought. You can't force me into a marriage of your choosing. I won't do it."

"You will," her brother replied frankly. "Or you'll lose everything you have."

"I will not." Alessa wouldn't let Joel break her down. "I'd rather be poor and on the streets than walk down the aisle and marry Dean Artino."

Joel chuckled. "Would you rather be dead? Or that Abriella was? Maybe you don't care about your life, but consider hers, too, Alessa."

Abriella gasped sharply. "Joel!"

Alessa clenched her teeth so hard her jaw ached. "You bastard."

"Ouch," Joel murmured. "That's low. Come on, little sister. You're better than that."

"You don't know a goddamn thing about me," Alessa retorted.

"I know enough. It's called sacrifice. Be the martyr, Alessa. Every good family needs one."

Abriella gave their brother the middle finger. "Go to hell, Joel."

Joel grinned. "Someday. Today, however, is not that day."

"Why didn't you tell me?" Alessa asked.

Sara shrugged, keeping her gaze down. "I was ashamed, Lissa."

"I wouldn't have cared."

Well, she might have cared a little.

"I know," Sara said, a small smile forming. The sadness in her gaze didn't leave. "You were always like that, even as a child. You never saw the bad in people, only the good. You have a sweet heart."

"How many people know?" Alessa asked.

Sara picked at her fingernails. Alessa didn't think she had ever seen her mother so embarrassed before. "Very few. People who had been close to Terrance and those that were very close to my father."

"Did you ... love him?"

"God, no," Sara said quickly.

"No?"

"Not a bit."

"But you were sleeping with him," Alessa pointed out.

It felt weird and awkward for her to be having this conversation with her mother like this was just another gossip session. Terrance—dead or not—was still Alessa's grandfather and her mother was still her mother. She'd grown up around them and never once had she witnessed the two act anything other than platonic and respectful toward one another.

"You don't have to love someone to have sex," Sara said frankly. "And I was young and stupid. I was enamored with who he was and the things he did. I got caught up in a mess and before I could get myself out of it, I ended up pregnant with Joel."

"Oh."

Sara waved Alessa's shocked expression off. "Terrance always treated me well. My father was enraged and disgusted. I'd shamed him terribly. The deal they struck for my marriage to Peter was mostly brought on by Terrance for my benefit and to get me away from my father."

"Joel said something ..."

Sara sighed, her gaze narrowing. "Joel says a lot of things. He's always had his opinions about his biological father. I know how he feels about what I did. I tried with him, but he was close to my father growing up and the man never hid a damn thing from Joel. It's almost like he poisoned Joel against me as he grew up."

That sounded right, considering Joel's words against his mother.

"I'm sorry, Mom," Alessa whispered.

"Don't be," Sara replied sadly. "I don't know where I went wrong or how I could have done better for Joel, but he is who he is. Peter cares a great deal for him but we've come to a point where it's better to just let him do his own thing. We have very little say because of my father."

Alessa cringed. "He said Peter hated you."

Sara laughed softly. "At first, maybe he did a little. He hated being pushed into a marriage and fatherhood before he wanted it. He despised marrying a woman who had been involved with his father."

"But?" Alessa asked, knowing it was coming.

"It took a while, but we eventually moved past all of that. We were friends sharing a home for a long time. We didn't even sleep in the same bedroom. And one day, things changed." Sara took a deep breath, shrugging like all the weight on her shoulders had gone with that confession. "And then Abriella came along."

"And me," Alessa said.

"And you."

"What about Dad?"

"What about him?" Sara asked.

"Do you love him?"

Sara's tender smile felt like a private moment Alessa was intruding on. "He gave me two children, a life of my own, and a friend when I had none. Yes, I love him very much."

Alessa thought back to her childhood and knew her mother was telling the truth. Her parents had always been close, from what Alessa could remember. She couldn't even bring back moments when she witnessed them fighting.

Sara reached over and caught Alessa's hands with her own. "I'm sorry about your brother and what he's doing."

Alessa frowned. "I don't know how to do this—pretend like I'm okay with this."

"The same way I did, Lissa. You grit your teeth, smile, and do what you're told."

Those were terribly cold words coming from a woman who had been forced into her own marriage, but Alessa understood her mother's position. There was practically nothing Sara Trentini could do to get her daughter out of the arrangement Joel had made for the future engagement between Alessa and Dean. She had no say—she was just a woman.

"Mom—"

Sara squeezed Alessa's hands, quieting her daughter. "I'm sorry."

"That doesn't help."

"I know. It didn't help me, either," Sara said.

"I think this will work out just fine," Walter Artino said. "I'm pleased you agree, my boy."

Joel nodded, flicking out his napkin before placing it over his lap. "I think so, too. Terrance had seriously considered the match before his death, but he held back on it just in case something better came along."

Dean scoffed. "We're a strong family, Joel. There's not many better than us."

Joel barely graced Dean with his attention as he replied, "Well, with Ben gone, the Artinos certainly have the ability to step up to the plate and take the crown for the DeLuca side. I will give you that. It'll be interesting to see how far your family is able to go with Ben dead and Dino DeLuca out of the picture."

"Out of curiosity," Walter said, swirling the wine in his glass, "... who else was your old man looking at for her?"

"Theo, for one," Joel said.

"Oh?" Dean asked.

"Yes. But he declined."

Alessa felt like she was in a daze, as if a giant cloud of smoke had come into the room, covered her in it, and was holding her in its smothering grip. She couldn't believe this conversation was happening with her right there in the room like she didn't matter to these men at all.

Because in reality, she didn't.

Alessa Trentini was nothing more than a commodity. Something to be bought and traded for a good price and the right last name. Which was exactly what they were doing. She wanted to scream and shout at Joel. She wanted to deny his demands and threats, but the invisible noose tightening around her throat and Dean's hand, firmly gripping her knee under the table, kept her quiet.

"Was there another?" Walter asked.

"Not from the Outfit."

Alessa somehow managed to find her voice. "Who?"

"Someone from the Sorrento family in Vegas," Joel replied flippantly. "It would have made a good match, but they're incredibly well-connected to the Marcellos in New York."

"Mmm," Walter hummed.

Alessa blinked. "That was a problem?"

Christ.

She would have taken a future marriage to any man ... *any fucking man*

... but the one touching her right now.

"Of course it was a problem," Joel said, chuckling. "Max Sorrento wasn't willing to let his family mingle in marriage with ours if it might provoke the Marcellos into severing their ties. A great deal of his business is integrated with New York."

"A lot of his business is integrated with ours, too," Walter said.

Joel waved it off. "Don't worry. We'll take our shot at the Marcellos the first chance we have."

"When will that be?" Dean asked, his hand traveling higher on Alessa's leg.

"We clean our house first before we worry about others," Joel explained.

Dean squeezed Alessa's thigh.

Somehow, though she didn't know how, Alessa didn't jerk away from his touch. It took everything inside of her that she had not to do it. Dean Artino made her sick to her fucking stomach. He acted like he already had some kind of claim on Alessa even though Joel promised the engagement wouldn't happen for at least a couple of months.

"Stop," Alessa hissed too low for anyone else besides Dean to hear.

Dean smirked and squeezed her thigh again.

Why? Alessa wanted to shout that one word to the ceiling. Her grandfather hadn't been dead five days. His body probably wasn't even completely chilled yet, and her brother was promising to marry her off already.

Joel wasn't giving Alessa a choice and he knew his threats on the people she cared about the most would be good enough to manipulate her into compliance. Alessa was choked. Her heart raced in her throat, threatening to send her food spilling all over the table

"You look stunning tonight," Dean said quietly.

Alessa fought off the shudder crawling up her spine. She focused on the plate of food in front of her instead of Dean, who continued watching her. "Thank you."

"I'm glad to see the bastards let you back in your home," Walter said from three seats down.

"Yes, me, too," Joel said.

Abriella frowned beside her brother. "They'll be back, won't they?"

Joel shrugged. "The officials said they had what they needed from the office space and they already took the security footage, not that there was anything to see. The killer deleted it all. I haven't had the time to clean the office properly, though."

Alessa choked on the pasta in her mouth. Coughing, she pretended like her brother wasn't giving her the dirtiest look at the other end of the table.

"Haven't had it cleaned?" she squeaked out.

"It's a process to have it back to normal," Joel replied. "There's a company that'll come in and clean the blood up so you can't even tell the difference."

Alessa doubted that. Terrance had suffered a gunshot point blank to the face. Thankfully, she hadn't seen the mess in the office, but her mother had. Alessa heard her mother plainly say things like *blood* and *matter* after finding the body.

"Besides, I haven't decided what I want to do with the space," Joel added as he stabbed his fork into the pasta mess on his plate.

"The Will hasn't been read," Abriella told their brother quietly.

Joel flashed a confident smile. "It doesn't have to be, remember? I already told you where this house came from and that it would be coming to me. It's mine. Terrance's Will is a matter of semantics. I don't care to wait for it, it's already mine with him dead."

Alessa cringed. "So, it's still … up there right now?"

Joel cocked a brow. "Yes. Although the biggest part of the mess is gone. There are no chunks and bits hanging off the wall now."

Jesus Christ.

Why were they even in this house right now?

"Oh," Alessa mumbled.

Abriella sighed. "Joel, come on."

"What?" their brother asked. "She asked."

"You're fucking disgusting," Abriella spat.

"Be nice to your brother," Walter warned. "He's the only one holding all the keys to your kingdom, my dear."

Abriella didn't even bother to hide her glare, but she stayed quiet all the same.

"Enough of this," Walter said, slapping his hands on the table. "We're supposed to be celebrating tonight, not in a mood. Isn't that right, Joel?"

Joel smiled. "Is it. So, let's eat and we can get to that."

Alessa met Abriella's gaze. Abriella was pissed off, no doubt about it.

"Have you given anymore consideration to who the killer may have been?" Walter asked.

Joel didn't look like he gave a damn as he said, "Well, I suspect it came from Riley. Who exactly did the hit is another matter altogether. I'm not concerned. They did what they came to do and it's over with. I'll reap the rewards while the rest of the Outfit fights amongst themselves."

"It should be an interesting show to watch," Walter noted.

"I hope so," Joel replied.

"Eat, Alessa," Dean said, his tone offering no room for argument. This man had little to no control over Alessa, but tonight, he was suddenly acting like he did. "You could use a few extra pounds on that tiny frame of yours. How you don't blow away in the wind, I don't know."

Walter laughed crudely, showing teeth and tongue. "Oh, my boy. Be grateful she is small. You won't have to worry about her turning into a cow like your mother did by the time she was thirty."

Alessa's mouth popped open, disbelief filling her to the brim.

Dean's father was a loud man and large in stature. During the dinner, one that Joel had initiated and ordered Alessa and Abriella to attend, Walter Artino took center stage. Alessa couldn't remember a time when the man had ever tried to be the dominant man in the room, but he was making up for that in the tenfold tonight.

Maybe because Terrance wasn't there to be the head of the table, and Joel didn't seem to mind letting Walter act as if he controlled the room.

For the moment, anyway.

Abriella's lips curved downward in her disgust. "And where is your wife tonight, Walter?"

Walter shrugged. "At home where she belongs."

Alessa couldn't sit at the table for another second.

"I, uh … excuse me," Alessa said, pushing away from the table. Dean finally let go of her leg, but not without scowling.

Joel arched a brow high. "Where are you going?"

"I need to use the bathroom."

Dean sighed. "Hurry back."

Right.

In his fucking dreams.

Alessa took her sweet time in the bathroom washing her hands and fixing her wayward curls. The less time she had to spend with Dean and his awful father, the better. By the time she made her way back to the dining room, she found Abriella just outside the entryway, hiding against the wall.

Abriella put two fingers up to her lips. "Listen."

Alessa nodded, sliding in beside her sister. "What are you doing out here?"

"Joel was getting antsy about how long you were taking."

"Too bad for him."

Abriella snorted quietly. "Yeah, well, I told him I would come find you."

"I could have her move into my penthouse," Dean said inside the dining room. "I wouldn't mind being able to keep a closer eye on her until the wedding. Consider it, Joel. It would be one less body you'd have to watch."

Alessa tensed all over. "I don't think so."

Abriella shook her head. "You're not even engaged to him yet. Don't worry about it."

How could she not?

Joel cleared his throat. "For now, she'll remain living in the apartment with Ella. They're close and I don't want to separate them until I have to. Plus, it wouldn't look good on my sister if she was shacked up with a man before she was even engaged to him. Besides, you're intentions are showing, Dean."

Dean laughed loudly. "What intentions?"

"Wait until the wedding night. Or at least until I let you put a ring on her."

Walter joined in on his son's amusement. "Joel is not stupid, my boy."

"Better to try and fail; that's what you always told me," Dean replied. "You can't blame me for trying."

"I get it," Joel replied. "But the fact remains, she will stay where she is for now. My problem with moving her has very little to do with how you'd treat her or that she'd miss Abriella, but rather, Alessa would cause issues. She isn't entirely in agreement with this whole thing. The less problems I have to deal with right now, the better. She stays with Ella."

"Fine," Dean muttered unhappily.

"And what of the DeLuca family?" Walter asked.

Joel scoffed. "What of them?"

"Have you considered my suggestion?" the older man asked. "They're hanging on by a thread as to where, and with whom, their loyalties lie, Joel."

"Dad makes a good point, Joel. Strengthen what ties you have there. Cull any affection they may have toward the Conti family."

"I will," Joel said. "I have a plan."

"Which is?" Walter asked.

Joel hummed under his breath. "Don't worry. It'll be put into action soon enough. With what they have left, they'll have no choice but to stay on my side of the line."

"And the Rossi family?" Dean asked.

"Tommas is ... a good friend of mine," Joel replied simply. "Next to Walter as my underboss, I think Tommas would make one hell of a front boss for the Outfit."

Abriella's hand found Alessa's and squeezed tightly.

"How long will that last?" Alessa asked her sister.

"I don't know," Abriella whispered. "Tommy doesn't trust Joel at all right now."

"Tommas' father is a loose cannon," Walter pointed out.

"Maybe so, but I have not reached a point yet with Tommas Rossi where I want to hurt him just because I feel the need to spill blood."

Yet, Joel had no issue with hurting his sisters for his own benefit.

The hypocrisy burned like nothing else on the back of Alessa's tongue.

"And if Laurent Rossi continues on the path he's made for himself, I won't have to do a damn thing," Joel added. "He's digging his own grave, my friends."

"By the way," Dean drawled, sounding entirely bored.

"What is that?" Joel asked.

"I got that information you wanted on Dino DeLuca."

"Did you?"

"Yes," Dean said. "Chicago XM, 96.5. His favorite station. I took a drive with him and every time I tried to turn the radio, he threatened to cut my hands off and then put the station back."

Alessa swore she could hear the smile in her brother's voice when he said, "Perfect."

"Why not Theo?" Walter asked. "With Dino already working on prison time, you would practically wipe out—"

"Either one would serve my purposes," Joel interrupted smoothly. "And Theo is still young; he's loyal to the Trentinis. You shouldn't skip church on Sunday."

"Oh?" Walter asked.

"Yes, be there," Joel replied. "I hear it's going to be a *blast*."

What in the hell was that supposed to mean?

CHAPTER FIVE

Meet me under the willow.

That was all the text said.

Adriano didn't know how to refuse Alessa a damn thing, so he took the risk and went. He heard the sounds of Alessa's footsteps long before she slipped under the low lying branches.

Alessa shifted on her feet and hugged her midsection. "I didn't think …"

"That I would come?" Adriano asked.

"Yeah."

"Well, I did."

Alessa laughed, but even the sound was sad. "You always do, right?"

"Run after you while you push me away and leave me behind? Yeah."

"Ouch, Adriano."

Adriano shrugged. "It is what it is, Lissa."

He was a little bitter. This girl was everything to him and he never tried to hide it. But ever since the night of the wedding a few evenings ago, Alessa hadn't contacted him at all. She didn't answer his texts and ignored his calls.

It pissed Adriano off.

"Why aren't you at your place tonight?" he asked.

Alessa frowned. "Joel had a dinner with the Artinos and demanded Abriella and I come, too. It ended late. Joel decided we should stay instead of heading back to the apartment."

Adriano's gaze narrowed. "Joel *decided* you should stay? Since when does he decide things for you, Alessa?"

"Exactly."

"You're going to have to be a bit clearer than that," Adriano said.

Alessa wouldn't meet Adriano's gaze. "Since we found out our grandfather is actually his father."

Adriano turned to stone. "I don't think I heard you right, Alessa."

"You did. And he hates Terrance. Everything he says and does shows it."

Whoa.

"He's not giving us a choice in anything," Alessa added quietly.

Adriano didn't like what Alessa's words implied.

"Did anybody see you come around?" Alessa asked.

"No," he responded. "I parked a few blocks away and jogged down the backroad before coming in on the property. We're good."

Alessa sighed. "Thanks. I'm sorry I didn't answer you back the last few days."

"Are you?"

"Yes," Alessa said. "But I've been … stuck in my own head, trying to figure out what I was going to do. I thought I should let you know so you can stop worrying about me and move on to your own thing, Adriano."

"You are my thing," Adriano replied. "Don't you know that?"

Alessa dipped her head down, keeping her face out of his view. "I can't be your thing."

"Stop it with that shit. None of this matters to me. It never has."

"I can't be *your* thing," Alessa repeated firmly. "Not anymore. Not now."

"Hey." Adriano took a step forward, and Alessa answered it by taking a step back. "What is up with you?"

Alessa shrugged. "It's been settled. I'm going to have to marry Dean Artino. The engagement and wedding date isn't official, but I'm sure Joel will be an asshole and send an invitation to your father. I wanted you to find out from me and not someone else through the grape vine."

Air cut through Adriano's lungs with a searing burn. A ball of rage and possessiveness swirled in his midsection hard and fast, threatening to take him under with the current. Alessa was, and always had been, *his.*

Like fuck was he going to hand her off to some useless bastard like Dean Artino.

Over his dead body.

It wouldn't happen.

"No," Adriano said in a growl, stepping closer to her.

Alessa blinked up at him. "W-what?"

"No. You're not marrying *Dean.*"

"I don't think you understand, Adriano."

"Oh, I understand perfectly fucking well." Adriano couldn't help but notice how Alessa didn't back off the closer he came. Once they were toe-to-toe under the willow tree, she had to look up at him to hold his gaze. "I get it, but it's not happening."

Alessa's tongue peeked out to wet her lips. "Right now, it's just the promise of an engagement between Dean and me soon, but Joel assured me the wedding would happen within the next few months. I don't get a choice and it's not fair to you, so let me do what I have to. Okay?"

"No."

"Adriano—"

"No," he repeated darkly.

The pressure building in his gut only seemed to grow in intensity until it was spilling into his chest. A sudden surge of anger and jealousy danced hand in hand. Adriano was three seconds away from hunting the Artinos down and killing them all.

"Scum," Adriano said, barking out a laugh.

"Who?"

"Dean and his dumbass father," he explained. "Fucking cowards. They're the worst kind because they wait until people are weak and then they strike. They use the pain and vulnerability of others to propel themselves upward. Otherwise, they wouldn't have a fucking chance in hell of getting higher by their own hand—no, they have to break everyone else's backs on the way up. Fuck them."

They didn't get to take what was his.

Alessa wasn't theirs.

Dean wasn't fucking *worthy*.

Adriano would *kill*.

"I'll be okay," she said softly. "You know that."

Those six words broke whatever control Adriano had. She wouldn't *be okay* without him. Alessa couldn't be okay with anybody but him because nobody gave a fuck about her like he did.

Like a bolt of lightning had struck right under his feet, Adriano moved fast to close the last three inches keeping him from Alessa. He grabbed her wrists in both his palms and yanked her hard into his body. Alessa stumbled in her flats, but Adriano kept her upright with his hand to her lower back.

She stood inches shorter than him, short enough that he always had to bend down whenever he wanted to taste her mouth, but he never cared. He liked that she was short and small to his much taller and more muscular frame. It let Adriano feel like he was her protector in some crazy way.

His mouth crashed down on hers with punishing force. Alessa's eyes widened right along with her soft lips, letting Adriano spear his tongue into her heat. Their teeth and tongues scraped and tangled as he kissed her harder, deeper. With every strike of his tongue along hers, Alessa melted into his embrace a little more until he could feel her body giving out under the weight of their kiss.

Adriano let her fall, holding her all the while. Alessa grabbed onto his gray T-shirt and pulled him closer. He fisted his hands into her hair, tasted her flavor burst along his palate, and watched the blues of her eyes darken as her knees hit the ground.

On her knees looking up, Alessa exhaled heavily. Adriano was leaning down with his fingers still firmly tangled in her hair. He used one hand to cup her cheek before driving it down over her racing pulse point on her neck.

Alessa shivered. *"God."*

"You know it has got be something fucking good to take you to your knees, Lissa."

She whined under her breath, sweet and needy. "That's not fair. You never play fair with me. You always win."

"Because you're mine," he murmured.

"I can't be yours."

"Too bad."

Alessa's lashes fluttered as Adriano ran his hand down her neck again. He kept his other hand firmly seated in her hair, keeping her in place. She trusted him. He didn't know how to hurt her.

Wetness coated Alessa's bottom lashes, but she didn't try to wipe the tears away. Adriano bent down again and kissed her softer the second time.

"I'll be okay," she whispered as he pulled away.

"No, you won't," Adriano muttered.

Alessa swallowed hard. "Probably not."

"You're not his. You're not marrying him."

"No," she agreed.

"And why not?"

Adriano waited, still and quiet. He let Alessa have her time and boundaries. He let her build as many walls as she needed around her heart to keep him from reaching too deep. He took his goddamn time with her so that she knew exactly what she wanted.

There was no mistaking anything about them. She wanted him.

"Why not, Alessa?" Adriano repeated. "Tell me."

"Because I love you. And I have for a long time."

Adriano tugged Alessa back to her feet. He held tight to her face, refusing to let her go. Tilting her head back so he could stare down into those wide eyes of hers, he found home.

"Do you know how long I've wanted to hear you say that?" he asked gruffly.

"A long time."

"Yeah."

"I don't know what to do about Joel," Alessa admitted.

"I'll figure something out," he said thickly.

"I missed you."

"I didn't chase off the jerk, huh?"

Alessa laughed. "Dean is such an asshole."

"Yeah, he is."

"And he kept … touching me," Alessa practically spat out.

Adriano burned red hot inside. "Touched you?"

"All night at the dinner. And I heard Joel talking to them when I came back from the bathroom. Dean was trying to convince him to let me live with him before we're even actually engaged. I can't do that, Adriano. I would rather die."

"Don't say that," Adriano demanded, letting his thumb trail along her bottom lip. "Never say that."

"He's a pig!"

"*Hush.*" Adriano pulled her into his embrace and let Alessa bury her face in his chest. Holding her close was better. "It won't happen. I'll make sure of it."

Adriano simply needed a plan. There was only one place he could go to make it all happen: his father.

"But my brother and the Outfit—"

Adriano shook his head, quieting Alessa's rebuttal instantly. "Needs a new boss. It won't be Joel."

Especially not after Joel tried to light Adriano up with the shooting. Adriano decided not to mention that to Alessa. She didn't need to know, for one thing. And for another, there was no absolute proof it was Joel. Like the coward he was, Joel wouldn't admit a damn thing. He liked letting other people take the blame.

Alessa blew out a heavy breath, looking up at him again. "Did your father do it? Terrance, I mean."

Adriano lifted one shoulder in response. "He says no."

"Why do I hear a *but* in there somewhere?"

"Because I don't believe him, Lissa."

Alessa's face fell. "Oh."

Adriano hated the pain on Alessa's pretty features. It was like a knife to his gut, opening up his insides for the world to see. "I'm sorry."

"It's not your fault."

"Maybe, but that doesn't make it any better. I don't entirely trust my father, either." Adriano scowled, wishing he had a different option when it came to getting help for Alessa. "He's playing some kind of game I don't want to be a part of."

"I know he's angry about your mom."

Adriano scoffed. "No, he isn't. He plays that part well, but it's just a front. You can't believe or trust anyone in this business, Alessa. Especially not my father."

Alessa spread her hands wide over Adriano's broad chest. "I don't want to talk about all of this right now. You're here and that's what matters."

Adriano grinned. "Oh?"

"Very."

"I'm still pissed," he said honestly.

Alessa nodded. "I know."

And if Dean touched Alessa again …

Adriano shuddered with his rage, unable to hide it.

"Hey," Alessa whispered sweetly, her fingers skipping over his clenching jaw. "I know that look, Adriano."

Chuckling, he asked, "Do you?"

"All too well." Alessa flashed a quick smile. "Don't be jealous."

"I can't help it. And that man doesn't understand the word no."

Alessa glanced away. "I'll handle him."

"Somehow, right?"

"Somehow," she echoed.

Fuck.

Leaning up on the tips of her toes, Alessa pressed a kiss to Adriano's mouth. It was fast and fleeting, but it still woke up every nerve in his body. His cock ached under his jeans. The need to have this girl all over him thrummed hard and deep.

"Kiss me like that again," Alessa whispered. "You're right. It's always best when you put me on my knees."

"Dirty girl." Adriano smirked. "Is that all you want?"

"We'll see."

Adriano pushed against the small of Alessa's back, driving her into him. He kissed her, stealing kisses before she gave them, and turned them around to walk her backward. She tasted like sin on his tongue, just like always.

Alessa broke the kiss just as her back hit the trunk of the willow. "What—" Her question abruptly cut off as his hands drove under the skirt of her flimsy dress. The sound of her gasp melted into a low, airless moan when Adriano fisted her panties and yanked them down around her thighs.

"Jesus Christ," she said, laughing. "You're impatient."

"I don't like waiting, Lissa."

"I know. You never did."

Alessa spread her legs wider. Her thighs shook, but Adriano wasn't sure if that was because of him or her nerves. Cupping her bare pussy in his palm, he could feel her juices seeping onto his hand. She was soaked and hot to the touch. Her sex felt like warm satin against his skin. He squeezed the supple, wet flesh.

"Shit, you want me bad, Alessa."

"So bad."

"So wet," he murmured against her lips.

Alessa sighed the sexiest sound as he swept two fingers through the lips of her pussy, dragging her wetness up to her clit. "For you, always."

"Just me, pretty girl."

Adriano caught her first cry with his lips and muffled the sound as he circled her clit with light strokes. Alessa's second cry whispered over his jaw when he teased his fingers down to her entrance and thrust inside to find her wetter than ever and clenching hard around his digits.

"Fuck, Adriano."

"Mmm. Love that," he said through gritted teeth.

Alessa's teeth bit down into her bottom lip. Her hips canted into his hand over and over, meeting every plunge of his fingers. He could feel her arousal coating his digits and smearing to her thighs. He loved seeing her pussy sticky and slick with her come. The sounds of her juices and pussy sucking his fingers in for more was fucking glorious. Spreading his fingers wide on the withdrawal, he could feel her tremble a little more.

"Love that," Adriano repeated. "My name in your mouth, Alessa. That's all I ever need to hear—all I ever *want* to fucking hear. No one else does this for you, hmm. Just me."

"You," she breathed.

He was the only one who had ever touched this girl. Adriano knew it. He didn't need Alessa to confirm it. Nobody had her, knew her sounds and tastes and the way she fucked like he did.

Catching her wrists in his palm, Adriano pinned Alessa's arms on the tree high above her head. She tilted her head back, exposing the pale expanse of her neck to him. He bit and licked a line up her neck, over her racing pulse and up to her jaw.

"Don't you move," Adriano ordered.

Alessa swallowed hard, nodding. "Okay."

"Let me fuck this beautiful pussy of yours with my fingers, stay still, and I'll give you everything you need."

Alessa watched him under her thick lashes as he nipped her jaw. "*Mmm.*"

"Do you want to come?" he asked huskily.

"Yes."

"Hmm?"

"Please, Adriano," she pleaded.

His strokes inside her pussy had been gentle, teasing touches meant to work Alessa higher and closer to coming. Adriano liked nothing better than seeing her squirm and moan under his want. He knew her body and what she liked. He knew exactly how to touch Alessa to make her stutter, shake, and come undone in seconds.

Alessa was sex on legs to Adriano. Pure sin. When she was chasing her orgasm, the girl just didn't give a damn. She was wild in her movements, frantic in her chase. She rode his hand as hard as he fucked her with it.

"There," Adriano said, curling his fingers with the next thrust. He knew the spot inside her walls and hit it perfectly. The next stroke of his fingers over her G-spot had her juices soaking him even more. "Right there, Lissa. Christ, feel you holding me so fucking tight."

Alessa's eyes flew wide. "Oh!"

"Get it, Lissa," Adriano urged gruffly. "Let go for me, give it to me. I want your come all over my hand, covering me. *Come.*"

She came hard with her teeth clenching and her fingernails digging into his palm. Adriano caught her broken shout with his mouth, swallowing the sweet sounds she made as the walls of her sex shuddered around his fingers.

"Fuck, fuck, fuck," Adriano groaned, loving the feeling of Alessa.

It never got old.

Nothing with her ever did.

Alessa's chest heaved with her heavy breaths. "I bet I look like a fucking mess right now."

Her hair was mussed, her lips pink from his kisses, and her dress crinkled from his handling.

"No, you look sexy as fuck," Adriano said.

Alessa laughed. "You would say that."

"Of course. I don't know how to lie to you, Lissa."

"I like that."

Adriano smirked wickedly. "Good to know."

"Abriella said she would cover for me if needed and Joel was already sleeping when I snuck out, but I should probably get back."

No way.

"Nope," Adriano said. "Run away with me for the night."

Alessa's eyes widened. "You're joking, right?"

"No. You said it—your brother is sleeping and Abriella covered for you. I'll get you back before morning. We've done this before. Who is going to know?"

And he missed her. So badly.

Alessa glanced over her shoulder, peering through the thick branches of the willow tree. The Trentini mansion loomed in the background. "This is reckless. Right now, doing that would be stupid."

"Maybe," Adriano agreed. "But they've already ruined everything else. We're not going to be one of them."

Turning his hand over, Adriano offered it to Alessa. She took his hand without hesitating.

"Run away with me for the night," he said again.

"I don't know how to say no to you, Adriano."

"You always did before."

Alessa laughed. "No, I'm just a really good liar."

Damn.

Alessa grabbed Adriano's hand and tugged. "Come on."

"I hate that fucking thing, Alessa."

"But I don't."

Adriano chuckled deeply. "All right. Chill, woman."

Navy Pier was still wide awake with people and lights despite being a little after midnight.

"Hold up," Adriano said, stopping at a booth designated for selling tickets.

Turning to the girl waiting behind the Plexiglas window, he ordered two tickets.

Alessa grinned as Adriano paid for the required tickets and slipped the printed out stubs into his back pocket. Adriano wasn't fond of being one-hundred-fifty feet in the air inside a rocking cage. Heights weren't his favorite thing. But he agreed to let Alessa pick whatever she wanted to do for their night away, and she wanted the Ferris Wheel.

What Alessa wanted, Adriano gave. Especially if it made her smile.

Adriano tucked Alessa into his embrace as they waited in line. He constantly scanned the crowd of people, looking for someone who might recognize them. He didn't notice anyone.

It wasn't such a surprise. The families inside the Outfit were so busy trying to tear one another apart, or rather, keep from being torn apart that they probably didn't have any interest in being out having fun.

That, and it was too dangerous. Even Adriano felt strange being out in the open. Like he had to look over his shoulder for a man waiting for his mark.

"Hey," Alessa whispered.

Adriano glanced down at his lover, smiling as her fingertips traced his lips. "Hmm?"

"I'm here, Adriano."

"I'm very aware of where you are at the moment, Lissa."

"So be with me," she said.

Adriano dropped his worries instantly. "Yeah, okay."

As the man controlling the gate for the Ferris Wheel waved the couple in, Adriano dug into his pocket and pulled out the tickets and his wallet. He quickly shoved a hundred dollar bill between the tickets and nodded at the people waiting behind them in line. Each carriage could hold several people, but Adriano wanted to take Alessa up on the ride alone. The guy smiled and nodded before holding up his hand to stop anyone else from following behind Alessa and Adriano.

When the door closed and latched, Alessa eyed the people wearing grumpy expressions. Adriano guided her to the bench on the far side of the carriage and sat down. Alessa snuggled into his side, letting Adriano hold her close.

"You paid him to let us in alone, didn't you?" she asked.

Adriano shrugged. "Yep."

"You just don't want people seeing you freak out over the height."

As the Ferris Wheel began to move again, Adriano tipped Alessa's head back and kissed her, claiming her mouth with demanding strikes of his tongue. He was a starved man when he kissed Alessa—her mouth and kiss was the water sedating a thirst that beat inside his body. By the time he let her go, Alessa was flushed and breathless.

"No, Lissa. I didn't want people seeing me doing that."

"Oh," she mouthed, still grinning. "You're bad tonight."

Adriano scoffed darkly. "I'm bad every night."

"I never get to see it."

"Someday you might."

Alessa winked but said nothing.

Once the Ferris Wheel had made a quarter of its loop, it stopped again. Adriano looked down over the side wall but he couldn't see very far beyond the roof of the carriage below. He got the same view looking up.

"You're looking the wrong way," Alessa said.

"Oh?"

"Yes, see—" Alessa pointed straight out over the pier where the lights of the grounds cascaded in colors. "—look there."

Adriano didn't take his eyes off her for a second. "Yeah, the perfect view."

Alessa tucked her head into Adriano's shoulder and quieted as the Ferris Wheel began to turn again. The ride made one entire rotation and just as their carriage came close to the very top for a second time, rain began to fall down fast from the sky. Wind rocked the carriage, swaying it gently from the force. The rain quickly turned into a pounding torrent. At least the roof and mostly enclosed space kept them safe from getting too wet.

"Jesus," Adriano muttered.

Alessa laughed. "Scared?"

"No, but if I see lightning, we're climbing the fuck down."

"Sure we are."

Adriano held Alessa a little tighter as the ride stopped completely. They rested at the very top of one-hundred-fifty feet. It wasn't uncommon for the ride to stop if a storm dropped down suddenly, just for safety. The carriages down below couldn't be seen through the sheet of rain.

Alessa shivered.

"Cold?" Adriano asked.

"A little."

Before he could even try to correct that for her, Alessa climbed into his lap. Adriano was lost the moment Alessa's lips touched his. There was nothing soft or innocent about her kiss. She was forceful and demanding, her teeth scraping along his lip as her tongue dove into his mouth. Her breathing was harsh and ragged, pushing her sweet tits into his chest.

Adriano pushed the skirt of her dress higher and she worked at the button and zipper of his pants. Air cut past Adriano's lips in a hiss when Alessa's hand slipped under his boxer-briefs and wrapped around his cock.

Hot, smooth, and soft.

Her quick, firm strokes worked him from the base to the tip, hardening his cock. The idea of sex outside, in a public place, only made his lust thrum deeper. They certainly couldn't be seen. Not with the rain and the wind pounding down like it was while they were high in the air.

That didn't make the thought any less hot or intense.

"This will be new," Alessa whispered.

Adriano cocked a brow. "Who's the bad one again?"

Alessa only grinned.

"Shit," Adriano mumbled as her fingernail dragged over the head of his cock. The tip of her finger smeared his pre-cum down along the underside of his shaft. "Stop teasing me, Lissa. Either you want to fuck, or you want to make me come. I'm good with both but make up your goddamn mind."

Adriano helped Alessa resituate herself on the bench seat so that both of her ballet flats rested on the cold metal along his hips. Hooking his thumb along the seam of her panties, he moved the fabric to the side and swept a finger across her slit. The sliver of her pink flesh, wet, soft, and hot, drove him insane.

"I want to be buried inside you, Lissa."

"Hurry up and fuck me then."

"You're still on the pill, yeah?" he asked.

Alessa nodded. "Yes."

Perfect.

"Soaked," Adriano noted, teasing her pussy with light touches.

Alessa sighed, rocking her hips into his hand. "You're wasting time."

No, he wasn't.

Not with Alessa.

Adriano grabbed her waist tight and pulled her down onto his cock. Her snug heat covered every inch of his dick in seconds. He didn't feel the coldness of the rain or wind, just the feeling of Alessa's pussy wrapping around his cock.

The best fuck he'd ever had was this girl.

Crazy wild.

"Holy shit," Adriano forced out.

Alessa's pink lips popped open, a quiet cry escaping her heaving chest. "*Adriano.*"

"Mmm. Again, Lissa. My name in your mouth just like that." Adriano lifted her fast and pulled her down on his cock harder the second time, lifting his hips from the bench to add to the friction. "Christ, you're perfect."

"Missed this," she breathed as his hands found her breasts over top of her dress.

Adriano slipped a hand under the flimsy fabric and beneath her satin bra to pinch her nipple. He pulled the capped sleeves of her dress down, letting her tits spill out of her bra. Alessa had gorgeous breasts, as far as he was concerned. They fit his hands perfectly and her pink nipples were just the right size for him to take into his mouth to bite and suck.

Without missing a beat, Adriano teased and nipped at Alessa's breasts while he grabbed her ass and lifted her up and down on his cock. Her hands slipped off the rail and found his back and neck. Through his shirt, he felt her fingers dig in while her nails scored thick, stinging lines across his neck. The dim lights on the Ferris Wheel and carriage was just enough to filter through the rain and darkness, letting Adriano get the best view of Alessa riding him.

"Fuck, look at you," Adriano mumbled, watching his dick disappear over and over again into her pussy.

Just the sight alone made him want to come. With her panties pulled aside, her arousal coating his dick and smeared all over her folds, and her little clit poking out, begging to be touched, it was sexy as fuck.

Alessa's tongue peeked out to wet her lips. "Yeah?"

"God, yeah."

Her quiet whispers of *more*, and *God*, and *fuck me, Adriano* made him only want to fuck her harder. Fuck her until all she could feel was him and they were in an entirely different place—somewhere beautiful and wicked.

Alessa shuddered all over. "My *God.*"

"So perfect."

He loved Alessa best when he was bare and could feel every inch of her pussy holding him snug inside her walls. She fit him beautifully. He filled her totally.

"Ride me faster," Adriano demanded. Alessa's teeth cut into her lip as he fisted her hair and yanked her head back. "Ride me, Lissa."

Alessa used the wet steel bar of the carriage wall to grab onto as she began a rhythm on top of Adriano that would get them to a fast peak. Adriano pulled her in for a bruising kiss, wanting his girl to feel him on her for days after they were done. The best pressure built in his spine as her cries turned louder in his ear and breathless with her need.

Yeah, so perfect.

Alessa came quaking, crying out, and tightening around him all over. Adriano followed close behind, grabbing onto her tighter than ever.

"Don't let me go," Alessa whispered.

Adriano watched the sight of his semen mingle with her fluids.

She was his all over.

He was all through this girl.

"I don't know how to let you go, Alessa."

Adriano nearly barged inside his father's office but managed to stop himself just in time. Being an asshole wasn't likely to get him what he wanted from Riley. Checking his watch, Adriano noted the early morning time. Evelina said earlier that their father had been in the office since he woke up and hadn't even asked for a coffee yet.

Knocking three times on the door, Adriano waited.

"Yes?"

"It's me, Dad."

"Come in," Riley said, his voice muffled behind the thick oak door.

Adriano entered his father's office and stood a little straighter at the sight of Riley overlooking photos spread out across his desk. "Good morning."

"Good morning," his father greeted. "I called you last night, but you didn't pick up."

"I was out."

"Without your cell phone?" Riley asked.

"I took a night to relax. What is that?" Adriano asked, waving at the pictures.

"Joel Trentini has been busy, it seems."

Adriano forced back his irritation at the mention of Joel. "Oh?"

"Very. I've had someone tailing him since Terrance's death, just to see what he might do. Wining and dining the Artinos, chatting up Theo DeLuca on the side, and getting cozy with Tommas Rossi. Although Tommas isn't such a stretch as they've always been friends, I suppose. Nonetheless, Joel is a busy boy."

"It's only been a few days, Dad. Maybe they're giving their condolences."

Riley snorted under his breath. "Sure. And Joel's soaking it up."

"So?" Adriano asked.

"So, he's trying to gain allies, Adriano. I cannot let him get so far ahead of me in this game that he believes he can stand up to me at the table. That little bastard is not boss material and I won't allow him to think he is, either."

The 'little bastard' comment struck a chord with Adriano. He didn't want to outright ask his father if he knew the truth about Joel Trentini's paternity. Not yet, anyway.

Riley glanced up from the pictures and asked, "What did you need, son? You haven't been around since our last discussion."

Their last discussion being when Adriano was nearly killed in the rental car. It didn't end well, especially when Adriano refused to retaliate on Joel just because his father said so. Adriano had more to lose than his father understood. Alessa, most importantly. Going after Joel could very well put Alessa in a dangerous situation.

He couldn't do that.

Adriano steeled his nerves and decided to just go straight for the kill. Even if that meant giving up the things he believed in when it came to the Outfit so that his father could gain whatever it was he wanted. Adriano didn't care. As long as he got Alessa in the end and she was safe, Adriano didn't give a fuck.

Not about anyone else.

"I'll do whatever you need," Adriano said quietly.

Riley raised a single brow. "You're going to have to explain that, son."

Adriano gestured at the photos, shrugging. "This, the Outfit, and your plans."

"I never said I had plans, Adriano."

"You don't have to. It's obvious."

Riley sighed, eyeing his son curiously. "I'm listening."

"I'm not going to fight about it or take any sides but yours. You want loyalty, you've got it. You want a compliant son that'll do what you say and need, here I am."

"And what you do want in return?" Riley asked.

Adriano cleared his throat. "I didn't say I wanted something."

Riley laughed, throwing Adriano's words right back at him. "You don't have to. It's obvious."

"Alessa," Adriano murmured. "Joel is going to marry her off to the Artino asshole. Right now, it's just the promise of an engagement, but that could change any day."

"Dean?"

"Yes."

Riley nodded once. "Interesting. He's definitely working his angles by strengthening the closer allies he already has in his pocket. And we can safely assume you don't want the marriage to happen."

It wasn't even a question.

"No," Adriano admitted.

Riley stood straight, drumming his fingers to the desk. "I will see what I can do."

"Dad—"

"No arguing, Adriano. For now, it's the best I can do. We'll see how agreeable you are when the time comes for you to step up. Just remember, the worst gift might be exactly what you wish for, my boy."

What was that supposed to mean?

Adriano didn't care or ask. He got what he wanted.

That was all that mattered.

CHAPTER SIX

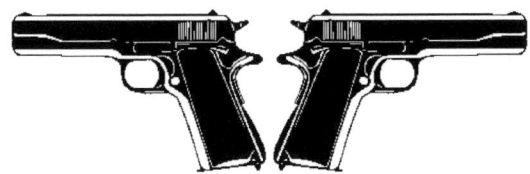

"**Y**ou should answer him back," Abriella said.

Alessa refused to grace her sister's know-it-all attitude with a response.

The phone in Alessa's hand vibrated with another text. She passed the screen a glance, knowing who it was and what he wanted. Adriano's messages to her over the last three days since she saw him last were vague at best. Simple *heys* and little else.

This text was nothing like his others: *Talk to me.*

Frank, bold, and demanding.

Just the way Alessa liked Adriano the very best.

She shuddered at the unexpected ache rising between her thighs.

"Do you think he did it?" Alessa asked. "Killed Terrance?"

Abriella cocked a brow. "Riley?"

"Yeah."

"According to Tommas, he said Riley denies it," Abriella said. "Which is interesting, if you think about it."

"Nothing about this shit is *interesting*, Ella."

Abriella glared. "I didn't mean it like that. I just meant that Riley doesn't have a reason to lie about it, Alessa. If he did it, it's done. What is there to hide? Nothing."

She had a good point.

"No one else had a reason to go after Terrance," Alessa said. "Riley did."

"What difference does it really make?" Abriella asked. "You know, when you go messing with a man, you're accepting his crazy, too."

Alessa laughed. "Oh?"

"Yeah. Including his family. You can't blame Adriano if Riley is at fault for this."

"I don't blame him," Alessa replied honestly.

"Then what is up with you?"

Alessa wished she had a good answer.

"I don't know what to say to him," Alessa finally decided on saying.

"Start with hello," Abriella replied.

"Easy for you to say."

It wasn't Abriella's man whose father had likely killed their grandfather.

"What is the point?" Alessa asked.

"You're going to have to be a bit clearer than that, Lissa."

"It'll never happen. Me and him, it just won't. Why bother continuing with something that's only going to seriously mess with my head and heart? Doesn't that seem like I'm asking for trouble?"

And now Alessa also had Dean looming in the back of her head like a little poisonous tumor that was slowly killing her. It had been just a couple of days since the dinner, but the man was already trying to stake his claim by showing up outside of Alessa's college and apartment every chance he could. It was annoying.

"We've all got a little bit of a masochist inside us," Abriella said. "Besides, you know me. I'm more than willing to urge you on in bad behavior."

Alessa scoffed. "The rebel, I know."

"Hey, you're just cleaner about it than I am. Don't act like you're some kind of angel, Alessa."

She definitely wasn't one of those.

Abriella's cell phone rang, cutting their conversation short. Alessa was grateful for that. She didn't know how to explain to her sister that admitting she loved and wanted Adriano Conti, regardless of what problems it could bring or what his father might have done, would be like locking herself into a personal hell she couldn't get out of.

They couldn't be.

They just *couldn't.*

Alessa wished her heart would start listening to the rational side of her brain.

"Hey," Abriella said as she answered her phone. "Where are you?"

"Who is it?" Alessa asked.

"Tommas," her sister mouthed.

Alessa rolled her eyes. While Alessa was wavering on her own issues, Abriella didn't seem to have a damn problem knowing what she wanted. Abriella didn't seem to mind the risks involved with taking what she wanted, either.

"I *know*," Abriella groaned.

Alessa watched her sister pace the length of the living room. Abriella, with a cell phone stuck to her ear, looked like she was at her wits end.

Joel had all but demanded the Trentini sisters move out of their apartment and come back home, but somehow, Abriella convinced their brother to lay off. They needed space and time to process everything, she'd said. Joel fell for it.

If Alessa could help it, she wouldn't be moving back home any time soon.

"You'll be there on Monday, right?" Abriella asked.

Alessa frowned.

Monday was their grandfather's funeral. Alessa shivered, the sound of her mother's scream reverberating through her mind. Sara found Terrance's body in his office. His face had been blown off from the gunshot to the face. There were no witnesses. The security video that constantly recorded in the home and outside for the front and part of the backyard had been wiped. It was like no one had even been there.

Except someone had.

"I miss you," Abriella mumbled.

Alessa hated seeing her sister cry. Abriella Trentini wasn't an emotional person. She was too good for that nonsense. But the feud between the families had taken away the one thing Abriella wanted more than anything—Tommas Rossi.

That man might as well have been Abriella's drug.

Withdrawal was a bitch.

"I *can't*," Abriella snapped, surprising Alessa by the anger heating her tone. "Every time I make a goddamn move, someone is right on my ass, Tommy."

"If you don't, you know I'll come to you, baby."

Alessa heard those words loud and clear. She raised a brow in question to her sister, but Abriella gave nothing away.

Abriella turned her back to her sister. "Tommy ..." She sighed and said, "Yeah, all right. Just don't be stupid. Your fucking father is stupid enough for everybody."

Tommas' laughter was all Alessa heard from the call before her sister hung it up. Abriella turned fast and tossed the phone to the couch, glowering.

"What?" Alessa asked.

"He wants me to go out," Abriella said, blowing out a heavy breath.

"Really?"

That was kind of ballsy. Not that anything about the relationship between Abriella and a man eight years her senior was innocent.

"I should go," Abriella said, glancing at the darkness outside. "I could sneak out the back and grab a cab. Cover my face, just in case."

"Abriella—"

"Stop," Abriella interjected fiercely. "Don't even start with whatever you're going to say."

"All right. I won't."

Abriella nibbled on her bottom lip. "He's dead, right? Granddaddy is dead, so nobody is going to say a thing about us going out right now. Everyone is way too focused on who is killing who and who is going to kill who next."

"Joel," Alessa pointed out quietly.

Abriella scowled. "Fuck Joel. He's useless, Alessa."

Sure. Until he pulled his weight as their older brother. He seemed to like doing that a lot lately.

"I was just saying," Alessa said.

"Before you try to talk me out of it, maybe you should come, too," Abriella said, smiling slyly.

The idea was tempting.

"And if someone sees us?" Alessa asked.

Abriella shrugged. "We're drowning our sorrows."

Sure they were.

Alessa didn't give a damn. "Let's go."

Before they left the apartment, Alessa sent out one text to Adriano: *I'm going out. Tommas' place.*

Adriano could do with that what he wanted.

Tommas waved a finger over Alessa's head. She batted it away, but the man acted like she hadn't done a thing.

Nonetheless, the bartender still noticed his gesture.

"Yeah, boss?"

Tommas tipped his head in Alessa's direction. "Keep her sober. One more after this, but she's cut off. Got it?"

"Fun sucker," Alessa mumbled around the rim of her glass.

"Twenty-year-olds are not legal in my club," Tommas retorted.

"Got it, boss," the bartender responded.

"You'll be okay?" Abriella asked her sister.

Alessa tipped her gin and tonic up for her sister to see. The one good thing about Tommas Rossi's crazy relationship with Abriella was the man's club. Alessa was a few months shy of her twenty-first birthday, but she never got carded at Tommas' place.

"Perfect."

"Good. Text me in a couple of hours and we'll head out before it gets too packed in here and someone notices us," Abriella said.

"Will do."

Abriella disappeared into the crowd with Tommas. Alessa turned her back to the crowd and sipped on her drink, deciding her sister's words earlier sounded pretty damn good. Drowning her sorrows for the evening was a decent plan.

Alessa wasn't sure how long she sat at the bar, but she felt someone creep in behind her long before she heard the person. A warm, large hand grabbed the curve of Alessa's waist and held tight as another swept her hair to the side and familiar, hot lips pressed to the back of her neck. A lust that was all too wicked burned through her body instantly.

Adriano barely had to do a thing and already, Alessa wanted and needed him.

"Your hair is down tonight," Adriano murmured.

Alessa shivered. "It is."

"And you're wearing blue."

"I am," she agreed, grinning.

"What is underneath?"

"Blue lace."

"Damn," Adriano mumbled against her skin.

His teeth nipped a sensitive spot behind her ear. Alessa jerked on the stool when Adriano's hand slipped around her side and in between her thighs. His hand disappeared under her skirt before his fingers swept under the thin fabric of her panties, brushing her sex with a gentle touch. No one around them seemed to notice what was happening.

"Feel this," Adriano said, chuckling deeply. "You're wet and hot, pretty girl."

"So wet," Alessa whispered.

A single finger slid through her folds again before dipping into her core. Alessa's legs tightened around Adriano's hand, giving her the best pressure on her clit.

"Needy," Adriano said.

"Yes."

He added a second finger, crowding her body further and keeping them from view. Alessa had chosen the far end of the bar which meant she was mostly alone anyway, but there was still a whole dance floor of people just twenty feet away. Alessa tried to take another drink from her glass but ended up using it to hide the way her lips contorted with bliss as Adriano thrust his fingers in and out of her sex slowly.

"I love the way you fuck my fingers, Alessa," Adriano said darkly in her ear. "Love the way your body rocks into my hand like you can't fucking get enough of me. Ride my fingers, Lissa. Soak them up good and wet for me so I can get a taste of you tonight."

"Oh, my God," Alessa breathed.

"Come," Adriano said in her ear, using his free hand to grab her shaking thigh. "Come, Lissa. Let me feel it. I want to taste it. Chase it for me, show me how badly you want it. *Come.*"

Alessa's body lit up like fireworks under Adriano's demanding strokes. She came undone with short, panting breaths and her face tilted down so no one could see. As her body calmed, Adriano pulled his hand out from between her thighs as auspiciously as he could manage. Alessa could feel his smug smirk as he kissed her cheek.

"This public sex thing is starting to get good," Adriano said, a hint of satisfaction deepening his words. "We should do this more often."

"You're terrible."

Adriano hummed a sexy sound as Alessa turned on the stool in just enough time to see his wet fingers disappear into his mouth. Her sex clenched at the sight alone. Adriano winked as he cleaned off his fingers and held Alessa all the while.

Now, all she could think about was getting his mouth on her pussy.

Alessa bit down hard on her lip to stop those thoughts.

"You taste good, too."

"Oh?" she asked, more turned on than ever.

"Great. Dance with me while this club is still quiet and we've got some time together."

Alessa's smile fell. "That's all you want to do?"

Adriano shrugged. "No, I'd really like to take you out to the Camaro and fuck you silly but I also want to feel normal for five minutes. And I love the way you dance, Lissa."

How was she supposed to say no to that?

Alessa was lost in the feeling of Adriano's hands gliding over all the curves of her body as they moved together on the dance floor. Dancing with Adriano was a lot like fucking Adriano, Alessa knew. He was controlled, demanding, and always got her sweating for more. With her ass tucked into his groin as their hips moved to the beat, Alessa was happy.

They were just another couple on the floor.

For a few minutes, they were *normal.*

Under Adriano's urging, Alessa turned to face him.

"Hey," she said, smiling.

Adriano laughed. "Hey."

"*No!* Not in my club!"

The shouts from Tommas Rossi chilled Alessa to the bone. Adriano's grip on her hips tightened momentarily before she was grabbed around the waist roughly and pulled backward. Alessa shouted her shock, her gaze flying up to meet Adriano's as he too was pulled away from her. Alessa's arms were jerked behind her back to pin her in place as she was dragged even further from Adriano.

Adriano's shouts cut her straight to her heart. He struggled with men Alessa didn't know. A fist landed on Adriano's midsection with enough force to send him to his knees. Another landed on the side of his jaw, sending his head flying to the side.

"Stop!" Alessa screamed. "Don't hurt him, *please!*"

Adriano could take care of himself, as far as that went. But when he had four men holding him down and beating on him, it certainly wasn't fair. Alessa's heart was in her throat as blood began to fly. Panic took the air straight from her lungs as she screamed at the men to stop again.

No one listened.

A girl didn't fucking matter.

"Lissa, go," she heard her sister yell from somewhere in the crowd. "Just go!"

Alessa looked for Abriella but couldn't find her. In the fast movements of the people surrounding them, Alessa barely recognized anyone. The sickening voice of Dean Artino in her ear sent Alessa's anger spiraling out of control.

"You just don't know how to behave, do you?" Dean asked.

Alessa tried to fight against Dean's hold, but it was pointless. She couldn't see Adriano through the swarm of people anymore, either.

"Not in my club!" Tommas shouted again.

A single, loud pop echoed in the space. Three more quickly followed, answering the first. Alessa knew that sound better than anyone. The gunshot sent people screaming and scattering. Glasses shattered across the floor and Alessa's heels crunched on the shards as Dean forced her closer to the club's side exit. The gunfire worried her to no end. The screaming was so loud that Alessa's ears rang. A sickness rolled in her stomach.

Where was Adriano?

Her sister?

Who had shot the gun?

"Stop fighting or I will beat your ass black and blue," Dean threatened.

Alessa stilled. "You wouldn't dare."

"You think? Move, right now."

Despite every single inch of Alessa that screamed for her to fight against Dean's order, she let him drag her out of the club. The very moment after the cool air of the outside soaked into Alessa's lungs, she found herself shoved into the closest wall roughly. The side of her cheek scraped against the bricks as Dean forced her head into the wall.

She reacted by striking Dean in the side of the face with her closed fist.

"Let me fucking go," Alessa hissed.

His haughty laughter pissed her off further, but she didn't get the chance to smack him again. Dean caught her flying fist and slammed it into the wall, too.

Dean leaned in close, teeth bared and sneering. "Did you think I wouldn't find out that you were out tonight, Alessa?"

Alessa forced back her rising panic. She wouldn't give Dean her fear or tears. He didn't deserve them and it was all he wanted, anyway.

"I didn't do anything wrong," Alessa spat.

"Oh, you know better than that," Dean muttered.

Alessa's cheek burned. She could feel the bricks making bloody lines along her skin. A million thoughts raced through her mind, but all Alessa could think about was how to get out of the situation she was in. Only a few things would scare Dean enough to make him back off.

"Don't you dare mark me more than you already have, Dean. Joel will kill you, regardless of what I did."

Dean's grip loosened momentarily. "You little bitch."

Alessa laughed. "You've already marked my face, asshole. You'll be lucky if he doesn't mark yours for it."

It worked.

Dean let her go. Just as fast, his fist slammed into the brick wall right beside Alessa's head.

"You are stupider than I thought," he growled. "Still messing around with the Conti prick, huh?"

Lie, Alessa's mind screamed. "No. He just showed up and I agreed to a dance."

Dean scoffed. "To a Rossi's club."

Alessa pushed her back as close to the wall as she could and met Dean's glare. "I don't know who Tommas does business with, Dean!"

Before Alessa could move out of the way, Dean grabbed her face hard enough for it to hurt. His fingers dug painfully into her cheek as he came close enough for Alessa to see the rage swimming in his gaze.

"Rossi should be careful of the garbage he lets in, Alessa," Dean murmured quietly. "And you should be mindful of your behavior in a public place. If I ever catch you dancing with another man, nothing will stop me from teaching you exactly who you belong to. Do you understand me?"

Alessa released a shaky breath. "Yes."

"Good. Let's go. I'll make sure you get home safely."

Like hell.

Alessa wasn't going anywhere with Dean Artino.

"My sister is inside."

"She will be taken home immediately. Your brother has already been contacted. Joel is currently replacing the useless enforcers that had been watching you. A man will be outside your apartment building in an hour. Abriella will meet you there."

"But—"

Dean yanked Alessa away from the wall roughly, quieting her rebuttal. "You're coming with me right now."

The door opened before Dean could pull Alessa further down the alleyway.

"Artino, we've got to get out of here," the man said.

Dean's grip on Alessa loosened. "Why?"

"Mitch is dead."

Alessa froze as Dean finally let her go.

"What?" Dean asked.

The man just shrugged like it didn't make a difference.

Mitch Artino happened to be Dean's cousin and a made man in the family. Alessa hadn't noticed him inside the club, but she'd been mostly focused on Adriano and getting away from Dean.

"You heard me," the guy said. "Stray bullet got him. Red, white, and blue will be showing up soon. We need to beat feet to the pavement."

"All right," Dean muttered heavily. "Meet me around front in thirty."

The guy passed Alessa a fleeting glance. "And her?"

Dean's smile was cold and cruel. "Don't worry. She will make it home just fine. Won't you, Alessa?"

Alessa glared. "Yes, Dean."

"Remember those words, Alessa. They're all I ever want to hear come out of your mouth."

"I had much better things to deal with tonight," Joel said, his face reddening. "And then I get a call about you two being at a club!"

Abriella crossed her arms and glared at their brother. "Oh, poor Joel had to work his sisters into his very busy schedule. My apologies."

Joel took a step forward, his fists clenching at his sides. "That mouth is going to get you in trouble, Ella."

Abriella didn't even flinch. "I doubt it."

"What in the hell were you doing at Tommas Rossi's club?" Joel asked.

"We wanted to have some fun," Alessa said quickly, trying to figure out a way to defuse her brother's anger. "It's been a difficult week, Joel."

"And Tommas has a decent, safe club," Abriella added.

Joel glowered. "This stunt you two pulled isn't going to happen again. That I can guarantee. This apartment is gone, do you understand that? It's gone. You're to be back living at the mansion before this coming Friday. If you leave this apartment between now and then, a driver will be waiting."

Alessa wasn't surprised. "Who called you?"

"A friend that came into the club and noticed Adriano was there," Joel answered, smirking. "And speaking of that little bastard, you had better start talking and fast, Alessa. According to Dean, you and Adriano looked awfully cozy."

"We were dancing."

That was her story and she was sticking to it.

"Why?" Joel demanded.

"Because we're friends."

Joel scoffed darkly. "You two are not friends. You will never be friends with that man, Alessa. Understand that and heed it. He is a Conti—*nothing* to us and *nothing* to you. Sever whatever ties you might have had with Adriano because after today, it's over."

Alessa forced herself to stay quiet.

"And," Joel drawled, pointing a finger at Alessa. "Dean strongly believes there is more to you and Adriano than what you're letting on, Alessa."

"There's nothing," Alessa said slowly, forcing herself to stay calm. In reality, her heart was beating out of control as her brother looked her over like he was searching for any sort of lie in her words. "We're just friends, Joel. Honestly. I'm not an idiot."

"I—"

"Look at me, Joel," she interrupted bitingly. "Look at my face. Dean did this. He saw something innocent and went insane. There's nothing between Adriano and I. There has never been anything between us."

Every single word she spoke was a lie.

It fucking downright ached to do it.

Joel didn't look entirely convinced or pleased. "I'll be watching you, Alessa. If you disobey me, I'll make sure Dean gets his wish before the engagement even happens. Is that understood?"

A cold shiver ran down Alessa's spine.

"You're an asshole," Abriella spat.

Joel sneered. "This isn't news."

"We just wanted to have a little fun, Joel," Alessa said.

"Maybe so, but you knew better. As far as Adriano being at the Rossi club, it certainly answers a few questions for me that I've been wondering about. Tommas isn't being as truthful as he seems."

Abriella opened her mouth but shut it just as fast.

There was enough hate, distrust, and violence to go around. No matter what anyone said or did, it would only grow.

"Before Friday, this apartment needs to be emptied," Joel repeated. "A car will be here in the morning to pick you up at eight sharp for church. Do not keep the driver or me waiting. Neither of you will like what happens if you do."

Without another word, Joel vacated the sisters' apartment. Alessa glared daggers at the closed door, wishing it would implode on itself. Abriella's aggravated sigh brought Alessa's attention back to her sister.

"Where in the hell were you?" Alessa asked.

Abriella waved her hands high. "At the club!"

"Where, Ella?"

"In the back office with Tommy," Abriella said quietly. "We were having a smoke and talking."

And apparently being too busy to notice someone storming the club looking for them.

Alessa's anger was boiling. "Did you see what they did to Adriano?"

Abriella flinched. "He'll be fine."

"Someone shot a gun and someone else died!"

"I didn't see who did that, Lissa."

Alessa huffed, too pissed to think straight. "You know what, I'm over this night."

"Lissa, wait," Abriella said when Alessa turned away from her sister.

"What?"

"I'm sorry. Okay? I really am, Alessa. We were honestly just chilling out and talking. Tommy and I don't get to do that a lot anymore. One of his guys came into the office going on about Dean showing up with his people. We got out of the office as quickly as we could and tried to find you. I figured you would probably try and get Adriano out tonight or whatever."

Alessa's guilt ate at her insides. "It's not your fault. I knew better."

"You shouldn't have to know anything. Adriano is a great guy."

"I almost got him beat to death tonight," Alessa argued.

"Don't worry, Dean will get his," Abriella replied. "Trust me."

"How?"

"He's not made. Adriano is. Your possible future status to Dean doesn't matter, he should have known better than to attack a made man like that. If Riley lets that go unanswered, he's only asking for trouble."

Alessa hadn't expected her sister to sound so agreeable to Riley Conti. "Which side are you on, Ella?"

Abriella shrugged. "Tommy's."

Well, that answered everything.

Not.

"I am sorry," Abriella said. "I feel like I have to look out for you sometimes, Lissa."

"You don't, Ella."

"Yeah, I kind of do. Joel is a dick. Mom and Dad are useless. I used to have Granddaddy wrapped around my finger, but now he's dead and we're stuck with what is left."

Alessa smiled sadly. "We have each other."

Abriella nodded. "Exactly. So, I do have to look out for you. Simple as that."

Without a doubt, Alessa loved her sister. They'd always been close and shared everything. There were no secrets between the two.

"I can't marry Dean," Alessa said. "Look at what he did to me, Ella."

"I know," her sister whispered.

"I know right now it's just the promise of an engagement, but Joel could change that any day and then I'm stuck with that asshole. What am I going to do?"

"We'll figure something out, Alessa."

"Do you believe that?"

"I believe that." Abriella grinned and added, "Just nod and smile for now. That's what Dean wants. But he's stupid and bound to fuck up. Let him."

"We'll see. How's Tommas doing with everything, anyway?"

Abriella's eyes dimmed. "You know I love you and that you're a great roommate, right?"

"So you always say."

"But this isn't home," Abriella said softly. "And Tommy is alone at home."

Yeah. Alessa got what her sister was saying without saying it. Abriella often spent more time away from their apartment than she did in it. Alessa always covered for her when Abriella stayed at Tommas' place, an apartment that he rented especially for Abriella even though he owned his own home. Unfortunately, with the Outfit in an uproar like it was, Abriella couldn't afford to take those kinds of risks.

Tonight was the perfect example.

"Don't worry about it, Alessa. Just get some sleep."

Alessa laughed. "I should."

Abriella made a face. "Church, bright and early."

"The joy. I can feel it."

Alessa gave her sister a tight hug before leaving Abriella alone in the living room. Padding down the hallway to where her bedroom was at the very end, Alessa rubbed at her sore, bruised cheek. By morning, she was sure it would look terrible. Not even makeup would hide that mess completely.

Alessa yanked open her bedroom door and froze right where she stood.

Adriano pushed up from the edge of her bed with the grace of a predator. "Hey."

What?

A slow smile tugged at the corners of Adriano's mouth. The left side of his bottom lip was split and a reddish bruise was beginning to form on his jaw. The sight broke Alessa's heart but hell, he was alive.

"Hey," she finally managed to say.

Adriano laughed as Alessa slammed her bedroom door shut. "Joel sounds pissed."

"He is."

"I still have your spare keys."

Alessa nodded. "I guess so."

"This is probably stupid."

"You being here?" she asked.

"Yeah," Adriano said.

"It's reckless."

"Do you care?"

"No," Alessa replied.

Adriano took two long strides forward, coming to stop in front of Alessa. His fingers ghosted over the scratches and bruises on her face. "Did he do this?"

Alessa didn't need to ask who he meant. Adriano knew. "Yes."

Rage bloomed in his green eyes, but Adriano hid it well.

His words, however, hid nothing.

"I'll kill him."

Alessa had nothing to say to that except, "I love you."

"I love you," Adriano echoed.

"There was a gun …"

Adriano's gaze flicked away from hers fast. "Yeah, mine."

Oh.

"I wouldn't have brought it out, but they didn't give me a choice," Adriano added quickly. "They were all around me. I needed them off."

"You don't have to explain," Alessa murmured.

"Don't I?"

"No."

Because she loved him.

Adriano cupped Alessa's cheek with a gentle touch. "I'm always going to protect what is mine. You understand that, don't you?"

Alessa nodded. "Yes."

"That means I'm going to do whatever I have to so that you're safe and happy, Alessa. Nobody else matters to me. If that means I have to throw myself headfirst into this mess with the Outfit, then that's what I'll do. I've tried to be neutral—I can't be after tonight. And sometimes, it's not always going to be pretty the way I do it."

"It doesn't have to be."

"Good," Adriano said. "I just needed to make sure you understood that."

"I'm not looking for a good man."

"Just yours, huh?"

"Just mine," she agreed.

"I needed to be here, to know you were okay," he said, his tone softer than Alessa had ever heard it before. "I promise I'll get out of here without anyone ever seeing me."

"There's an enforcer at the door, apparently."

Adriano chuckled. "There's a roof exit and a next door building only a couple feet away. I'll jump across and exit there."

Alessa was impressed. "Smart man."

"Very."

"Kiss me, Adriano."

He didn't disappoint.

CHAPTER SEVEN

"Let me see it," Riley demanded.

Adriano tilted his head up, giving his father access to the bruise and cut he sported from the previous night's fight at Tommas' club.

"Jesus, son."

"Yeah, I know."

It still hurt like a motherfucker, too.

Adriano wouldn't show it.

"Christ, you're one-hundred-ninety pounds of muscle and—"

"And Dean had four fools jump me from behind," Adriano cut in fast. "What in the fuck do you expect, Dad?"

"Mitch ended up taking one of your bullets, huh?" Riley asked.

Adriano shrugged. "They didn't give me a choice."

"Well, nobody saw a thing, so we'll use that to your favor at the moment."

"Nobody ever sees anything," Adriano muttered.

Riley didn't respond to that. "Dean has grown a mighty set between his legs over the last week if he thinks something will excuse him from attacking a made man."

"Is that all you're worried about?" Adriano asked.

Riley laughed lowly. "You were at a Rossi's club."

Yeah, Adriano had been waiting patiently for this. "I was."

"With Alessa."

"Coincidence, nothing more. She happened to be there when I showed up," Adriano lied.

Riley's mouth drew tight in his annoyance. "I'm sure."

"What are people saying?"

"That you were at a Rossi club and that speaks to the Rossi family's allegiance," Riley said.

"To us," Adriano filled in.

Riley smiled confidently. "Yes. So, I will overlook your little fuckup with the Trentini girl as this puts me in a better place than I was yesterday.

And I will demand something for … *this*," Riley said, waving at Adriano's face. "What a mess, son."

"My face?"

"No, the Outfit. Although you could have used a good ice pack last night. It might have helped."

"Maybe," Adriano said.

Riley raised a single brow high. "Where did you go after the show at the club? I sent men out to your apartment and to some of your friends' places. You should have come directly to me."

Adriano didn't miss a beat. "I decided to lay low for a while."

"Where?"

"Somewhere safe; where no one would come searching for me," Adriano said.

Riley took a deep breath and eyed his son over, looking for a lie. Adriano was used to this with his father. The man had been doing it ever since Adriano was a kid. It never worked.

"Is that so?" Riley finally asked.

"It is."

"Still a damn mess, son."

Adriano agreed. "What is Tommas saying about last night?"

That's what Adriano really wanted to know. Tommas hadn't invited Adriano to the club. Adriano caused a lot of issues for the guy by bringing trouble in. The Capo could easily spill the truth, saving his own ass in the process.

"Tommas has been pretty neutral in this whole thing," Riley said instead of answering Adriano's question.

"I know. His father isn't."

"Laurent is like a fly you can't kill. I've been waiting for the alcohol to eventually drown him, but maybe I'll have to speed up the process. Nonetheless, I assumed Tommas' friendship with Joel would keep the two close. I think this may drive the wedge I need in between them."

"You didn't answer me," Adriano pointed out. "What is he saying?"

"Nothing. He is saying nothing."

Maybe Tommas Rossi didn't want to save his own ass. Or maybe he had something else to save.

Evelina tiptoed around her father and brother, a jar of something skin-toned in her hand. "Let me see."

"Makeup?" Riley asked.

"Look at him, Dad. This will just hide the bruising for now."

Riley sighed. "Fine. But make it good."

Evelina didn't even try to hide her glare. "Go away."

"Going. Thirty minutes left, so hurry. Both of you."

Adriano met his sister's gaze as she dabbed a bit of makeup onto a sponge. Once his father was out of the room and far from hearing range, Adriano said, "Thanks."

"You're welcome," Evelina said, smiling. "You worried the shit out of me when the phone call came through about the club. Dad had guys going crazy out there looking for you, Adriano. I thought Dean might have … never mind, but it scared me."

"I got out of there just fine," Adriano said.

"Still!"

"Sorry, Eve."

Evelina frowned, dabbing the sponge along his cheek. "Where did you really go last night?"

"Alessa's."

"Seriously?"

"Yeah," he replied. "I just used her spare key. No one was home when I got there."

Evelina didn't look very impressed. "She's going to end up getting you killed, Adriano."

He doubted it. But even so …

"It would be worth it," Adriano said quietly.

"Would it?" she asked.

"Entirely. Love's crazy like that."

"I'll take your word for it."

"Twenty-five minutes!" Riley shouted from the kitchen. "Stop messing around and hurry the hell up. I have cars and men waiting. I do not want to be late and miss the look on Joel's face when he sees us."

Adriano groaned. "Fuck this day."

"He's just on edge," Evelina said.

The Conti family was about to thrust their way right back into the Outfit with a bang. Adriano wasn't exactly impressed with his father's plan to put Joel on edge by showing up at the church where the DeLuca and Trentini families attended, but he agreed to do whatever his father wanted. This was what Riley wanted.

Adriano pushed down the rising aggravation and let his sister finish dabbing on the last bit of foundation. "If the Artino asshole is there, I might kill him, Eve."

He figured someone should be aware.

"Dean?" Evelina asked.

"Yes."

"The guy is a pig," she said dismissively.

He was, but he was also dangerous.

"He hurt Alessa."

Evelina flinched. "Physically?"

"Yes. If you think my face looks bad, you should see what he did to hers using a brick wall, Eve. They might not be officially engaged or anything, but it's basically a sure thing, so she's intended to be his wife and he hurt her. He can't even keep his goddamn hands to himself before he has got a ring on her finger. Imagine what it would be like for her after he strapped her down into a marriage and behind the privacy of closed doors."

Evelina's gaze dimmed. "Oh, Adriano."

He hated pity.

"I might kill him if he shows up today. He won't have his little bastards holding me back."

"Play the good boy," Evelina told him softly. "Give Dad what he wants to get what you want."

Adriano needed someone to talk to about his situation with Alessa. Evelina kept his secrets. It worked.

"You make it sound like I'm selling my soul," Adriano said.

"Maybe you are."

"Alessa owns it anyway, Eve."

"Is love worth that?" she asked.

Yes.

"Just remind me to keep cool, huh?"

"Will do, little brother." Evelina grinned. "What a way to make our entrance back to church, huh?"

Yeah, bruises and all.

Adriano stood stoic and quiet at his father's side. He was the pillar of a cool, calm composure, just as his father had asked. Evelina stood at the other side of their father. Riley, between his children as the head of their family and dressed in all black, smiled as Joel Trentini caught sight of the Conti family standing at the bottom of the church stairs.

Joel's mouth opened to say something but quickly snapped shut.

Adriano knew what the man was seeing. Well over half of the Conti crew had gotten up early and dressed appropriately for church that morning. They stood behind the man they considered their boss and his children, waiting for him to make the first move.

Adriano forced himself not to let his restlessness show. He hadn't been inside a church since his mother's funeral. The grief-fueled ache hadn't disappeared, even if he was too busy to notice it lately.

He couldn't ignore it now.

"Let's go," Riley murmured.

Adriano matched his father's pace as they began their trek up the church steps. He could hear the men behind them walking, too. Bells rang out loudly, warning the start of Mass and the gathering of the parishioners. Joel Trentini's rage swam behind his piercing gaze as his jaw clenched and his hands shook.

Alessa stood a few feet behind her brother at her sister's side.

It took all Adriano had inside not to look at her for long.

At the top of the stairs, Riley took his daughter's hand and patted it. "Find us a seat inside, Eve. Somewhere close to the front."

Joel scoffed when he heard that.

Adriano knew the Trentini family had always taken first pick of the front pews at their church. The DeLucas usually took the next few rows back.

Riley acted like nothing had happened. "Go, Eve."

"Sure," Evelina replied.

Once his daughter had disappeared inside the church, it didn't take long for people to wander out after seeing her. Men from the DeLuca crew stood off to the side, watching the silent scene unfold with wariness. A few looked Adriano over, probably noting the cut on his bottom lip and wondering where the bruises were.

Evelina had done a damn good job of hiding them.

Adriano immediately found Dean Artino in the crowd of men. Like the coward he was, Dean stayed hidden behind the men with his asshole of a father like they were his first and only line of defense. Adriano had news for him—when it came to the Outfit, you were nothing if you weren't made.

They wouldn't protect Dean.

Adriano smirked when Dean's eye caught his. Dean sneered but Adriano's expression didn't waver. Cocking his brow, Adriano reached up and touched his split lip with his thumb before dropping his hand just as fast.

Dean didn't miss the action.

Adriano hoped the asshole knew he'd get him back for the marks and the cheap shots. He'd make damn sure Dean would pay for every bruise, scratch, and drop of blood he spilled from not only Adriano, but Alessa, too.

Fuck you.

Conti men always win.

Like the man could hear what was inside Adriano's mind, Dean dropped his gaze.

Adriano felt the tension skyrocket as his father stepped forward.

"Good morning, Joel," Riley greeted serenely.

Joel's gaze narrowed. "Was your church unavailable this morning,

Riley?"

"No, not at all." Riley's answer was simple and brazen. "How are you?"

"Well," Joel all but forced out.

"And your beautiful sisters?" Riley asked, tipping his head in Alessa and Abriella's direction.

"Fine."

"Ah, that's good to hear. I'd heard you're considering arranging a marriage between young Alessa and the Artino family."

Joel's cheek ticked. "And if I am?"

"Oh, my boy," Riley said in a way that sounded chiding. "An Artino? An unmade Artino, Joel? Terrance would have been sorely disappointed in you for that."

Alessa gave nothing away. She found Adriano's stare, her tongue snaking out to wet her lips. He couldn't help but wonder if she could still feel him days after their last fucking. Did she still have the marks of his fingers on her ass and the tender ache between her thighs like she always did when he fucked her hard and fast?

Adriano needed to get away from those thoughts and fast. He shoved his hands in his pockets as Riley's favorite man, Kolin, stepped up beside him. They intended to appear unafraid and unbothered by the presence of Joel and his allies. Riley wanted to seem higher, above the drama and nonsense.

Adriano wasn't sure if it was working or not.

Walter Artino barked out a laugh and stepped through the throng of men. "You've got a lot of nerve saying anything, Riley."

Joel held up a single hand, quieting Walter instantly. "Is that so, Riley?"

"I think so." Riley glanced over the men standing in the church entrance. "And whether or not you're willing to admit to it, Joel, your father never would have approved of a future match between Alessa and an Artino. Terrance would have had a fit if he were alive."

Silence covered the crowd.

Speechless, Joel could only glare in response.

Riley smiled coldly. "Oh, had you not told them yet of your parentage?"

"A great deal already know," Joel spat.

"You mean the Artinos," Riley replied.

Adriano couldn't help but be a little enraptured by his father's show. Riley Conti wasn't backing down and he was more than willing to play dirty. He wanted respect and he wanted to throw Joel completely off his game.

In Adriano's opinion, Riley was succeeding.

"And this mess last night," Riley continued quieter.

Joel's teeth clenched so hard that his molars crunched. "I'd heard."

"I think your men owe my son an apology, Joel."

Walter scoffed. "Like hell."

"Joel," Riley said, firmer the second time. "Regardless of this feud between us, your unmade man made an attack on a made Outfit *principe* simply for dancing with a woman who isn't even his fiancée yet. Now, I understand a no touch policy, but Alessa and my son have always been friends. Adriano kept a watch on her all through high school. Never once did your father take issue with the closeness between the two. Terrance always knew it was innocent. Just like the dancing last night was innocent. And my God, look at her poor face."

All the eyes turned on a very uncomfortable looking Alessa. She cupped the side of her cheek with her hand, her gaze turning downward. Adriano's rage pulsed hard and fast through his veins. Makeup did nothing to hide the bruises and scratches on her cheek.

And then, Alessa's lashes fluttered as she lifted her gaze to meet Adriano's. There was a smug satisfaction swimming in her irises. Like she was taking some enjoyment out of Dean's actions being shamed.

"I wasn't aware Alessa's injuries were caused by Artino," Joel said slowly.

The lie was boldfaced and terrible. Anyone with two brain cells could see it.

"Then you are an idiot, and I feel for the poor treatment your sister is sure to receive at her future husband's hand because you look the other way," Riley murmured. "Look at her face. She has the bruise marks of his fingers on her cheek. Refusing an apology to my son I could understand … maybe. But your own sister, Joel?"

Joel looked absolutely enraged. "I appreciate the information."

Riley shrugged. "Do with it what you wish, my boy."

Despite not being totally in agreement with his father on a lot of things, Adriano had to admit his father was putting on a good show. Riley had effectively put Joel into a position where he had no other choice but publically shame Dean for his actions or privately discipline him for them. Either way, abuse towards women in the Outfit had never been acceptable. Not when people were made aware.

It didn't make a difference with the war between the families dividing them all, women and children should always be held above reproach. They were the untouchables. The men of *la famiglia* would surely demand some sort of justice for Alessa's marks.

Dean would pay.

Adriano prayed to God he would be the one to deliver it.

"As for my son's apology," Riley drawled, taking a step toward Joel.

"What of it?" Joel asked.

"He will accept one from you, of course. Won't you, son?"

Adriano nodded once, giving Joel a passing glance. "Of course. Seeing as how Dean is your man but still unmade in the family, an apology from you for his actions would be fine. I will offer forgiveness if the apology is appropriate."

Riley smirked over his shoulder at Adriano like he approved. "Well said."

Joel's shoulders straightened. "You're asking for a lot."

"I'm asking for the very same thing the rest of the men in this family would demand, Joel," Riley replied frankly. "And do not for one second believe that any of these men would allow Dean's actions on one of their highly regarded and respected sons in the Outfit to go unanswered."

Quietly, confirmative murmurs started to pass through the crowd.

Adriano could practically feel the pleasure his father took in that.

"Dean will be handled," Joel said.

"And my apology?" Adriano asked, smirking.

Joel's fists clenched a little tighter. "Perhaps we could discuss that on another day."

Adriano held back a scoff. "Today is just as good as any other, Joel."

"You're treading thin ice, Conti."

"Oh, I'm sure we can sit down at another time and work this all out," Riley said, stepping in front of Joel as if to block Adriano from the man's sights. He was close enough to hold a hand out to Joel, waiting for the man to shake. Joel looked down at Riley's offering with obvious distain. "Friends always have a way of working these things out, don't they?"

Joel's eyes flashed around the crowd of people. It was clear he was trying, and failing, to figure out a way to save his face and position.

"Maybe we could sit down at some point," Joel said, still refusing to take Riley's hand.

"How about this coming Friday?" Riley asked, smiling widely. "And of course, we'll be there to pay our respects to Terrance tomorrow."

"You'll be there—" Joel's words cut off as his face turned beet red. "You're crossing a line, Riley."

"Am I? Terrance was one of my oldest friends. Despite everything that happened over the last couple of months, I would like to say goodbye to him, Joel. Are you refusing me that?"

"Like you refused us at your wife's funeral?" Joel asked bitingly.

"Any man in this church who was there to witness my first few days after my wife's death would be stupid to say I was in my right mind. I was grieving and it showed."

Joel laughed bitterly before his voice turned lower and threatening. "And after, when you had Terrance killed, what then?"

Riley didn't even blink at the question. "I never had my friend killed."

"Liar," Joel muttered.

Murmurs passed through the crowd again.

"And shooting up the guests in our driveway the night we welcomed home the Rossi twins," Joel added. "What of that, Riley?"

Riley didn't answer.

Adriano's father had denied that to him, but Riley refused to confirm or deny his involvement in the shooting that killed Lea Rossi and Ben DeLuca to anyone else who asked. And for good reason, it drew fear.

"Or the shooting of the Rossi business last month?" Joel asked.

Another incident Riley wouldn't confirm or deny.

Adriano's father seemed to like letting people make assumptions and draw their own conclusions about his involvement in things.

On one hand, Adriano believed his father had been involved with some of those things, but on the other, he wasn't sure. It didn't seem like Riley to go off half-cocked, killing whoever. But Riley was looking to move higher and he just might do whatever in the hell he needed to so he could get there. Adriano suspected that was just what his father wanted people thinking, too.

Riley smiled. "You're making a point for me without even trying, Joel. Do you realize that?"

Adriano took the chance to watch the men, gaging their reactions to the conversation. Most seemed entirely focused on Riley and Joel, while some watched the men standing behind the Conti family.

"You can throw whatever names at me you want, Joel, but a liar is not one of them. Between the two of us, we both know who deserves that title. I did not order the hit on your father. I was angry and distraught, but not enough to kill him. You, on the other hand, have certainly gained a lot in the last week since his passing."

Attention flew to Joel in a flash. Adriano hadn't known ahead of time what his father would say or bring up in their first meeting with the families and Joel, but Riley was pulling out all the stops for this, apparently. Especially if he was blatantly suggesting Joel had been the one to order the hit on Terrance.

The men of the Outfit would have to be stupid and blind not to seriously consider Riley's words against Joel. They had merit. They had worth. Just as much, if not more, than Joel's accusations against Riley did.

"Are you still living in Terrance's home?" Riley asked.

"My home," Joel corrected sharply.

Riley's lips pursed. "As far as I know, as I'm included in Terrance's final Will and am expected to be at the reading on Tuesday, his Testament hasn't been read yet, Joel. That home still belongs to your father."

Joel sneered. "Which one?"

"Terrance, of course. I don't mince words like you do."

Ouch.

Adriano's respect for his father's unfazed attitude climbed a notch. Regardless of Joel's arrogance or rudeness, Riley stood firm and cool.

Like any good boss would do.

Adriano did a double-take of his father then, realizing something. Riley would make a good boss for the Outfit. He had all the skills, temperaments, and ability to lead. He commanded attention, and then he kept it. Riley reminded Adriano a lot of Terrance.

But what would they all have to give up for Riley to become the boss?

"That home is mine," Joel repeated, flicking his wrist in Riley's direction as if to dismiss him. "You're running off at the mouth and nothing more."

"Just like the Outfit is yours, too?" Riley asked calmly.

Joel looked as if someone had shoved a lemon in his mouth. "I beg your pardon?"

"How angry over Terrance's death are you really, Joel? How often have we all watched you tear into that man, battle against his requests, and challenge his position? How many times did he reach out to you only to have you push him away? You're not angry, but you are smart."

"Careful," Joel said with fire in his gaze.

Riley didn't relent. "Yes, you are very smart. What a convenience Terrance's death is for you, my boy. Keep using it. Maybe it'll get you somewhere."

Joel spluttered for a response but came up with nothing.

Riley continued smiling like this was just another day for him.

"Dad, we should join Eve," Adriano said. "I'm sure the priest would like to start Mass."

"We should." Turning his attention back to Joel, Riley asked. "Are you coming?"

"You are unbelievable," Joel spat.

"It's easy to act like a boss when you have no competition to stand against, my boy. Welcome to the real world. You have big shoes to fill, Joel. And you don't even come close. All of these men know it."

With that, Riley dismissed Joel and walked straight on past to the doors leading into the main floor of the church. Dino DeLuca leaned against one of the ornate doors with an amused grin playing at the edges of his mouth.

"DeLuca," Riley greeted.

"Boss," Dino murmured.

The quiet chatter of the people behind them stopped all at once.

Before Terrance's death, it hadn't been uncommon for people to greet Riley with the title of boss. Being the front boss for the Outfit, Riley always had a certain measure of control and respect. But with Joel and Riley feuding over the highest position the family had, it left a lot of things out in the open.

Dino had plainly offered his opinion on the topic by referring to Riley as his boss.

Riley offered Dino his hand to shake. Dino took it.

"Where is the happy couple?" Riley asked as Dino released him. "I'd heard Lily and Damian were expected to show today."

"My sister and her new husband are late this morning," Dino explained. "They were coming directly from their week away, so I'm not surprised that they're reluctant to leave the hotel. Hopefully when they do show, they'll be quiet about their tardiness and not draw attention."

"The last thing Damian Rossi ever does is draw attention, Dino." Riley laughed. "Nonetheless, I understand their reluctance to rejoin the real world. My apologies for missing the wedding."

Dino shrugged. "No harm done. My sister would appreciate some time with her friend, however. Eve and Lily have always been close, Riley. It's a shame to ruin friendships simply because men can't work out their differences."

"I'll see what I can do," Riley replied. "She is a Rossi now. We have to consider that."

"Oh, I'm sure they'll come to their senses."

"And what about you, Dino?" Riley asked. "Have you come to your senses, yet?"

"I'm getting there," the man answered.

Riley smiled tightly. "I hope so. Although after today, I'm certain we will all know exactly which side you're on."

Dino didn't respond. Adriano caught the gaze of Dino's younger brother Theo who was leaning against the far wall. Theo watched the exchange in silence, but disgust was clearly written in his furrowed brow. Quickly, Adriano found Alessa again, too. She was still and quiet, taking everything in like she usually did without inserting herself. Alessa knew her place and to get what she wanted, she had to follow along. As for the men behind them, Adriano ignored them.

Let them make of it what they wanted.

It was what Riley needed, anyway.

"Church?" Adriano asked behind his father.

"Church," Riley agreed.

"Eve, go let the driver know we're ready to leave," Riley said to his daughter.

"Sure," Evelina replied.

"Ask him to bring the car up to the front steps. I'm not in the mood to walk across the parking lot."

Evelina nodded, gave Adriano a smile, and started her trek down the front steps of the church right behind Dino DeLuca. The man had been talking to his sister and new brother-in-law. Lily and Damian Rossi didn't show up to the church until almost thirty minutes into Mass, but they kept their entrance quiet as they took a free pew in front of Dino and Theo.

Adriano turned away from the sight of Damian pulling his wife in for a kiss that was not meant for others to see. It felt as if he was intruding on a private moment.

Church had gone by quietly, for the most part. Adriano had very little patience for Sunday services preaching forgiveness and love when he was distracted by his own issues and the pretty girl two pews over.

It took all that Adriano had inside him not to reach out and grab Alessa's hand as she walked past him with her sister at her side. Alessa glanced up at him through those thick lashes of hers, her eyes glittering with the reminders of love and sex. The simple, innocent look was more than enough to get his cock hardening.

Alessa's sensual little smile sealed the deal.

He could almost forget about the bruises and scratches on her cheek. Almost.

Dean stayed close behind Alessa, glaring at Adriano the entire time. When Dean's attention was distracted by his father, Adriano gave Alessa a quick smile.

"Hey," she mouthed.

Adriano winked.

"Oh, Joel," Riley called.

Joel's back stiffened as he started walking down the steps. Turning, the younger man asked, "Yes?"

"Friday, hmm?"

"I will see what I can do, Riley."

Riley laughed. "There is no seeing, only doing. I'm not offering you room to argue about the meeting, Joel. It needs to happen."

"Perhaps other things need to happen even more," Joel replied. "Have you considered that?"

"Do not forget that I am still a made man in this family," Riley said coldly. "And my button is worth far more than yours will ever be, Joel. I have already offered the sit-down. There is no man in the Outfit who will shun my request and if you do, it will not end well. I can promise you that. Friday, my restaurant in Melrose, be there."

Joel scowled. "I—"

"Be there, Joel."

Adriano could fill in the blanks his father wasn't saying. If Joel didn't show, it would give Riley the perfect excuse to end the man without any possible backlash. Adriano wondered why his father was giving Joel any handouts at all.

Then again, maybe Riley expected Joel to shun him.

"Fine, Friday," Joel said.

Riley nodded, dismissing Joel like he had earlier.

Adriano searched the parking lot for his sister. Evelina was just jumping into the backseat of the black car as Dino DeLuca began to back his white Bentley out of the parking space directly across from their driver's car.

And then Adriano was blinded.

It was so goddamn *loud.*

And *hot.*

Fire, shattering glass, and screams.

His mind couldn't comprehend the sight he was seeing across the parking lot. He didn't understand the fireball or the flinging glass and metal. He didn't know what the sound was or why the white Bentley was covered in red flames and black smoke.

The screams got louder.

A bomb.

Adriano's mind finally caught up with the scene going down.

Panic for his own safety bubbled up along with the fear for his sister who was inside a car only fifteen feet away from the bomb.

Riley hit the ground when Kolin pushed him down.

Adriano did the only thing that made sense. Alessa was still in arm's reach for Adriano, so he grabbed the back of her dress and yanked her further away from the sound and flying debris. Her cry of shock sliced him straight down to the bone, but he just kept pulling her closer and walking backward. He needed to get her away from that, or anything that might come next.

In the background, Adriano could hear someone shouting.

A familiar voice.

A pained voice.

A heartbroken voice.

Lily Rossi.

"*Dino!*"

Adriano pushed Alessa inside the church right behind Damian Rossi who had his fighting, screaming wife in a bear hug. The man kept apologizing to her, over and over. Alessa stared at Adriano, wide-eyed and frightened.

"Don't go," Alessa whispered.

He stepped away from her.

Alessa's voice echoed louder. "Don't go."

Adriano didn't want to.

He turned away and bolted for the steps, straight for his sister.

CHAPTER EIGHT

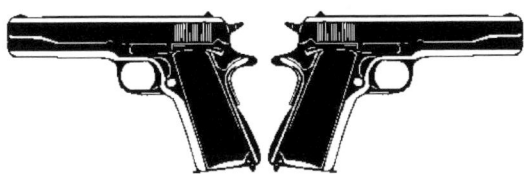

Alessa stayed pressed into the corner, watching the men pace back and forth in the living room. The Artino family ranted on and on about Riley showing up at the church and his demand of an apology. Dean spewed his vile words, waving a hand at Alessa and swearing her marks were by her own cause.

Alessa stayed quiet.

She had nothing to say.

Nothing she could say would matter.

Abriella, leaning against the far wall across from Alessa, caught her sister's eye and frowned.

She could still smell the smoke.

She could still feel the heat.

"That bastard," Theo choked out.

Joel didn't move from an inch from his seat in the large recliner at the head of the room. "I'm so very sorry, Theo."

No, he wasn't.

Alessa's mind screamed the truth: Joel did this.

Joel did it.

Joel.

Alessa wasn't surprised that Theo had fallen into Joel's trap. As it was, everyone suspected Riley's involvement in a number of things. The shooting that killed Lea Rossi and Ben DeLuca. The attack on the Rossi business and the retaliation on Laurent's crew.

Riley Conti had done nothing to confirm or deny his involvement in those things. People pointed to him, and he said nothing in response.

Why wouldn't everyone think he had done this, too?

Fear was the perfect motivator.

Alessa wasn't sure what to believe regarding everything else. Had Riley done the other shootings and killings? She didn't know

But she knew Riley didn't kill Dino.

Who would believe her?

"My brother ..." Theo trailed off with a pained grunt, his teeth clenching. "My brother, Joel."

"He'll answer for this," Joel promised calmly. "Riley will answer for this."

"Did you hear what he said to Dino before the service?" Theo asked, his voice cracking on the final word. "That we would all know, Joel. We would all know which side my brother was on after today. He fucking told us right then!"

"I heard him," Joel said.

"We all heard him," Walter muttered.

"Why the fuck would Riley go after my brother, huh?" Theo asked, his frustration boiling over. He threw his hands high, facing Joel as his shoulders heaved with every breath. "Why Dino? There was no reason for that, none at all!"

Alessa knew the truth. Abriella knew the truth.

Joel, Walter, and Dean knew the fucking truth.

Theo didn't.

Alessa's heart broke for the man.

"Of course there was a reason," Joel said quietly.

Theo scoffed. "Oh?"

"Yes. Riley clearly wanted to make some point. You knew your brother was leaning toward the Conti side of things, Theo." Joel shrugged in the chair, looking his fingernails over as he added, "And I brought it up to you, too. Dino couldn't be trusted entirely."

"He was loyal to me," Theo spat.

"You believe he was, and I'm almost positive Riley did, too. Somehow, the man is getting information." Joel eyed the mostly silent men in the room, never once sparing his sisters any of his attention. "Perhaps Riley's point was to show that even those who think they might have a leg in this game, those who are close to him, are not safe from his wrath if he decides to level it on them."

Theo's body trembled. "I want that man to pay."

"As I said," Joel murmured, "he will."

No.

Alessa shook her head but forced her mouth to stay quiet.

No.

Riley Conti didn't do this.

She wanted to tell them—tell Theo—but who would believe her?

Alessa caught Abriella's stare again. Even her sister looked worn and unsettled. If Abriella couldn't manage to save face and keep strong, what did that say for Alessa? What did that say for their family and the Outfit?

Joel had finally gone too far.

You shouldn't skip church on Sunday ... I hear it's going to be a blast.

Joel's words. Not Riley's.

Why had her brother done this?

"If this doesn't show the Outfit that Riley Conti cares for no man and cannot be trusted, I don't know what will," Joel said quietly.

Joel played his game well, Alessa realized. His words said it all. He'd killed a man simply to drive Dino's family closer to theirs by using their pain, grief, and fear. Joel ended someone's life to further his own, not because that man deserved to die.

It was disgusting.

It left a terrible, smothering chill running through Alessa's body.

A false sadness covered Joel's expression. His frown looked real. Even his tired, watery gaze seemed true. Nothing was. Joel was a liar.

A filthy, untrue, turncoat liar. A dirty player in the Outfit's games.

Because he couldn't win otherwise.

Alessa wouldn't let him win.

She'd make goddamn sure of that.

"We'll get him, Theo," Joel said.

Theo nodded. "We better."

"We will, Theo. Mark my words."

Alessa felt Adriano's presence in the church before she even saw him. It was like comfort and home had just walked into the room to pick her up and take her with him.

Dressed in all black, Adriano walked down the aisle between the pews. The suit Adriano wore was appropriate for the funeral. His hands were clasped at his back and his head was bowed just enough to keep his eyes from Alessa's view as he passed her by. Silent and resigned, Adriano barely graced anyone with his attention.

Alessa wanted him to look at her.

Just fucking *look* at her.

She'd tried to call him, needing to hear his voice and make sure he was okay. She wanted to tell him what she knew about Joel and the things he had done. Adriano needed to know that Joel was planning something on Riley.

But how could she tell him if he wouldn't talk to her?

The funeral went on as planned, despite the bombing from the day before. The location for the service had changed to a smaller church, one Alessa's grandfather used to attend when he was a younger man.

Somehow, Adriano must have gotten the change of venue for the service if he showed up. He showed up alone, interestingly enough. Alessa didn't miss the fact that Riley and none of his men had accompanied Adriano to the service.

Adriano came alone. He came unprotected.

He didn't look the least bit frightened as he stepped up to Joel with a sympathetic frown and offered his hand, quiet apologies for their loss, and nothing more.

It was brazen.

Bold.

Crazy.

Completely insane.

And guessing by the look on Joel's face—the unaltered rage churned with shock—this was just another game to the families.

Dean stood beside Alessa, keeping her firmly in place. She couldn't skip out or try to catch Adriano as he left. Dean wasn't likely to leave her side.

Abriella's hand found Alessa's. Without a word, her sister squeezed.

Someone was there.

People were watching.

This is how you win in a war. Play dirty.

Adriano passed by Peter and Sara who stood at the casket, offering them the same he did Joel. Abriella and Alessa stood in the front pew, directly across from Terrance's casket. Briefly, Adriano paused at the casket, murmuring his goodbye to an Outfit boss.

When Adriano spun on his heel, turning his back to the casket, his gaze caught Alessa's. She searched his eyes, needing to find something there staring back. Something familiar. Something comforting and loving.

Anything.

Alessa found nothing.

Adriano looked cold.

It burned her, searing through her heart and soul with a devastating intent.

Abriella squeezed Alessa's hand again.

Just another game.

Adriano had to play his, too.

Christ.

Alessa hoped that's what it was.

Abriella slipped inside Alessa's bedroom silently. "Hey."

Alessa didn't look up from her phone. She was waiting for a call or text, but nothing came. Nothing except useless platitudes and apologies from college friends and distant relatives about the death of Terrance. Certainly not the phone call or message Alessa wanted, at least not from the right person.

Adriano.

Alessa sighed, shoving her phone down to the blankets. "Hey."

Abriella waved at the door. "The house is still packed full."

Great.

"Still?" Alessa asked.

"Very," Abriella confirmed. "And it'll probably keep going most of the night. Joel is already drunk, but I'm not sure if that's because he's an idiot, or because he's pissed off about Adriano showing up at the funeral after the bomb."

Alessa tried not to be annoyed, but she really just wanted to go home to her apartment, away from the prying eyes of the guests and mourners. As was custom for a family after a funeral, the Trentinis arranged a dinner and quiet party for guests to celebrate Terrance's life. Quiet being the key word.

Apparently no one got that message.

It wasn't uncommon for the parties to get loud, even if it was brought on by a funeral. Given the bombing a day before, and Adriano's show today, a great deal of the Outfit's families had shown up alongside friends and relatives.

Alessa just couldn't stand it anymore. She had needed to get away, and the very first chance she could, slipped upstairs to her old room.

Well …

New room.

By the end of the week, she supposed she would be living in this space again.

It felt like the old her—a younger, more naive Alessa.

"Adriano won't answer my calls," Alessa said.

Abriella frowned. "Give him a couple of days. Maybe he's just out of it right now. Eve is in the hospital, too."

Yeah, Alessa heard. Evelina had taken a few bumps and cuts from flying debris. The front and side windows of the car she had been in when the bomb went off had exploded. The Conti driver had been badly burned.

"I want him to know," Alessa said. "I need him to know that I know who did this."

"This is going to backfire," Abriella muttered.

Alessa glared at her sister. "I don't care. Adriano probably thinks I blame his family for this. I need him to know that I don't."

"No, I meant Joel."

"What?"

"Joel," Abriella said again. "He's trying to turn people against Riley. I think it's going to backfire."

"How so?"

"Fear is a great motivator, Alessa. The stronger man always wins."

"But all these people are here, Ella."

Abriella shrugged. "Middle men. Unimportant men. Go back downstairs and take a look around, Alessa. The right men, the ones Joel should have, didn't follow the family back to the dinner."

"Laurent is here," Alessa said.

"Tommas isn't," Abriella replied just as fast. "And everybody knows he makes the important calls for the Rossi side."

"Theo is here for the DeLucas. Walter, too."

"Theo is grieving. He's lost a great deal of people. His uncle, his brother, and in a way, his sister is married off to a family who isn't showing a lot of support to the Trentini cause. But a lot of the DeLuca crew is keeping their distance from Joel. It's the same thing as the Rossi crew.

"Walter, on the other hand, is using this tragedy to climb higher," Abriella said, looking entirely unbothered by the fact they were stuck in a mess. "He thinks Joel will take him there. As far as Riley goes, he has the biggest crew. The Conti side of the Outfit has always dominated the streets because he's the front boss with a closer hand to the men. Riley had a great deal of support and if his crew starts moving in on the others, they'll bow down because they don't have a choice."

Alessa chewed on her lower lip. A mess wasn't good enough to describe the shit show surrounding them. Everything Abriella said simply told Alessa that the fighting would continue until someone got what they wanted. A higher seat. The better title.

Where in the hell did that leave her?

Where did that leave Adriano?

All over again, Alessa was left with the distinct feeling that she and Adriano just couldn't be. Something was always going to stand in their way. Someone would always be waiting, ready to step in and stop them.

Alessa didn't want to think that way but the nagging pain in her chest, reminding her of how far apart Adriano already was from her, wouldn't leave.

Joel was still planning to marry Alessa off the first chance he could.

The families were still feuding.

Adriano still wouldn't answer his damned phone.

The Outfit might be a ruined mess, but her life was a hurricane.

Pity party for one right here, Alessa thought.

She shook it off, knowing it wouldn't do her any good.

"What am I supposed to do, huh?" Alessa asked. "How is this supposed to work out?"

Abriella grabbed the doorknob and pulled open the door as she said, "Wait, Alessa. Something else will happen. It always fucking does. That is one guarantee we can always count on in this life."

Waiting was the killer.

Alessa padded through the bottom floor, making her way toward the large kitchen for a drink of water. Thankfully, all the guests had left the property, but it was well after one in the morning. She'd stayed hidden up in her room until she was sure the mansion had cleared of people.

Another positive: Dean hadn't come looking for her.

Passing by the living room, quiet murmurs and womanly giggles stopped Alessa in her tracks. She didn't try to hide the fact she was standing in the large entrance, but none of the people inside noticed her there, either.

Joel sat in the leather recliner at the head of the room. A woman rested on his lap, draped across Joel and the chair. Alessa recognized her as the daughter of one of Walter's men. Chloe was her name. There was only a handful of times Alessa could remember seeing her brother with a woman. And it sure looked like he had a whole handful of the girl in his lap, considering Joel's hand was up her skirt and her legs were spread wide.

Chloe didn't act like there was anyone else in the room, watching the show she was putting on with her legs opened, her panties down around her knees, and her skirt pulled up high.

Someone else was in the room, though.

Dean was sprawled across the couch with a glass of whiskey in his hand, laughing loudly. The amber liquid in his glass spilled to the floor and he rolled into a sitting position. It certainly didn't help that Chloe was starting to shudder and gasp like she was enjoying it all.

Alessa bet the girl's father would absolutely die if he knew what she was doing tonight. Then again, maybe Chloe's father thought messing around with Joel would get him higher.

Games.

They all fucking played them.

They all had their own to play.

"What are we going to do about Riley, huh?" Dean asked.

Joel shrugged, his hand still moving between Chloe's legs.

Alessa was just grateful the woman was turned the opposite way from her. Unfortunately, the pulled down panties and spread legs was enough to make Alessa's stomach roll.

"Be specific, asshole," Joel said.

A slur coated his words, telling Alessa her brother was drunk.

Or still drunk from earlier.

"Adriano and the club thing," Dean explained.

A very noticeable bulge in Dean's slacks caught Alessa's attention. Dean was clearly enjoying the show between Joel and Chloe. That was even more disgusting to her.

"We're going to make you, of course," Joel said flippantly.

Dean grinned. "Yeah?"

"Walter suggested it. Getting you the button will clear that nonsense right up. And it looks good for my sister to be getting hers with a made man when the time comes, anyway."

"Perfect," Dean said, rubbing his hands together. "When?"

"Soon. Just act fucking surprised when you get the call. All right?"

"Got it, boss."

Alessa couldn't let that happen. She clenched the still silent phone in her hand a little harder, willing Adriano to answer one of her many messages back.

Chloe's loud cry was swallowed up by Joel grabbing the girl's face, pulling her up high, and shoving his tongue down her throat. Alessa turned away, not wanting to see that or what was going to come next.

Apparently, she didn't have to see anything. Their next words were enough.

"What do you think, Chloe?" Joel asked, his tone dark and deep with drink. "Are you up for a little fun tonight? Two, maybe?"

"Maybe," Chloe echoed.

"Whiskey dick goes all night," Dean said, almost like he was warning the girl.

Yuck.

That was the man Joel planned on trying to marry her off to eventually.

Right. No way.

It wasn't going to happen. Alessa didn't care what she needed to do in order to get Dean gone from her life forever, she would do it. The information she learned tonight, and the little bit of understanding she had when it came to the Outfit and initiating members, was the perfect chance to help Dean along ... far away from her.

Even if that meant he would be going six feet under.

Alessa had never spilled blood. Her hands had never once been dirty. She'd fucking bathe in it if that meant getting the hell away from Dean and the Artinos.

Play dirty.

This is how you win in a war.

But what would winning mean?

Alessa was willing to risk it.

"Yes or no?" Joel said.

"I'm still waiting on that from you, Joel," Chloe murmured. "We keep fucking and messing around, but you don't want to talk about real life."

Joel laughed. "Oh, Chloe. You need to forget about that shit."

"Be grateful you're sitting on his lap at all, babe," Dean said, chuckling.

Chloe scoffed. "I'm good enough to fuck, but not anything else, huh?"

"You don't wife a whore, sweetheart," Joel replied.

Ouch.

Alessa kept walking.

"Who are you texting?"

Alessa didn't get the chance to hide her phone from Dean before he snatched it from her grasp. "Dean!"

Dean waved her off, scrolling through her iPhone and the few vague messages Alessa hadn't deleted from the last hour. Adriano's contact name and information had always been disguised as someone else. She had always been careful to delete their conversations from the main inbox as well as the history and text files. Plus, she always kept her messages to Adriano short, sweet, and without any real detail to give away who he was.

Nonetheless, Alessa's anxiety still pounded deep.

"Give me the damn phone," Alessa said.

Dean gave one last look at the screen, rolled his eyes, and handed it back over. "Who is Rain?"

Quickly, Alessa slipped her phone back into her pocket. "A girlfriend from school."

"A new friend or just someone?" Dean asked, walking over to the office door. He looked out into the hallway and checked the hall. "Still quiet."

Alessa didn't care if the hall was quiet or not. "Why does it matter if she's a new friend or not?"

"You haven't been texting her for very long but the contact was made years ago."

Shit.

Alessa racked her mind for an appropriate excuse. "We met a long time ago at school, exchanged numbers, but never really hit it off. Her grandmother died. I just found out this morning from a mutual friend when I picked up some stuff before coming here. I was trying to get a message to her. To say sorry, you know."

It was a good enough excuse. Joel had allowed her driver to take Alessa to meet up with a friend to get some of the assignments and notes that she'd missed from her summer classes.

Dean leaned against the doorjamb and eyed Alessa curiously. "That seems nice of you."

"Does who I am scream 'bitch'?"

"No."

But she was a damn good liar.

"To me, on the other hand, you're downright nasty," Dean added.

"I wonder why," Alessa muttered under her breath.

Dean chuckled. "I always liked difficult women."

Jesus.

She wanted to get away from this man as quickly as she could. Why Dean had even been invited to Terrance's Will reading, Alessa wasn't sure. It wasn't like Dean or his father had a place in the Will.

Still, Joel asked them to come along.

Despite his son acting as his lawyer for well over a decade, Terrance had went outside of the family for his final wishes to be documented and carried out. The executor of the Will explained to the family that Terrance had asked for each person to have their reading done alone. Alessa's inheritance from her grandfather's estate had already been read and explained, alongside Abriella's and their parents'. Now, she was just waiting for Joel and Riley to finish theirs.

She'd hoped Adriano would show up today since his father had to come, but being stuck inside a private office space with Dean wasn't allowing her any time to go search for him.

"Are we almost done here or what?" Alessa asked.

Dean shrugged. "Waiting on your brother, Lissa."

"Alessa. It's Alessa."

"Lots of people call you Lissa."

Not you.

Alessa just stared at Dean, hoping her displeasure was clear for him to see. "It's Alessa, Dean."

Dean spun on his heel to face her completely with his arms crossed and a passive expression. "You know, I might not be such a bad guy in the end of you'd just try. I've never hid my intentions or interest in you, Alessa. We could be good together, this doesn't have to be a fight every fucking step of the way."

"You mean while you fuck everything with a hole between its legs and then come home to me for more?" Alessa asked sweetly. "Because I'm not interested in that, Dean."

"That's awfully presumptuous of you, Alessa. Who said I'm not faithful?"

The scene she witnessed the night before with her brother, Chloe, and Dean said it all. The man was a vile pig. Alessa wouldn't be another one of his conquests or a permanent notch on his bed post. She wasn't his fiancée yet and if she got her wish, she would never be.

Dean grinned. "How many men have you been with, anyway?"

One.

Adriano.

"None of your business," Alessa replied.

"You might enjoy a real man, you know."

She had one, but even still …

Alessa scoffed. "I'll make sure to find one, Dean."

Anger clouded Dean's features. "Will you, now?"

Instinct demanded Alessa take a step back and put some distance between her and Dean. Pride kept her in place as he moved closer, standing toe to toe with her.

"Have you forgotten so quickly what the last little show with a man who wasn't me earned you, sweetheart?" Dean's hand came up lightning fast, but the stroke he leveled on Alessa's cheek was tender and soft. It still burned like acid on her skin. "Find that man and see what happens, Alessa."

She refused to let the memories or the lingering pain from her injury caused by Dean overwhelm her with fear. Dean didn't deserve to see it. Men like him thrived on a woman's compliance and terror.

He wouldn't win.

Not with Alessa.

Dean dragged his hand along the side of Alessa's blue jumper, pulling the thin strap down over her right shoulder. His gaze darkened at the sight of her black, satin bra. He raked his stare straight down to the spot between her legs, licking his lips as he smiled salaciously. Dean hid nothing.

Vile wasn't a good enough word.

"Do the panties match?" he asked.

Disgust spilled into Alessa's throat and she forced the shudder back.

"Go to hell, Dean."

"Well, do they?"

Alessa wouldn't give him what he wanted. She stayed quiet as he fixed the shoulder of her jumper, letting his fingers linger for too long.

Without a doubt, she would not marry this man.

Somehow, she just *wouldn't*.

Dean didn't seem to mind. "This is all mine, Alessa. No one else gets to see it. Pretty soon, I'll have a ring on your finger making it fact. Remember that."

"Have you forgotten what I told you?" Alessa asked, keeping her expression unreadable.

"What is that?" Dean asked.

"It'll be the last goddamn thing you ever get to see."

It wasn't a lie.

Dean smiled a cold sight. "Don't be like that, Lissa."

"It's Alessa, Dean. And if you want me to speak to you, I suggest you learn it and fast."

"I'd prefer you spoke as little as possible."

Alessa refused to grace him with another response. She moved toward the door, intent on finding her sister or parents. She didn't have to stay alone in a room with Dean if she didn't want to.

Dean grabbed her wrist with enough force for it to hurt. With a rough tug to bring her closer, Alessa nearly stumbled in her flats.

"Where do you think you're going?" Dean asked.

Anywhere away from him.

Alessa steeled her spine—another lie was coming. "To the bathroom."

"There's one across the hall."

"It's for men and the women's bathroom is out of order on this side of the office."

Dean sighed, glancing at the clock on the wall. "Ten minutes, Alessa. I'm supposed to be keeping an eye on you today. Get back here before your brother does. Understood?"

Alessa yanked her wrist out of Dean's grasp. "I don't need a damned babysitter."

"Today you do."

"Why?"

"Conti is in the building."

Alessa rolled her eyes, more frustrated than ever. "I'm aware Riley is here today."

"Then you know why your brother wants to keep you safe."

Safe.

Right.

Joel was an idiot. What could Riley possibly want with Alessa?

"Can I go?" Alessa asked.

Dean nodded and waved at the opened doorway. "Hurry back. I'll go check on your brother. Ten minutes, Alessa. And then I'm coming to find you."

Perfect.

CHAPTER NINE

"We're going to head down to the docks tonight and supervise some of the crew while they get the newest shipment readied for the streets," Kolin said.

Adriano nodded; he wasn't really listening. "Whatever, man."

"Hey."

"I said whatever," Adriano repeated.

"Adriano," Kolin barked.

The warning in the man's tone caught Adriano's attention instantly. Kolin rarely, if ever, raised his voice. He was the kind of man who didn't need to shout and act like a fool to gain someone's attention. Good leaders used their better skills to command men.

Just hearing Kolin raise his voice to Adriano was enough to snap him out of the stupid daze. Adriano shoved his hands into his slack pockets, shook off the hazy feeling, and gave Kolin the respect he was owed.

"Sorry," Adriano said quickly. "I'm edgy here."

"I can see that. What did I say we were going to be doing tonight?"

"Docks, shipment, streets, got it," Adriano said.

Kolin frowned. "What is up with you, kid?"

"Just because you're double my age, doesn't make me a kid."

"Anyone over twenty-five years younger than me is a fucking kid," Kolin replied.

Adriano knew better than to argue with his Capo. He had worked under Kolin for the better part of his teen years by his father's demand. Kolin was a decent Capo to work for and he didn't let shit pass him by. As Kolin's right-hand man for the Conti crew, Adriano had just as much respect and control as the Capo did. But Adriano didn't have the Capo title to go along with it like Kolin did.

Kolin Bastoni might have been Riley's first cousin, but he never let Adriano get away with a thing just because the two had family ties. When Adriano had been put up for the button at just eighteen by his father, to the disgruntlement of a lot of older Outfit men because of his young age, Kolin had been the one to step up and vouch for Adriano.

Adriano appreciated the fact that Kolin took him under his wing to teach him the streets and the Outfit life when his father was too busy being the face of the family as the front boss. Kolin called him a natural.

You'll make a damn good Capo, kid. These are gonna be your streets someday.

Adriano was good at it—watching the men, making money, and running the streets. He loved it. Riley wanted Adriano higher. Kolin knew Adriano wanted to stay right where he was good. Running the streets and a crew, eventually getting the title of a proper Outfit Capo, and nothing more. Why did everyone seem to think the only way to be happy in the mafia was to hold the highest seat?

Who in the hell wanted that kind of target on their back?

Adriano trusted the guy. But Kolin was, like he would always be, loyal to Riley first. Adriano didn't plan to run off at the mouth about his personal issues. Kolin had never been one to stand for a man whining, anyway.

"Seriously, you're pouting like a fucking baby," Kolin said, pulling a cigarette out of his silver case. "Little boys pout, kid. Fix that or I'll knock it off your face with my fist."

Adriano grinned, unable to stop it. "Have I told you how much of an asshole you are lately?"

Kolin lit up the cigarette and blew out a heavy puff of smoke. "Made you stop pouting."

"Not in the mood to get a punch in the face today."

Because Kolin was a dick like that. He didn't make empty promises and if he threatened to punch Adriano with a good one, he'd fucking do it.

"No, I wouldn't think so. You've still got a mighty bruise from Artino's pricks."

That, too.

Adriano sighed and glanced around the parking lot. For obvious safety reasons, Riley wanted a couple of men to trail him when he went to the reading of Terrance's final Will. Kolin agreed because he had nothing to do. Adriano jumped at the chance because he knew Alessa was going to be here.

Quickly, Adriano found Joel's driver standing beside a black Mercedes along with Peter and Sara Trentini's vehicle parked in the next stall in the parking lot. A red Mustang, one that made Adriano's rage flare like a wildfire, was parked two stalls down from his father's car.

Dean Artino.

If there was one person on the earth that Adriano wished he could kill without repercussions, that man was it. Riley was holding off on allowing Adriano the hit. It pissed Adriano off like nothing else.

As long as Adriano didn't bring up Alessa's name in a conversation, Riley was willing to talk. He would discuss the Outfit, Joel, their plans, but not Alessa. Riley wouldn't even broach the goddamn topic.

Adriano did everything his father demanded, but Riley still wouldn't give him what he wanted.

Alessa.

Christ.

There was a very thin line between jealousy and envy. Envy was wanting what some other fucker had. Jealousy was worrying about that fucker taking away what was yours.

Adriano had always called Alessa his. Because she was.

Dean Artino was getting to stake a goddamn claim because of Joel's stupidity.

Adriano was starting to believe the line between jealousy and envy just didn't exist for him anymore. He fell into both categories like an idiot with arms and legs flailing. Alessa was his, everyone else called her someone else's, and a prick was trying to take her away.

Yeah.

Idiot in both categories flailing like a fool with no help in sight.

Fucking perfect.

Kolin's voice was a deep timber dragging Adriano from his thoughts. "Talk to me, Adriano. I'll shrink your head today."

Adriano needed to get Kolin away from the idea that there was something wrong. If Kolin sniffed that shit, he would dig at it like a dog going for its bone. And then he'd run to Riley.

Don't poke the bear, as the saying went.

"Why in the hell are we working the docks tonight?" Adriano asked.

Kolin shrugged. "We have to get back to work sometime. Your father wants the crew running as normally as possible through the coming weeks. It gives off the impression he's got everything under control while the Rossi, DeLuca, and Trentini crews are still struggling to catch up after everything that's happened."

"Yeah, but—"

"No buts, Adriano. Be there or I'll come looking for you."

Adriano scowled. "Yeah, I got it."

Kolin's phone buzzed, drawing the man's attention away. He tossed his unfinished cigarette to the ground as he pulled the cell phone out of his pocket and glanced at the screen.

"Your father is almost finished," he informed.

"Great."

But not really.

Adriano hadn't even gotten a glimpse of Alessa that morning. He had wanted to call her for the last two days, but his phone ended up damaged the Sunday of the bomb. Unwilling to part with the memories he had on that stupid iPhone, he sent it away to get fixed.

Kolin's phone buzzed again. "And you're needed inside, Adriano."

What?
"Why?"
"Not sure. I don't ask questions, kid."
Wonderful.

"Sit," Riley demanded.

Adriano took the large chair beside his father and gave his attention to the lawyer on the other side of the desk.

"You may leave, Riley," the lawyer said.

Riley scowled. "Why? He's my son and Terrance was my friend. Surely whatever he left for Adriano isn't that secretive."

The lawyer didn't seem affected by Riley's tone. "I did not make the rules for this Will reading, Conti. Terrance was very specific in his instructions that each person be read their portion of the Will in private with me and me alone. I'm sorry if that displeases you, but you are not the one who paid me."

Huffing, Riley pushed up from his chair and exited the room without another word. He closed the door a little louder than was necessary.

The man passed over a thin, ivory envelope to Adriano and then looked at the papers in his hand. Flipping the envelope over, Adriano noted the Trentini wax seal and a yellowish stain along the edge of paper where it was closed. It wasn't thick or particularly heavy, but Adriano wondered why Terrance would leave him anything at all.

"A letter, to be delivered upon the result of my death, to Adriano Riley Conti," the lawyer read aloud. Peering through his thick spectacles, the man squinted at Adriano. "I was not informed of the contents of the letter, young man, and according to this, neither has anyone else. It is intended for your eyes only and has been double sealed across the folded edge for the added insurance of privacy. The wax seal comes from Terrance and only Terrance."

Adriano checked the wax seal over again. It matched the large signet ring Terrance had always worn bearing the Trentini coat of arms with a lion lunging, three swords, and the flag beneath.

"You are one of two men who received something like this," the lawyer said. "There is also a small trust—very small, a few thousand, nothing more—to explain away the fact you are included in this reading. Terrance's request was that those who received his letters get them without the knowledge of others. He had no desire of making the contents, whatever they are, publically known. That includes your father, Adriano."

Adriano rested back in the chair, the letter burning his curiosity further. "Oh?"

"According to Terrance, especially your father. I suggest you put it away until you have time to read it in private."

Taking the risk of ruining the perfect wax seal, Adriano folded the envelope and shoved it into his pocket.

"I need to have confirmation from you that it has remained sealed," the man said.

"It's not been opened," Adriano replied, sure of that fact.

"I should hope not," the lawyer replied. "It's been in my safe along with this Will for years."

"Years?" Adriano asked quietly.

"Terrance knew what he wanted." Wincing, the lawyer added, "With provisions, of course. Bearing in mind his father-in-law's demands and whatnot. Terrance had a great deal of possessions and family titles that belonged to solely him. Those, he did with what he wished."

"And if the seal had been broken?" Adriano asked, curious.

"Then his request in the letter, whatever it is, would be already filled or void and you wouldn't have received it or the trust at all."

That explained everything, didn't it?

Adriano pushed up from the chair. "Thank you. I'll be—"

"There are a few things left for your father," the lawyer interrupted, flipping over the pages on his desk. He waved at Adriano. "Ask him back in for me. You may leave, young man."

Dismissed.

Adriano liked this. Too many Will readings took place with all the family and recipients present, fighting over what was given and crying about their losses. Not all of that crying was for the dead, either.

Outside the office, Adriano found his father waiting.

"Well?" Riley asked.

"You're wanted inside." Adriano laughed, shooting his father a look. "When you die, make sure you have him for an executor, huh?"

Not a lick of humor answered Adriano back from his father.

"I will meet you at the front desk, son," Riley said.

Adriano left his father behind. The long, bright hallway was quiet. Adriano didn't notice anyone, including Joel or the rest of his family, but the waiting rooms were closed shut.

The letter in his pocket irked his curiosity.

Why would Terrance leave him anything, but especially something like a letter?

At the first bathroom Adriano came to, he pushed the door open, noting the unisex sign and closed it. The bathroom was obviously intended for employees of the law practice, considering it was small with only one toilet, a single sink, and a large vanity mirror lit up with white lights.

Pulling the letter from his back pocket, Adriano cracked the wax seal and ripped open the corner. A cream colored paper rested inside. Opening it up, Adriano read the first few words.

Adriano,

Should this letter find you, my boy, then I have clearly failed.
And should this letter find you, then my end has been met.
I saw you two once, under the willow—

Before Adriano could read more of the words, the bathroom door was pushed open again, smacking him square in the back.

I saw you two once, under the willow …

Oh.

"Shit," Adriano muttered.

He quickly shoved the letter inside the envelope and put it back inside his pocket. Stepping away from the door, he turned and pulled it open.

Alessa stood on the other side with wide eyes and a growing smile. Everything he needed was right there in those blue eyes.

Everything.

Being this close to Alessa reminded Adriano of how much he had missed her. Seeing her at the church and then the funeral wasn't enough. He had needed to play a part on both those days and that hadn't allowed for risks with her.

Alessa blinked.

Adriano kept holding the door open, waiting for someone to call her name and drag her away again.

No one did.

Familiar.

Home.

Love.

Like the old tune they were, Adriano could only think to say one thing. "Hey."

Alessa smiled wider. "Hey."

She wore a blue jumper that was loose around her frame, showed off her legs, and dangled down one of her dainty shoulders.

Young.

Beautiful.

Crazy.

They were so fucking crazy.

"I called and messaged you a dozen times. You didn't answer me back," Alessa said quietly.

"Broke my phone."

"A house phone wouldn't work?"

"Did you want a Conti number showing up on your phone if somebody grabbed it off you?" he asked.

Alessa frowned. "Point taken."

"I have a burner, but you never did answer unknown numbers."

"I might have," Alessa said, "if I thought it was you, Adriano."

"You couldn't be sure."

"Stop making excuses. I was worried."

The indignant cock of Alessa's brow tipped Adriano over the edge. He reached out, snagged both her wrists in his palms, and yanked her inside the bathroom without thinking about who might be watching in the hall.

Alessa came without argument.

Adriano kicked the bathroom door closed, hit the lock on the knob, and then pulled Alessa into his chest.

"Stupid man," Alessa whispered.

"Crazy man," Adriano growled.

It was all he could give before taking her mouth with his. The kiss was so forceful, so bruising, that Alessa's quiet gasp echoed in the silent bathroom. Adriano pulled her closer still, wrapping his fingers in her flimsy jumper as her hands tangled up into his hair.

Hard and aching, Adriano's cock dug into Alessa's stomach. It wasn't enough. Not nearly enough. The friction of her toned midsection rubbing against his erection through his slacks did nothing to soothe the need pulsing through his body.

"Fuck, fuck, fuck," Adriano muttered, knowing how goddamn reckless this was.

He didn't care.

"Let me touch you," he said, licking at the corner of her mouth and down to her jaw. He hated her bruises and wanted to kiss them away. "Just one touch, Lissa. I *need* it."

Needed her.

"Oh, *God.*"

Adriano was already tugging her jumper down her small frame, wanting to see her skin under his hands. He pulled the jumper all the way down to her waist and then yanked her bra straps over her shoulders, too, letting her tits spill out into his hands.

Tiny, pink nipples hardened under the pads of his thumbs. Adriano rolled his fingers over the rosy buds until Alessa was arching into his touch and backing into the sink.

"That's more than one," Alessa moaned.

"And taste and lick and fuck," Adriano said gruffly, licking his lips.

She was beautiful in his hands. Perfection.

"I don't have time for that, Adriano," Alessa said, her air catching on the last word. "Shit, *yeah.*"

Adriano bent down and caught her right nipple between his teeth, tugging on the hardened bud and flattening his tongue over the top. He drove his hands down her stomach and under the jumper bunched around her waist to find satiny panties wet with her arousal.

"Christ, you're always ready for me, Lissa."

"Hot."

"Hmm?"

"You get me hot," she breathed.

Adriano lifted Alessa off the floor and set her ass on the sink counter. Digging his fingers into her round ass, he pulled her pussy into his hard dick and grinded his pelvis into her body. "Feel that, Lissa? That's how fucking hot you get me."

"Fuck."

"I'd sure like to."

"Wait," Alessa said, sucking in a breath as she pulled away.

Adriano felt like he'd been burned. "What?"

"Wait a second." Alessa leaned back, putting more space between them than he wanted. "Just … talk for a second. Talk, Adriano."

"What?"

Way to turn into a fucking parrot, Adriano.

"I have to tell you something," Alessa said, opening her palm to his chest, keeping him from leaning in again. "And I only have a few minutes before that asshole is going to come looking for me."

"Dean."

"Yeah."

Adriano let out a disgusted, angry sound that came off a hell of a lot like a growl. "Fucking Christ."

Alessa frowned. "I know."

Instantly, he was cupping her face and running his thumbs over her sexy lips. "Stop that nonsense. Smile, Lissa. For me, you smile."

She did.

"Perfect," Adriano murmured. "Talk and be fast about it."

"Hey!"

"Kidding." He kissed her softly. "We can talk, Lissa. Nothing else."

Alessa grinned. "Maybe I want to."

Adriano groaned loud and deep. "Who's wasting time now?"

"Fine. Your father didn't do it."

"Do what?"

"The bomb; Riley didn't do it," Alessa repeated.

Adriano froze, unsure of what he'd just heard. Everybody blamed his father for the bomb in Dino's car. Even Adriano placed the blame on Riley. In fact, he'd even assumed Riley sent Evelina to the car because he thought maybe people wouldn't think it was his fault if one of his own children was hurt in the incident, too.

Riley had been so adamant they go to the church that morning. He'd made a point of talking publically to Dino DeLuca.

"You're sure?" Adriano asked.

Alessa nodded. "I heard Joel talking to Walter and Dean about it but I didn't understand what he meant until it happened. And then Walter and Dean—"

"Went along with it," Adriano interrupted. "That's not surprising."

"No. Well yes, but no."

Adriano held onto Alessa's waist a little tighter. "Explain."

"Last night at dinner after the funeral, Joel was alone with Dean and …" Alessa trailed off, making a face.

"What, Lissa?"

"Chloe Belli, she was there with them both."

The way Alessa's voice dropped and her nose crinkled said more than she had to.

"Together? All of them?" Adriano asked.

"They were getting that way, but I got out of there fast." Alessa shrugged. "They didn't notice me but before I left, Joel said he was going to get Dean the button so he didn't have to answer for what he did that night at the club."

Cowards.

Adriano's rage flared again. The worry in Alessa's gaze compounded hard in Adriano's chest. He didn't want to use her as some kind of middle man between their families, feeding him information. But she'd offered and now he had to use it however he could.

"Thank you," Adriano said.

"Yeah?"

"So much, Lissa."

Alessa's smile was a sweet sight. "Love wins, Adriano."

Well, theirs would.

"Kiss me," she demanded. "Kiss me and touch me like you promised."

"Time," he reminded her.

"We have a little. Please?"

How could he deny her when she asked so nicely?

Adriano couldn't.

Quickly, he stepped back and pulled Alessa off the counter. Before she could react, he turned her, slammed her hands to the countertop, and kissed a path down her spine. "Don't fucking move, Lissa."

Alessa squirmed under his hands. "What—"

"Don't move those hands," he warned.

"Okay."

"One taste, sweet girl." Adriano let go of her hands so he could pull the jumper down over her ass to her knees. Alessa's ass, covered in black satin with a lace trim, was high in the air. He tugged her panties down with his teeth until they were at her knees, too. "I want one taste of you today. I want your come in my mouth. Does that sound good to you?"

Alessa's legs trembled as Adriano bit into the swelled flesh of her ass. "Yes."

"Yes?"

"*Yes*, please."

Adriano dropped to his knees, putting his face level with the sliver of her pussy and her beautiful, rounded ass. Using his hands to spread her ass cheeks, he could see the lips of her pussy were already wet with her sweet smelling arousal.

Her sex was pink, quivering, and the wider he spread her ass, the more he could see. Her tiny, pale clit poked out, begging to be nibbled and sucked.

"Fuck, Lissa," Adriano said, a moan already building.

Christ.

He hadn't even tasted her yet.

His mouth was already watering.

"You're fucking beautiful, Lissa."

"*Mmm*." Alessa shook her ass, her hands slipping on the counter. "Please, Adriano."

"Don't move and fucking hell, try to be quiet."

Alessa laughed softly. "I'll try."

"Do."

Without warning, Adriano buried his face into her pussy and attacked her wet, hot slit with hard and fast strokes of his tongue. He nipped and sucked on the fleshy lips of her sex, drawing them into his mouth to clean off the juices soaking her pussy. Her tart flavor flooded his mouth and the moan he'd been holding back finally released, deep and dark.

"Christ ... oh, fuck," Alessa whispered.

She rode his face, backing her ass into his mouth as he found her clit and sucked it hard between his teeth. Using his tongue to drive hard into the pulsing little nub, Adriano could tell Alessa was already working toward a quick orgasm under his fucking.

He ate her like he was starved.

Because he was, for her.

Starved for her taste, the way she called his name, and how she shook when she came. Starved for the sweat beading down her spine, the sound of her fingernails digging into the counter, and the way she begged for more.

"Holy shit," Alessa gasped.

Adriano was lost in her quiet, soft sounds. Her gentle whispers of *there* and *just like that.*

She kept her hands on the counter, holding tight like it was a lifeline.

"Come," Adriano demanded against her clit. "Give it to me, Lissa. I want it, sweet girl."

He let go of her ass with one hand, thrust two fingers up into her slippery sex, curled them roughly into her G-spot, and sucked her clit into his mouth hard again.

Alessa's final cry was airless and choked.

It washed over his senses like liquid gold.

Not wanting to, but knowing he had no choice, Adriano kissed up Alessa's ass and naked back, pulling her panties up as he went. Pulling out a few paper towels, he cleaned the arousal smeared on her thighs, before tossing the used tissues to the garbage can. He fixed her jumper without a word, tried to smooth the mess he'd made of her curls and then met her gaze in the mirror.

Her teeth had smudged her lipstick and her slivers of tears had messed her mascara. Alessa was out of breath and looking thoroughly fucked.

"I want more," she whispered.

"Me, too."

A sharp knock on the bathroom door, followed by Dean's voice, snapped Adriano out of his daze.

"Come on, Alessa. Your brother is ready to leave," Dean hollered through the door.

The handle jiggled, but Adriano knew the fool wouldn't get in. Adriano had been smart enough to lock it, after all.

"Shit," Alessa mumbled, her eyes wide with panic.

"Alessa!"

"Coming, just let me wash my hands," Alessa shouted back.

Adriano reached over and flushed the toilet, giving more credibility to her words. The whoosh of the water drowned out their words for a moment.

"Crying," Adriano said. "You were crying."

It would work.

"I look like I just had sex," Alessa hissed.

She did.

Adriano shrugged, turned on the water, and got his hands wet. He rubbed his thumbs under her eyes, wetting them like the water was more of her tears. It smeared her liner and mascara further, but it looked real.

"I need you to hold onto something for me," Adriano said quietly.

Alessa's brow furrowed. "What?"

Not once had he forgotten about the letter, but Adriano didn't want to have it on him. He had a lot of work to do and there was less of a chance someone might notice it if he put it in safe keeping until he had time to handle it.

Ridiculous, maybe, but Adriano wasn't taking the risk of his father finding it.

"This," Adriano said, pulling out the letter. He tucked the folded envelope into the pocket of her jumper. "Keep it safe for me. Okay?"

"Okay," Alessa said.

With his fingers to his lips, Adriano slid against the side of the wall. When the door was opened, it would keep him hidden from view and block him from the mirror.

"Love you," he said with a wink.

Alessa gave him a fleeting smile, mouthed the words back, and flung open the door. She didn't waste time leaving it open. Instead, she walked out to meet Dean, flicked off the light and closed the door as she stepped out.

Adriano could still hear their muffled conversation out in the hall, but it grew distant.

"That was fifteen minutes," Dean grumbled.

"I—"

"Never mind, I can't stand a crying female."

Adriano chuckled when Alessa muttered, "You're a dick."

"Yes, but I'm going to be your fiancé soon," Dean replied.

Alessa laughed sharply. "Only in words and only to you and Joel. I'm not yours and I'll never be, Dean."

"We'll see about that."

"Don't forget what I told you about what will happen if you *see* anything on me, asshole."

That was his girl.

Alessa didn't always realize it, but she was tough as fuck.

"They're letting me out today," Evelina said, smiling at her brother.

Evelina's happiness was infectious. Adriano couldn't help but smile back.

"I heard. That's why I'm here. Waiting for the okay to steal you away."

Adriano wasn't used to seeing his sister sad and in a hospital bed.

It fucking sucked.

"You don't have to be here. Dad will send someone to get me. I know you've got work ... or whatever."

Adriano rolled his eyes. "The Outfit. I have the Outfit, a bruised up sister, and a father that won't get off my ass."

"How did the Will thing go yesterday?" Evelina asked. "Dad didn't say much about it when he visited last night."

Adriano shrugged, flipping his cell phone over and over in his hands. He'd finally gotten the damn thing back that morning before running over to get Evelina from the hospital. "It went okay."

"Just okay?"

"Went without issue," he informed his sister. "Dad and Joel passed one another by with the usual glares. Dad reminded Joel about a sit-down this coming Friday."

"And Dean?" Evelina asked.

Adriano snorted. "He's still alive."

Evelina grabbed her brother's hand, stopping his fidgeting. "For now, Adriano."

"Hey," Adriano said, arching a brow at Evelina. "Don't worry about the Outfit's affairs, huh?"

"Why, because I'm a girl and I don't matter unless someone wants to marry me off?"

Adriano turned his sister's hand over in his and squeezed. "No, because you ended up in a hospital bed, and you've got far more important things to worry about."

Evelina smiled that smile of hers again. "Oh, like what?"

"Maybe moving into the spare room in my apartment."

"Dad—"

"Agrees that you need some time to relax. Trying to stay out of his way, the Outfit, and now you had to drop your summer classes ... it's a lot, Eve."

Evelina sighed. "I wouldn't mind staying at your place for a while."

"Great."

Adriano could keep an eye on his sister and make sure she was away from their father's ridiculousness as the pressure on the Outfit increased at the same time.

A knock on the hospital door interrupted the siblings' conversation. Adriano was stunned to see his father standing in the doorway and a familiar woman behind him.

Lily Rossi offered a small wave to a quiet Evelina. Lily didn't look like she wanted to be standing anywhere near Riley and really, Adriano didn't blame the girl. After all, Riley was the one being blamed for Lily's brother's death. It had only been three days since the bombing.

Fresh wounds had a way of bleeding easier than others.

"Hey," Lily said, stepping past Riley into the hospital room.

Evelina chewed on her cheek and shot Adriano a questioning look.

"Eve," Adriano said, his hand tightening around his sister's again.

What was up with her?

Evelina glanced between her father and her friend like she didn't know what to do. Adriano knew right then what the problem was. The last time Evelina had made an attempt to see Lily, Riley had nearly beaten her.

And now, there he was, standing at the door with Lily.

Adriano dropped his sister's hand and stood to greet their unexpected guests. "Hey."

"Son." Riley waved at Lily as he said, "Her husband is hanging around somewhere and I've agreed to a short meeting between the two. As a favor to Dino, of course. He asked before his unfortunate death and I'm not one to refuse the wishes of a dead man."

Lily flinched, anger heating her gaze. It faded fast, but Adriano had still seen it all the same.

"Thanks," Lily said, avoiding looking at Riley with all her tiny might.

Adriano gave his sister a quick hug. "I'll be back. All right?"

Evelina smiled. "Okay."

"Let's take a walk, Adriano," Riley said.

Adriano followed his father out of the room, closing the door behind them.

But not before he heard Lily say, "Your father is an asshole."

Riley either hadn't heard or ignored the comment. Adriano chose not to ask. He didn't entirely disagree with Lily's statement.

"Damian Rossi is around somewhere," Riley murmured, surveying the quiet hospital hall.

"So you said."

"Then you know to be careful of your words."

Adriano nodded. "Sure."

"You skipped out of dinner last night."

"Had work at the docks," Adriano lied.

Well, half-lied. Adriano needed time to think after the things he learned from Alessa. He used the docks as an excuse to get away from his father for a while.

"You've been avoiding me since the bombing at the church," Riley said.

"I have not."

"You have. Ask, Adriano."

Adriano's confusion climbed higher. "Ask what?"

"If I set the bomb. Everyone else is too frightened to ask. I think they believe they'll be next."

"Do you blame them?"

Riley smirked wickedly. "No, but it works out well to my favor. Ask."

"I don't have to," Adriano said.

"Oh?"

"No."

"Why is that, son?" Riley asked, his hand coming up to clasp Adriano's shoulder and stop him from going further. "What do you know that I don't?"

A lot.

Adriano chose to tell what would benefit his father.

"Joel did it," Adriano said. "He's also seriously considering making Dean after the upcoming sit-down to help him avoid punishment for what he did."

Riley's expression remained passive. "Is that so?"

"Yes."

"I wondered because I sure as hell didn't kill Dino. That little ... *bastard.*"

Adriano met his father's gaze head-on. "Aren't you going to question me now?"

"On where you got your information?" Riley asked.

"Yes."

Riley laughed. "Oh, son. I don't have to. Your heart talks louder than your brain does."

Adriano didn't know what to make of that. "It helps you."

Didn't it?

"Maybe so, but in the end, I doubt it will help you, Adriano. This is a lesson you're clearly going to have to learn the hard way, my boy."

CHAPTER TEN

"**M**om wants us over there for supper in a little while."

Alessa kept digging through the boxes that someone had carelessly tossed into her old bedroom at the Trentini mansion. "Why?"

"Welcome home or something," Abriella said, sounding entirely bored already.

"Yay." Alessa didn't bother to hide the sarcasm coating her tone. "Because we're so glad to be back."

Abriella laughed lightly. "Try to make that sound good for Mom and Dad at least."

Alessa couldn't promise that. Despite giving his sisters until Friday to move home, Joel had men waiting to pack the apartment up that morning. Their apartment was torn apart, shoved into boxes, and shuffled away until all that was left were white walls and bare floors.

"Damn," Alessa muttered, pulling out a silk dress from one of the many boxes. "Look at this."

Abriella glanced over the snagged side of the dress. "What did they do, shove it in there with the fucking hanger on it?"

"Apparently. It's ruined, like half of the rest of this stuff." More annoyed than ever, Alessa dropped the dress back into the box. "Dinner, you said?"

"In their wing," Abriella confirmed. "Without Joel."

"Thank God."

"Only because he's got stuff to do tonight, I guess."

Whatever. Alessa would take it. A night off from their brother was better than nothing.

Abriella eyed Alessa's mess. "Are you good in here?"

"As good as I'll ever be," Alessa replied.

For now …

"Okay. I'm going to go do something," Abriella said.

"Lock the door on your way out," Alessa told her sister.

Once her sister was gone, Alessa flung her body back on the bed and sighed loudly. Alessa hadn't even gotten the time to process one change in her life before another one was coming around to bite her. The privacy and independence she had by living away from the Trentini mansion had been ripped away in a few hours.

Just like that.

Gone.

Alessa felt suffocated already.

Glancing to the side at the pile of boxes lining the wall, Alessa frowned. She had too much to do and no desire to do it. The buzz in her pocket broke her daze. Alessa pulled out her phone and typed in her pin to check the message.

Phone is fixed.

That was all the text read. But the words along with the recognizable number was more than enough to know who the message came from.

Alessa couldn't help the smile forming as she typed back, *Good to know.*

A call rang through just as Alessa hit send on the text. She picked the call up instantly.

"Hey."

Adriano's deep timber greeted her in the most familiar way, "Hey."

"Adriano, you need to go grocery shopping," Alessa heard in the background of the call.

Evelina.

It was good to know Evelina had finally made it out of the hospital safe and sound. Asking anyone about Evelina's condition after the bombing only led to side-eyes and disgusted grunts. As if Alessa should know better than to ask.

"Would you quit your bitching, Eve? Christ, you've only been here for two hours and already I need new sheets and my dresser is a mess. Now it's the fucking kitchen. What next? I love you but stop it. I am not your pet project."

"Until I have something better to do, yes, you are," Evelina replied sweetly.

Evelina's happy response made Alessa laugh.

The sound of a door closing echoed through the phone.

"Maybe this wasn't such a good idea," Adriano said faintly.

Alessa's heart dropped. "Calling me?"

"What? *No!*" Adriano chuckled loudly. "God, no, Lissa. I meant having Eve here at my place for a while."

"When did that happen?"

"Today. I convinced Dad that she would be one less person he would need to worry about. I wanted to give Eve a break in the process."

"She's been through a lot the last couple of days," Alessa said.

They all had, really.

"Yeah, she has," Adriano agreed. "She knows, by the way."

"About what?"

"Us."

Alessa bit her inner cheek. "Oh?"

"Yeah. She's entirely for this. Me and you. She's also crazy but whatever. Surprising, I think."

"Not really. Eve hangs around with Abriella—" Or they used to before the mess with the Outfit started. "—so she's not entirely innocent to the game, Adriano."

"I'm aware of what my sister does … or did. The fact remains, she was really angry at first about Mom. Angry with your family, I mean. I just figured she would be more like Dad and lean to his side of things."

"Maybe not everyone in this whole thing is as ruined as you believe they are, Adriano."

Adriano snorted. "By the end of it, I bet they will be."

"Silver linings. Find one and color it blue, Adriano. Blue is prettier to look at than a shiny gray."

"I love the way you think, Alessa. And blue is always nicer when you're wearing it."

Alessa grinned and buried her face in the pillow to muffle the low moan building in her chest. Just the sound of his voice was enough to set her on edge and promise something wicked. Memories of the day before when he'd bent her over the sink and ate her pussy like he was a starved man flew into her mind. She could still feel his languid laps at her pussy lips before he'd attacked her clit in a way that made her nerves sing. A pulse started to throb between her thighs and Alessa rubbed her legs together in an effort to soothe the ache.

It did nothing.

Nothing but Adriano ever helped with that little problem.

"Fuck, stop, Adriano."

"Stop what, Lissa?"

"You know what."

His chuckles rocked her to the core. "What are you wearing today?"

"Stuff."

She wasn't doing this with him. Not right now and not right there. Uh-uh.

It wasn't going to happen.

"Anything blue?" Adriano asked, his tone dripping with sex and sin.

"Jeans," Alessa said, unable to stop herself.

"Skinny?"

"Tight as fuck."

Adriano groaned. "Just the way I like."

"Stop it."

"I can't. I miss you." Adriano sucked in a harsh breath, adding, "And you left me hard yesterday, Lissa. So hard I couldn't fucking think. For the rest of the day, the only thing I could taste was your come in my mouth. I could still fucking smell you on my hands, okay? That's what you left me with. I had to take care of that alone and it did nothing. Talk to me."

Alessa whined under her breath and turned on the bed so her back was to the mattress. "You don't play fair."

"I never have, babe."

He broke her resolve just like that.

"Blue jeans, a band tee and—"

"Which one?" Adriano interrupted.

"Metallica. From one of their old tours, not the new ones."

"Because they played better when they were high," Adriano said.

Alessa laughed. "So you always say."

"I got you that shirt."

"Never told me where," she whispered.

"A thrift place, actually. It was encased in this shadow box because it was signed."

Alessa glanced down at the black T-shirt, void of any signatures. "There's never been a signature on it."

Adriano hummed lowly. "Because when I took it out of the box, it smelled funky. Like it'd been sitting too long. I wanted to see you wear it, not hang it up on the wall. I washed it—it was just pen ink on the white letters. It came out."

"Damn."

"You still wore it."

"I still do," Alessa replied, smiling wide.

"Where are you?"

Alessa was brought back into the present with a bang. "At the mansion. We moved out of the apartment this morning."

"Good to know," Adriano replied. "But that's not what I meant."

"Oh."

"Yeah. Where in the fucking mansion?"

"Bedroom."

"Yours?" he asked.

"Of course."

"God does love me. Tell me what is underneath that shirt, Lissa."

"Black bra, satin with lace trim."

"Matching panties?"

"Thong, actually," she replied. "These jeans are too tight for lines, Adriano."

"Goddamn. Painted on?"

"Might as well be."

"Fucking *hell*."

Something heady and delicious heated his tone. Alessa couldn't help herself—the damn bedroom door was locked and she had the entire floor of the wing to herself, basically.

Apparently Adriano wasn't waiting on Alessa to get her mind in the game. "Hurry up and get your hands down your pants, pretty girl. I want to know how wet you are right now, how you feel under your fingertips and then I want to see if the sound of my voice can make you come."

"Yes," Alessa said instantly.

"Hmm?"

"There's no wondering about it. I know it can."

Adriano laughed. "Hurry, Lissa."

Alessa worked the button open and unzipped the zipper. She hadn't lied. Her skinny jeans were tight, so she pushed them down until she could kick them off.

"Talk to me," she demanded playfully. "Or I'll hang up the phone."

"Don't you fucking dare. That would give me just the reason I need to come over there, Lissa."

Alessa stilled on the bed. Rough, callous, and crude. Adriano was usually well-spoken, although she'd witnessed his temper come out a time or two on other people. She decided to poke his bear a little more. "Then you better talk."

"Spread your legs wide," he ordered. "Feel yourself through the lace, babe."

She did as he asked, jolting the moment her fingertips grazed over her lace covered sex. The thong did nothing to protect the sensitive, tender flesh from her touch. She was wet already and soaking through the panties.

"Tell me what that feels like, Lissa."

Alessa swallowed hard. "Wet. And so good."

"My fingers stroke," he murmured quietly. "They stroke you from the back of your pussy straight up to the clit. Do you know why I like doing that so much?"

"No."

"Because you shake, Lissa. Your pussy fucking quivers from me. I love seeing all your juices smearing all over the pink lips of your pussy as I stroke you and touch you. And when I taste you? Fuck, when I taste you, it makes it even fucking better. I've got all of you to clean then. Every single drop, baby, I like to lick it all off. I love the way you taste in my mouth and how it keeps on coming the more I lick."

Alessa shuddered, still running her fingers over her sex. "I want to touch."

"Please do."

Her fingers skipped under the gusset of her thong to find the silky lips of her pussy wet and hot to the touch. She was tender as her digits glided through her labia over and over, dragging her arousal around her slit and up to her clit.

"Let me guess," Adriano whispered. "You're burning up down there, your little clit is hard against your finger, and you're wetter than you thought."

"Yes."

"Fucking beautiful."

"You can't see," Alessa said, licking her lips and still holding the phone tight to her ear with a shaking hand. "You can't see me at all."

"I don't have to, baby. I've got every fucking inch of you memorized. I've seen all the spots on you, I've touched them, and tasted them, and Christ … You're in me, now, Lissa. I can't get you out if I fucking tried."

"God."

"Love your sounds," Adriano said.

She swore there was a hint of smug satisfaction in his words.

"Are you grinning?" she asked.

"Very much. And stroking my cock, thinking about your pretty mouth being wrapped around it. Shit, do you know what you look like when you suck my dick, Alessa? Amazing. So fucking sexy. I love it when your lips are painted red and they're wet with my come. You stain me all over and I can't get that nonsense off no matter how hard I scrub."

Good God.

That was wicked.

Filthy sinful.

Alessa loved it.

"Fuck yourself with your fingers," Adriano said, softer than before. "You must be wanting it bad by now. I bet your juices are just flooding your fingers, needing it. I want to hear all the sounds that come out of your mouth while you do."

"How hard are you?" Alessa asked, pressing two fingers deep into her pussy.

Her inner walls hugged her digits hard. She couldn't believe how turned on her body was but it shouldn't have been a surprise. Adriano had always done this for her—he'd always been the only fucking one for her.

Alessa's fingers working her pussy certainly weren't Adriano's. He knew her body better than even she did. While her digits were slender and graceful, his were long and nimble, knowing how to make every little stroke and press send her flying higher toward a precipice of bliss.

"I need to know," Alessa added quietly, a whimper breaking past her trembling lips. "Tell me how hard you are."

"So hard. Swollen even. I need to come," Adriano said huskily. "I'd love to shoot my load down your throat, but this is good, too. And I'd really like to do it hearing you call my name, Lissa. Make that a reality and fast."

"Oh, my God."

Alessa couldn't have stopped if she tried. Adriano's filthy mouth and quiet demands were enough to make Alessa work her sex a little faster. Harder strokes inside her pussy and then quicker circles on her clit until her thighs burned and shook. The beginning whispers of her orgasm crawled across her skin, promising bliss. She twisted in the bed, her thighs clamping around her hand and still holding the phone tight.

"So close ... so close, Adriano."

"Fuck, yeah. Those sounds are going to kill me, Lissa."

Even his voice had turned rough. Harsh whooshes of his breaths crackled in the speaker.

Alessa came hard, gasping for air and trying to muffle the sound all the same.

Adriano's gravelly groan followed close behind. "Shit, shit, shit."

Sighing, Alessa turned back on the bed and squeezed her eyes shut. "Okay ... that was a great way to let me know you got your phone back."

Adriano's laughter filled the phone. "Yeah?"

"So good."

"I made a fucking mess."

Alessa grinned. "I'd clean it up for you if I was there, you know."

"I shouldn't ask. I *shouldn't.*"

"I would lick every drop of it—"

"Fuck, don't tease me. I can't handle it right now," Adriano warned.

Alessa glanced to the side, noting the boxes in her room again. "Reality sucks."

"This was a good break, hmm?"

"Very. Thank you."

"Never thank me for that, Lissa," Adriano said. "Text me later, yeah?"

"You know I will."

"And get rid of the texts."

Alessa rolled her eyes. "Of course."

"I love you, Lissa."

"Love you," she echoed, still smiling.

Hanging up the phone, Alessa clenched her fist tight around the device. A dirty thought passed through her mind, making her giggle. Before she could second guess her choice, she turned on the camera on the phone, knowing damn well her face was flushed, her makeup was likely smeared, and she probably looked thoroughly fucked. She shot off a picture and then sent it to Adriano before deleting all of their conversation in the messages and text files.

Habits.

She couldn't break them if she tried.

Not a second later, another text came through from Adriano: *Fuck yes. Christ. We're doing that again, but on video chat.*

Alessa laughed out loud.

Whatever you want, Alessa typed back.

Oh, I want, came the response. And then another dinged: *I want it all.*

Damn.

Alessa had a feeling Adriano was talking about more than just their phone sex. She hated that their entire world was so fucked up right now. She couldn't help but be bitter that the people around them were so selfishly focused on their needs and moving themselves higher in the Outfit that no one gave a fuck about anyone else.

Adriano was *hers.*

He'd always been hers.

Why couldn't she have him?

Frustrated but refusing to let it ruin the natural high Adriano had just given her, Alessa went through deleting their last couple of texts. She quickly got redressed and decided to just get the awfulness over with by unpacking more boxes or as many as she could.

The first three boxes were mostly knickknacks and framed photographs that had adorned the sisters' living spaces. Nothing of much importance and most of it would have to be packed away in storage until they were into a new place.

Popping open the fourth box, Alessa pulled out some clothes that needed refolding and put away. A garbage bag at the bottom of the large box, filled with dirty clothes, reminded her that she needed to do a load. The Trentini mansion had a full staff on hand to cook, clean, and take care of all the chores in between, but Alessa preferred to take care of her own things. She'd always been like that.

Pulling the garbage bag out, she dropped it to the floor. The top popped open, showcasing the jumper she'd worn the day before. The white corner of something familiar stuck out of the left pocket. She knew better than to pry, but Adriano had given it to her.

Right?

Alessa's curiosity got the better of her. She snatched the letter out of the jumper and noticed immediately that Adriano must have opened it and read it at some point. The wax seal was broken and the flap had been ripped.

The familiar wax seal made her heart stop for a split second. She knew that signet because it was the same one that adorned several things in the Trentini mansion. Her grandfather had worn a ring with the crest embedded on the top.

Their family crest.

Alessa's confusion jumped higher the longer she stared at the envelope. Clearly Adriano had read it and didn't care if she did, too. Not if he had given it to her opened for safe keeping. Even still, a wariness settled in her gut as she pulled the letter out and opened it up.

Instantly, she recognized the handwriting as her grandfather's.

Adriano,

Should this letter find you, my boy, then I have clearly failed.

And should this letter find you, then my end has been met.

I saw you two once, under the willow. You and my Alessa. It was the day of her seventeenth birthday and she was smiling. All day, she hadn't done much of that at all despite the people and the party. And then you came—she smiled for you.

So, I saw you there and I knew. Love is an interesting beast and young love is even worse. As you should know by now, Adriano, a match of the heart doesn't guarantee you a match at the altar. Not in the Outfit. Not to men who want only to better their position and their families. How could I deny her smile, though?

I couldn't.

I call Alessa mine, you see, because I was never very good at turning away from Sara, even if it meant I was selfish and someone was sure to hurt. If my end has come before my second son's, then I am sure that some of my misdeeds will come to light. Joel's paternity, for one.

He's waited a long time for this.

I own that—him.

I tried.

I am not sorry. Not for him though I tried.

That woman gave me three children and I've not been able to claim even one of them. I was there to see their first steps, to give them my last name, and to provide for them in the best ways I could. I've loved them terribly ... from afar and through their eyes, as a grandfather. Giving them more or admitting my wrongs would have put my family front row and center for Sara's father's anger and retribution, and for her shame. I've not been the boss forever, after all. I had a wife of my own to protect. Two women I adored that I couldn't dishonour.

And then there's Joel. Even bad men have good intentions. Joel never has.

I love my children, but I am not required to love their behavior.

I've tried, and you should know that. I tried to give Alessa what would make her smile and that was you. For a time, that meant ignoring the passing looks, late nights, and the closeness. It meant excusing your affections as innocent. It meant covering your lies when you were not very good at it.

Your father has never hidden his intentions. Not as well as he would like to think he has and certainly not as well as I've hidden mine. He would like to be higher and

Alessa would never get you there. Even if she was the granddaughter of the Outfit's boss.

If this letter has found you, my boy, I've failed to give Alessa what makes her smile.

I'm sorry.

Don't be the next one who fails her, too.

—T. Trentini

Alessa should have stopped reading long before the end. She should have folded the letter back up the moment that sinking feeling in her stomach wouldn't leave.

She didn't.

She couldn't.

In a few hundred words, a couple of short minutes, her entire life was different.

Just like that.

Her mother lied.

Her grandfather lied.

Her *father* ...

Alessa, shaking and with tears welling, roughly crammed the letter back inside the crumpled envelope.

Adriano knew. He'd gotten the letter, read it, and didn't say a thing. Instead, he'd given it to her so that she could read it. Sure, he'd told her in a way, but it still pissed her off all the same.

He *knew*.

... she smiled for you.

I have clearly failed.

Alessa couldn't breathe. Her chest hurt and her heart ached.

I've loved them terribly ... from afar.

Why?

Alessa shoved the letter into her pocket, ignoring the way her hands trembled and how her tears fought to fall. She desperately tried to correlate the man she knew as her grandfather to be her father. She couldn't.

Peter Trentini raised her.

But her mother? Married, sleeping with her old lover, and lying all the same. She birthed children and passed them off as another man's. It was foul and wrong. So fucking wrong.

Alessa grabbed her phone off the bed and dialed the first number she could think of. Because even if she was pissed, Adriano was still the only person she thought could withstand her confusion and anger.

"A little early for you to be calling back, isn't it?"

"You knew," Alessa said the moment Adriano picked up the call. "You knew and you gave me that fucking thing, knowing I would read it alone. That hurts. That makes you just like him. A goddamn *coward*, Adriano."

"Whoa, hold up."

Those three words froze Alessa's blood in her veins. "Excuse me? Where do you get off doing that to me?"

"Lissa, stop," Adriano growled.

"Why did you do that?" she cried.

Hurt was not a good enough word for what she felt. It could never be enough.

"Go. I'll meet you in the car, Eve," Adriano said, his voice faint. Then, he was back to the call in an instant. "I don't know anything, Alessa. Talk to me."

"The letter—"

"You read that?"

Alessa's tears poured faster. "Yes."

"Fuck, Lissa."

Oh, no.

No.

"You didn't?" Alessa asked in a whisper.

"You interrupted me in the bathroom. I only saw the first couple of lines. I figured you would get the hint and keep it hidden for me. My father was way too interested in the fact I had been included in the Will. According to the lawyer who gave the letter to me, it was intended for my eyes only and I was to make sure it remained private. Lissa—"

"My life is wrong. It's a lie."

Adriano cleared his throat on the other end, asking, "How?"

"They lied to me."

"Who?" he asked.

"My parents."

"Peter and Sara?"

Alessa shook her head, knowing damn well he couldn't see it. "No, Terrance and Sara. They've been doing this for years. They played a game around everyone else, and we were just products of it. Like fucking chess pieces. They moved us here and there as they saw fit to hide the awfulness of their lies."

"Slow down," Adriano murmured.

She couldn't. "I was so pissed off at Joel because he called my mother a whore for her mistakes when she was younger, but he was right. Nothing he said was a lie, Adriano."

Adriano grew quiet on the other end for longer than Alessa liked.

"Say something," she demanded.

"Your father is ... *was* Terrance."

It wasn't even a question.

"Yes."

"Shit," Adriano muttered.

"And that makes my mother a lying wh—"

"Don't do that," he interjected, his tone gentle and smooth. "Don't ever do that to her or him, Lissa. You don't get that right. I love you, pretty girl, all the way around the world and back but you don't get to do that. You can't possibly understand their situation or motives. Maybe it hurt and maybe it didn't. Maybe they were selfish and wrong and foul. But you don't get to say because they loved you. They always loved you."

"But—"

"Deny it."

Alessa couldn't. "This hurts."

"It will." Adriano sighed before saying, "I want to read that. It was meant for me. Don't get rid of it, please."

Her guilt climbed higher. "I shouldn't have opened it."

"Yeah, well, I should have just kept it on me but it made me fucking edgy. Everything makes me edgy."

Alessa swallowed hard. "Everything?"

A hint of a smile colored up Adriano's words as he said, "Not you."

Yeah, she knew there was a reason why she called him.

A knock on the bedroom door forced Alessa to end the call out of panic and nothing more.

Abriella's voice on the other side made Alessa scowl. "Ready to head over to the other wing?"

"No," Alessa said under her breath.

That meant facing her mother and father while pretending nothing was wrong. Alessa didn't think she could do that.

"Alessa?" Abriella asked, knocking again.

"Coming."

Alessa pushed the food around on her plate, keeping out of the light conversation flowing around the table between Peter, Sara, and Abriella.

Did her sister know the truth, too?

After all, Abriella had known about Joel's paternity before Alessa did.

All through the dinner, conversation between the family members had been mundane and safe. There was no discussion of the Outfit and certainly no talk about Joel. It was almost like Alessa's parents wanted to keep all that nonsense out and pretend like it wasn't happening.

How in the hell was that even possible?

She also couldn't help but watch her parents. She'd always thought Sara and Peter loved each other. Sara said she loved Peter. Alessa's upbringing was filled with memories of her parents being happy, close, and always together.

They played their roles well.

Even when they didn't have to, Alessa supposed.

"Alessa!"

Jerking her head up, Alessa met her mother's gaze from across the table. "What?"

"I've called your name three times," Sara said quietly.

Alessa's gaze snapped between her mother, father, and then her questioning sister. "I ..."

Need to get the hell out of here, her mind finished when her mouth wouldn't.

"Would it be all right if I headed back and say goodnight early?" Alessa asked.

Adriano's words were still repeating heavily in the back of her mind: *Don't do that to them.*

She understood why he said that. She knew that her life had been a good one with parents and grandparents who loved her dearly.

Their secrets, on the other hand, were an absolute killer.

"Is something wrong?" Peter asked. "I know you have a lot going on, Alessa, but we're here to talk, sweetheart. What is the problem?"

"Everything," Alessa muttered, pushing out from the table and standing.

Abriella cocked a brow. "Lissa?"

"Please, excuse me," Alessa said, spinning on her heel to leave her uneaten food and confused family behind.

Alessa didn't even make it to the locked corridor that separated the main wing of the Trentini mansion from her parents' wing before Sara caught up with her.

"Alessa!" Sara grabbed her daughter's arm and pulled hard enough to stop Alessa from opening up the door that was usually locked. "Hey, look at me."

Alessa's stare burned as she leveled it on her mother. "What else did you lie about?"

Sara jerked away from Alessa as if she'd been slapped. "I beg your pardon?"

"Do you really love Dad or have you gotten so used to lying every time you speak that even you believe it?"

"Alessa ..."

"Was Abriella why everything changed one day?" Alessa asked, sneering. "Remember when you told me that, Mom? One day, everything changed. Was she why? Did you fuck up again like you did with Joel? Would Peter have known? Did you lie to get him closer, to make him believe? Was Abriella why?"

Alessa's questions and accusations came out as a rapid fire assault. One after the other. Bang. Bang. Bang. She couldn't stop the word vomit if she tried.

Sara stepped back from her daughter, pain and shame lighting up her familiar blue eyes. "Alessa, don't you dare."

Alessa scoffed.

Hard, loud, and rude.

She didn't even care.

"Don't worry, Mom. I'll keep your secrets. I have to, right? Otherwise, we're all just stuck swimming in your pool of disgrace, soaking in your embarrassment. None of us deserve that, not even Joel."

Sara's tears began to spill, tracking lines over her cheeks. "I'm sorry."

"Are you?"

"Yes," Sara whispered, nodding. "But I loved him."

Alessa laughed. "Which one?"

"Both."

Christ.

Alessa couldn't do this.

Sara didn't give her the opportunity to run away a second time. Alessa watched as her mother turned and disappeared back down the corridor without another word. It was only then that Alessa noticed her sister standing at the far end with her arms crossed. Abriella said nothing. Alessa didn't need her to. The look on Abriella's face, an expression churned with confusion and pain, was more than enough. She hadn't known.

She did now.

"Abriella …"

What could Alessa say? Her anger had spilled over. She'd clearly hurt her sister.

"You're right," Abriella said. "You need to get out of here."

"I—"

"Joel's gone. Don't leave the property. I'll cover for you if he comes home early."

Alessa wasn't sure what she should say. Abriella should've been angry, but she wasn't.

"Thanks," Alessa whispered.

"No," Abriella murmured. "Thank you."

Alessa hit the damp grass running. She wasn't entirely sure what she was running to, but it felt better than walking and far better than breathing.

The phone in her hand buzzed.

Over and over.

She didn't need to look at it to know what it said. She could feel his presence a mile away.

I'm here.

Under the willow.

I'm always here.

She'd texted Adriano and then waited as long as she could before she needed to just get the hell out of that house.

Alessa had a feeling she'd always be running in one way or another.

But she would make damn sure she was always running to him.

CHAPTER ELEVEN

Adriano held Alessa tighter, enjoying the silence of the darkness as it fell around them. Pulling the corner of the blanket snugger around Alessa, he let her sink into his embrace. He usually kept a blanket in the backseat of his Camaro, just in case. While it wasn't cold for a late August day, the rain was enough to be chilly.

"I was awful," Alessa said.

Adriano didn't bother to ask what she meant. Alessa had already explained the confrontation she had with her mother and what little came of it. Nothing except more hurt.

Alessa's shoulders heaved, pressing her back harder into Adriano's chest. "I don't know what is wrong with me."

"Nothing. You're confused."

"You're biased."

Adriano chuckled. "Maybe so, but you're entitled to be a little angry, Lissa."

"Why didn't he want us to know? Terrance, I mean."

Thinking about the letter he'd finally gotten the chance to read in full, Adriano figured the answer to that question was obvious. "He had a wife to protect and a family to keep in good standing. It's one thing to run around with a *goomah*, but it's entirely different to be sleeping with your son's wife, Alessa."

"Appearance is everything."

"To a lot the men in the Outfit, yes."

"Appearances are deceiving," Alessa mumbled.

Adriano hugged her again. "Sometimes."

"Have you ever … done that, I mean?"

"Done what?" he asked.

"I know we never put labels down or whatever, so I guess there isn't much for me to say if you were with other girls."

"No," Adriano said. "Never, not once. You didn't label me, but you were always mine. I'll do a lot of bad shit, but running around on you isn't one of them."

"Am I a hypocrite?" she asked.

Again, he knew exactly what she was talking about without asked. "Because of Dean?"

"Yes."

"You're not even engaged, yet. It's just a promise of something in the future. You didn't agree to that. You've never agreed to that. You've said from the start you wouldn't follow through with that," he replied, hoping his point was clear.

"We're still expected to get *engaged*." Alessa spat the word out like it was vomit. "And I've been with you several times since that happened."

"Show me a ring and it'll stop."

Alessa's laughter was light. "Oh, is that what it'll take?"

Adriano cleared his throat. "Maybe a wedding dress, a priest, and a gun to my head, too. I'm here for this all the way to the bitter end, pretty girl. I always have been."

"Damn."

"I'm not letting you go, Lissa. I don't give a fuck about Dean Artino."

Alessa sighed. "Thank you for coming."

"You know I always will."

"I was awful to you, too," she whispered.

Adriano pressed a kiss to the nape of her neck. "Actually, I'm happy you called me first instead wondering and hating me. We got the bullshit out of the way quickly. There's enough drama around us without adding to the crazy."

Alessa fingered the leaves hanging from one of the low lying branches. "You should go soon. I don't know when Joel is coming home."

"Not yet."

He didn't mind the risk.

"Not yet," she echoed.

"What do we know?" Riley asked.

Kolin sidled up beside the car with a coolness that could rival any made man in the vicinity. There happened to be quite a few Outfit men in the area, considering the sit-down that was about to go down a block away at one of Riley's restaurants.

"We know the restaurant is clean and clear," Kolin said.

"One-hundred percent?"

Kolin nodded. "The boys didn't take their eyes off it once since you told Joel that's where you wanted the meeting."

Adriano couldn't shake his odd feeling.

"Your driver will be ready to pick you up at the door the moment he sees you once this sham of a meeting is over. But I do think it would be better to walk down and take them off guard by not arriving in a vehicle like they suspect you will."

"I like that idea, too," Adriano said. "Who else showed up?"

"Laurent and a great deal of his crew," Kolin explained. "Seems the Rossi crew is dispersed outside doing whatever it is they want. I have people on them."

"And the DeLuca side?" Riley asked.

"Just Theo. But he hasn't made any effort to go inside. And the Artinos are inside."

Adriano frowned. "Dad, you could always tell Theo that you weren't involved with his brother's death."

"I like it better this way," Riley said as he clipped the end of a Cuban cigar. "Besides, young Theo is just one man in the DeLuca crew."

"Heading it at the moment," Kolin reminded Riley. "And Laurent?"

Riley waved dismissively. "We will handle him when the times comes. For now, let's get this sit-down over with."

Adriano pushed the back passenger side door open. "Lead the way then."

Kolin reached in through the window, stopping Riley from getting out. Adriano waited for his father and the Capo to finish before he moved away from the car.

"Are you good?" Kolin asked quietly.

Riley laughed under his breath. "Are you asking if I'm nervous, old friend?"

"No, I'm asking if you're safe, Riley."

"Trust no one," Riley murmured. "I'm good."

Adriano had no fucking clue what his father and Kolin were talking about, but he figured if it was for him to know, they would have let him in on it already.

Kolin nodded. "Good. Say the word, Riley, and I'll finish this shit the proper way."

Riley sighed heavily. "Bullets won't solve the underlying issue with these men."

"I think it would solve a world of their problems, Boss. After all, it stems from Joel."

"I want him to do it to himself, Kolin. It might take a little longer for Joel to dig his own grave, but don't worry, I'm sure he will shoot himself in the foot a few times along the way."

Riley waved at his friend to move away from the door. When Kolin did, Riley opened the door and joined his son on the side of the street.

Adriano fixed the knot on his tie, feeling suffocated in the humid air outside. "It's hot."

"Mmm," Riley hummed in agreement. "It's a very good day for this. Don't worry, Adriano. Stop minding the small things."

"What should I concern myself with then, Dad?"

"Helping me shoot Joel in the foot, of course."

Adriano chuckled.

Yeah, he should have known that.

Adriano's carefully hidden anger flared to life as he watched Joel hold a hand out to help his sisters, one at a time, out of a black car. No one had said a thing about Alessa or Abriella being invited to the meeting. They didn't have a reason to come, frankly.

Laurent Rossi stood from his seat although his son stayed seated. Tommas Rossi didn't give his father or the arriving Trentinis any of his attention as they made their way inside the restaurant. In fact, Tommas continued talking to his cousin Damian as Laurent greeted Joel and his sisters.

Adriano surveyed the men loitering outside the restaurant. Theo DeLuca was amongst the men, keeping one eye on the windows and the people inside while maintaining what looked like some kind of conversation with a few men of his crew.

Dean and Walter Artino sat quietly in the corner, looking smug as fuck and entirely unbothered by the fact a sit-down was about to occur just feet from their table. Adriano supposed Theo didn't need to be inside if the Artinos were standing in place for the DeLuca family. It was too bad Theo didn't realize Walter and his cunt of a son were looking to take over for Theo completely, not on a part-time basis.

Adriano stood with his father as Joel approached their table.

Alessa and Abriella followed close behind their brother.

"Look at that," Riley said.

"Dirty pool," Adriano murmured.

"Yes, but smart. I've not given Joel enough credit, clearly. Bringing along his sisters is sure to keep things peaceful between all the men at this meeting."

"Maybe that's what he wants," Adriano said.

Riley scoffed. "I'm sure."

Kolin stepped in front of Joel, blocking the man's path to Riley. Without a word, Kolin went about checking Joel quickly before taking the man's suit jacket and laying it over a chair. It showed Riley that Joel was clear of weapons.

All the while, Adriano watched Alessa from the corner of his eyes, taking in her appearance and tired gaze. Clearly, she hadn't slept much after he left her the night before. An unexpected ache started up in Adriano's chest. He rubbed at the spot, hoping it looked like he had an itch or something.

Riley's voice broke Adriano's daze.

"Not even a gun?" Riley asked Joel.

Joel smiled falsely. "Oh, I don't believe I'll be needing anything of the sort today, Riley."

Riley's expression didn't change. "I'm sure. Sit, my boy."

Joel managed to find some kind of gentlemanly bone by pulling out the chairs at the table for his sisters. Then, Joel took a seat for himself before a man Adriano recognized as an enforcer for the Trentini crew came to stand behind him.

Alessa watched Adriano through her lashes, quiet and pretty. Knowing he needed to keep his feelings for Alessa in check when people were near, Adriano focused his attention on anyone else but her.

The ache in his chest increased.

Kolin took his spot to stand behind Riley, silent and formidable.

Adriano, at his father's left, leaned back in his seat as Joel waved a skittish server over.

"Surely we can drink?" Joel asked Riley.

Riley nodded. "On the house, of course."

Joel flashed the waiting server a charming grin. "Whiskey, four fingers; neat."

The girl scampered off. Adriano didn't blame her. The restaurant had been cleared of normal patrons for the meeting, but the workers were asked to stay in case they were needed.

"Terrance always said there was nothing that couldn't be solved over a drink and a few words," Joel said, still smiling falsely.

Riley smirked. "And a gun, Joel. If you would have listened to him more, you might have heard the rest of what he was trying to tell you. Anything can be solved between normal men over a few drinks and words. With men like us, anything can be solved with a drink and words … or a gun."

Abriella snorted indelicately. "Or a marriage."

Riley offered Abriella a serene smile. "Or that. I hear you're back at the mansion, my dear."

Joel's gaze narrowed in on Riley. "How—"

"We are," Abriella replied, interrupting her brother without batting a lash. "I'd like to say it's good to be home and all …"

"But I don't imagine it is because you probably weren't given a choice," Riley finished for her. He flicked a look in Joel's direction before going back to Abriella. "How close am I?"

Abriella simpered him with a smile. "Bang on."

"I usually am, Ella."

Joel scowled. "Enough of this. She isn't here to make chitchat, Riley."

"Then why did you bring her here today?" Riley asked, loud enough for everyone to hear. "Because you see, I happen to find Abriella interesting when she opens up that mouth of hers to talk. She's got a dark humor that's difficult to find in a woman, not to mention, she isn't hard on the eyes."

Abriella laughed. "Thank you."

"Ah, you've earned those compliments, my dear," Riley replied. "But Joel here, he's obviously brought you along for this sit-down with other intentions. If he expects you to sit, shut up, and look pretty, then you're not doing very damn much for me here."

Silence answered Riley back from Joel.

Riley, apparently, wasn't looking for a response. "Which leads me to believe you're not a distraction, but perhaps his failsafe for something. It's a terrible thing when a man doesn't have enough confidence in his own standing that he has to bring along not one but two females in order to ensure his safety with another man. Terrible indeed."

Joel openly glared. "You have—"

Riley waved Joel's words off, whatever it was he planned on saying. "Oh, don't bother denying it, Joel. You are the only man inside and outside of this restaurant that believes the men in the Outfit are stupid and easily manipulated. Keep believing that, my boy, and they'll run you straight into an early grave."

"I highly doubt that," Joel muttered.

"As I said, keep believing it, Joel, while the rest of us stand around and watch as someone digs six feet down into dirt where your casket will rest."

Adriano damn near laughed, but managed to hold it back somehow. Without even realizing it, Joel had given Riley an opening to start in on. And like the fucking shark Adriano knew his father to be, Riley would bite on and rip out a bloody, messy chuck, leaving Joel scrambling to pick up the pieces.

It was Riley's game. He played it especially well.

Alessa's gaze jumped between Joel and Riley. Adriano caught her stare in between, held it for a brief second, and then dropped it just as fast.

"You're mighty arrogant today," Joel said.

Riley chuckled. "No, Joel. I'm arrogant every day. I've earned this right. Someday, you might have the benefit of saying the same, but not today."

Adriano stayed quiet at his father's side, grateful there was nothing between Joel and Riley that might possibly get caught in their heated glares. Even the men gathered around the room, watching the two front runners vying over the boss's seat in the Outfit couldn't help but stare, enraptured and likely confused.

Who would win this one?

The server broke Joel and Riley's staring contest by setting the glass of whiskey to the table with a loud clink. She disappeared into the back of the place just as quickly as she'd came.

"Is the engagement between Alessa and Dean still going through?" Riley asked, passing a look in the Artinos direction.

"Of course, eventually," Joel replied. "When the time is right. Why shouldn't it?"

Riley raised a single brow high. "A few reasons."

Joel didn't look like he gave much of a damn. "Like what, Riley?"

"Well, for one, because bosses typically okay an arrangement between families and there is no official boss to do that, Joel."

"I am more than capable of making those decisions for my sisters."

"Alessa is young," Adriano said before he could stop himself. Alessa's head snapped up, her pretty blue eyes widening with shock. "You're planning to marry her off before she's even had time to graduate college or do anything, Joel."

He knew better. Riley had been specific in his instructions that Adriano stay quiet during the meeting and learn from it.

Joel's gaze cut to Adriano. "I would love to know when my sister's welfare became any of your concern, Conti."

Riley pinched his son's thigh under the table hard enough to bruise. It kept Adriano quiet.

"He, like any man in this family, has a right to an opinion where there is concern for someone else," Riley said, almost like he was daring Joel to deny it. "And there is a great deal of concern to go around with this match you're preparing to make between Alessa and Dean. Which brings me to my second point, Joel. You're going to end up marrying your sister off far below her reaching. That is disgusting."

"I beg your fucking pardon, Conti?" Walter barked from the corner.

Joel held up a hand, quieting the man. "Which one is too low for you, Riley? Dean or his father?"

Riley laughed. "Both, my boy."

"Perhaps a marriage would be the chance for them to advance."

Christ.

Joel was stupider than Adriano thought.

"Does young Theo DeLuca realize that's what the marriage is intended for?" Riley asked quietly. "Does he realize there are men moving in on him under the guise of a promised engagement? Or are you using the distress he's feeling over his brother's passing to help the Artino cause along?"

Hushed murmurs passed through the men in the restaurant.

Too bad Theo was outside.

Adriano was sure the man would be filled in eventually.

Joel scowled. "You—"

"My God, Joel," Riley said, sighing. "You are nowhere near ready for the role you're attempting to take from me. And you are nowhere near the man I am, so your useless attempt at marking me inept and incapable is entirely pointless. Save yourself the trouble, step down before I have to force your hand into it, and save what face you might have left for your men. If you have even the slightest ounce of respect for your family and your crew in this game, you will take my advice before I rip what sense of dignity you have left away. I've let you have your shows, shooting up my son's car and making nice with other families, but I'm done with all that nonsense, Joel."

Flicking his wrist in Joel's direction, Riley added, "I have given you every available chance to step down to me in the easy, honorable way. I can't help but wonder if you even understand that stepping down for me to take the seat would be far from a failure on your part, but instead, an incredibly smart move. I have offered you my hand and a spot in this family even with Terrance—your *father*—dead in the ground. I have given you far more than any other man in this room would have, trust in that. After today, I don't know that I'll be willing to offer you the same thing again."

Silence echoed in the room. Not a fucking soul made a sound or moved an inch.

Adriano swore he heard Joel's teeth clench across the table.

Alessa sucked in a quiet breath, eyeing her brother from the side. Even Abriella seemed to watch Joel with a little more interest, like maybe she was curious about what his reaction would be to Riley's statement.

Riley didn't give Joel the chance to say anything as he stood fast from the table, tossed down three one-hundred dollar bills for the waitress, and straightened his jacket.

"This is done, Joel," Riley murmured calmly.

Never once had Adriano's father raised his voice. Not once had he physically threatened Joel or used the men he brought along to scare him into compliance. Riley didn't need any of that. As much as Adriano hated to think that his father had only used Mia's death as a way to advance his position in the Outfit, he couldn't help but admit what he knew was a fact.

Riley would make a damn good boss.

Any man in the room would be damn stupid not to see it.

Leaning over the table, Riley smacked his index finger to the wood grain. "And before you go running off at the mouth about how loyal many of these men are to you and only you, Joel, let me correct your very misunderstood and wrongly fed assumptions. There is not one man in this room who has looked at you and wondered what you will gain him. They are not looking at you because they believe you can and will lead them properly, but because you are weak enough for them to manipulate exactly how they see fit for their own needs.

"And eventually, whether the men want to admit it or not, they're aware of what chasing after you will do to them," Riley continued, his face blank and unreadable. "They will chase themselves straight down a fucking rabbit hole right along with you, my boy. Manipulating you will only get them so far and when you're nothing more than a shell of what they've molded and created for their purposes; then they're left with nothing more than a hopeless, incompetent boss unable to hold his own gun or shoot his own bullets. What will they do with you then, Joel? Tell me."

Joel stood from his chair fast enough to send it flying backward and clattering to the floor. His rage spilled over like it usually did when Joel didn't like what he was being told. Clenching his fists at his sides, Joel's entire body shook.

Adriano had seen this very thing happen one too many times where Joel was concerned.

He wasn't even surprised.

Shooting his own foot.

"Careful, Joel," Riley warned quietly. "*Your* incompetence is showing. If you can't handle one little sit-down with a man who hasn't even raised his voice to you, how do you think you'll fair sitting at the Commission against men like Dante Marcello or Maximo Sorrento. Do you think either of those bosses will bow to your hissy fits simply because you stomp your foot and demand it as so?"

Riley barked out a laugh, "Think again. They would have you buried in a makeshift grave before you even realized you were dead, boy. Men like them have little use for children in business. And that, Joel, is all you are."

Even Adriano had to check his father at that. Riley Conti had just gone from fighting for a boss's seat to essentially stripping Joel of any pride and respect he might have had with nothing but *words*.

"You *cocksucker*," Joel hissed, his face reddening.

"Ouch." Riley flashed a wicked smile. "Try again, Joel. That's nothing I haven't already heard before."

Joel scoffed. "Something else? How about a little truth slinging for your side, too? I think your words are the one and only thing you have to show in this room, Riley. How terrible and awful it must have been for you to lose your wife—you're certainly moving on quickly enough, though, aren't you?"

Riley's jaw ticked. "Do not walk that line, Joel."

"I think I should. Someone should," Joel spat back. "You seem to have a great deal of information about my dealings and allies in this, so why don't we talk about what I know regarding you, Riley? I hear you like them young. Courtney is her name, isn't it?"

Adriano's back stiffened like someone had shoved a steel rod up his spine. Still, he gritted his teeth and stayed quiet. All the eyes in the room had turned on his father.

Riley shrugged, unaffected. "Do you think I'm the only man here with a piece of ass on the side? Think again. I could ask you about Chloe and her father, but I'm sure Ronnie is like the rest of them. No doubt, he's pimping his daughter out to you in hopes of moving higher. Once you have your fill, both he and she will be left behind."

"I'm sure your wife would have loved to know she was just another whore that had been given a little more than the rest, Riley," Joel said, sneering. "Caught your last name, birthed you a couple of kids, and got fucked all the same."

Adriano lifted out of his seat slowly. There was a lot of shit he would listen to and take, but his mother being slandered sure as fuck wasn't one of them. He ignored the way Alessa's face crumpled for him, likely knowing how much her brother's words stung.

While Joel might have come into the restaurant unarmed, Adriano certainly had not. Adriano wanted the man to know it, too.

"Say that again," Adriano said coolly, flashing the gun at his waist. "Go on, do it."

Riley clapped a hand on his son's shoulder. "Don't bother. Joel is simply proving my point, son."

Adriano's molars ached from his jaw clenching so damn hard. "If you say so."

"I do, Adriano." Turning his attention back on Joel for a moment, Riley dismissed the man with a flick of his hand. "Enjoy your drink and please, get your sisters something to eat before you go. The restaurant was closed today for this meeting but there's no point in wasting it. However, my men and I will be going. Consider my words, Joel."

Joel's gaze narrowed in on Riley. "You're hoping for a lot."

Riley smiled his cold grin again. "Hopes are reserved for men who have something to dream of. I have no doubt that all my dreams will come crawling to my feet in due time. Good luck, Joel. You'll surely need it after today."

Kolin held out a suit jacket for Riley to put on before he left the table without another word. Adriano followed his father and the Capo, taking his strides slowly as a few Conti men stood from their seats at various tables to leave as well.

Like promised, there was a black car parked alongside the curb to take Riley away.

Adriano heard the ding of the restaurant's front door just as the passenger side was opened for Riley to get in. Tossing a glance over his shoulder, Adriano froze. It was just a brief second. Enough to turn his blood to ice.

The shine of black metal and the click of a safety was all Adriano needed to *know* ... Laurent Rossi raised the weapon and aimed through the crowd of men, pointing directly at Riley. No one seemed to notice what was happening. Maybe they all thought it was just another Conti man making his way out from the restaurant after every other guy had.

Who cared?

Adriano heard himself shout, but it sounded distant even to him. "Gun!"

People moved fast.

Time moved faster.

Adriano lunged toward his father, but he wasn't nearly fast enough. And there were far too many men in the way, trying to either help someone or get the fuck out of the gun's scope. The barrel of the gun flashed brightly, quiet pops following. A pain seared across Adriano's left bicep as he grabbed for his own gun and turned it on Laurent.

His weapon fired, snapping hard in Adriano's hand over and over with the kickback. Glass shattered as his bullets ripped through the glass windows of the restaurant. Unlike Laurent's gun, Adriano's had no silencer. The bangs echoed through the quiet street and screamed in his ears.

Then again, maybe those screams weren't from the noise of his gun at all.

For a brief moment, Adriano took his finger off the trigger.

Oh, God.

Alessa.

She was in that fucking restaurant and he was firing at it.

Adriano dropped his weapon to his side and pushed toward the black car and through the swarm of men protecting his father.

"Dad!" he shouted.

"Move, move—go!" someone barked.

More shots fired.

From who, Adriano wasn't sure. He didn't even fucking know if his had hit their target. Someone pushed his back hard, sending him flying through the opened passenger door and into the back seat of the black car.

Adriano's hands slipped on something wet and warm when he grabbed for his father. A morbid red stained Adriano's hands.

Blood.

But who did it belong to?

Adriano searched Riley for any sign of blood or a wound needing attention. "Where is it?"

Riley didn't answer.

"Shit," Riley growled, pain crossing his features as he winced. "Kolin …"

The car's door slammed shut as the vehicle lurched forward. Adriano's back hit the seat hard as the car's tires squealed when it took a sharp turn far too fast.

"Kolin!" Riley called again.

"Yeah, boss," Kolin said from the front passenger seat.

Adriano could smell it.

Rusty and tangy.

Heady and thick.

Fresh and wet.

Blood.

CHAPTER TWELVE

The ricochet of shattering glass and the background of volcanic noise was all Alessa heard before she hit the floor. A searing pain sliced her cheek when someone's hand hit the back of her head and forced her down.

"Stay the fuck down!" Dean snarled.

Where had he come from?

The last she saw, Dean had still been sitting in the corner with his father.

Abriella … Adriano …

Alessa was torn between her sister and her lover. She settled for the person she knew was closest and prayed that Adriano was okay.

"Abriella!" Alessa screamed, reaching for her sister. Abriella should have been there. She was one seat away at the table when the bullets started flying. "Abriella!"

No one answered her back.

More bodies hit the floor. Men covered their heads. Pop. Pop. Pop. Her heart raced, leaping into her throat. A sickness curled around her senses as tires screeched outside.

"Get off of me!" Alessa cried.

"Stay there," Dean barked.

"*Ella!*"

Alessa didn't give a damn about Joel. She had a sneaking suspicion he probably planned for the meeting to go down this way. He'd been sitting at the table between Alessa and Abriella, but he smiled when Laurent stood from his table with a gun in hand, following behind the Contis.

Somehow, Alessa rolled to her back even with Dean's weight on her.

"Let me go!"

Dean glared. "You have to stay—"

She slapped him hard, shocking him enough for her to push him off. She didn't give a damn if he was protecting her and the gunshots were still loud outside. Rolling over to her knees, Alessa searched for her sister as Dean's arms wrapped her waist and pulled her down to the glass filled ground again.

Alessa was stuck staring at her sister. On her back, Abriella choked and jerked, spitting out red saliva as crimson pooled around her back. Terror saturated Alessa, keeping her stricken and immobile.

"Ella," Alessa whispered.

Quiet, gasping cries echoed from Abriella. Alessa tried to crawl to her sister's side, but Dean's strong hold around her middle was relentless.

"Oh, my God ... let me go," Alessa begged. "Ella!"

It was just a blink and Tommas Rossi was there. His black shoes skidded across the floor before his hand slammed into the table, pushing it out of the way.

Tommas' attention was only on Abriella. "Slow breaths. Not too fast, Ella."

Dean finally let Alessa go.

It was only then she realized the gunfire had stopped. Alessa crawled on hands and knees across the four feet that separated her and Abriella. She stopped just short of the bloody mess, scared to touch it.

Damian Rossi came to his cousin's side, tugging off his suit jacket. "Chill, Tommy."

He spoke the words quietly—warningly.

"I'm trying," Tommas said under his breath.

"And failing," Damian muttered. "It's coming from her back."

"Yeah," Tommas grunted. "Let's get some pressure on that to stop it from bleeding more than it already has."

"Ready?"

Tommas nodded. "On three."

"Call for an ambulance!" someone yelled.

"One, two—"

"Three," Damian interrupted his cousin and lifted Abriella on her side.

The sickness Alessa felt only got worse as she caught sight of the bullet wound bleeding out from Abriella's back. Damian shoved his jacket underneath and pressed his hand to the injury, keeping firm pressure.

"Back down," Tommas ordered.

Damian lowered Abriella to the floor.

"Ow," Abriella mumbled.

"That's good," Tommas whispered. "Feeling pain is good. It means you're not going into shock."

"For now," Damian added softer.

"I don't like you much," Abriella told Damian.

Damian smirked. "You're not required to."

"Good thing Lily married you," Abriella said. "Otherwise, no one would put up with your ass."

"Stop talking," Tommas ordered. "Try to be calm."

"Hey," Abriella whispered, touching Tommas' mouth with her fingertip.

Tommas smiled but it faded fast. His words were too quiet for anyone else to hear. "I'm going to fucking kill him, Ella. After this, he's so gone, girl."

Who?

"Careful," Damian warned his cousin.

"Hush, Tommy," Abriella soothed. "You worry too much. I tell you that all the time."

Alessa searched for Joel in the questioning, worried faces beginning to move with phones pressed to their ears. Joel's tired, angry laughter filled the mostly quiet restaurant. With devastation all around and his sister dying on the floor just feet away, all Joel could do was laugh.

"Fucking hell," Joel said, his fingers digging into the leather bench as he stared outside at the street. "That cocksucker."

The people outside must have dispersed. Tires screeched again. A siren echoed in the background, telling her help was on the way.

"Laurent got out good," someone said. "Beat feet to the pavement quick and his car was parked down the way."

Joel scoffed. "Useless. That's what he fucking is."

"Maybe so, but someone got something bad out there. It happened kind of fast, boss," Dean said, ignoring Alessa on the floor. "Give him some credit. Look at all that fucking red out there on the ground. Wait and see who it came from, Joel."

Red ...

Oh, God.

Adriano.

Alessa's heart screamed out for him, needing to know he was safe and okay.

"Riley took something," Walter added, righting a table before he sat down on a chair. "I saw it when it hit him."

"Right," Joel said faintly.

Their conversation went on like nothing else was happening. Like Abriella wasn't bleeding to death on the floor.

But Joel ... he didn't care a damn ounce about his sisters.

Nothing.

Glancing around the restaurant, Alessa watched as the men cleared out. They said nothing, but the shock, anger, and confusion racing across all their faces was enough to tell her that none of them knew this would happen. Joel had shown his colors, as mean as they were.

But the Outfit was like it always was. It wasn't a one for all or all for one thing.

Save your fucking asses.

"I think the bleeding is staunched," Damian said, bringing Alessa's attention back to her sister. "Try not to move much."

Abriella wasn't listening. Alessa could tell by the way her sister looked around, dazed.

"Ella," Tommas said harshly. "Eyes open, sweet girl."

"It's worse than it is," Abriella mumbled.

"I think you took a bullet straight through your back and into the lung," Tommas replied quietly. "That's kind of bad, Ella. And I need you to keep looking at me."

Abriella laughed bleakly. "I've only ever looked at you. Who the hell else is going to save me?"

Alessa felt numb. Or like maybe she was floating up above and watching those down below move around her prone, quiet form. She stared blankly at the tiled floor of the emergency room. Her tears finally subsided. Her eyes still hurt and felt swollen. Shock had finally set it.

Several people had attempted to sit down in the empty chair next to hers and chat. Her parents had rushed to the hospital the moment they got the news about the shooting, but Alessa couldn't even bring herself to talk to them when they tried.

Nothing.

Just a shell.

Between worrying for her sister who had been in surgery for three hours with no word on her condition, and wondering about Adriano's current situation, Alessa was overwhelmed. She had given up and given into it.

She didn't know how to do anything different right then.

A form settled into the chair beside Alessa's. She passed the person a fleeting look, but did a double take when she realized who it was.

Tommas.

"You're still here?" Alessa asked quietly.

Tommas chuckled dryly. "Where else should I be, Alessa?"

Alessa took inventory of who was still in the waiting room. There were a lot of her brother's men, some of the Rossi crew, and a few family members.

Joel had gone long ago. His quick departure hadn't been a shocker.

"I don't know, Tommas, I just thought—"

"My whole life is lying on an operating table with a bullet in her body because her brother is a fool," Tommas interjected calmly. "And at the moment, I'm doing my best to keep my cool. But in here ..."

Tommas pointed at his chest, growing silent.

"Yeah?" Alessa pressed.

"I can't breathe."

"Oh."

Tommas shrugged. "So, I'll stay until I can't anymore or I get word. But then I'll have to figure something out so that I can get in and see her."

"You shouldn't have to sneak around."

"I've always had to sneak around with Ella," Tommas muttered. "She'll be okay. Abriella doesn't give up anything if she doesn't want to."

Alessa felt lighter just hearing him say that. "I hope so."

"Ah, there's no hoping about it. I know. The way you were looking over here, dead to the world, I figured someone needed to tell you, too."

"Thank you."

Tommas offered her a small smile and nothing more. He stood from the seat and resumed his spot across the waiting room with his cousin.

Alessa's phone buzzed in her hand. She glanced down at the screen, recognizing the familiar number and disguised contact for Adriano.

I love you, it read.

Tommas hadn't been the only one who couldn't breathe.

Alessa finally took a real breath.

"Ew," Alessa grumbled, letting the tapioca fall off the spoon. "Oh, my God. It looks like squishy, wiggly puke with fish eyes in it or something."

Abriella laughed. Her cheeks pinked with a healthy, happy glow. Alessa couldn't help but join in with her sister's joy. Just seeing Abriella alive and well was the best thing ever.

It had been a little over a week since the restaurant shooting, but Alessa hadn't been able to sleep for a single night since without dreaming about it. A single four-hour surgery had saved Abriella's life. Barely. The first night was a touch-and-go kind of thing.

"So, you don't want it, either?" Abriella asked through bouts of giggles.

Alessa pushed the tiny glass bowl away with the tip of the spoon. "No thanks. But you need to eat something. That's why they bring you three meals a day, Ella."

"It doesn't matter." Abriella waved her hand and winked. "Tommy is going to sneak me in take-out later."

"Oh?"

"Yep. He smooth-talked a nurse into letting him in after visiting hours. I would be jealous, you know, if he wasn't doing it for me."

"Playing with fire," Alessa murmured in warning.

"Worth the burns," Abriella replied quietly. "Besides, if he didn't get in here that way, he would find another way. At least like this, no one has to figure out an excuse for Joel to explain away Tommas right now."

Alessa scowled at the mention of their brother.

"Still sour?" Abriella asked.

"Yes."

Of course.

How could Alessa not be when it came to Joel?

The asshole had only managed to make his way into the hospital over the last week to visit with his younger sister twice. Joel even made a fuss about taking Alessa into the hospital to stay with Abriella during visiting hours. Alessa downright refused to stay anywhere near her brother for longer than necessary.

Plus, going to see Abriella kept Alessa away from Dean. It seemed like he had been around a lot over the last week, too.

Alessa glanced down at her hands, hoping to hide her displeasure from Abriella. The last thing her sister needed was to hear Alessa whine.

"How are you feeling today?" Alessa asked quietly.

Abriella shrugged. "Better. The IVs are gone and now I can take an oral dose of antibiotics. I'll be out before the weekend."

That was good news.

God knew Alessa needed some.

"What is wrong?" Abriella asked.

"Nothing," Alessa replied quickly.

"Liar, liar," her sister teased in a sing-song fashion. "Now, quit sulking or tell me why you are, Alessa. It's more than Joel, obviously. After all this time, we're used to brushing his nonsense off our shoulders. Talk to me."

"Dean," Alessa whispered.

Well, he was part of it. Alessa decided giving her sister something was better than giving her nothing. Since Abriella had been in the hospital all week, she didn't know what had happened over the last few days.

Abriella's distaste was written all over her face as she said, "That asshole again."

"Look at this garbage," Alessa said, lifting her hand.

A large, gaudy diamond ring sparkled in the stream of light coming in from the window. It was far too big for Alessa's small hand, not that she cared much about the size. It was the meaning of the ring that felt like someone had tied a noose around her throat and pulled as hard as they fucking could.

It finally happened.

Joel finally gave the okay for an engagement.

Dean wasted no time.

Abriella's gaze widened briefly before narrowing into slits. "When did that happen?"

"Last night. He came over to talk with Joel. Somehow, it seemed like a good time to get one on me," Alessa explained, sighing. "His words, not mine. I couldn't refuse. Joel wouldn't let me. I am not marrying that man, I don't care what anyone tells me I have to do. It's not happening."

"A good time to *get one on you?*" Abriella scoffed loudly and slapped the bed with her palms. "He's a tool."

"I'm aware."

"But nothing new," Abriella added quietly. "So, I get why this is annoying you, but what else is there, Alessa? What else aren't you saying?"

"Joel picked a date for the wedding," Alessa informed. "November second."

Abriella cringed. "Three months?"

"Yeah. And according to Joel, I need to get serious about what I want, or he'll just hire whoever to do it for me and I won't get a choice."

"Do you care?"

Alessa snorted. "Not a damn bit."

"Good."

But it still sucked. Now, with an official engagement, a wedding date set and looming sooner than Alessa was comfortable with, she didn't have a choice but to face reality. There was no way out of this arrangement. It didn't matter what Alessa said, she knew the truth. She was going to be forced to marry Dean, even if that meant she would be dragged down the aisle kicking, bloodied, and screaming the whole way.

Fuck Joel.

His desire to have a higher position meant everyone else around him suffered.

Abriella eyed Alessa from the side. "We'll figure something out."

"You keep saying that."

"Yeah, well, you keep saying you won't marry him," Abriella replied frankly.

"Willingly," Alessa muttered. "I won't marry him willingly."

"Then you won't marry him at all." Abriella gave a short nod like she was willing her words a fact. "I'll make goddamn sure of it." Abriella reached over and grabbed Alessa's hand. "Has Adriano seen this yet?"

Subconsciously, Alessa flinched away from the question.

"I'll take that as a *no*," Abriella said slowly.

"A huge no."

"Why not, Lissa?"

Alessa frowned and tugged her hand out of Abriella's grasp, wanting to pretend the ring wasn't there. "Hard to show him when I haven't seen him since the restaurant shooting."

It was the truth.

Adriano had sent Alessa a few vague texts over the last week. It was enough to tell her that he was alive, safe, but Alessa missed Adriano. He was her calm in the storm.

"Not at all?" Abriella asked.

"None. He sent me a couple of messages, but nothing big. It's like he dropped off the radar this week or something."

"Or maybe someone else did," Abriella said.

Alessa's brow furrowed. "Huh?"

"Tommy likes to talk sometimes," her sister explained, refusing to meet Alessa's curious gaze. "And he doesn't trust anyone but me, so he goes off at the mouth sometimes because he needs to get it out."

"So?"

"So, Riley is out, Lissa."

"Like out how?" Alessa asked, still confused.

"Gone. Poof. His men have backed off this last week. They had been moving in on the Rossi and DeLuca streets here and there, gaining friends and pulling men in. Riley had worked the streets hard because he's got loyalties there whether Joel wants to admit it or not."

"But this week he hasn't," Alessa said.

"No, this week he's no-fucking-where, Alessa. Completely gone."

The memory of the bloody sidewalk outside the restaurant filled Alessa's mind. It had been such a morbid shade, so violent in color.

"Someone said Riley took a couple of bullets," Alessa said.

Abriella's lips drew into a thin, contemplative line. "Tommy might have mentioned that, but he couldn't say for sure. It happened fast. Riley's guys shot back and then Laurent had men outside waiting."

"Are you saying Riley might be dead?" Alessa asked.

"I'm saying nobody knows and his streets are quiet, his men aren't talking, and if that's the case, Joel got every damn thing he wanted."

Alessa felt sick.

Everything about the situation screamed bad news to her.

"What would that mean for Adriano?" Alessa asked.

"If something did happen to Riley and they're trying to keep it quiet?"

"Yeah."

Abriella chewed on her inner cheek before blurting out, "Whatever Joel wanted, I guess. He would make the call on the Conti crew if they didn't have the strength or allies to fight back."

"Well … damn."

"He's still working on getting that Capo title, too," Abriella added. "So, without that, he doesn't have a whole lot of clout with leaders for the other crews. He's just a kid to them. Adriano's best bet would be to—"

"Follow the herd," Alessa interrupted.

Abriella laughed under her breath. "Basically. I don't think he's the type, though."

Not at all.

"Dino DeLuca's funeral is tomorrow," Alessa said, wanting to change the topic.

"I heard. Are you going?"

Alessa nodded. "With Dean, unfortunately."

Abriella offered a small smile. "Give Lily a hug for me. I might hate my brother, but she loved hers."

Dino DeLuca's funeral was like a bad reminder of Terrance's for Alessa. With a body so badly damaged, there was a closed casket. Soft music filled the church as bells rang and incense burned. Blessings were said, apologies given, and the day progressed with the usual heaviness of grief.

Alessa's black dress fit the day, like most everyone else. She'd given Dino's sister Lily the apology and words from Abriella. Lily took it all in stride, but the girl seemed out of it. She looked tired, sad, and angry all at the same time. Her husband Damian never left her side once in the front pew.

It all felt surreal to Alessa.

Another funeral.

Another day.

More black clouds and clothes.

More tears.

Dean sat quietly beside Alessa. She didn't trust him. Not with a damn inch. Dean was a lot like Joel. They were cut from the same cloth. Dean didn't do anything that wasn't to his benefit. He likely—stupidly—believed that if he could get closer to Alessa, she would let him in.

That wasn't going to happen.

The last few guests made their way from the pews to give a final goodbye to Dino and hand their condolences over to the family before the service moved to the cemetery. A hush fell over the crowd of mourners.

Confusion settled in Alessa as she glanced around, wondering what had caused the disruption.

Alessa noticed a figure darkening the entrance to the church.

Just like Terrance's funeral.

Well, in a way. At least this time, Adriano hadn't come alone like he did to Terrance's.

Adriano, wearing a black suit and flanked by several men, walked down the row of pews and kept his gaze trained on the altar where a shined oak casket rested. Theo DeLuca stood from the front pew with a rage lighting up his gaze and his fists clenching into tight balls at his sides.

Theo obviously still blamed the Contis for his brother's death.

Alessa knew the truth, but it did no good.

Quietly, Lily stood with her brother, put a hand to his shoulder, and whispered something in his ear. The tension in Theo's posture didn't relax, but he gave his sister a tight nod and faced Adriano as the two men stood toe-to-toe.

Hands shook.

Soft words murmured.

Alessa couldn't hear a thing. She was far too interested in watching the way Adriano seemed to ooze confidence and remorse all at the same time.

Then, Adriano turned to Joel who had come to stand on the other side of the DeLuca family. More conversation passed between Joel and Adriano, but Alessa was too far back to hear. Nonetheless, her brother's face flickered with no emotions, not even his usual cockiness.

What was happening?

Walter slid in beside his son. Dean's attention left Alessa and turned on his father.

"I wonder where Riley is," Walter mused.

"Those are some big guns Adriano brought along from the Conti crew," Dean said.

Walter nodded. "They are."

Alessa took note of the half of a dozen men who had followed in behind Adriano. The men had dispersed themselves around the floor of the church and kept their eyes on the meeting at the same time.

"He's a bit young to be having a say with them," Dean said.

"Smart kid," Walter replied. "Do not let Adriano Conti's age fool you into a comfortable zone, son. Adriano has spent the last half of a decade under the feet of some of the most powerful men inside the Outfit. His ability to stand on his own and take what he wants should not be overlooked because of his youth. You would be an idiot not to realize how good of an ally he could be without his father making the calls."

Alessa couldn't help but notice Dean's scowl at the very suggestion of

Adriano being an ally to him.

"Eventually," Walter continued, "the Outfit is going to be controlled by a younger generation of men, son. And if this war continues to take the older men who make the calls now, then that day might come sooner than any of us think. Once Riley Conti is gone, if he's not already, Adriano will step up as he should. Mark my words, Dean."

"Unless he gets killed first," Dean said coolly.

"Foolish men who make foolish mistakes end up dead."

"Your point?"

"Adriano has not yet made a mistake."

"What about his father?" Dean asked bitingly.

"What about yours?" Walter shot back.

"I—"

"You follow me, son. He follows his father. As he should. That's how it is. Even Joel understands that Adriano can't be blamed for his father's actions. And speaking of Joel, look at how he followed his father through life despite hating the man. We give our loyalties where they are due—to the men who raised us, Dean."

"You're awfully fond of him," Dean grumbled.

"Oh, stop it," Walter replied sharply.

Alessa's cell phone rang in her clutch. She cringed, realizing she had forgotten to turn it off before entering the church. It was rude of her. Alessa felt her cheeks heat up. She pulled the phone out and silenced it, but not before noticing it was her sister.

"Excuse me," Alessa said, waving her phone for Dean to see. "Abriella might need something."

Dean nodded, satisfied with the excuse.

Even though she didn't want to go further away from Adriano than was necessary, especially after not seeing him for over a week, Alessa made her way out of the main hall. She stepped into one of the private rooms that was usually used for meetings or families and called her sister back.

Abriella picked up on the second ring. "You were still in church, weren't you?"

Alessa laughed. "Yes."

"Sorry, but I have good news. I'm getting released early tomorrow instead of the weekend. I wanted to tell you right away and Tommas, too. I know Tommy is there at the funeral, so I was hoping you could somehow pass the info along."

Alessa growled playfully. "Getting me to do your dirty work, now?"

Abriella whined. "Lissa, I'm sick and I almost died, so you have to—"

The cell phone was snatched from Alessa's hand before her sister could finish whatever she was going to say. Turning fast on her heel, Alessa came face to face with a smirking Adriano. Somehow, he'd managed to get inside the private room and close the door without her hearing a thing.

Adriano put the cell to his ear. "Ella?"

Alessa's mouth went dry as Adriano's lips curved wickedly, and he looked her over. She could hear her sister in the background of the call, but she couldn't discern what was being said.

"Yes, I know," Adriano said quietly. "I'm glad to hear your voice. Get well. She'll call you right back."

Adriano handed the phone to Alessa. She put it back in her clutch, unsure of what to say.

"One of my guys mentioned which direction you took. I had to use the bathroom and took a wrong door. Imagine my luck," Adriano said slyly.

His guys.

Alessa didn't miss those choice in words. "Reckless—that's what you are."

"Us," he retorted.

Before she could say another thing, Alessa found herself pushed back into the closest wall. Her spine ached from the force as Adriano's lips found hers and his hands fisted into her curled hair.

Alessa gasped when his teeth bit hard enough on her bottom lip to leave a mark. Adriano kissed her harder, deeper. Like he was starved and thirsty and she was the buffet spread out for him to take what he wanted. His tongue claimed her mouth, his teeth smearing her lipstick.

"Christ," Alessa breathed when he drove his hands down her sides.

"That's bad. We're in church."

"That's what is bad about this?"

Adriano chuckled darkly. "Well ..."

Alessa found her hands pinned above her head. Adriano's fingers ghosted over her wrist and palms, promising and sweet.

"I'm going to be busy for a while," he told her. "Another week, maybe."

"I noticed that already."

"But I'll be around."

Alessa nodded. "I'll be waiting."

Adriano gave her another sinful smile, kissed the tip of her nose, and let her hands go. "Don't wait, just be ready."

She didn't have the first clue what he meant.

Adriano kissed her hard once more, fixed a wayward curl, and left Alessa confused and turned on like nothing else alone in the private room. With shaking hands, Alessa pulled out her phone to call her sister back.

The lack of something sparkly caught her eye instantly. Her engagement ring was gone.

Alessa's breath caught in her throat. "Oh."

Sneaky. So jealous.

Adriano must have took notice of the piece and acted.

Oh, she loved him and hated him for it.

Selfish man.

Alessa wouldn't try to deny it made her even hotter. Except now she had to explain where it had went to Dean. She hoped her acting skills were up to the job.

Somehow, Alessa felt lighter with the ring gone. Adriano probably knew that, too.

Dammit.

She loved that man.

CHAPTER THIRTEEN

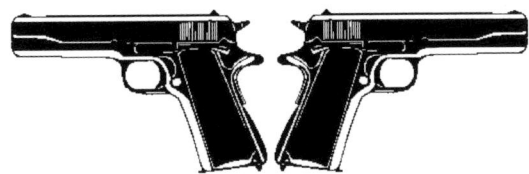

Adriano opened up the trunk of his Camaro and eyed the wrapped up form. Duct Tape covered the oblong shape in a spiral, insuring it would stay tucked in and not come apart once dumped. Six feet long and rolled in blankets and garbage bags, the shape of a body was unmistakeable. Thankfully, there was no smell to the corpse. Not yet, anyway.

"Ready, Skip?" Rickie asked.

It took Adriano longer than he was willing to admit before he realized Rickie was talking to him. Maybe because the whole Skip thing put Adriano on edge and he wasn't accustomed to being graced with such a title.

Adriano nodded. "Yeah, let's get this done and over with."

Stones had already been added inside the blankets and clothing of the person within. When they dumped the body into the water, it would sink to the bottom and stay there until it decayed into nothing but bones. Wrapped up and sealed like it was, the weights couldn't get out. Two holes at the top and bottom section of the form would let the gasses disperse without forcing the wrapping apart or sending the body floating to the top.

Adriano had done this more than once. In fact, the man inside the blankets and garbage bags had taught him all the tricks to keep a body hidden under water without it being noticed.

Kolin Bastoni.

Nothing about this was easy.

Kolin hadn't even made it to the damn clinic after being shot in the back repeatedly when he tried to get Riley into the car. Adriano found it hard to believe that two weeks had passed since the incident. It still felt like yesterday to him.

Adriano thought the Capo deserved a proper funeral. The right kind of goodbye for a wise-guy of an older generation——one who had taught Adriano how to be a wise-guy in the new generation.

Riley disagreed.

Keeping Kolin's unfortunate end a secret from everyone but the people who had been inside the car would mean speculation and assumptions could run wild. Riley wanted that sort of mess, just to see how Joel might react. Or rather, not react.

"Feet or head?" Rickie asked.

Adriano beat back his frown. "I'll take the head."

Just another job, Adriano reminded himself.

Heaving Kolin's deadweight out of the car wasn't much of an issue. As long as he didn't think about what he was doing, Adriano was fine.

"Throw it out as far as you can on three," Adriano said.

Rickie nodded. "All right. You count, Skip."

"One, two ..." Adriano swung the body outward with Rickie's motion and said, "Three."

The mass hit the water fifteen feet below with a loud splash. Adriano wasn't worried about anyone hearing or noticing. This particular place had been on the Conti payroll for as long as he could remember.

"Did you hand over the cash when you came in?" Adriano asked, still staring down to make sure the figure was sinking.

It did. Slowly.

"Yeah," Rickie confirmed.

"Good. Then I'll see you later when I get to the warehouse."

"Sure, Skip."

Adriano swallowed hard and shoved his hands into his pockets, watching the murky water disguise and hide another death. Long after Rickie was gone, Adriano could still hear the guy's words in the back of his mind.

Skip.

Skip, Skip, *Skip*.

Adriano had waited a long time to be called that.

He wasn't sure if he was ready for it. He wasn't sure if others were ready for it.

"I suppose you're going to get your spot quicker than you thought," Riley said.

Adriano stared at the body wrapped in black garbage bags inside the six foot long freezer. "What?"

Riley slammed the freezer lid down, hiding Kolin's dead corpse. "The title to go along with the button, son."

"I don't know what you're talking about."

"I'm going to give you a pass on the distraction since it's been a long day and all," Riley murmured, turning to face his son. His father still wore the bullet proof vest that had saved his life during the shooting. Two bullets were lodged in the chest of the Kevlar. "But correct whatever issue you have and quickly, Adriano. There's a whole crew of people you need to manage alone now that Kolin's culled. We have to keep moving forward, don't bother with what is behind. You get that?"

Adriano nodded. "Sure."

"I think it sounds good. Youngest one in the family that I can remember."

"Huh?" Adriano mumbled, still not able to shake off the fact that Riley had hid a family member's body inside his freezer. "What, Dad?"

Riley sighed harshly. "Seriously, correct that shit, Adriano."

"I will."

"Good, because Capos don't have time to sit around and sulk when someone gets whacked, son."

Capo.

Well, damn.

Adriano blinked out of the memory, feeling much older than his twenty years. Inside his left pocket, he felt for an object that he'd been holding onto for a while. Pulling the diamond ring out that he'd slipped off Alessa's finger when she'd been too distracted by him at the church, he eyed the piece.

Disgust.

That's how he felt looking at it.

Entirely, completely disgusted.

Dean didn't get to put a ring on Adriano's woman. He sincerely hoped the fool didn't give her any issues about *losing* it. Adriano would probably take the replacement, too.

With one more look at the piece of jewelry, Adriano tossed it into the water. It hit the water with a plop.

"Good fucking riddance."

"Anyone talking?" Adriano asked.

Rickie scowled around the cigarette in his mouth. "A little."

"About what?"

"You know what, the same shit. Kolin hasn't been around and all that. I mean, I know why he isn't around. Some of them suspect why he hasn't been around. It makes for a bad crew, Skip."

Adriano nodded and shoved his hands in his pockets. The best way to ward off someone's concern was nonchalance. He wasn't Kolin's right-hand anymore. He was the crew—the head of the Conti show. A lot of the guys probably wondered about it all, but now it was just time to confirm it for real.

He had to put his game face on.

The mask.

Twenty-years-old ...

A fucking kid to some people. That's all he was.

People gave Theo DeLuca shit all the time for his age and the fact he was a second Capo to the DeLuca crew. So, how would people react to Adriano with his age?

Don't give them a chance to.

Adriano could practically hear Kolin in the back of his mind.

It helped.

"There's a little issue between Con's guys and Steve's," Rickie informed. "Same shit, different week."

Con was a man, a year older than Adriano, who had also been close to Kolin in his own way. Not as close or with as much control as Adriano had over the crew, but there had been a friendship between them nonetheless.

Problems could come from that.

"Thanks for the info," Adriano said. "Go in, I'll be there in a minute."

Without a word, Rickie disappeared into the warehouse with a cigarette still in his mouth. Adriano reminded himself that this was just another step. One more thing to do. Three quarters of the men on the Conti crew were young like him and Rickie. Street guys, smart guys. Young guys. The other quarter were people of Kolin's generation that mostly worked out of businesses and in other trades. They weren't the ones Adriano had to concern himself with as far as making his position as the Conti Capo clear.

They would pay their dues no matter who showed up to collect.

Stepping inside the warehouse, Adriano gazed over the men who had shown up. It wasn't a required meeting for the crew, but he'd put word out and a great deal of the guys showed up. Thirty or more, anyway. Whoever hadn't come would find out the suspicions about Kolin's end and Adriano's new position the next day.

Word traveled fast on the streets.

A few of the guys turned as Adriano approached, looking him over with wary eyes.

"Where is the Skip?" Con asked from the far corner.

"He won't be coming tonight," Adriano said.

Or any other night, he held back from adding.

Adriano passed the guys a look, noting the wariness they sported was beginning to churn with understanding. If a meeting of a crew was called, it was usually done by the Capo and he would be there.

Kolin wasn't there.

Adriano was.

"Is there a problem?" Adriano asked calmly.

Going for his usual comfort of nonchalance, Adriano cocked a brow and rested his shoulder against a crate.

Con stepped forward. "Yeah, I came to talk to the Skip."

Adriano nodded once. "You're looking at him, so talk."

Silence answered that back.

And then Con had to go and ruin it. "Kolin—"

"Is at the bottom of a river currently. It's an unfortunate end for him, but that's the nature of the Outfit. It's a beast, man, what else do you want me to say?"

Anger and confusion slipped over Con's features.

Con wasn't made in the Outfit. He had no real claim or stake.

Adriano needed a sacrifice, something to mark his claim and make sure everybody knew he wasn't fucking around when it came to his spot as a Capo. Kolin had always told him that violence should only be used to draw control when absolutely necessary. All other means were best used first.

That didn't apply in situations like these.

Violence—this was how a Capo took his spot.

Simple.

Bloody.

Just like that.

"I asked if there was problem, Con?" Adriano asked.

Con's gaze narrowed. "No, of course not."

Adriano glanced to Rickie. "There's a problem. Seems you've been causing Steve issues again. What's that, the sixth complaint I've heard about that shit? There's enough problems in the Outfit right now without my crew adding to it by fighting amongst themselves. So yeah, Con, we've got a fucking problem."

Con opened his mouth to say something, but Adriano was already done talking.

Yanking the gun from the waistband of his pants where it was hidden by his jacket, Adriano cocked back the hammer and aimed. It wasn't Con's fault, not really. The little issue between the men could be solved with a few words or somebody's ass getting kicked. Blood didn't need to be spilled. But Adriano had to make a point. He wanted no trouble when it came to being the Capo for his crew. Con was a good one to use to make everything clear.

Nobody moved or said a word.

"I'll answer to Skip or Capo," Adriano said quietly. "I suggest no one forgets that in the future."

Pulling the trigger back inside the warehouse was the best choice Adriano had.

That didn't mean it was easy.

"Where in the hell are you?" Riley asked, his tone edging sharp like a razor.

"Working," Adriano replied, never taking his eyes off the dark road in front of his parked vehicle. He flicked the lights off on the Camaro just to be safe. "Isn't that what a Capo does, Dad? We fucking work. We go out and check up on shit. We keep up-to-date with the crew and then report back when there's something to say. What more do you want from me?"

"Updates," Riley barked.

Adriano rolled his eyes and palmed the tension headache starting to throb at the base of his skull. "The guys are nervous and twitchy. They're working, but barely. Some think that the Trentini and DeLuca side of things might skip in on the streets and light someone or something up. They've got reasons to be worried."

"No, they don't," Riley responded quietly. "No one is stupid enough to overthrow an already settled crew. Would they overthrow the leader of it and take over that way? Yes. But it's not the same. You should be explaining that to them, Adriano."

Adriano should do a lot of things.

Like hang the fuck up on his father, for one.

"You're the one who wanted to disappear for a couple of weeks, Dad. Back off. If you're ready to step back out and say everything is okay and good, then do so."

"Not yet. I'm waiting on Joel."

"Waiting on him to do what, Dad?"

Riley chuckled. "Patience gets a man everywhere."

Adriano always thought men like them took what they wanted, when they wanted it. Mostly, he was just tired of the runaround he was getting from his father on a lot of things. Like dealing with the Artino assholes.

"Did you get the other job done tonight?" Riley asked.

Kolin, he meant.

They always used burner phones, but breaking the habit of talking vaguely or just in circles was hard to break.

"Swimming with the fish," Adriano confirmed.

"Thank you. Stop by tomorrow and we'll discuss some things."

"Like what?"

"Whatever I want, Adriano. Tomorrow."

Riley hung up the phone before Adriano could get another word in edgewise. Adriano didn't mind, really. Checking his phone, Adriano noticed a text had come in while he was talking with his father.

Two minutes, it read.

Adriano grinned, and hit the gas, moving his car further down the dark road with his lights still turned off. The glow of the moon was enough to see where he needed to go. Up ahead, he watched a tiny figure step out of the treeline. If someone followed that trail in the woods, it would lead straight to the back property of the Trentini estate.

Hitting the brake, Adriano leaned over and pushed the passenger door open. Alessa tossed her messenger bag inside first before climbing inside herself. Her sweet grin was the only fucking thing Adriano had wanted to see for the last week.

The quick meeting at the church hadn't been nearly enough.

He'd texted Alessa earlier, just wanting to check up on her. She'd followed it up with a demand for Adriano to come get her for the night. It was stupid—way too reckless. He didn't say no. But they were the only thing he knew how to save in this mess. When everyone else was picking up the ruined pieces of what was left, Adriano and Alessa would be okay. More than okay, even.

Somehow.

"What makes tonight a fine night to sneak out, Lissa?" Adriano asked.

"Joel is out for the night. Somewhere, I don't know."

"Don't you think it'd be important to?"

Alessa laughed. "I don't even care."

Maybe she didn't.

Adriano wasn't going to complain.

"Eve is staying at my place," Adriano said.

"I already knew that."

Adriano chuckled. "Then you know to keep it down to a dull roar."

"Oh?"

"I have time to make up for," he explained.

"What are you waiting for?" Alessa asked as she closed the door.

"You," Adriano murmured.

Alessa smiled wider. "I'm here."

"Yeah, but I'm always waiting on you for one thing or another. I don't mind."

Something woke Adriano from the dead sleep he was in. Nothing in his apartment had made a sound, and Alessa's rhythmic breathing at his side said she was still sleeping soundly. But the oddest sensation crawled over

Adriano's spine, like someone was watching him.

Sliding his hand under the pillow, he grabbed the magnum that was always there. Turning fast in the bed, he cocked the hammer back and aimed. The barrel of his gun pointed directly at the chest of Damian Rossi.

Adriano felt his heart clench painfully at the sight of Damian's gun aimed and ready, pointing straight at a sleeping Alessa.

There was a reason why people called this man Ghost, after all. Adriano's apartment was as safe as it would ever be, but Damian had his ways. This did not make for a good situation. As far as Adriano understood it, Damian only showed himself during a job if he didn't plan on the victim seeing him leave.

"Evening," Damian greeted almost soundlessly.

Adriano's mouth was dry as he replied, "I'd say it's early morning."

"Getting there." Damian looked over the couple and the messy sheets. Adriano shifted in the bed and tugged the sheet a little higher over Alessa's naked shoulders. "This is an interesting sight."

"Is it?"

"Very. Doesn't she have her own bed to sleep in?" Damian asked, watching Alessa closely.

Jealousy burned white-hot through Adriano.

"Don't you have your own wife to stare at?"

"Touché." Damian chuckled lowly. "Adriano, I have very little interest in your girl here, trust that. I'm happily married, remember? But if the Trentini girl puts you on a steeper edge while we chat, I certainly don't mind using it to my advantage and making you uncomfortable."

"Is that so?" Adriano asked.

"Fear often has a way of dragging out the truth where it might not otherwise be offered."

Adriano's jaw clenched. "Then why are you here?"

Damian smiled grimly. "We need to have a little chat."

"Oh?"

"Yes." Nodding at the gun in Adriano's hand, Damian said, "Put it back where you found it, please."

"Like fuck."

Damian cocked the hammer back on his gun. Alessa shifted at the loud clack. Cringing, Adriano quickly stuffed his magnum back under the pillow as quietly and with as little movement as possible.

"Happy?" he asked the hitman.

Damian shrugged. "We'll see how this discussion goes."

"Perfect."

"How did she end up here tonight?" Damian asked.

"Does that matter?"

"A matter of curiosity."

"Curiosity killed the cat, Damian."

"Stalling killed the man, Adriano."

Point taken.

Adriano scowled. "She snuck out of the Trentini place, and I met her at the back road with the lights turned off. That enough for you?"

"You're really toeing the line between crazy and downright insane with this girl, Adriano. The general consensus is that if she gets you killed, it wasn't worth it."

Adriano disagreed entirely. "Your opinion, Damian."

"And I'm usually right."

"What do you want?" Adriano asked, tired of the chitchat.

"She sleeps like the dead," Damian noted, nodding at Alessa.

"Not really."

Long night, Adriano held back from adding.

He couldn't hold back his smirk even if he tried.

Damian sighed and shook his head. "I get it. Never mind."

"Good."

"Your sister is sleeping down the hall," Damian said like it was an afterthought.

"I got my Dad off her back."

"Fascinating. Let's have that chat before daylight comes and one of the two wakes up," Damian said.

"Will you drop your gun?" Adriano asked.

"No."

Well …

Adriano kept one eye on the weapon, one on Damian, and his hand on Alessa's side under the blanket as he said, "Talk."

"I need some information," Damian explained. "On your father."

Adriano barely held back from barking at Damian to go fuck himself. He figured that wouldn't be the best thing to say to the man holding the gun. "I have nothing to say about him."

"Too bad. But if you're trying to hide the fact that he's alive, don't bother. I'm already aware. I have friends in every man's house. Your father's included."

Dammit.

"Does anyone else know?" Adriano asked.

"A lot of people suspect. No one has confirmed anything. I suppose that works out well to your father's favor, if this is his goal, I mean. And if not, but for whatever reason he is hiding away, then he's making Joel look mighty good. Riley might want to take a second look at his choices right now."

Adriano chuckled. "Nice try. I won't tell you his plans."

"I'm not asking for them."

"Riley holds my loyalty, Damian. Take that as you may."

"I didn't ask that. Let's not waste time with runarounds."

Fuck.

"What do you want to know?" Adriano asked.

"My wife is very upset," Damian said quietly, never taking his heavy stare off Adriano as he spoke. "And you see, when Lily Rossi is upset, I am upset. I don't like to see her cry and I've been known to hurt those who cause her tears."

Adriano didn't blink. "So?"

"So, her brother was murdered a little over three weeks ago with a bomb that was planted in his car. I have to console my wife in her brother's home while being bothered by a nosy police detective. Lily can't even get a goddamn break from her pain because now, even Dino's home is hers and she can't get away from it all. A lot of people believe your father ordered that hit on my wife's brother. In fact, Riley isn't even denying it, considering he seems to be using it to his advantage with everyone's fear."

"Your point?"

"Did your father plant that bomb, Adriano?"

A little second-guessing through the vine could be a good thing …

"No," Adriano said, knowing it was the truth.

Damian's gaze narrowed. "No, huh?"

"Nope."

"You're very sure of those words, kid."

"Because Joel did it," Adriano said, not giving a fuck who the guy told. Joel could waste all the time in the world trying to deflect whatever this conversation started. Adriano didn't give a shit. "And as far as anything else my father has done or will do, I'm not aware. I'm not made aware until it happens. Sometimes he denies certain things, sometimes he doesn't say a word. Riley has a way about those kinds of things, and he doesn't give an honest damn if I believe him or not. But if you're looking for someone to blame for Dino's killing, look to Joel."

"Joel is closely aligned to the DeLuca family, Adriano. Now you're just making up lies to waste my time. That is going to earn you—"

"I am not lying," Adriano interrupted coolly. "Alessa told me. Even the walls have ears, Damian. Joel wanted to sever any possible ties the DeLucas might have had to the Contis. He wasn't concerned with losing a man who was already half gone to the system, anyway. With everyone blaming my father for the other shootings, why wouldn't they blame him for this, too? Now look, Theo DeLuca is in a rage and closer than ever to Joel and his fools. The Artinos are trying to climb over the backs of the DeLuca family to get closer to the top."

Damian's jaw ticked. "Joel got exactly what he wanted."

"Partly."

"What is that supposed to mean?" Damian asked.

"Watch my father, Damian. He can't be trusted. You're right, he's going to use this. Fear brings more than truth, it also brings out the cowards."

Damian smiled but the sight was cold. "This was a good chat. Let's do it again sometime."

"Not if I can help it."

"Well, you really won't get a choice, kid."

Shit.

Adriano passed Alessa another glance, grateful for her tiredness. "One more thing, Damian."

"What is that?"

"Is your cousin planning to head the Rossi family?" Adriano asked.

Damian smirked. "How should I know?"

"I think you would."

"Tommas is his own man," Damian said simply.

"Maybe, but with the distrust between him and Joel right now, Tommas could really use a shift in his own position to get him to safer grounds."

Damian didn't give away a thing as he said, "My cousin has had most of the control over the Rossi crew and involved families for years. His father is too much of a drunk to be held responsible. Laurent would run us into the ground."

Adriano smiled, wondering if Damian even realized his mistake. "Us, huh?"

"My family," Damian replied quickly.

Too quickly.

"You don't take sides because you already have one, don't you?" Adriano asked.

"I have people I watch out for," Damian said instead of answering.

"Tommas, for one."

Damian's eyes flashed with a warning. "For one. We looked out for one another growing up."

"How much do you charge for a hit, Ghost?"

"More than you can afford for the shit that's going on right now, Adriano. The last thing the Outfit needs is more trouble because someone wants to settle another score. Let the issues work themselves out on their own. Natural selection will run its course like it always has."

Adriano scoffed. "Try me."

"Depends on who it would be for," Damian said.

"For Tommas."

"Absolutely not."

Adriano shook his head. "Not for him, but *for* him, Damian. It would benefit us both to put Tommas in a higher position right now. He might run the Rossi crew, but he doesn't have the official weight behind him because his father is alive."

"A hit on Laurent ..."

"Like I said, it would benefit us both."

"How so?" Damian asked.

"My father needs a little more of a shove from the Rossi side, if you know what I mean."

Damian nodded. "You're admitting that Riley is well and good, then?"

"I'm admitting my father would make a better boss than Joel Trentini."

"Point taken. What if I said there are men who might be better than your father?"

Adriano smirked. "Hey, as long as I get what I want, I don't give a shit about anybody else."

"Feeding your own wants is a bad game to play. Selfish boy."

"Like you aren't?" Adriano asked.

Damian shrugged. "Depends on the prize, Adriano. And I won the biggest when I married my wife a month ago."

"Consider the benefits of the hit, Damian."

"I am. While Tommas is under suspicion from Joel, Laurent is still hanging tight to the fact he is loyal to the Trentinis. Killing Laurent would certainly make Joel point the finger at Tommas, while Tommas pointed the finger at Joel. Either way, you're shoving Tommas straight to Riley's side. I see your point."

"Do you?"

"Yes. That doesn't mean I will agree to do it, Adriano."

"It's an interesting idea," Adriano said.

Damian frowned. "I'm against the idea of manipulating my cousin into someone else's path simply because your father wants a hand out here."

"My father isn't asking. I am. But if you want my honesty, he's discussed the option of taking out Laurent after what he did at the restaurant."

"You do realize this is a bit like playing Russian Roulette, right?" Damian asked. "There's always one bullet in the chamber, Adriano, and you might be the fool who gets it."

"Everybody needs to pick a side, Damian."

"My cousin doesn't need to take a side, he has one."

"Oh?" Adriano asked.

"Yeah, his."

"Consider it, Damian."

Damian shoved his gun into the waistband of his jeans. "Eighty-k."

"That's your price?"

"Have it in cash within twenty-four hours, get someone to drop it off at Dino's—" Damian winced. "—*my* new place, and I'll do the job. I'd probably take less, but I think I'll make it two. Eighty-k seems fitting for a double hit on people I don't care much for."

Adriano arched a brow in question. "Who is the second one?"

"Might as well put my aunt out of her misery, too."

Damn.

Cold as ice.

So cold it burned.

Adriano wasn't even surprised. Hitmen weren't in the business because killing made them feel something. They did it because they felt nothing at all, and someone had to do it. Even so, Adriano knew Damian's wife Lily. She was a sweet girl with a nice personality, and she wasn't all too fond of the Outfit or its dealings. Just the idea of her being head over heels for a killer like Damian was one huge fucking contradiction.

"How in the hell did someone like Lily fall in love with you?" Adriano asked.

Damian chuckled. "Naturally. Like breathing."

"Or bleeding."

"Exactly."

Adriano awoke to the best pressure tightening around the head of his dick. A wet heat engulfed his shaft as his eyes flew wide to find Alessa between his legs, her pretty pink lips wrapped around his cock, and staring straight at him.

A groan slipped from his lips as he fisted the bedsheet with one hand and grabbed her hair with the other. "Good morning, beautiful."

Alessa released his cock with an audible pop. "Good morning."

"Lick me."

"Mmm, anything you want, Adriano."

Christ.

Fuck yeah.

"That sounds perfect coming out of your—" Her tongue licked from the base of his dick all the way up to his tip as her fingers wrapped around the bottom of his cock and squeezed. "*Shit!*"

"Again?" Alessa asked sweetly.

"Again," he demanded throatily.

Alessa's tongue was a wet, textured paradise on Adriano's cock. She licked and flicked a path on the underside of his shaft against the sensitive vein until his dick was throbbing and the pre-cum beaded at the tip. Through her dark lashes, Alessa watched him silently as she cleaned the pre-cum off with fast strokes of her tongue to his hole.

"God, that feels fucking good," Adriano muttered. "Shift up here and let me see that pussy of yours while you suck me, Lissa."

She twisted on the bed, giving Adriano the best view of her pussy and ass. Soft, smooth skin met the palm of his hand. He ran his digits over her folds with light touches, smearing her arousal through the lips of her pussy and up to her clit.

"Suck me," he said again.

Alessa's took his cock into the heat of her mouth until her nose was nestled against his trimmed public hair. For a second, Adriano just wanted to feel his cock down her throat and have her lips tight around his dick while her saliva soaked his length. He held her hair tight, keeping her there. Her cheeks hollowed around his cock, sucking him hard as her throat contracted.

"Fucking hell," Adriano grunted.

He let her go. Only because he wanted to keep her hair out of the way while he watched the show.

Alessa started a fast bobbing rhythm on his dick that was sure to make him come and fast. Adriano let her do what she wanted, loving the way her mouth felt as she sucked him off. He fingered her pussy with two digits knuckle-deep while his other hand piled her hair high on the top of her head.

"Shit, suck that cock, Lissa," Adriano said, a pressure building in his groin. He used his thumb to press along the hood of her clit while he fucked her pussy in time with her beat on his cock.

The moment her thighs began to shake and her sex turned tight under the thrusts of his fingers, Adriano knew she was coming. Alessa's cry muffled around his cock but it was enough to send his own orgasm hurtling fast to the end.

"I'm going to come," Adriano warned.

Alessa's mouth left his cock, leaving his orgasm behind.

"Fuck, what—" Adriano's words cut off abruptly as Alessa shifted fast in the bed, climbed on top of him, and straddled his cock. She sat down, letting the hot satin lips of her pussy slide against his length and she rolled her hips up and down his cock. Her fingernails scored into the muscles of his abdomen. The biting pain made him groan. "Fuck."

"So wet," Alessa whispered, still rocking and rubbing on him. "Feel how wet you made me."

"I can," Adriano forced out.

And fucking hell, was she ever. The pressure of her bodyweight pressing down on his cock while her fluids provided all the friction for his length was delirious.

So crazy.

Adriano couldn't breathe.

"Don't stop doing that," he ordered.

Alessa flashed him with a sinful grin. "Never."

All over again, his orgasm was fast approaching. He was going to come like this. Like this … with her rubbing her pussy on him and whispering his name.

"Christ, what are you doing?"

"Enjoying the show, Adriano. Do you know how good you look when you come? I love seeing it. I *want* to see it. Let me see it. *Please.*"

"God, that's dirty," he muttered.

Alessa licked her lips, pressed her palms to his chest, and rolled her hips a little faster. "Let me see it."

The pressure in his spine was undeniable. Adriano couldn't have fought back the need to come even if he tried. Cursing harshly, he grabbed her hips, digging his fingers into the soft flesh of her thighs as he moved her faster on top of him. It didn't take long at all for the coil in his gut to unwind with release. His come shot out in thick, ropey streams, splashing up his stomach and chest.

Adriano's head slammed back into the pillow, his teeth gritting to hold back the shout of Alessa's name. "Fuck, fuck …. *Fuck!*"

"Love the show," Alessa murmured.

High on nothing but her, Adriano watched in fascination as his lover began to lick him clean. Alessa worked her way up his stomach, her tongue swiping away at every drop of his come. She took her sweet fucking time and he didn't mind a bit.

She looked happy, so blissed.

Worked over.

Thoroughly fucked.

His.

By the time she finished cleaning him, Adriano was hard again. Alessa, still soaking wet and straddling him, let her fingers dance across his pecs.

"You missed your alarm," Alessa said.

Adriano cocked a brow. "Did I?"

"It went off ten minutes ago. I heard it and woke up."

"Thanks for getting me up, too."

Alessa winked. "I figured this was a good way to wake up."

Oh, it was.

Adriano let his thumb travel down Alessa's toned stomach, past her navel and straight to her clit. It was hard and warm under his touch as he circled her clit with gentle swipes.

Alessa sighed, rocking her body into his thumb. "You're going to make me come again."

"That's the plan. You're not the only one who enjoys the show."

"Mmm. Since when do you miss your alarm?" she asked, breathless and soft.

Since someone woke him up in the middle of the night and he had a hard time falling back to sleep. Adriano decided not to mention Damian's presence the night before. It wouldn't do any good except maybe put Alessa on edge.

"You woke me up, so that's all that matters."

Almost.

Adriano thought about Damian's demand. "I have to make a detour before taking you home today. That okay?"

Alessa swallowed a whine as a tremor rocked her thighs. "Perfect."

"You sure? Your brother—"

"Yes. Abriella said Joel didn't come home last night. Apparently he left a message saying he'd be back in the evening. I called her after I woke up. It's only five."

Adriano checked the clock, noting she was right.

"We have to get going," he murmured.

"Not yet." Alessa lifted off his body, held the base of his cock, and lowered down on his length with a slowness that was sure to kill them both. Her heat and tight channel hugged his cock in the best way. Fucking heaven. A wet, hot heaven. "Fuck, right there …"

He grabbed her waist and turned them around fast so Alessa was under him. Her legs spread wider, letting him get deeper with every hard thrust. She pushed her hands into his wild mess of hair and pulled, arching off the bed.

So beautiful.

One more wasn't going to hurt anything.

A few more minutes wouldn't kill anybody.

"Harder," Alessa breathed. "Fuck me harder, Adriano."

Sweet Christ.

"One more time," Adriano mumbled. "And then we have to go."

Alessa nodded, but her eyes were already dazed and her stomach clenched with her need to come. "One more."

CHAPTER FOURTEEN

Alessa melted into the bed, content and blissed. Adriano's arm curved her lower back as he kissed a path over her sweaty cheekbone.

"God, don't start us again," Alessa warned, feeling out of air and hot at the same time. "I don't know how to say no to you, Adriano."

Adriano hummed against her shoulder, smirking wickedly. "It can't be that late, Lissa."

"Jesus."

His hand slipped between her thighs, widening her legs without a word. Alessa found herself propped up to her knees, her face buried into the blankets, and Adriano behind her. His cock found heaven and home, driving her up the bed with the first thrust of his body against hers. He took her hard, rough, and fast. Deep, quick plunges that reached every possible inch it could.

Alessa felt him everywhere.

She fisted the bedsheets as he grabbed her hair and yanked her upward into his chest. The sting in her scalp was lovely. The sound of their flesh meeting was even better.

She was sticky.

Dirty.

Sweaty.

She smelled like him and sex.

It was fucking wonderful.

Adriano's mouth found her neck and his teeth marked her skin. It was enough to send her into another orgasm that left her drained of energy and gasping for air.

"Fuck, I love feeling you come," Adriano growled into her ear. "So hot and tight, Lissa. And my name in your fucking mouth—nothing sounds like that. *Nothing.*"

He wasn't the only one.

She felt his pace pick up, his body driving into hers even faster and harder.

"Come," Alessa begged. "Let me feel it. I want to feel it, Adriano."

He came with a thick groan, pushing them both down to the bed. Alessa felt his cock jerk with spurts deep inside her tender pussy, filling her full.

"*God*," she breathed, happier under his weight. "So good."

Adriano mumbled his agreement.

Alessa laughed. "We have to get up."

"We will," he assured. "But I like this."

"This?"

"Us. In a bed together. Nothing else matters. I like it."

Alessa smiled into his arm as he rolled them over so she was tucked into his side. Adriano's fingers ghosted down her arm before coming to a stop on her finger. Alessa stilled, remembering the piece of jewelry that should have been there but wasn't because Adriano took it.

"How'd this go over?" he asked.

"No one has noticed yet."

Adriano barked out a bitter laugh. "Seriously?"

"They're all too focused on other things to be bothering with me. I've passed them by a lot over the last week. I'll figure out something when they do notice."

"Don't let him put another one on there, Lissa."

Alessa glanced up at him. "I don't have a choice."

Adriano's gaze darkened. "I'm the only fucking man who gets to put something on that finger of yours. You're mine, Lissa."

Alessa wasn't going to argue that fact.

"Promise me," Adriano said quietly.

"I won't let him put another one on me."

"Why?"

"Because I'm yours."

"Shit."

Alessa heard Adriano's curse just as she closed the bedroom door.

"Uh, hey, Eve," Adriano said loudly.

Alessa cringed.

Maybe their one more time had turned into two or three.

The small hallway that led out to the kitchen and living room of the loft apartment kept Alessa hidden well enough. She turned to go back into Adriano's bedroom, but stopped when Evelina started talking.

"You are not nearly quiet enough, Adriano," Evelina said.

Alessa's cheeks turned pink at what Evelina implied.

"I don't know what you're talking about," Adriano muttered.

"Right," his sister drawled. "Where is she?"

"I don't know—"

"Alessa!"

Crap.

Alessa walked out into view of the kitchen and leaned in the small entryway.

Evelina looked her over and nodded like she knew something was up. "You're quite a sight this morning."

Alessa shrugged. "Yeah, well …"

She needed a shower, a hairbrush, and a facecloth to clean the smeared makeup she sported. Alessa wished she could find it in herself to care about her appearance.

"Walk of shame," Evelina said to Adriano. "I can't believe you were going to let her leave here looking like she just spent the night with someone. Are you stupid?"

Adriano glared. "I didn't want to wake you up."

"And we have to leave soon," Alessa added.

"Too late, I'm already up," Evelina replied. "And seriously reconsidering staying here if I have to wake up like that again."

Adriano cleared his throat. "Sorry."

"You know what is sad about it all?"

"What?" Adriano asked.

"I wasn't even surprised and I didn't even have to wonder who it was you brought home. That … says a lot, Adriano."

"We good?" he asked.

"We're good. And of course, I'll keep my mouth shut."

Alessa laughed under her breath. "Thanks."

Evelina nodded at Alessa before pointing at the hallway. "I bet you know where the bathroom is. You'll find what you need in there."

"Five minutes," Adriano said to Alessa.

She'd make it two.

With a detour still to take, they were running out of time.

"Stay put," Adriano said. "I'll be five minutes, maybe ten at the most."

Alessa leaned over and kissed him quickly. It was only a quarter to eight in the morning. "I'll be fine."

"And quiet, huh?"

She got his point without needing to ask.

Dino DeLuca's home and property rested just outside of the Chicago city limits on a private estate. After Adriano made a stop at a warehouse and came out with a black bag and no answers, he'd driven them straight to Dino's place.

Or, it used to be Dino's.

"I heard Lily got the house and property," Alessa said.

"She did, apparently," Adriano replied. "Theo picked up the businesses and some trusts. Dino had it all settled and ready. Odd how that worked out. Like he knew or something."

"We all know, Adriano."

"Hmm?" he asked.

"We all know it's where we're going to end up. Dead, I mean. It's just a matter of when and how. I'm more surprised when a man in the mafia doesn't have something set up in case of his death. Men like that think they're untouchable. That's a bad place to be."

Adriano frowned in his seat. "That's an awfully morbid way to look at it, Lissa."

"I see it like it is."

"And say it like it is," he said.

Sometimes life was too brutal to think about it differently.

Alessa didn't like to live in the clouds. Sometimes, when she was with Adriano, she found herself there all the time. High up, looking down. So high, actually, that nobody could reach him or her.

She knew that was wrong.

Somebody would reach them. They weren't the untouchable ones.

"Hey," Adriano whispered.

Alessa let him catch her chin between his forefinger and thumb. He turned her head so they could stare at one another. The flecks of color in his green irises drew her in like a moth to the flame. Fitting, since they were both waiting to be burned in one way or another.

"Hey," Alessa said back.

"You're a special kind of crazy beautiful. You know that, right?"

Alessa smiled. "I do now."

"This is all going to work out, Lissa. You and me, it'll work out."

"I'd like to think so, but … more often than not, the bad guys win, Adriano."

"We are the bad guys."

Were they?

"As long as I'm bad with you," Alessa said, grinning.

"Cute." Adriano sighed, eyeing the quiet, large home. "This is just one more step in everything. One more goal to hit before we're closer to the end."

"I'm almost tired of running to it. Isn't that what we're doing; running?"

From responsibility, fears, and life. They ran. Maybe he liked to use the excuse that they were running toward something, but she figured they were constantly running away.

Adriano smirked. "Just keep running, Lissa."

"Why should I do that?"

"I like the chase," he said.

Alessa blinked, feeling his thumb roll over her bottom lip soothingly. "Love you."

"Always," he echoed. "I'll be back in five, like I said."

"Go. I'll wait, Adriano."

Adriano got out of the car, tossed her a wink, and closed the door. Alessa watched in the rear-view mirror as Adriano popped the trunk and pulled out the black bag. He didn't even make it half way across the driveway before the front door opened to the large home. Damian Rossi stepped outside. The two men met one another in the middle.

Despite knowing better, Alessa rolled down her window to listen.

"That was quick," Damian said.

Adriano shrugged. "I think we all have our reasons for wanting to get this done, Ghost. Better to do it fast, like ripping off a Band-Aid."

Damian eyed the car, his gaze falling on Alessa. "Why did you bring her here?"

Alessa wasn't offended by the question, but she had to admit, Damian could be a little intimidating. For the most part, the man stuck to the shadows and out of the spotlight.

"We woke up later than we should have and this was easier," Adriano explained.

Alessa was confused. Adriano talked like Damian had somehow known she spent the night with Adriano. How could Damian possibly know that?

"Lucky her brother is out of the city."

Well, that answered one of Alessa's questions regarding Joel's whereabouts. Even Abriella hadn't known where their brother disappeared to for a day.

"Is he?" Adriano asked.

Damian scoffed, jerking a thumb in Alessa's direction. "Like you don't already know."

"I don't know where he is, asshole."

"Vegas, apparently."

Adriano's brow shot up as he shot a look over his shoulder at her.

"Vegas?"

"Sorrentos. Maybe he's trying to buy votes or something."

"That's the wrong family to be going to for that," Adriano said.

"Joel has a mighty sense of entitlement, a big head, and enough cockiness to carry him through a meeting with Maximo Sorrento. One meeting, anyway. Two might cost him more than he's willing to give, like his life. After all, Max has little to no patience for spoiled boys. Look at what he did to his own son."

Adriano chuckled. "And then Max will head back to the Marcello crew in New York."

"Like I said, buying votes," Damian replied dully. "Or trying."

"I'll pass the info along."

"Do what you will with it, kid."

"Thanks," Adriano said.

"I didn't expect you to get here this quick," Damian said.

"Or you didn't expect me to get the money."

Damian shrugged like it didn't make a difference. "Semantics, Adriano. Out of curiosity, do you often keep eighty-k of cold cash just sitting around for a rainy day?"

Eighty-k?

That was a lot of money. The black bag in Adriano's fist caught her attention again. It made a lot more sense.

"No, but a friend of mine did," Adriano replied. "And I figured since he can't use it anymore and I was the only one who knew about his stashes of cash, I might as well put some of it to use."

"A friend?" Damian asked.

"Sleeping at the bottom of a river."

Alessa frowned at those words. She was starting to think maybe she should roll the window back up, but she didn't.

Damian chuckled coldly. "Well, that's unfortunate."

"It was." Adriano's tone held a great deal more feeling about the topic than Damian's did. "But it is what it is."

"I heard a rumor this morning," Damian said, looking Alessa's way again.

"I'm listening," Adriano replied.

"There are new boots on Conti territory."

Adriano stilled. "Oh?"

"Are we going to play stupid?" Damian asked. "I thought we were past that, Adriano."

"There's a little truth in every rumor, as the saying goes, Damian."

"Well said." Damian sighed heavily. "You'll make a good Capo if you stay the fuck out of trouble. You're young, yeah, but that's all right, too. You've been doing this under Kolin for years. No man in the Conti crew has ever worked as closely with him as you did. I bet they're not even looking elsewhere for a Capo but right at you. You'll be fine out there—the guys like you. But you need to keep your head above water and right now, you're pretty goddamn close to drowning, Adriano. Do you get what I'm saying?"

"Sure," Adriano muttered. "But considering she's the only thing that keeps me breathing, I don't mind being pulled under with her."

"Poetic," Damian said dryly.

"Are we going to do this thing or keep chatting?"

Damian smiled, flashing his white teeth in the process. "There's no need. You're too late."

Adriano's shoulders stiffened. "We made an agreement, Damian. Twenty-four hours; eighty-k. I followed through. Why won't you?"

"Because I don't need to, kid." Damian surveyed his quiet property before saying, "There was a big story on the news this morning."

"Stop skipping around and get to the fucking point. Why in the hell won't you follow through on the hits?"

Hits?

Alessa's heart practically leaped into her throat.

"Because I don't need to. At least not on one. Laurent Rossi was found late last night by his wife after she was woken up from one of her many drunken stupors by the sound of a gunshot. Laurent had his head blown apart and was dead on the kitchen floor by the time Serena got to him."

Adriano just stared at Damian like he didn't believe a word the man was saying.

"So, there's nothing needing done," Damian continued, still smiling. "Someone already did it. Serena is still there. If she follows her usual pattern like I believe she will, Serena is liable to drink herself into her own grave. Especially now that her husband isn't there to rush her to the hospital when she needs her stomach pumped."

"You're serious," Adriano said.

Damian shoved his hands in his pockets in the most unbothered fashion. "Yes."

"Who did it?"

"That, Adriano, I do not know."

"Is that the truth?" Adriano asked.

"For this, I have no reason to lie," Damian said.

"Well then." Adriano shifted on his feet, still tense. "My father had planned nothing on Laurent, not yet. He was waiting and said it wasn't time."

Damian grinned. "Keep your ear to the ground, Adriano. You hear a lot there."

"What is that supposed to mean?" Adriano asked.

"Someone did this for a reason. They're looking to help somebody. That means something is about to happen and soon." Damian glanced back at his house. "I'll leave you to it. My wife doesn't like waking up alone and it's been a rough couple of weeks for her."

Adriano nodded once, but he still looked unsure. "Yeah, all right."

"Godspeed, Adriano. I have a feeling this war is not even close to being over. And when the families really go to the mattresses, there's not a soul in Chicago who won't feel it."

Alessa didn't want to let go of Adriano's hand. He kept one on the steering wheel and his other locked with hers, resting on the seat between them. Tenderly, his thumb swept over her knuckles again and again.

When the car rolled to a stop, Alessa didn't move.

Adriano eyed her from the side knowingly. "Back to life, Lissa."

Alessa sighed. "Confession time?"

"Shoot."

"Last night was the first time I've slept without nightmares."

"Since the restaurant," he said quietly.

"Yeah."

Adriano looked her over without sympathy. Alessa appreciated that in a way. He didn't coddle her or tell her false platitudes. "Give it time."

"Time."

"You're not going to forget, but it'll get easier. Less nightmares, more sleep. Less time spent thinking about it because you've moved on to new things. That's life, Lissa."

"My sister almost died," Alessa said, staring down at their connected hands.

"Some of my bullets might have gone inside that restaurant," Adriano admitted.

Alessa sucked in a deep breath, nodding. "I want this to be over. I don't want to lose someone else I love in this mess."

Adriano leaned over and kissed her softly. Ghosting the pad of his thumb over her cheekbone, he murmured, "We won't be one of them. I'll make sure of it."

"Okay."

"Back to life," he repeated.

Alessa smiled, feeling better already. She had a part to play, too.

"How many people do you think are playing games in this?" Alessa asked.

Adriano shrugged. "A lot. And we're no different than them, Alessa."

She knew he was right.

"Text me later," Alessa ordered teasingly, before kissing him quickly again.

"Will do, pretty girl."

Before Alessa could find another excuse to stay in Adriano's Camaro, she dropped his hand, grabbed her messenger bag, and got out of the vehicle. The cool September air chilled her through the skinny jeans and long-sleeved Henley she wore. Alessa waved to Adriano as she stepped inside the treeline onto the familiar trail she had used more times than she cared to count.

Glancing over her shoulder, she knew Adriano couldn't see her through the thick brush. Even still, he sat with his car running for a good few minutes. About the time Alessa knew it would take her to get to the back property.

When he pulled finally pulled away, she watched him go.

And missed him already.

Alessa jogged the path back to the Trentini property. She slipped under the rear side of the old willow tree, shoved her bag into a hollow spot on the trunk, and then emerged from the other side. Alessa crossed the six acres of backyard property quickly. She was thankful Terrance had been a proud man when it came to his land. Landscapers had long ago come in and made beautiful pathways with trees, rock gardens, and bushes. More than enough to keep Alessa hidden as she walked back to the house.

Climbing the stairs that led to the rear large deck meant for entertaining a good one-hundred guests or more, Alessa pulled the keys for the back door from her pocket. The sound of a throat clearing made Alessa stumble in her walk. The keys dropped from her hand, falling to the wood deck with a loud jingling clatter.

"Shit," Alessa mumbled.

Sara Trentini sat on the rocking bench with a book in her hand and her head turned down like she was thoroughly engrossed in reading. The cock of her mother's eyebrow as she regarded her daughter told Alessa that Sara had probably been waiting for her.

"Mom," Alessa greeted.

Sara's lips drew thin as she looked Alessa over. "Same clothes as yesterday?"

Alessa chose not to answer that question.

"Your brother isn't home yet," her mother said.

"I know," Alessa replied simply.

Sara didn't look all too impressed with that answer. "I don't know where you've been, Alessa, but you can't expect me to hide your secrets when I find you sneaking around."

Alessa tried not to sneer and failed miserably when she replied, "Like you sneaked around with Terrance for years?"

Sara sucked in a sharp breath, her gaze narrowing. "Now that's quite enough, Alessa."

"You're right, it is. You don't deserve that, I'm sorry."

"Thank you," Sara murmured.

"But those who live in glass houses shouldn't throw stones, Mom. And if I don't pass judgement on your mistakes, then don't begin to lecture me on mine."

"I learned from my errors, sweetheart."

Alessa snorted. "Did you, or did you just learn to be more careful?"

"Alessa!"

"It was an honest question, Mom."

"Well, it was a little bit of both," Sara admitted.

Alessa was surprised to hear her mother confess anything in that regard.

Sara swallowed hard and then nodded toward the back door. "Go inside. Your sister is feeling awful this morning. She's got some pain in her back and had shortness of breath when she woke up. She called me through the intercom, wanting me to check her over. I asked her about you. Abriella is a damned good liar when she wants to be, but I went looking because something didn't feel right.

"And when I couldn't find you anywhere in the wing, I went back to Abriella and demanded she tell me where you had gone," her mother finished.

Alessa steeled her spine, refusing to let her mother wear her down. "So?"

"You know, when you girls were just little, I always hoped you would be close. I wanted you both to have what I didn't—a good, close relationship with your siblings. Joel managed to screw that up royally on his side, but you and Abriella ... you two are exactly what I had hoped for."

"Are we?"

"Yes, she would protect you right to the very bitter end," Sara said, laughing under her breath. "But that also means you don't get to be selfish, Alessa. Not right now with what your sister went through. You don't want me to throw stones, then fine. You want me to keep my mouth shut about seeing you come home in the early morning looking like you've been out all night, then fine. But you need to be here for your sister right now, not feeding whatever craziness you have going on."

Guilt wrapped Alessa in a smothering grip. Her mother was right.

Alessa took that as her cue to leave her mother and go inside. As she opened the door, her mother cleared her throat once more.

"Yes?" Alessa asked.

"Did you have fun?"

The question had been posed quietly, but innocently.

Alessa couldn't have lied if she tried. "Yeah, I did."

Sara smiled. "Be careful, Lissa."

"I am, Mom."

"I hope so."

Two weeks passed in relative silence. Alessa was grateful for the break. She barely noticed the month of September and it was gone already. Joel returned from his unknown trip to Vegas without a word and said nothing about where he had gone when he did get back. He did lock himself in his office for most of that night but Alessa didn't bother to try and find out why.

Chances were, Joel's trip hadn't gone as planned.

He liked to sulk in private like all spoiled men.

At least Adriano had kept Alessa entertained with random texts and quick calls when he got the chance. She figured he was busy though, because every time he called, there seemed to be a lot of noise going on in the background.

"I'm starting to think you're milking this being shot thing up as much as you can," Alessa said, teasing her sister.

Abriella sighed dramatically, her face contorting in fake pain. She had situated herself on the couch in the large library with a bowl of ice-cream and a book of poetry. "More ice-cream, Lissa. I demand it! For my poor injured self, I mean."

Alessa laughed. "You're practically all better now."

She barely managed to dodge the pillow that Abriella threw.

"Don't make me get off this couch, Alessa," Abriella warned playfully.

"I'm not getting you anymore ice-cream. That's your third bowl."

Abriella pouted. "Damn."

"But I will go distract Joel with something for at least ten minutes so you can call Tommas and not worry about being interrupted."

Her sister's face lit up with joy.

"Yeah?" Abriella asked.

Why not?

Abriella was always covering her Alessa.

"Yeah," Alessa confirmed.

"I officially love you again."

Alessa grinned. "Good to know."

As Abriella pulled out her cell phone, Alessa slipped out of the library. She went in search of Joel, knowing exactly where her brother was. In his office, like usual. Thankfully, Dean had been busy for most of the week and when he had been at the Trentini mansion, he'd been too distracted by kissing Joel's ass to notice Alessa.

Or notice her still missing ring.

Alessa knocked on her brother's office door and shoved her one hand in her pocket to hide the missing jewelry. It had become a habit, but she knew sooner or later, someone would catch her little secret.

"Yeah, it's open," Joel shouted.

Alessa pushed open the door. Joel sat in a chair with his booted feet propped up on the edge of a desk. He watched a news broadcast. Another one revolving around the Outfit and the newest murder the officials were linking back to the families.

Laurent Rossi's.

Alessa wondered if her brother killed him, too. Joel's words that day at the restaurant had certainly gave off the feeling he was pissed at Laurent for missing his mark on Riley.

"What, Alessa?" Joel asked, never taking his eyes off the screen.

"Nothing."

Joel watched her from the side, but didn't respond. Alessa watched the newscast with him in silence until Joel had enough and asked, "Do you have a reason to be in here?"

"Nope."

The phone on the desk rang.

"Then get out, Alessa."

Not a problem.

Alessa heard her brother's voice traveling down the hall while she walked away.

"Yeah, that's not a rumor, we're opening the books," Joel said. "But I want it being whispered like one. I'm not sure when. Another week or so, as there are some guys out of town for business. I'm hoping, if the bastard is still alive, that the suggestion of nominations will drive Riley out."

Alessa knew those words …

Opening the books.

She *knew* them. She shouldn't, but she wasn't a fucking idiot.

Opening the books meant someone was going to be nominated to join the family. There was only one man her brother talked about giving the button: Dean.

"Lissa?"

Alessa blinked awake to someone shaking her shoulder and calling her name.

"Yeah?" she asked, her throat dry.

Abriella stared down, curiosity lighting up her familiar blue eyes. "Did you fall asleep in the middle of the afternoon?"

"I must have."

"Are you doing that a lot lately?" Abriella asked.

"I'm bored as hell in this house doing nothing. You get to go to school and get out of here. I don't." Alessa had went on the defensive immediately, even though she knew there was no reason to. Abriella's question was innocent enough. "Sorry, Ella. I didn't mean that."

Abriella kept watching her with that same curiosity as she readjusted the strap of her messenger bag around her shoulder. "It's okay."

"You're home early."

"I had a headache and called the driver," Abriella explained.

"Oh."

"And found you here."

Alessa pushed up from the couch, feeling like the nap wasn't nearly enough. "I'm up. What is going on?"

"Dean is in the kitchen. Miss Cathy is making him some food or whatever. I guess he was waiting for you to wake up. Something about a date?"

Alessa cringed. Dean was forcing her to go on dates with him whenever he felt they should.

It'd only been a few days since she learned her brother was getting serious about opening the books to give Dean his button, but it put Alessa on edge. She was trying to get more concrete information on the whole thing before she let Adriano know.

So far, nothing.

"Great," Alessa muttered, standing from the couch.

"Maybe you can convince Dean to let me tag along."

Alessa smiled. "Good plan."

"It'll keep him from being a dick, anyway."

Maybe.

Alessa left her sister and found Dean leaning over the island in the large kitchen. He chatted with the cook Miss Cathy until he noticed Alessa in the entryway.

"Princess finally woke up, huh?" he asked.

Alessa might not have been bothered by his words if the sarcasm didn't ooze from them. "Sorry, I didn't realize you were coming over."

Dean lifted a brow high. "Don't you have anything better to do in the daytime than sleep?"

She chose to ignore his words.

The fluffy, sweet cherry cheese Danishes on the counter called to Alessa. She crossed the space quickly and reached for one of the fresh pastries set out on the wax paper.

She realized her mistake the moment Dean's eyes narrowed in on her hand, but it was already too late to hide her missing engagement ring.

"Where is it?" Dean asked, his voice going dangerously low.

Alessa snapped her hand out of reach and hid it behind her back. "I—"

"Where is your fucking engagement ring, Alessa?"

Miss Cathy glanced between the two rapidly but said nothing. She really couldn't say much, not if she wanted to keep her job.

"I just—"

"She was making bread with me yesterday and we lost it in the dough," Miss Cathy said for Alessa when she couldn't come up with something. "We tried for hours to find it and ended up throwing out all the dough. She was supposed to help me remake all the bread today for Joel's party on Monday, but she fell asleep. It was an honest mistake, Mr. Artino."

Alessa nodded quickly though every word had been a lie. "Yes, the dough. I'm sorry."

Dean's eyes flashed with rage. He hid it well enough, but even the way his fists clenched at his sides was enough to tell Alessa he was pissed. Really, really pissed.

"I paid a great deal of money for that ring," he said quietly.

The memory of having her face slammed into a brick wall ran through Alessa's mind. She had to placate Dean, or his anger could show and he'd lash out at her physically again.

"I'm sorry," she repeated.

It was the only thing she could think to say.

Dean reached out and snatched Alessa's arm so he could see her hand. Without warning, he squeezed her fingers hard enough for her bones to creak. It fucking hurt. She held back the whine but couldn't hide her flinch.

"I will have you a new one by next week," Dean said. "I have enough going on this week without you adding to it."

Alessa swallowed hard. "Okay."

But it wasn't. Not at all.

Dean's fingernails dug into Alessa's palm, marking her. "And you will not lose the second one. Is that understood?"

"Yes."

She could practically feel his rage seeping from his hand to hers.

"Let me go, Dean," Alessa demanded softly. "You're hurting me."

He did. Silently, Dean left the kitchen without another look back.

Alessa flipped her hand over. The imprints of Dean's fingernails had cut into her palm and marked her red. If he'd pushed a little harder, she might have bled. It was probably going to leave bruises.

Tears welled in Alessa's eyes as her hand throbbed. She couldn't marry that man. This would be her entire life with him—abuse and fear.

"My God, Alessa," Miss Cathy whispered.

"I'm okay," Alessa said, waving the concern off.

She wasn't okay by any means. If Miss Cathy hadn't been there, Alessa had a feeling that Dean's violence would have made another appearance.

Alessa's stomach finally gave into the fear she had been hiding, rolling with sickness. She barely made it to the garbage can before she was sick and shaking. As she wiped the vomit from her mouth, Alessa decided right then and there that she wouldn't have to worry about Dean doing this to her again.

Ever.

CHAPTER FIFTEEN

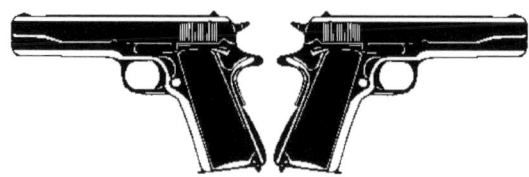

Adriano walked into Slips, a sports bar, giving the familiar bouncer a nod as he passed the man. Quickly, he found the man he was looking for sitting at a far booth with his black books spread out, three cell phones resting beside each book, a pen in one hand, and his eye on a flat screen television playing the latest on the Chicago Cubs.

"Ryan," Adriano greeted as he sat down on the bench across from the man.

Ryan didn't take his eyes off the screen. Bookies had a way about them. "Skip."

"What kind of line are we running this week?"

"Twenty-five percent. That's the only way we're going to make any fucking money since we're not working with the DeLuca or Rossi crews currently."

Adriano scowled at that. For every gambler that wanted to put money down on a game, he had to put an extra twenty-five percent down, too. That way, the bookie for the Conti crew wasn't losing out, even if he had to pay a lot out. Unfortunately, having high percentage lines on bets meant some gamblers wouldn't come back.

"And what is the pool looking like?" Adriano asked.

"Seventy-k at the moment," Ryan informed. "But we've got that big game next week. I'll get the difference made up."

"Good."

Ryan finally graced Adriano with his attention. "Don't you think it's a little ironic, Adriano?"

"What is that?"

"You're not even legal to sit in this bar, yet there you are."

Adriano chuckled. "I've been coming here with Kolin since I was sixteen, man."

"Still, it's funny. That's all I'm saying."

Glancing around the bar, Adriano felt a little uncomfortable. He was firmly tucked into the South side of Chicago, a territory the Conti family had always controlled. But Slips was closer to the far South of Chicago, where they didn't control. In fact, the DeLuca side of the Outfit controlled the far South. It just made him edgy to be close to another family's lines when everyone was in a big uproar.

"What has got your panties in a twist?" Ryan asked.

Apparently Adriano's discomfort wasn't going unnoticed.

"Nothing, man. Just choose a different joint, would you? Somewhere close to the middle of the South until this shit blows over. Even closer to the Southwest."

The West and Southwest side of Chicago was mostly controlled by the Rossi crew, although the Contis had been known to slip in on their streets from time to time when it was needed. The Rossi crew was a hell of a lot less likely to cause a ruckus if someone showed face on their side.

"Sure, whatever," Ryan muttered, going back to the television.

Being a Capo was not as glamourous as it may have looked to the outside. Men worked for years to get their button, and then they hoped and prayed for the chance at an actual position inside the Outfit. Like being a Caporegime was the end all, be all.

It was fucking tedious.

Snail-slow, penny-counting tedious.

There were so many little details to manage with the crew and all the while, an eye had to be kept on every man, making sure the money came in on time and shit was running smooth … tedious. Adriano didn't remember it being this much work when he followed Kolin around.

"Who are you looking at to win?" Adriano asked, nodding at the television.

Ryan held up a hand as one of his three phones rang. He didn't even look at the phones, just grabbed the one screeching and picked it up.

"Yeah, Ry here." Ryan nodded, scribbled something onto one of his books and said, "That's going to be twelve-twenty-five."

Adriano waved at the waitress passing their table and asked for a drink.

"Listen, the line is twenty-five, so either you pay or don't," Ryan barked. "Make it up, it's not my problem. You know where I'm at. I'll be here for the rest of the night."

Ryan hung up the call and tossed his phone back to the table.

"The high lines are going to fucking kill us," Ryan said after a moment.

"Maybe not. If they want to play bad enough, they'll pay."

"True. We good?"

Adriano nodded. "I'll be back next Friday. Don't fuck me on the bottom line, Ryan."

The bookie smirked. "I would never."

"I should hope not. The last bookie got his fingers cut off for skimming. Kolin made a necklace out of them and made the guy wear them for a week before he finally put the fool out of his misery. I watched—it was interesting."

Ryan's amusement faded fast. "It'll all be on the up, Skip."

"Make sure of it."

"I'll have the books all out so you can see," Ryan said.

Adriano knew the guy wouldn't screw him over, but sometimes, he felt the need to remind people of what would happen if they tried. Fear was a great motivator in that way. Standing from the table, Adriano took the drink the waitress brought to him.

"On the house, Conti," the girl said.

Her smile was too wide and she seemed to have tugged her shirt down a little lower from what it was before she disappeared behind the bar.

Adriano wasn't interested.

"Have a good night, Tori," Adriano said.

He downed the whiskey in one go, handed her back the glass, and made his way out of the bar. The early October night was chilly and a wind whipped harshly, making Adriano tighten his leather jacket and shove his hands in his pockets.

Winter was coming way too soon.

Adriano slid inside his unlocked, still-running Camaro. Nobody was stupid enough to steal his baby in these streets. They all knew who he was on sight. And they knew his car. Turning the heaters up a little higher, he enjoyed the hot air blasting into his face as he surveyed the busy street filled with people. Chicago was a melting pot for all different characters.

He pulled his coat off and tossed it into the passenger seat. His night wasn't even close to being over yet. Another group in the Conti crew was planning a heist on a truck of electronics later that evening and a shipment of narcotics had finally passed through the right hands and got on their territory.

Adriano needed to oversee all that shit.

Yeah, tedious.

The ring of his cell phone from inside his jacket pocket brought him from his thoughts. Adriano almost ignored it, figuring it was just another one of his guys wanting something else, but he searched for the phone anyway.

Adriano didn't bother to look at the screen as he picked up the call with, "Yeah, Conti speaking. Get it out and fast. I'm fucking busy."

He put his car in forward and began to maneuver the vehicle out of the tight space.

"Adriano?"

Alessa's soft, timid voice made Adriano slam on the breaks.

Something in her tone was off. It tasted of distress and he didn't like that at all.

"Alessa?" he asked.

"He did it again," Alessa whispered.

A car honked their horn behind Adriano. He rolled down his window enough to flip them the middle finger.

"Who did what?" Adriano demanded.

"Dean," she said quickly and quietly. "Not like the last time, but he might have if—"

"The last time," he interjected. "Like the club last time?"

"It wasn't like that."

What the fuck was it like then?

Adriano's rage grew into a hot ball in his midsection. "What happened?"

"He noticed the ring."

Fuck.

"And?" he pressed.

Alessa's laugh was bitter and sad. "He squeezed my hand hard enough to leave bruises and he cut my palms with his fingernails."

Sweet Jesus.

Adriano's anger blew out of control, but his guilt was close behind. He knew better than to take that goddamn ring away and leave Alessa to deal with the consequences, but his selfishness and possessiveness demanded he take the fucking thing.

"But he was angry, Adriano. He would have come at me had someone not been there. I know it."

"When did this happen?"

"This afternoon," Alessa explained.

"And you're only telling me now?"

"He forced me out to dinner with him, but I got Abriella to tag along. And then he cut it short, saying something about work or whatever."

Thank fucking God, Adriano thought.

"Who was around when it happened, Lissa?"

"The cook. She explained it away with an excuse about me losing it making stuff for Joel's party next week."

"Party?" he asked.

"I don't know what she's talking about," Alessa said. "But Joel mentioned opening the books a few days ago."

Adriano's jaw ticked as his hand tightened around the steering wheel. There had been rumors on the streets about the books being opened, but no one had any real confirmation about it.

"If she's cooking, that means she intends for it to happen there, right?" Adriano asked.

"I would think so."

Adriano's initiation into the Outfit had also happened inside the Trentini home. He could remember in fine detail the events of that night. His palm had been cut from the tip of his index finger all the way down to his wrist. He then watched his blood pour across the face of a burning saint as questions were thrown at him one after the other from more men than he cared to count.

The scar was still there, but faded.

The honking of a horn echoed behind Adriano's Camaro. He flipped the idiot the middle finger again. The fool, whoever it was, could wait.

"I don't want him to do this to me again," Alessa said, a heat coloring up her words. "Ever, Adriano. I'm so fucking stressed out I can't even eat or stay awake in the daytime. It frightened me enough today that I got physically sick from it."

Adriano held his breath, refusing to let the string of cusses roll off his tongue like he wanted. That, and Alessa didn't need to hear it. Clearly she had a rough enough day as it was.

Dean wouldn't get the chance to do that to Alessa again.

Adriano would make sure of it.

"You're okay right now?" he asked.

"Yeah. I just needed to talk to you."

Dean earned his goddamn death tonight. He supposed it was time to give the Artino bastard exactly what he deserved. Adriano had waited far too long to deliver some pain on Dean as it was. He'd waited for his father's call, but Riley hadn't given it yet. Maybe he never would.

Adriano was done waiting.

You couldn't hurt an angel and expect to survive it.

Adriano checked the clock on the dash. "It's late, pretty girl. Get some sleep, hmm? I'll call you tomorrow after you've had some time to rest."

"Okay," she murmured, a hint of a smile in her tone.

"I love you."

He figured she needed to hear that again, too.

"Love you," Alessa whispered.

Adriano cruised the streets of South Shore, knowing he'd find who he was looking for if he was patient enough. Dean Artino was a fucking nobody in Adriano's world. He didn't have any real status or power, and Dean's father didn't scare Adriano, either.

But Dean was still a soldier for the DeLuca crew. That meant, if he was working, he'd be at one of his usual haunts or dirtying up the streets of his regular grounds. Dean seemed to favor the outskirts of South Beach.

That's where Adriano went looking for him.

The moment Adriano saw a face he recognized stepping out of a strip joint, he jerked his car over to the side of the road, left it running in hostile territory, and got out. Adriano left his gun in the car, figuring he wouldn't need it right then.

"Hey!" Adriano barked.

The enforcer Adriano recognized, a guy who worked for the DeLuca crew, turned at the call. The guy's eyes widened when he saw Adriano making his way across the parking lot.

It was fucking stupid.

So reckless.

Adriano knew better than to be causing issues in someone else's territory, but he couldn't calm the rage waging a war inside his head and heart.

Screw Dean.

It was over for him.

"Where the fuck is Artino?" Adriano asked.

The enforcer blinked. "What?"

"Artino, asshole. Where is he tonight?"

"Walter?"

"No, his useless cunt of a son," Adriano growled.

Adriano stopped walking when he was toe-to-toe with the enforcer. The guy was built like a brick shit house and tall, too. It didn't matter to Adriano. He was just as tall and built, too. All those years of football playing a line-backer toughened him up and he wasn't afraid of a hit.

"Are you fucking deaf?" Adriano asked.

"No."

"Then stop staring at me like I'm not speaking English, you idiot. Where is Artino?"

The enforcer looked Adriano up and down like maybe the guy was thinking of taking a swing. "I'm pretty sure I'm drunk."

"You don't know the difference?" Adriano asked, sneering.

"No, but there's a Conti on DeLuca territory and everybody knows Theo said he'd kill any fucker who was stupid enough to cross over."

Adriano smirked. "Theo isn't here."

"Good thing for you."

He wasn't worried about Theo DeLuca tonight. They would battle that shit out another day.

"Where is Dean?" Adriano demanded. "And if I have to ask again,

I'm going to break my knuckles on all of your teeth. Do you get that?"

"Last I heard, he was in Calumet Heights working some shit."

"Where in the Heights?"

The enforcer laughed. "You ever been there?"

Yes.

It was not a particularly safe place at night sometimes.

"I didn't realize I was playing twenty questions," Adriano said.

"You'll find him," the enforcer replied. "Dean likes to make people think he owns the place. Just watch the streets, Conti. You shouldn't be here. Take that as your only warning."

Adriano was already walking back to his car before the enforcer had finished talking. He had a job to do, and that didn't include worrying about Theo DeLuca.

Adriano could feel the cold air wrapping around his still form as he sat in his car, waiting. He'd parked his car between two other dark colored vehicles, turned off the engine and cut the lights to keep from being noticed. Or rather, he hoped someone who recognized his old, restored Camaro would just pass it by.

So far, he'd done okay.

Adriano found Dean like the enforcer said he would. Apparently Dean was collecting payments from dealers on the corners with another man from Theo's crew. A guy Adriano knew Theo DeLuca kept close, like a best friend.

Sometimes, with things like this, it was all about the wait.

There was a problem with waiting, too. The longer Adriano sat there, watching Dean collect cash as the fool leaned against the window of a shoddy looking apartment building, the bigger his anger grew.

For the marks on Alessa's face that had faded.

For the ones Dean had put on her today.

For making Alessa scared or treating her like she was shit.

For Dean thinking he had any right to Adriano's girl.

For fucking breathing.

Adriano had a dozen more reasons. He had a whole list. These were good enough. These were more than enough to make his body numb with rage and his mind colder than ice. It was simply enough to kill the man.

Another car drove by the apartment building and slipped into the alley like the fifteen others had already done earlier in the night. Adriano watched as Dean and Theo's friend pushed off the building and disappeared into the alley behind the car to collect another payment.

Adriano moved then. He turned the car on and left it running as he got out, slammed the door, and crossed the road. By the time he came to the mouth of the alleyway, the car was already reversing out.

Money, bad money, always exchanged hands quickly. Nobody wanted to stay there longer than necessary.

Quick and dirty.

That's how the streets were run.

The two dark-skinned men in the car didn't give Adriano a second look as their car passed him by. He moved into the darkness of the alley to find Dean and Theo's friend stuffing cash into a black bag before they tossed it under a dumpster.

Theo's man turned around first, coming face to face with Adriano.

He'd apologize to Theo for this … eventually. Someday, if Theo ever gave him the chance to.

"Evening," Adriano said.

It was the only thing he gave in warning before he pulled his gun out, cocked back the hammer and put a single bullet between the man's eyes. The high calibre weapon had a mighty kickback, but Adriano barely flinched. Blood and matter flew backwards with the body before it dropped to the ground with a thud.

Dead.

Just like that.

Before the guy even hit the ground, he was gone.

The sound of the gun going off reverberated throughout the alley. This was the kind of area where cops showing up was commonplace. Pretty soon, Adriano knew he would hear the red, white, and blue coming. He had to get this done and over with, despite how much he wanted to make Dean fucking hurt.

Adriano didn't blink, he just turned his gun on a wide-eyed Dean.

"Evening," Adriano repeated.

It came off calm enough, but anyone with any brains would know that a calm Adriano was a dangerous one.

Dean's hand twitched before he reached for whatever was under his jacket. Adriano didn't hesitate to shoot again. The bullet entered Dean's wrist. His scream shattered through the alley.

Adriano moved forward as Dean scrambled backwards, falling to the ground in the process.

"Should have fucking known," Dean spat.

Adriano chuckled. "That she was mine? Yeah, you probably should have known."

"No, that she was still acting like a little whore with trash like you."

Trash.

That was a new one.

Adriano was more pissed off about the whore comment.

Dean grappled for the gun at his waist again with his good hand, but he was too late. Adriano kicked Dean in the stomach, knocking the weapon far away. He then slammed his booted foot down on Dean's injured, bleeding wrist.

"Shit!" Dean howled. "Fuck you, Adriano."

"Try again," Adriano taunted, putting his weight down on Dean's wrist. "Something to make this quicker, maybe."

"I hope she was worth it," Dean jeered.

Adriano bent down and shoved the barrel of his gun into Dean's mouth as he grabbed him around the throat and squeezed. The guy struggled, refusing to open his mouth all the way. Adriano pulled the gun back just far enough for it to hurt when he smacked the butt straight into Dean's teeth.

Dean shouted before spitting blood, saliva and chipped teeth to the ground. It gave Adriano the opening he needed to shove the gun far enough into Dean's mouth that the man gagged around the barrel. Adriano squeezed Dean's throat again, using the weight advantage he had over the guy to keep him pinned to the ground.

"I'd do so much fucking worse to you," Adriano hissed. "I'd cut your fucking tongue out for breathing a bad word about Alessa. I'd break your fucking fingers for touching her in a way that hurt her. I'd take a hammer to your face for looking at her, asshole. I would make you beg to die."

Dean clenched his bloody mouth around the barrel of the gun, staring Adriano in the eyes.

"But I get to keep her," Adriano murmured, smiling coldly. "And you don't. So this works, too. Lights out, Dean."

Adriano shoved the gun in harder until it touched the back of Dean's throat and then he pulled the trigger. He couldn't remember a time when killing had ever felt better.

"Hello?"

Alessa's tired, groggy voice made Adriano smile. He didn't know why exactly he had called her, but the very second he had gotten back into Conti territory, his girl had been the one and only person on his mind.

"Hey, Lissa," Adriano said, pulling his car over into a vacant parking lot.

"Adriano?"

"Who else calls you at twelve at night, babe?"

Alessa laughed quietly. "No one. I thought you told me to sleep. I can't do that when you call me, you know."

Adriano grinned, ignoring the blood on his hands and the worry in his mind. He'd made a rash decision. He had let his anger control him and did something he was surely going to have to pay for. Killing Dean and Theo's man was unlikely to go unanswered in some way. Neither of them had been made men, but someone would be pissed.

Dean's father, for one. Theo, for two.

Worth it.

Adriano's anxiety was still hard to ignore. "I just wanted to hear your voice."

"Oh?" Alessa whispered.

"Yeah. Best thing ever, Lissa."

"Mmm, you're smooth."

"My mom used to say I was slick," Adriano said.

Alessa grew quiet for longer than he liked before she said, "You don't really talk about her anymore."

"It hurts a lot when I do, so I just don't."

"Talk now," she demanded softly.

"I miss her and it's not easier, but I don't blame anyone," Adriano said honestly. "I don't want apologies from people or their pity. My mom has nothing to do with this war, Lissa. I won't make it out like she does. That'd just be a ruin to her memory. She was better than bullets and blood, you know?"

"Yeah," Alessa said. "I do."

"I wish other people understood that, too, but now they're too focused on positions and greed and killing. But I can't say anything in that regard, so, oh well."

"What do you mean?"

Adriano cleared his throat, glancing out the window at the quiet, dark street. "You don't have to worry anymore, Lissa. Not about Dean. Okay?"

Alessa sucked in a deep breath. "Adriano ..."

"They might not identify him for a while."

Adriano shouldn't have said that.

"Yikes," she muttered.

Why didn't she sound surprised at all?

"Alessa?"

"Yeah?" she asked.

"You told me what he did today because you knew I would go after him, didn't you?"

Alessa sighed. "Yes."

Huh.

Alessa probably didn't realize it, but she had a lot of guts to be doing shit like that. Manipulation had never been in her game, but sometimes, a person had to do what they had to do. Adriano wouldn't fault her for using what she had at her disposal.

He certainly wouldn't blame her for using him.

"Lissa?"

"Yeah?"

"It was worth it."

Adriano shoved his hands under the scalding water and rubbed the bar of soap roughly between his palms, washing away the red stains. The water ran down the drain, diluted to a dull pink.

"Adriano?"

"Go to bed, Eve," he said without looking at his sister.

"Is that blood?"

Fuck.

"Go to bed."

Evelina moved further into the bathroom and flicked on the overhead lights instead of just the soft glow of the vanity mirror. "Oh, my God, Adriano."

"It's nothing," Adriano said quickly.

"You've got blood all over your shirt."

Yeah, well, there was a lot of after spray.

"It won't come out," Adriano said, dismissing his sister's concerns. "I'll just throw the shirt out."

"It's not yours, right?"

Adriano chuckled. "No. Does it look like I'm bleeding anywhere?"

Evelina didn't grace Adriano's attitude with a response. "Who does it belong to?"

"Someone. More than one, maybe."

"Adriano!" Evelina snapped.

He finally looked at his sister, noting her concern. "It's nothing, really."

"I'm calling Dad."

Adriano was going to argue, but he didn't. Riley would need to know. That was sure to be a fun conversation.

"Yeah, you should do that," Adriano said before he went back to washing his hands like nothing had happened. "And be fast about it. I'm fucking tired, Eve."

By the time Riley got to the apartment, Adriano had more than enough time to consider what he had done and what it all might mean. Instead of staying neutral in the war between the four Outfit families, he had made a serious statement by killing soldiers of another family's crew.

And by all accounts, for no good reason.

Riley stepped inside the apartment, leaving behind his enforcers as he closed the front door and rounded on his son. "What happened? Your sister was in a panic and said something about you coming home bloody. Who did what, Adriano?"

Adriano rested on the couch, sipping from a glass of water. "I did something, not anyone else."

Partly, he held back from adding.

"Weren't you working tonight?" his father asked.

"I went to see the bookie and then got side-tracked," Adriano replied.

"Doing what?"

"I went over to the DeLuca territory and finished some business."

Riley froze, eyeing his son with a burning anger that Adriano could feel from all the way across the goddamn room. "Tell me you didn't."

Adriano laughed. "All right, I didn't."

"Adriano!"

"You asked."

"Your smart mouth is about to meet the barrel of a glock," his father snapped.

Adriano checked his attitude, but couldn't help but mutter, "Yeah, that's what happened to Dean's mouth tonight, too."

"Fucking Christ."

Adriano chose to stay silent. He sat still, drank his water, and said nothing as his father paced the length of the living room. Adriano had convinced Evelina to go back to sleep before their father got there, just in case shit went south for whatever reason.

"I told you ... I told you, Adriano!" Riley shouted.

"You guaranteed me nothing," Adriano murmured, setting his glass to the coffee table and standing. "I gave you everything you wanted, Dad, and you did fuck all for me. I wanted one thing. For that marriage not to happen."

Riley barked out a laugh. "You're still pussy blind over that girl, son. She is a piece of ass, Adriano. There are a dozen more pieces of asses waiting at every corner of Chicago. Whisper your last name in their ear, and they'll climb all over you to get a chance."

Adriano brushed those comments off. "Alessa is not just a piece of ass. She's never been just that for me. And I'm not like you, Dad. I chose her, I want her. I won't do what you did to my mother—running around with every woman that would spread her legs and then fucking the ones who would abort the pregnancies when you paid them to."

Riley's brow shot up high. "I—"

"Fuck off, Dad. Don't deny it. You think I don't know about all that shit? You're a dog missing your collar. You couldn't even give mom the decency of wearing a fucking rubber when you were running around on her. I am not you. I don't ever want to be you."

His father seemed stunned and unable to talk.

"I asked for one thing when it came to Alessa," Adriano repeated quietly.

"Someone else," his father muttered. "He would have married her off to someone else."

"You could have settled this entire feud with a marriage between her and me!"

Riley gritted his teeth. "And what in the hell would that teach you, Adriano? That your soft heart matters to me; or to the Outfit, even? That your feelings are important to the family? None of that will ever matter, son!"

Adriano shrugged. "Fact remains, I took what I wanted. You didn't follow through, so I did. Dean's dead and another solider for the DeLuca crew happened to be caught in the crossfire. Handle it, Dad. That's what bosses fucking do."

"Watch your tongue."

"You want to be a boss, so be one."

CHAPTER SIXTEEN

Alessa rested against the cool tile on the bathroom floor, wishing her upset stomach would settle. Ever since her encounter with Dean two days earlier, Alessa had been struck with nausea. At first, she brushed it off as stress. Then, she figured maybe it was something she ate.

She glanced at the little calendar on her phone, showcasing dates she didn't want to see right before her eyes.

Oh, God.

What had she done?

She was not going to get away with this. This could not be hidden like everything else she had done with Adriano.

A knock on the bathroom door jerked Alessa from the daze she was in. She pushed up from the floor, grabbing her phone at the same time. Quickly, she flushed the toilet again, just to make sure everything from the last vomiting round had gone down.

Earlier, while watching Miss Cathy fry bacon for breakfast, Alessa found herself running for the closest bathroom without warning.

She knew it then.

"Lissa?" Abriella asked.

Alessa clenched her hands into tight fists, trying to maintain some sense of control. "Yeah?"

"You okay?"

Lie, lie, lie.

"Perfect," Alessa said, as cheerful as she could manage. "Just give me a few and we can go out shopping like you want."

Abriella had convinced Joel to let them take a driver and enforcer so they could make a day out of going to the mall.

"Are you sure you're good?" her sister asked.

"Yep."

"Miss Cathy said—"

"Abriella, I'm fine," Alessa said shortly.

Without even a goodbye, Alessa heard her sister walk away from the bathroom. Five minutes later, she left the privacy of the space, too. She walked through the large home, heading toward her bedroom, and still looking at her phone and counting days all over again.

Surely she had made a mistake.

She *must* have made a mistake.

Somehow.

Twenty-five ...

Twenty-six ...

Twenty-seven ...

Alessa wanted to stop counting. She wanted to stop seeing what she was seeing. But she couldn't and the proof was right there. Maybe if she just looked away and pretended like it wasn't happening ... She couldn't do that. In a way, because she didn't want to. And in another, because her mind was screaming her mistakes as loud as it could.

Jesus.

Thirty-four days.

Once she was in the privacy of her own bedroom, she closed the door, and then disappeared into her attached bath. Alessa tossed her phone into the sink before pulling open the medicine cabinet and stared at the little blue pack. She was almost scared to open it, but she did, anyway.

Alessa was already four days into her sugar pills this month. The placebo pills were supposed to be used on the days of her menstrual cycles. A cycle she hadn't had for thirty-four days and was just now realizing her error. She hadn't even realized that she missed her cycle last month, too.

This was bad.

So, so bad.

Alessa felt sick all over again. Sliding to the floor of her bathroom, she stared at the pills, numb.

Alessa barely managed to hide the pack of birth control pills under her leg as her mother opened the door to the bathroom. Sara stared down at her daughter with a cocked brow and questions on the tip of her tongue.

Alessa could feel them already without her mother saying a thing.

"Abriella called me an hour ago," her mother said.

"Oh?"

Had it been that long already?

"Yes," Sara said quietly, bending down. "Here."

Alessa stared at the white and pink box her mother held out. "I ..."

Can't take that, she wanted to say.

It'll be real.

I'll get him killed.

"Your sister told me some of the stuff that's been going on with you lately. Sleeping all the time, being snappy, and not feeling particularly well. I knew what her concerns were without her saying a thing, so when she called me today, I made a quick trip to the store. No one saw me. I didn't say a word. Take the pregnancy test, Alessa."

"I can't," Alessa whispered.

Sara frowned. "You have to. We'll figure it all out, but right now, I need to know if this is what it is."

Alessa blew out a shaky breath. "I fucked up."

"Me, too," Sara murmured. "Three times, but I never regretted one of you."

"I'm sorry, Mom."

Sara smiled. "Lissa, I never expected my mistakes to go unpunished. But I hoped that the fact I loved you would override the things that brought you into this world. There was nothing that could be done for me back then. I was under the control and bending to the demands of the men in my life without ever considering what was best for me."

"I'm sorry," Alessa repeated, not knowing what else to say.

"Take the test."

"It's not Dean's."

Sara nodded. "I didn't think for one minute that it would be."

"I don't want to get him killed because I fucked up," Alessa said.

"Adriano?"

Alessa was kind of surprised her mother knew who her lover was. "Yes."

Sara laughed quietly. "Terrance always said that man would be the one to get you. I didn't know why and he never offered an explanation, but he knew. I guess he was right."

"What am I going to do?"

Her mother pushed the pregnancy test into her hand. "Take it and we'll work the rest out later."

Would they?

Once her mother was gone from the bathroom, Alessa tore open the package with shaking hands, read the directions with hazy eyes, and did what she needed to do. While the test sat on the counter, the reading windows facing up, she already knew what it was going to say.

It was pretty goddamn sad that the two pink lines lit up the screen almost instantly.

Pregnant.

So fucking pregnant.

God.

She was twenty-years-old and *pregnant*.

Alessa waited the required minutes she needed to, but it was already confirmed.

"And?" her mother asked the moment Alessa stepped out of the bathroom.

Abriella sat on the edge of the bed, surprising Alessa. She hadn't known her sister came to her room, also.

"Yeah," Alessa managed to say through her wavering emotions. "It's positive."

Abriella didn't look surprised. "How're you feeling?"

"Awful."

"It'll be all right," Abriella said.

"I don't think it will," Alessa replied bleakly.

She still had to tell Adriano.

How would that go over?

Sara disappeared into the bathroom and came out with the pregnancy test and all the evidence. She even took Alessa's pack of birth control pills.

"What are you doing?" Alessa asked.

"I'm going to destroy this," her mother explained. "And I'm going to give you a couple of weeks to figure out what you want to do about this, Lissa. It's up to you, whatever you want or need, I'll help you."

Alessa didn't understand.

"Anything," Sara pressed gently.

"I don't want to … get rid of the baby," Alessa whispered.

Of course, she didn't. It wasn't just hers, but Adriano's, too.

Alessa couldn't breathe again and her body went numb all over.

Abriella watched her sister warily like she could read Alessa's mind. "It's going to be okay, Lissa."

Alessa held back the tears stinging her eyes. "You keep saying that, but I don't think you're right."

No one had a response for that.

"I can't believe I'm going to be an aunt," Abriella said quietly.

Alessa eyed her sister from the side, willing her to shut the hell up. It didn't work.

"How did that happen, anyway?" her sister asked.

"Well, when a man and woman take their clothes off, and the man sticks his boy part—"

"Alessa," Abriella hissed.

"—into the woman's girl part, his seed finds her egg, and a baby is made."

"Cute."

Alessa shrugged. "I try."

Having a little fun seemed to make the situation easier.

"I know how a woman gets pregnant, smartass."

Alessa smirked. "Then you know how this happened."

Abriella sighed. "No, I meant, how did you end up knocked up, Lissa? Because I remember being the one who took you to the clinic for birth control pills so this kind of thing wouldn't happen at all."

"I missed one or two back in August," Alessa said, avoiding her sister's stare. "I didn't even realize that I missed a cycle last month. It's been a shitty couple of months, all right? Stop judging me."

"I'm not judging you!"

"You are, with your judge-y little eyes."

"Alessa," her sister groaned. "Stop it. And I don't have little eyes."

Alessa laughed quietly and picked at the loose thread on her sweater. "I just messed up. It happened, Ella."

"When are you going to tell Adriano?"

"Soon."

The sisters' conversation was interrupted by the sounds of footsteps in the large entryway of the Trentini mansion. Alessa caught sight of Theo DeLuca as he strolled past the entertainment room looking like he was ready for a battle. He hadn't even rang the doorbell, although Alessa supposed someone must have let him through the front gate.

"What is up with him?" Abriella asked.

"I don't know." Abriella grinned slyly. "Let's go find out."

Abriella didn't give her the chance to argue before pulling Alessa up from the couch and dragging her along.

"None of our business," Alessa said as they followed the direction Theo had gone in the large home.

"Maybe not," Abriella agreed. "Except there's a lot of nonsense going around right now and the more information I have, the better it could end up."

"Like how?" Alessa asked.

Abriella didn't answer. What game was her sister playing? Alessa suspected it might have had something to do with Tommas Rossi. It usually did where Abriella was concerned.

The sisters sneaked down the third floor hallway that led to Joel's office. The space had once been Terrance's, and where he was murdered, but Joel took it on as his own, redecorating and remodeling. Alessa tried to stay out of the space as much as possible.

Staying a few feet down from the double French doors and close to the wall, Alessa listened with her sister as Theo started talking.

"We've got a fucking problem, Joel," the man said.

Joel sighed harshly. "Yeah, I'll call you back."

"A problem," Theo repeated.

"And what is that?"

Alessa had a feeling she knew exactly what the problem was. Dean hadn't been around for two days. Usually, he stopped in just to talk with Joel. Alessa knew where he was—dead.

It was time for everyone else to know it, too.

"Have you seen Artino around anywhere?" Theo asked.

"I've been busy," Joel said. "Big night coming up and all."

"Walter hasn't called you, Joel?"

"No. Why?"

"One of my guys went missing two nights ago," Theo said. "He was working like he was supposed to be, collecting dues and shit over in the Heights. Artino was supposed to be with him, earning his fucking keep and all that."

"So?"

"So, nobody's heard a thing from either of them."

Alessa heard Joel's chair squeak like he was standing from it.

"Don't bother," Theo said. "I already tried calling Dean. I talked to Walter before I even came over here and he said that his son hasn't called him since that night. He's starting to get fucking twitchy. He put guys out to look for him."

"Shit," Joel muttered.

"There's something else," Theo said.

"What now?"

"There was a shooting around the place my guy was supposed to be," Theo explained. "Two men shot in the face, unrecognizable bodies and no identification on them apparently. I'd take a trip down to the morgue just to see for myself, but I don't want to draw attention that they might have been soldiers for my crew. The Outfit doesn't need any more attention than we've already got these last few months."

"Fuck," Joel growled. "You're sure?"

"Positive."

Joel cussed a blue streak before something crashed to the floor.

"What else?" Joel demanded.

"There was talk when I sent guys down into the Heights to get info," Theo replied. "But you can only take it so far, since most of the people in that area are either shooting or smoking something."

"I'm not in the mood for runarounds, Theo."

"A couple of people were sure they saw a dark colored, older muscle car in the area and an enforcer said he might have come face to face with Adriano Conti earlier that night. He didn't say what Adriano wanted, just that he saw him. But I think the guy was holding something back for whatever reason."

Alessa's heart stopped. The description of the vehicle couldn't exactly be considered vague when someone admitted to the fact that Adriano had been in the area.

Abriella grabbed Alessa's hand and squeezed.

"You all right?" her sister asked almost soundlessly.

Alessa nodded.

About Dean's death, Alessa had never felt better.

For Adriano, she was worried sick.

"It's just something fucking else," Theo said, his tone dark and hateful. "Another Conti mess we have to clean up. And you know what? I'd give Adriano a pass because he's young and made when my guys weren't, but his father probably made the call on that. Riley is overstepping his bounds, Joel. He needs to be handled."

"I'm working on that, Theo," Joel said.

"Work faster."

"Hey, you're not the goddamn boss here, man."

Theo laughed bitterly. "Neither are you."

"Watch it, Theo."

"Listen, Joel. I don't give a fuck who takes the seat as boss in this damn family. It can be you or any other man, but it better not be Riley Conti. If you don't start cleaning out his dirt, I will."

"What in the hell is that supposed to mean, Theo?" Joel asked.

"Take it however you want to."

"Talk to me, Lissa."

Adriano's voice was a soothing, deep melody in Alessa's ear. He couldn't possibly know how much she needed to just talk to him, but she didn't know what to say.

There was the pregnancy, of course, but she didn't want to tell him that over the phone. She wanted to be face to face with Adriano when he got the news. He deserved that. It wouldn't be fair to just blurt the information out over a hushed, quick phone call.

"Theo was here yesterday," Alessa said.

"Oh?"

"Someone saw your car and someone else said they noticed you in the area the night Dean and Theo's guy went missing."

Adriano hummed dismissively. "I'm not concerned about it and you shouldn't be either."

How could she not?

"That sounds a little like playing with fire, Adriano."

"I'm clear, don't worry."

"Easier said than done," Alessa whispered.

"Stop," he murmured calmly. "Let's move onto something different. You said Joel has a party coming up and he mentioned opening the books again?"

"Yeah."

"When?"

"This week. Thursday, I think," she replied.

"We'd heard some talk but nothing was for sure," Adriano said more to himself than Alessa. "I need a favor from you."

"Anything."

Whatever he needed, she would give.

"He's not kicking you out for the night of his party, right?" Adriano asked.

Alessa laughed. "Well, we're being sent over to Mom and Dad's wing."

"But you'll still be there?"

"Yes."

"I need you to unlock the back entrances and turn off the security cameras for the house that night," Adriano said. "Can you do that?"

Alessa didn't even hesitate. "I can do that."

"Good."

"What are you planning?" she asked.

"Me? Very little. My father? Something interesting. But just in case Joel goes crazy, it'd be nice to not to have it all on camera."

Alessa didn't like the sound of that at all. "Yikes."

"Stop worrying. Tell me something beautiful, Lissa."

"Like what?"

"I don't know, anything."

Alessa smiled. "I miss you."

"That's kind of sad."

"And I love you."

Adriano chuckled. "Now that's something beautiful."

"Anything yet?" Abriella asked.

Alessa shook her head. "Nothing."

"Damn."

Abriella went back to stirring the homemade chicken soup that Alessa had convinced her to make them for supper. Their parents had gone out for the evening, despite telling Joel they would stay in with Alessa and Abriella while the party was happening in the other wing of the mansion.

Alessa didn't mind their lack of presence, although her mother had been a great support for her over the last few days. She felt terrible about the judgement and hate she'd given her mother when she found out the truth of her own paternity. And not because Alessa was caught in a mess of her own making, but because she was finally understanding how difficult it must have been for her mother to carry a child for a man she loved, but not be able to give him the baby.

Not in a way that he could claim it as his.

"Did Mom get you those vitamins?" Abriella asked. "The pregnancy ones or whatever?"

"Yes, and they're like freaking horse pills."

Abriella made a face. "That big?"

"That big."

"Any puke spells today?" Abriella asked.

Alessa laughed. "No, but the night isn't over. Morning sickness is a myth, okay? It's whenever-the-hell-the-mood-strikes sickness."

Abriella grinned over her shoulder. "I'll remember that."

Something in the lilt of her sister's tone caught Alessa's attention.

"Are you planning on babies anytime soon?" Alessa asked.

"God, no. But someday, maybe."

"Don't you worry about who you're going to be stuck raising them with?"

Abriella stilled, her stirring stopping. "You mean, like who Joel might marry me off to?"

"Yeah."

"No, I'm not worried."

"He did it to me," Alessa pointed out. "Or tried."

Joel could still pick a new husband for Alessa. Her future was uncertain. A variable that was tossed in the air, waiting for Joel to point and decide.

She knew where she wanted to go. Straight to Adriano.

The little life growing within couldn't be ignored, either. It was Adriano's baby—his child. He should raise the child, not another man. And what kind of man would want to marry Alessa if she was pregnant with another man's baby, anyway?

"He can try," Abriella muttered. "I know what I'm doing."

"Do you?" Alessa asked.

"Yeah, and I don't care what it takes for me to get there. Joel isn't the only one in this family who will play dirty to get what they want. He's not ready for me yet, Alessa. Trust that."

What was that supposed to mean?

Alessa didn't get the chance to ask.

Her phone buzzed on the table with an incoming text.

Now, it read.

She had finally changed the contact on the phone so that it showcased Adriano's name. With Dean out of the picture, she wasn't concerned about getting into trouble if it was caught. Even Joel was liable to brush off a contact as long as there was no messages between her and Adriano to find.

Alessa glanced up at her waiting sister. "You ready?"

Abriella smiled. "Soup later?"

"Sounds good."

"Then yeah. I'll get the security turned off. You let them in."

Alessa and Abriella parted ways at the doors that separated the two wings.

"Don't let Joel see you," Alessa said, only half joking.

Abriella snorted. "Right. He's stuck so far up his own ass, he can't even smell the shit right now."

She wasn't wrong.

Alessa made her way to the back of the house as quickly and quietly as she could. Joel had every made man from the Outfit that he could inside the Trentini mansion. Well, all the made men from the Trentini, DeLuca, and Rossi families. As far as Alessa understood, and overheard over the last few days, Joel hadn't openly invited the Conti people.

Which made sense, since he didn't want to give Riley the chance at the seat.

Nonetheless, the guests were supposed to be on the bottom floor between the dining and entertaining area, but that didn't mean a few might not break off into their own corners. The back of the Trentini mansion had always been off-limits to guests during events and celebrations, but people, especially Outfit people, didn't particularly like to follow the rules.

Luckily, no one happened to be wandering the halls as Alessa came to the back doors leading out to the deck and property.

She waited a good five minutes to make sure her sister had lots of time to turn off the security. That way, when she unlocked the back door, it wouldn't send off the alarms when it was opened.

Alessa glanced out the window into the dark backyard, noting the enforcer her brother had set out there for the night. The man was smoking a cigarette and staring up at the sky like he was bored as hell.

She supposed that job probably was.

Knowing the man was far enough away that he wouldn't hear the door being unlocked, Alessa turned the deadbolts and waited. She didn't have to wait for very long. Almost immediately, figures began to emerge on the pathways throughout the back property. Faceless men, as Alessa couldn't exactly make out who they were.

But there was a lot.

Fifteen, she counted at first.

Then she noted three more.

They all wore black suits and each held a gun in their hand.

As the enforcer noticed the men coming toward him, he turned to bolt toward the house with a phone in his hand.

Alessa should have turned away. She should have closed her eyes.

She didn't.

The closest man, one Alessa did recognize, raised his gun with a long silencer attached, and fired one single shot. It didn't even look like he had aimed, but he didn't miss his mark. Alessa jumped as the bullet entered at the back of the enforcer's head, sending blood and matter flying. His body lurched forward before he slammed into the ground. Riley Conti walked on past his victim like nothing had even happened. Like he hadn't just killed a man.

Alessa moved back down the hallway, knowing she shouldn't be seen by the Conti men as they came into the house. Adriano had warned her to stay out of sight, be safe, and let whatever happened, happen.

She slipped into the closest bathroom and closed the door, leaving only a crack open, as she heard the back door open and men file in. Their footsteps were quiet—practiced. Their voices were hushed murmurs whispering down the hall to her spot, but she couldn't quite make out what they were saying.

Then, their sounds got closer.

"All the doors on this wing only," Riley said.

"Not the other, boss?" came a man's question.

"No," Riley said. "He's only entertaining on this side. I want all the doors handled. Drop his men if you have to. Someone needs to be out front at the gates. I want that man gone, too."

"Trentinis will take a mighty hit, boss."

"So be it."

"Anything else?" another man asked.

"No, just keep the guns up," Riley said quietly. "If Joel doesn't want to step down to me willingly, then I will strong-arm him into it. I am done playing games with a child. And that is all Joel Trentini is to me. It's the Conti time now. We've always had the upper hand here, so let's show him that we're willing to raise it a little higher."

"And the others?" someone asked.

"The Rossis are partial to us at the moment—keep them that way. The DeLucas are smart. Volatile right now, but smart. For the time being, they'll choose the safe route. One that won't get half of them killed. That means our side. We're simply tipping the scales to our favor."

"Sounds good," came a new voice.

Confirmative murmurs passed along the men.

"Then let's get this over with. I would love to be home before midnight," Riley said, a hint of a smile in his tone. "I'm sure we can finish this out within the hour."

Jesus.

Alessa put her back to the door as men began to file past her hiding spot. Their shoes barely made any sound at all as they walked down the long hallway that would lead to the middle of the home where Joel was entertaining his guests.

Once the footsteps had faded, Alessa opened the door of the bathroom and stepped back out into the hall. She knew she wasn't alone instantly. Adriano leaned against the wall a few feet down like he had been expecting her to show.

"Hey," Adriano said, grinning.

His green eyes seemed darker as he looked her over.

Alessa's heart swelled. "Hey."

"Still miss me?"

"Like crazy," she said softly.

"Still love me?"

"Always."

Adriano pushed off the wall and met her in three long, smooth strides. His hands grabbed her shirt and pulled her into his chest roughly a split second before his lips crashed down on hers. He kissed her harder, deeper. His tongue warred with hers, making her hot and weak at the same time.

How long had it been since she kissed him?

Too long.

Alessa let him steal that kiss, because that's exactly what he did. There was no give; there was just him taking.

Like he missed her.

Like he needed her.

Like she was all his.

Alessa supposed she was—she had always been.

"Stay out of sight, all right," Adriano said, fixing Alessa's wayward waves of hair. "I'll be worried, otherwise."

"I will," she promised.

Her secret was like a thunder rolling around in her stomach, wanting out.

"What is it?" Adriano asked.

Alessa laughed quietly. "How do you always know when I'm hiding something?"

She could lie her ass off to anyone if she wanted.

Never to Adriano.

He touched the spot between her eyebrows with the pad of his thumb. "You get a little line right here. It tells me you're thinking too damned hard about something or other. What is it, Lissa?"

The words stuck in her throat like they suddenly didn't want to come out. Alessa wouldn't give them the choice. They might not have another moment anytime soon. If Riley got his wish of forcing Joel's hand tonight, it could very well make things a hell of a lot more difficult between Adriano and Alessa.

She refused to tell him about the pregnancy over the phone.

"Alessa, I need to catch up with the rest of the guys," Adriano said.

Alessa nodded. "I know. Just … this is important, Adriano. Really, really important. More important than the Outfit or anyone else. Okay?"

Adriano frowned. "Okay."

"Don't do that—frown like that. You'll make me nervous."

Alessa already was terribly nervous.

"You're rambling."

"I am." Alessa blew out a heavy breath and whispered, "I'm pregnant."

Adriano's grip on her waist tightened briefly before it loosened just as fast. He swallowed hard and watched her almost warily. "What?"

"I missed a couple of pills and didn't realize—"

"No, stop that," Adriano muttered.

Alessa blinked up at him. "Okay."

"Don't excuse it like I'm going to be angry. I'm not angry. I'm …"

"Not angry," Alessa echoed.

"Pregnant?"

She nodded.

Adriano didn't ask for dates. He didn't ask if he was the father or if there was someone else. He didn't question her on a thing. Alessa knew he didn't have to because she had only ever been his.

She loved him all the more for it.

"Oh, my God," Adriano breathed. "A baby … *my* baby."

That was all he said before he held her face in his palms and peppered her lips with soft, light kisses.

"Love you, love you, love you," he chanted.

"You're not ... mad or anything?"

"No. Why would I be? So we're fucking twenty and stupid. We're not the first, Alessa. Trust me."

Alessa giggled, but the reality of their situation weighed her happiness down. "What are we going to do?"

"I don't know," Adriano said. "But we'll figure it out. It might take a little while, but we will figure it out, Lissa."

"I'm worried."

She needed to say that. She needed to get it out. Her mother and sister didn't seem to listen when she raised her concerns. They brushed it off and told her to wait it out. She wanted to hear something different—something concrete and promising.

"I'm scared," Alessa added when Adriano stayed silent.

Adriano ghosted the pads of his thumbs over her cheekbones. "Yeah, me, too."

CHAPTER SEVENTEEN

Pregnant ...

Huh.

Adriano felt almost numb as he strolled through the hallway leading to the main area of the Trentini mansion. He knew he should be worried, maybe even scared, but something inside wouldn't let him be either of those things.

Instead, he just shut it off so he could get through the night. Once he did that, and all was good, he could start putting together a plan for him, Alessa, and their unborn child. He'd gotten this far and did okay, he just had to go a little bit further.

"How in the fuck did you get in here?"

Adriano chuckled at Joel's indignant, angry roar. The fool might as well have howled the words like a crying child, unhappy at having their fun spoiled. Silence followed Joel's shouts, and then two soft pops echoed, like a gun going off with a silencer attached.

"Shit," someone cussed.

Adriano slid into place at the large entryway to the entertainment area. Men stood around, mouths agape and confused. Riley, with his back facing Adriano, stood a few feet ahead of his son with his arms wide like he was gesturing at the party.

One of Joel's men laid dead in the middle of the space with two bullet holes to the face and a puddle of blood pooling outward. A gun rested just a couple of inches from the dead man's outstretched hand. He must have come at Riley.

Adriano's father had been clear. No one was to shoot unless someone else did first or they were threatened. And then their bullets and guns would simply be used to make a point; to draw fear; to control.

Damn.

Adriano missed out on the first bit of fun.

"As you can see," Riley murmured, taking a couple of steps further into the room and glancing around at the quiet men. "I am very much alive and well. My son handled a few things on my end while I took a break to clear my mind and get things settled. But I'm back now, and ready to discuss business."

Joel scoffed. "Clear your mind?"

Riley acted like Joel didn't say a thing. He snapped his fingers at one of his enforcers and said, "Get me a drink, would you?"

"Don't touch a damn thing in this house," Joel barked at the man.

"Oh, but it's no fun to have a party without a drink. And you are having a party, aren't you Joel?" Riley asked, unbothered by the dead man at his feet

Joel's face turned red and his teeth gnashed together. "Who let you in?"

"That's unimportant."

"I think it is," Joel spat. "You were not invited to my home. You haven't been invited here since you killed my father."

Riley barked out a laugh. "Now he's your father? Because before, he was just the asshole who donated the sperm. I'm not surprised. You've got the chance to gain something with Terrance dead and your parentage out in the open, or so you think."

Joel's gaze narrowed. "This is my birth—"

"Birthright?" Riley interrupted calmly. "Is that what you're going to say?"

Joel refused to answer, but his fists balled tightly at his sides.

Adriano scanned the faces of the men, taking inventory and tallying numbers. He wanted to know who they were up against if someone turned on them tonight and also, who seemed to be leaning toward his father's side.

Most were quiet, gaging the scene with interest and worry. That was to be expected. Adriano quickly picked out the most important faces—the ones who would be valuable to their side of things.

Tommas Rossi. He stood in the far left corner with a glass of cognac lifted to his smirking lips as he watched the scene unfold. Tommas had a lot more to gain with Riley as the boss than with Joel.

Adriano found another face quickly.

Damian Rossi. The hitman leaned against the wall just a few feet from his cousin and barely graced Riley or Joel with any of his attention. But Damian had things to gain with Riley as the boss if Adriano's last chat with him was any indication.

Walter Artino, a secondary Capo for the DeLuca family but still carrying weight, moved closer to Joel. Adriano didn't give a fuck about that man. He could be handled easily and then his body would vanish before the night was over. Adriano just needed a reason to do it.

Adriano found the last man, the final one who could sway opinions.

Theo DeLuca. He was pissed and it was obvious. Adriano didn't blame the man. Theo probably still believed Riley's hands were all over Dino's death.

Riley still wasn't denying it, after all.

"Your birthright," Riley repeated. "Isn't that what you were going to say to me, Joel?"

Joel's jaw clenched. "You know it is."

"I know you're thirty-years-old and in need of a reality check." Riley dismissed Joel with a wave of his hand, saying, "The Outfit has never been about birthrights, Joel. None of the men in this room got where they are because their fathers were important men. They got where they are because they put everything but themselves first to earn it. You have done nothing but throw tantrums, make demands, and pull triggers."

"Bullshit," Joel hissed.

"Facts," Riley retorted. "The only reason you got your button at eighteen was because Terrance felt obligated to give it to you. It certainly wasn't because you deserved it. And if I remember correctly, there were at least ten men who objected to your nomination but despite their protests, Terrance went through with it. You never should have gotten it by the Outfit's rules, but people turned their cheek, knowing there was nothing they could do about it."

"You lying bastard."

Riley shook his head. "I do not lie. But your father? He regretted giving you that button every single day after, Joel."

"Let's not forget that he's the same man you killed to try and get where you are," Joel said, sneering.

Riley waved his arms wide again. "I never killed Terrance. I never ordered his hit. I had no reason to."

"You're showing us one now," Walter Artino put in.

"Wrong." Riley smiled coldly. "I'm here to fill an empty seat as the only man alive in this family that is worthy of sitting in it."

Joel scoffed. "You're not welcome here. You weren't invited. Leave."

"I'm a made man, Joel," Riley said. "Every man I brought with me tonight is a made man in the Outfit. Tell me this is not what I think it is, and we'll turn around and go."

"And what do you think this is?" Joel asked, seething.

"I think you opened the books. I know you spread the word over the last couple of weeks, wanting to draw me out like I was some scared little kitten afraid of you. Well, here I am Joel. I'm right here, my boy. I'm looking you right in your face and I haven't given you what you wanted, I have yet to bow down to your ridiculous shows, and I have yet to turn tail and run."

Joel's fists shook. "I …"

"Speechless?" Riley asked. "Come on, Joel. A good boss has an excuse or a deflection right on the tip of his tongue, always. Where is yours? Where is your reason to make me give this to you? Where is your worth, Joel? Come on, *give me anything!*"

Joel took a single step back, frustration writing heavily across his brow.

Riley smirked and said, "You want to open the books, so let's open them."

Nobody said a word as Riley's enforcer moved to the bar, poured a glass of forty-year-old cognac, and walked it to his boss. Nobody moved, blinked, and they might as well have not even breathed. It was like they were all waiting for the other shoe to drop.

Even Joel stood stunned and stupid.

That wasn't particularly new.

"There is a man at every door," Riley informed. "Each one is armed and willing to die to keep anyone from getting past them. There are six men in this room that everyone can already see with guns ready, but I would be willing to bet there are more just waiting to show. No one leaves this house until we are finished. And if you do wish to walk out now, I will make it easy for you and have you carried out in garbage bags. I hope that's clear."

"Is that how you're going to play this?" Joel asked quietly. "You're going to force yourself into the seat and take it because you've frightened them into giving it to you? You're going to strong-arm your way into a position you don't deserve?"

Riley turned enough to give Adriano a view of his father's amused profile. "Oh, Joel, you have a great deal to learn yet. I deserve this far more than you and I'm showing you exactly why that is. Can't you see that, you fool?"

"I see a man unable to get it the right way," Joel muttered.

"And the way you were going to take it?" Riley shot back. "Sneaky, on the down low, and without the approval of an entire crew worth of men? Come on, Joel, you know better than that. Your position never would have stood against me had I come at you for it."

Joel swallowed hard. "I don't know that at all."

"Well, I suppose we won't have to find out now, will we?"

"Is that why you had Laurent Rossi killed, too?" Joel asked. "Would his allegiance to the Trentini family have upset your scales?"

Riley barked out a laugh. "I didn't do that, either."

"Liar," Joel accused.

"He is not lying," came a quiet, sure voice from the corner.

All heads turned in Tommas Rossi's direction. The man sipped from his glass of liquor without gracing anyone the pleasure of his attention, almost like they didn't deserve it. He simply lifted his glass again and took another drink, completely unbothered by the situation happening around him.

"He is not lying," Tommas repeated.

"And how can you be sure of that?" Joel asked his once best friend.

Adriano knew the two men had divided over the last couple of months. Joel was so distrustful of those around him that he even pushed his friend away. Instead of holding those people close, people he should have wanted surrounding him, he brought people who would use and manipulate him in. People like Walter and Dean Artino.

"I'm sure of it because I know who killed my father and it wasn't Riley," Tommas said frankly.

"Who then?" Joel demanded.

Tommas smiled. It came off cold and callous. His next word was just as heartless. "Me."

A pin could have dropped and it would have echoed. That's how goddamn quiet it turned in the room. Those who hadn't been looking at Tommas certainly were now. The rest seemed to be gazing rapidly back and forth between the man in the corner and Joel in the middle.

"I killed my father," Tommas said, sighing. "It only takes one stupid man in a group of the best to sour them all, Joel. I watched him drink himself nearly to death for years and make bad decisions over and over without consequence. I felt his abuse and his foulness for years. And when he hurt something else of mine, and they suffered for his stupidity, too? I couldn't do that anymore."

"You—"

"Me," Tommas interrupted Joel, shrugging uncaringly. "And it was the best decision I have ever made. I warned him; he didn't listen. So, I ended it. Simple as that."

Wow.

Adriano felt like he'd just been picked up and dropped off in the Twilight Zone.

This was surreal.

Unbelievable.

Riley gave Tommas a nod and a smile. "It's always nice working with you, Rossi."

Tommas returned the gestures by tipping his glass in Riley's direction. "And you, old friend."

Joel glared. "How dare you?"

Tommas didn't give Joel a reaction. "I nominate Riley Conti as boss for the Rossi crew. I can assure you my men are in agreeance with the nomination and none will object at this time. I am more than capable of speaking for them, but if any man from my crew feels the need to confirm their agreement, feel free."

A beat of silence passed around the room.

Just a beat …

And then …

"Aye," came a voice.

"Aye."

"Aye."

It echoed over and over. Ten, twelve, and then fifteen.

Tommas' smug grin grew a little more as he watched Joel fume from across the room.

Even Adriano found himself smirking as the confirmative votes passed through.

"Aye," said another man from the Conti side.

Again, the word traveled through every man that had come along for the evening. All the made voices in the Outfit for the Conti side that could and would speak. Riley stood stock still, tracing his finger around the rim of his glass and looking at the golden liquid within as his seat was all but given.

He only needed the nomination. He only needed the second vote.

"DeLuca?" Riley asked quietly.

Theo sucked in a hard breath, rage swimming in his brown gaze. "I concede."

Riley smiled. "Concede."

"I don't object, I concede," Theo growled. "I acknowledge you, I don't approve of you."

"What that means is you're a smart man, Theo," Riley said, shrugging. "So be it."

"And my son," Riley added, waving back at a silent Adriano. "He has amends to make with you, Theo."

"For killing my men, yes. I've heard." Theo gave Adriano a passing look and then turned his attention back on Riley as he said, "I want nothing from your son as of now, but I'll take an apology from you when I decide to ask for it."

Riley tilted his chin up at the man. "I look forward to it."

"I wouldn't," Theo replied with a flash of his teeth as he sneered. "Aye, I concede to the seat."

"Aye," came the confirmation from another DeLuca crew member.

More followed.

Quietly, almost so low he couldn't be heard, Walter Artino spat out, "Aye."

When silence fell, Riley glanced up at Joel.

"You should be careful of those you trust, Joel," Riley said. "No one around you is safe, my boy. They'll only work for their own benefit, and you ran that course. Give it up willingly; give it up with some dignity. You tried—I'll give you that. You tried damn hard. I know about your little trip to Vegas, and your chats with the smaller families in New York. I know about your request to the Commission for my hit, a hit they denied. You can't do it, but you did more than most men would have. Take that from it and be happy I've given you that much.

"I'll let you keep a spot in the Outfit as a Capo with a crew to run and money to make. You will have the same voice as any other Capo in this room does. It is not a loss, Joel. It is not a failure as long as you make the right choice," Riley finished sharply. "Do not be an idiot. Make the right choice."

Joel openly glared but he still couldn't seem to form any words worthy of speaking.

Adriano could feel the shift in the room already happening. His father had it—he had gotten everything he wanted. Riley didn't wait for someone to just hand it over to him, no, he took it whether they were willing to give it or not.

Fear and respect walked hand in hand.

This was the mafia way.

"Object, Joel, I dare you," Riley threatened, smiling wickedly. "Object to my seat, and I'll blow your brains out all over these beautiful Oriental rugs. If you thought washing Terrance's blood off the wall was difficult, just imagine the artwork yours will make on this floor."

Joel clenched his teeth, refusing to speak.

"Object," Riley hissed.

Give me a reason, Adriano thought.

He only needed the one.

Just one to get what he needed—to get Alessa. With no one heading her house as the man for the Outfit, she was free to do as she wished.

Give me a fucking reason.

"Aye," Joel whispered.

It was done.

Celebration would be an understatement when it came to the aftermath of Riley becoming the boss for the Outfit. Adriano assumed his father would take his win in a quiet stride, not draw attention to himself, and lay low for a while, but Riley went in the complete opposite direction.

He celebrated openly. He put his name on the streets immediately, uncaring of the tradition that the Outfit had always held for a formal front boss to the operation.

It was almost like Riley was challenging someone to challenge him.

Adriano didn't really care.

He'd gotten what he wanted ... well, almost.

A week after his father had taken the seat, Adriano was no closer to Alessa. His thoughts were plagued with her and for her pregnancy. He was worried what would happen when her brother figured out their secret.

Adriano had yet to come up with a plan that might actually work for them.

There was always running away, of course, but Adriano wasn't the type. Alessa deserved more than that kind of shame, too. He didn't want to embarrass the family that had loved and cared for her—minus her brother—simply because Adriano didn't have a better way to correct their situation.

"Where is your head tonight?" Tommas asked, drawing Adriano from his thoughts.

"Hmm?"

"Far away in the clouds, like it always is," Riley muttered.

Adriano shot his father with a dirty look, picked up his beer, and downed the rest of it in one go. "I'm just thinking."

"About what?" Tommas asked.

"Unimportant things, likely," Riley answered.

"Back off, Dad," Adriano warned.

Riley shrugged and cut into his steak, turning his attention on Evelina. "Are you just about ready to leave your brother's place and come back home?"

Evelina smiled sweetly. "If home means my dorm again, then yes, I am."

"Evelina," Riley said coolly.

"It's over, Dad," Adriano said for his sister. "Let her live in her dorm and get back to life. What is the fucking problem?"

Riley scowled. "The problem is that Evelina still broke my rules, son. Regardless of the rest, I still don't trust her to follow my directions."

Evelina glared across the table. "Then I'll stay with Adriano."

"So be it, but you still have to follow the rules no matter where you live, Eve."

Adriano glanced up at the ceiling, wishing it would swallow him whole. He was over this entire dinner. It wasn't that he didn't like Tommas, because he did. And dinner with Evelina was okay, too. But Riley had a way of making things more annoying than they usually would be with his arrogant attitude that made an appearance at every turn.

Tommas had been invited to the dinner to talk positions, as far as Adriano understood it. It seemed like Riley was preparing to give the man a higher spot as an underboss. Tommas would make a good underboss for the Outfit. Adriano didn't deny that for a second. Tommas was a cousin of Adriano's, but only through marriage. His mother, Mia, had been the adopted sister to Tommas' mother, Serena.

But the dinner was semantics.

The enforcers at the entrances and next table was all for show.

Adriano and Evelina's presence was nothing but appearance.

This was just another game to Riley Conti. Sure, he played it well, but Adriano had better things to worry about. Like his girl and the baby she was carrying.

His baby.

Fuck.

Adriano's head was not in the game today.

The buzz of Adriano's cell phone drew his attention down to his lap. He checked the message, surprised to see it was a text with a picture. Opening the message, he came face to face with a smiling, winking Alessa.

She looked happy—luminescent, even.

And apparently in his apartment if the background was any indication.

Adriano didn't have the first clue how Alessa got to his place. Joel was still being a dick to his sisters, apparently, and keeping them on a tight leash. Alessa had a key to Adriano's apartment, but she would have needed to get out from under Joel's thumb first.

Whatever.

It didn't matter.

She was there and that's right where he was fucking going, too.

"What is that all about?" his father asked, never taking his eyes off his steak.

Adriano stood from the table and tossed his napkin down before shoving his phone into his pocket. "Business. It was good to see you, Tommas."

"And you, Adriano," Tommas replied.

"Eve, I'll see you later. The driver will get you back, yeah?" Adriano asked his sister.

Evelina nodded. "Sure."

Riley's gaze cut to his son. "What kind of business?"

Adriano smirked. "More important business than this."

Alessa was working at the stove when Adriano arrived at his place. He slammed and locked the door like somebody might come in and steal her from him. She laughed a musical sound when he caught her around the waist, picked her up, and set her down on the table.

"What are you doing here?" he asked, kissing her lips over and over.

Alessa sighed, tilting her head back and giving him better access to her throat. "Christ, keep doing that."

"Oh, I will."

In fact, he planned on doing a lot more.

Adriano pushed the wool dress she wore up around her hips as he kissed and nipped at her collar bones. She wore a pink cotton thong under her dress and black pumps on her feet.

"You shouldn't be wearing heels that high," Adriano said, pulling the shoes from her feet and letting them drop to the floor. "You'll break your fucking neck."

"Pregnant, not disabled," Alessa said, giggling.

Adriano yanked her to the very edge of the table and skimmed his hands higher under her dress until his palms were flat to her toned stomach. Alessa's eyes widened with mirth and love, and her pink lips split with the sexiest grin.

"Hey," she whispered.

"Hey, Lissa."

"So, Abriella and I went shopping and she lost the guys trailing us. She dropped me off here and she'll pick me up later. Sound good?"

Fucking hell.

"Sounds perfect," Adriano said.

"You didn't have anything else better to do today?"

"Nothing more important than seeing you, Alessa."

She grinned. "I needed to hear that. I missed you."

"I know." Adriano shot a look over his shoulder at the soup cooking on his stove. "Since when do you eat chicken noodle soup?"

"It's the only thing that doesn't make me want to vomit when it's cooking. It's homemade."

"I had enough shit in the fridge for that?" he asked.

"And the cupboards. Eve must have went shopping for you again."

Adriano chuckled, drawing her closer until their noses touched. "You smell like peaches."

"I was eating one before you got home."

"I like it," he murmured against her lips.

Home.

He liked the word home on her lips.

Like this place was theirs and not just his.

Adriano would take the taste of peaches on her tongue as he kissed her instead. Alessa let him wrap her hair in his fist, tug her head back, and kiss her mouth with as much force as he could muster. He wanted to own her mouth; he wanted her to feel him there for days.

Alessa's legs spread wider on the table as his hands slid down between her thighs. Adriano didn't want to waste time. They didn't have a whole hell of a lot of it as it was. Evelina could come home at any moment.

They were a ticking time bomb waiting to blow.

"Let me love you," Adriano said, kissing her again as he stroked her pussy through the cotton thong. "You're so fucking hot on my fingers and I'm barely doing anything at all, Lissa. Imagine how that's going to feel when it's my cock pounding into you."

Alessa licked her lips and nodded. "I so want that."

Christ.

Him, too.

"So hurry the fuck up and get on it," Alessa added.

Adriano laughed, hard and deep. He didn't know how to deny Alessa anything. Especially not when she asked like that.

"So wicked," he told her.

"You made me this way."

He had.

Adriano hooked his hands around her panties and tugged them down over her ankles. Spreading her wider and pushing her dress up around her waist, he had the best view of her pink, wet pussy spread out like a buffet on his table.

He wanted a taste. So he took it.

Dropping to his knees, Adriano gave Alessa a grin before he buried his face between her thighs and found her wet and hot flavor with his tongue. He dove in with fingers digging into her shaking hips, holding her in place, while his tongue tunneled into her tight, clenching channel.

Her surprised shout was loud and echoing. She weaved her fingers into his hair, pulling as she rocked her hips into his face with every plunge of his tongue. Adriano licked up to her clit, sweeping away her arousal and loving the way she tasted.

Nothing was better than Alessa.

Not like this.

"So fucking hot," Alessa whispered, staring down at him with hooded eyes.

"You want to come?" he asked, slipping his thumb into her pussy before teasing her clit with his tongue. Kissing the hood of her nub, he smirked. "Do you want to fuck my mouth and come, Alessa?"

She whined the sweetest sound. "Please."

"Of course, pretty girl."

Adriano's attention stayed on Alessa's beautiful face as he attacked her clit with his tongue while his thumb slid in and out of her slippery pussy. She was incredibly soaked and it almost seemed like her body was more sensitive to his touch. The faster he flicked his tongue to her sex, the harder she rocked her hips into his mouth.

Like she wanted that orgasm. Like she was chasing after it.

Fucking needed it.

It didn't take long at all before she was shaking all over and shouting his name.

"Adriano!"

Yeah, hell.

That's where they were going.

But it was going to be worth it.

Before Alessa had even calmed from her orgasm, Adriano had her laid flat on the table with her legs spread wide and his pants pushed down around his hips. He freed the hard length of his erection from his boxer-briefs and stroked his cock, watching Alessa beneath him.

"So beautiful," he said.

She was flushed, pink-cheeked, wet and ready for more.

"Now," Alessa demanded, hooking her legs around his hips. "Fuck me now."

Adriano slid the head of his dick along her fleshy folds and slammed home. Alessa sighed in bliss, her face contorting with her pleasure as her back lifted off the table. He grabbed her wrists in his palms, pulled her arms flat to keep her in place, and began to drive into her.

He wanted to fuck.

Hard. Rough.

He wanted to feel her come all over his cock.

"Get it again, Lissa," Adriano said, his voice thick. "Chase that again for me, pretty girl. Show me you want it."

Alessa's eyes flew wide, meeting his. Her lips popped open with his name on the tip of her tongue. "Give it to me, then."

Fuck yeah.

"How are you feeling?" Adriano asked, nuzzling the back of Alessa's neck with his mouth and nose. She smelled like sex and him. It was better than any fucking thing he ever smelled before. And she was soft, like silk. "Any better?"

Alessa smiled, turned her head just enough to kiss his cheek, and nodded. "A lot better."

She sat on his lap while he watched reality contestants on the television battle it out for a ridiculously small sum of money. He wrapped his arm around her waist, holding her a little tighter. Pretty soon, she would have to go.

"And this one?" Adriano asked, letting his fingers travel over her stomach.

"I had an appointment yesterday. They checked for the heartbeat."

"And?"

"All seems good."

Adriano let out a sigh he hadn't realized he'd been holding in. "Perfect, babe."

"Are you scared?"

"Of what?" he asked.

"People finding out."

Adriano laughed. "You know, right now, I'm more concerned about you and getting your through your first pregnancy happy, safe, and healthy. That's all that matters to me, Lissa."

Alessa looked over her shoulder at him, her eyes downward as she watched him through her lashes. "Really?"

"Yeah, really."

"You don't even realize it, do you?" she asked.

"Realize what?"

"How much good is inside your heart; how good *you* are."

He killed men.

He sold drugs and handled dirty money for a living.

He was born and bred mafia.

Good was the very last word he would use to describe himself.

"Am I?" he asked.

"To me you are."

"You're you, Lissa."

"And I'm yours."

Exactly.

CHAPTER EIGHTEEN

Alessa stepped out of the lecture hall and stood there, watching the students of Chicago State move from one hall to another while they chatted and laughed. She hadn't expected to get back to school anytime soon, not with the way Joel had forced her out of classes for Dean's sake.

But, with Dean dead, Joel didn't have a reason to refuse Alessa.

Thankfully, her brother didn't seem to have any immediate prospects for Alessa to move on with in another marriage deal, either. That, or Joel simply couldn't arrange one because he'd smeared his family with his actions and behavior toward the Outfit and the new boss.

Either way, Alessa didn't care.

She was at school; she had a life. Now that the Conti boss had forgiven Joel's actions, however it was Riley managed to do that, Alessa didn't have to worry about territory lines or being somewhere she shouldn't.

Well, as long as her babysitters were close by.

That was better than nothing.

Alessa made her way to the parking lot where her sister's Hummer was usually parked. Abriella still had another class to go, but Alessa didn't mind waiting. Unlocking the large SUV with the spare set of keys she had, Alessa climbed inside and pulled out an apple juice from her messenger bag to drink.

She just tipped the bottle up to her lips when her cell phone rang. She managed to pick it up on the third ring.

"Hello?"

"Hey, babe," Adriano said.

Alessa grinned at the sound of his voice on the other line. It'd been a week since she spent the day with him. Being away from Adriano didn't get easier for Alessa.

"Hey," she replied.

"Apple juice is a good choice," he said.

"What?"

"Apple juice is a good choice. Better than pop, I guess."

He could *see* her.

Alessa stilled in the seat, glancing all around to see if she could find him. She couldn't. "Where are you?"

"Close. I had business in the area and wanted to check on you," he explained. "It's your first day back, isn't it?"

"Yes."

"How did it go?"

"Good."

"No incidents with puke?" he asked, jokingly.

"Nope," Alessa said, happy over that little fact. "All is good."

"Great." Adriano sighed heavily. "You've got a plethora of guards around this school. Did you know that?"

"I suspected."

"It's fucking terrible."

"That's Joel for you," Alessa grumbled.

Adriano made a dismissive noise. "Fuck him. You've got another appointment at the clinic today, yeah?"

"Just a follow-up."

"A follow-up for what?" he asked.

"I guess they lost something in the files the last time and they want to get it all down again and correct. It's nothing serious, Adriano. They're just going to check the heartrate again. I'll even record it and send it to you. Don't worry."

"Hard not to, Lissa. That's my baby and I don't even get to be there."

Alessa frowned, hating that for him.

"And what about losing the guards so no one sees you go in to the clinic?" Adriano asked.

"Joel thinks we're having regular checkups. Over his head, Adriano."

"Good."

"I'll see you soon," Alessa promised.

Adriano chuckled. "You better."

She would.

"Come on, you must have thought of one name," Abriella said as Alessa climbed into the Hummer.

"It's really early, Ella."

Alessa wished Abriella would get off the whole baby kick. Hell,

Alessa was still trying to get used to the idea herself, but Abriella took it to a whole new level. What names did she like? What colors did she want? Did she want to know the gender or wait? Abriella was just trying to help in her own way by making the situation seem normal and Alessa knew that. But the fact was, it couldn't be normal. Ever.

Alessa still had to hide her pregnancy until she figured something out. How was that normal?

"A name," Abriella said again, more pointed the second time.

"Adrian," Alessa said.

"For a boy, okay. But what about for a girl?"

"Adrianne. With A-N-N-E at the end."

Her sister laughed.

"Fuck, you've got it bad," Abriella muttered.

Alessa didn't deny it.

While her sister fiddled with the stereo, Alessa texted the recording of the baby's heartbeat to Adriano like she promised earlier. The clip was only a few seconds long, but it was loud and clear and wonderful.

Adriano messaged back not ten seconds later with, *Perfect, Lissa.*

She wasn't sure if he was talking about her or the baby.

"Back home we go," Abriella said to herself, scowling.

"Thanks for taking me over here today," Alessa said.

The clinic had called Alessa in for another heartrate check, as something had been lost in the files the last time she had been in. They made her take yet another pregnancy test and also had blood drawn for an iron test.

Abriella shrugged as she reversed out of the private clinic and maneuvered the Hummer onto the road. "I didn't mind."

"You're putting yourself at risk of getting in shit for me."

"So? You're my sister. I'd do anything for you, Lissa."

Alessa glanced down at her hands in her lap. "I know."

"Hey, none of that frowning crap," Abriella ordered.

"Yes, Queen."

"Oh, fuck off with that nonsense. Even Tommy says it now." Abriella looked pissed off about her own statement as she added, "And even after I threatened him, he just kept on calling me it. I think he gets off on it or something. The bastard."

Alessa laughed almost half of the drive home. It was a nice reprieve from the worried state she had been in ever since finding out about the pregnancy.

Abriella pulled up to the gated Trentini mansion. "Would you go get whatever mail the guard collected today? I might as well do something nice for Joel and see if I can get on his half-decent side. Maybe I can get something from him if I do."

"Sure."

Alessa climbed out of the Hummer and collected the stack of circulars and bills that had come in for their home. Once she was back in the SUV, she tossed the pile on the middle seat, forgetting about them. She had no interest in trying to sweeten up her brother for anything.

It wouldn't do her any good now.

"What do you want to get Miss Cathy to make for supper if she hasn't already started?" Abriella asked as their vehicle moved through the opened gates.

Alessa's stomach growled at the mention of food. "Steaks. And potatoes. Maybe gravy, too. That sounds good."

"Really?"

"Baby wants what the baby wants, Ella."

Abriella snorted. "Or Alessa wants a reason to pig out and the baby is a valid excuse."

"Hey, don't you judge me."

"I am not!"

Alessa eyed her sister. "Ella."

"Okay, maybe I am a little. Not judging so much as … curious, maybe? You're petite. I can't imagine you getting …"

"Fat?"

"*Beautifully* round with child," Abriella said pointedly.

"Nice save."

"Thanks. But seriously, pregnancy isn't an excuse to be unhealthy and shove whatever into your face."

"I'm aware," Alessa said dully. "But I've just spent the last couple of weeks puking three times a day and this is the first one where I haven't felt like total shit. Just let me eat cake, Ella."

"Steaks," her sister corrected.

Maybe cake, too.

"How was school?" Joel asked, keeping his eyes down on the steak he was cutting into.

"Good," Abriella said.

"I was asking Alessa."

Alessa jerked out of her thoughts in just enough time to see Abriella roll her eyes.

"We go to the same school, Joel," Abriella said.

"Yes, but she's just returned while you haven't left." Joel flicked a look in Alessa's direction and asked, "So, how was it?"

"Fine," Alessa replied, uncomfortable by her brother's attention.

It wasn't like Joel to give a damn.

"No problems then?" he asked.

Alessa shook her head. "No. I'm starting a few weeks late into the semester, but that's fine. It's nothing I can't catch up on."

"You always were quick," Joel noted more to himself than Alessa. "Anyway, I'm glad to hear it. Sara pestered me with calls, worrying for whatever reason about your return today. I figured I should ask if she was so concerned."

"Mom, Joel," Abriella said. "She's our mom."

Joel's cold gaze traveled to Abriella. "To you. To me, she's just Sara."

Christ.

Alessa shoved a bite of steak into her mouth just to keep quiet. Sometimes, with Joel, it was all about picking the right battles to fight. This was not one she wanted to have with her brother. Alessa didn't care about her mother's past or choices. The now mattered more. It took her a little while to realize that, but she finally had and that was the most important thing.

Joel would get there, eventually.

Maybe.

"Nonetheless, she was worried," Joel continued, shrugging. "I don't understand why. This isn't your first time going to school. She acted like she was sending you off to kindergarten for the first time all over again. Ridiculous."

Alessa fidgeted with her fork and kept her eyes on her plate, more nervous than ever. Sara had called Alessa a few times throughout the day, but she was too busy with classes and trying to catch up on what she had missed to pick up the calls. Her mother was worried because of the pregnancy and stress she thought Alessa was experiencing. Alessa didn't blame Sara for her concerns, but she wished her mother would leave Joel out of it.

Then again, maybe Sara was trying to get closer to Joel in some way.

A throat cleaning broke the conversation between the siblings. Miss Cathy stood in the entryway between the kitchen and dining room with the pack of mail that Abriella was supposed to give to Joel earlier. It looked like more had been added to the pile—a large yellow envelope rested on the bottom.

"Mr. Trentini, this was left on the counter in the kitchen for you," Miss Cathy said.

Joel waved a hand. "Bring it in."

As quietly as she showed herself, Miss Cathy brought the mail to Joel and then left.

Thankful for the reprieve from her brother's attention, Alessa went back to enjoying the steak dinner in peace. The only sounds that could be heard in the dining room were Abriella and Alessa's cutlery scraping across plates while Joel ripped open mail.

Silence was nice.

Alessa wouldn't complain.

"What is this?" Joel asked.

Alessa's head shot up to see the larger yellow envelope in her brother's hand. He flipped it around, giving Alessa a view of the plain white label sticker on the front with their surname scrawled in messy handwriting. No address or even a return address was on the envelope that Alessa could find.

"Not sure," Alessa said.

She didn't remember that being in the mail pack she picked up.

Abriella shrugged across from Alessa and picked at her food. "Maybe Mom or Dad brought it over, Joel. Just open it."

"Maybe," their brother agreed.

Joel tore open the top of the envelope and pulled out the few papers inside. Figuring it wasn't important, Alessa let her brother read whatever it was in peace.

It didn't take long at all before Joel stood slowly from his chair. Alessa watched his hands clench around the papers as his gaze lifted and caught hers. Just like that, the entire room seemed to get hot and stuffy around Alessa. Her shoulders stiffened. Something was wrong.

Joel watched her like he wanted to fucking *kill* her.

"What is this?" Joel demanded.

"I—"

Joel began to read and with every word, Alessa felt the color drain from her face.

"Patient reported being over thirty days late in her cycle. A standard pregnancy test was performed. To confirm further, blood tests have been done. Heartrate of the fetus was one-hundred-thirty beats per minute. From the dates the patient provided, the pregnancy is approximately eleven weeks along and due date is May eleventh of this coming year."

"Joel—"

Alessa didn't, or couldn't, get any other words out as she stared at her brother. How did he get that information? Who gave him that package?

She turned to face a silent Abriella. Her sister wouldn't meet her gaze and Alessa knew it right then. Abriella had somehow gotten a copy of Alessa's file and gave it to their brother. Maybe that was where her missing information had gone that caused the second follow-up appointment.

Betrayal stung heavily on the back of Alessa's tongue.

"You bitch."

"Don't," Abriella whispered. "You don't know why, Lissa."

She didn't have to.

Her sister betrayed her. That was enough.

Joel's face reddened as his hands shook. With a disgusted shout, he tossed the papers down the table. They flew everywhere. Alessa didn't make a move to pick them up. She could see a couple of them from her spot.

Joel moved around the table, coming straight for her, and Alessa stood quickly from her chair. She backed up, knowing that look in Joel's eye. He was pissed and ready to blow. She did not want to be in the line of fire when it happened.

His gaze narrowed in on her like he was ready to kill. "Guess whose name is on the top of those documents?"

Alessa didn't have to. "Mine."

"Pregnant? You managed to get knocked up?" Joel roared.

"I—"Alessa stopped herself from saying anything further. She didn't want to call the baby a mistake. It wasn't the child's fault. "I did."

"That fucking bastard."

Alessa's eyes widened. "What?"

"Dean," Joel spat. "I demanded he wait and clearly he fucking didn't. Now he's dead and I'm left with you and this bullshit. How in the hell are you ever going to marry off with another man's child, Alessa? Huh?"

Sickness pounded at her insides.

No way.

Alessa wouldn't let anyone believe for one second that this baby was Dean Artino's.

"It's not Dean's," she said quietly.

Joel froze, a warning darkening his features. "I beg your pardon?"

He was only a few feet away from her. Close enough that he could reach out and grab her if he wanted. Abriella had yet to leave her chair, but she had stopped eating. Feeling unprotected like she was, Alessa wrapped her arms over her midsection.

"It's not Dean's child," Alessa said again, louder. "I wouldn't have gotten into bed with that man. Not even if you forced me into it, Joel."

Joel blew out a hard breath, his teeth clenching. "Who does it belong to?"

Alessa wanted to keep quiet. She tried. "Adriano."

A brief pause answered her back. It was enough to see Joel's features visibly contort with his confusion as he took that information in. And then ... it changed.

A slow, sly smile curved Joel's mouth as he nodded to himself.

"Adriano *Conti?*" her brother asked.

"Is there another Adriano we know?"

"No, Alessa. No, there is not." Joel laughed loud and happy. "Well done."

Well done?

What?

Joel pointed at Alessa. "You're forgiven."

"Uh ..." Alessa was stunned.

"And pack your fucking bags," her brother added.

With that, Joel left the room, still laughing the entire way.

Alessa turned on her sister, angry and confused.

Abriella glanced up from her hands with a watery gaze. "I'm sorry."

"Why would you do that to me?"

"You'll understand why," Abriella whispered. "Give it time, you'll see."

See what?

And what would happen to Adriano now?

"I can't believe you did this to me," Alessa said.

"Not right now. But you will. You're welcome, Lissa."

"Get those bags from the trunk," Joel ordered the waiting enforcer.

The man nodded and rushed to do what he was told.

Alessa stood in a familiar driveway, feeling more confused than ever as she stared at the large home.

"Here's how this is going to go," Joel said. "You're going to follow behind me, stay quiet, and do whatever the fuck I say. After I leave, I don't give a shit what happens to you, Lissa. That's all on Adriano and his father to decide."

"You're an asshole," Alessa muttered.

Joel shrugged. "Maybe so. As I said earlier, you're forgiven, but I won't be stained by your shame. The Contis, on the other hand, can hide it however they please. But if you want things to go smoothly, you will let me handle my side of it however I see fit."

Alessa didn't know what her brother was planning, but he had taken her to Riley Conti's home with a great portion of her belongings. It didn't seem like Joel had any intention of taking her back home, either.

"Take them to the front step," Joel told the waiting enforcer.

The man went.

"What are we—"

"Hush," Joel interrupted. "Follow me, Alessa."

Too tired to question her brother, Alessa followed along. She trailed up the stairs behind Joel as the enforcer dropped her bags at the bottom of the steps. Joel rang the ornate doorbell and the chimes echoed within.

Alessa thought it was odd that they had been able to just walk right up to Riley's front steps.

"Where are Riley's guards?" Alessa asked.

"We're peaceful," Joel said with a hint of bitterness coating his words. "They're watching us, no doubt, but they have no reason to send us away."

Alessa noticed a form darken the frosted glass of the front door. It disappeared before another came and the door opened. Riley Conti stood on the other side, his expression unreadable as he surveyed the people on his front step.

"Evening, Joel," Riley greeted.

"Evening, *boss.*"

Alessa cringed at her brother's tone. It almost sounded like he was mocking Riley's position.

"This is a surprise," Riley said, glancing over Alessa's quiet form.

"I bet. Where is your son tonight?"

"Working, Joel. Just like you should be."

Joel said nothing and instead, grabbed Alessa's arm and tugged her forward so she was standing in front of Riley. "Here, a mess for you to clean."

"A mess?" Riley asked.

"She's pregnant. Your son is the father."

Riley's brow shot up high as his mouth opened with a denial right on the top of his tongue. "Now, just you—"

"Don't bother denying it. They've been running around for years. A few phone calls was all it took for the mouths to start talking with what they've seen and what they know. You don't even look surprised, boss. My guess is that you knew, too. She was promised to be engaged and your son knocked her up at some point during that time. That's unacceptable, disgusting, and shameful."

Riley's jaw ticked. "And what do you expect me to do about this, Joel?"

Joel grinned. "Oh, I'm sure we can figure something out."

Alessa wasn't sure she liked the sound of that.

"But for now, a marriage to protect my sister and her child's standing will suffice," Joel added before Riley could say another thing. "I'm sure you agree."

Riley said nothing.

Joel waved at the bags on the step. "Her things. Your son can do with them what he wants."

With that, Alessa stood still and stunned as her brother turned on his heel and left.

Adriano cupped Alessa's cheeks in his hands and rolled his thumbs over her cheekbones in the sweetest, most soothing way. Alessa needed that. Waiting for him to get to his father's home had been nerve-wracking enough. Riley had said not one single word to Alessa, but he watched her like he was two seconds away from blowing her brains out.

"You okay?" Adriano asked.

Alessa nodded, smiling. "Better with you here."

"This was not what I expected to happen when Joel found out."

"Me either," she admitted.

"I wonder why," Adriano mused, tracing her lips with his thumb.

"Because he fucking wants to advance and this is a good excuse to use," Riley said as he entered the living room.

Adriano's shoulders stiffened and he scowled. "Not right now, Dad."

"Oh, I think now is the perfect time, son." Riley flicked a hand in Alessa's direction like she was a piece of garbage he was shooing away. "And what am I supposed to do about this, huh? Look what you've done, Adriano. Your stupid, foolish recklessness has cost me a great deal today."

"I think this is perfect," Adriano replied, never taking his gaze off Alessa.

She chewed on her inner cheek, feeling happy and worried all at once. Riley didn't seem pleased, but Adriano was over the moon.

Alessa was inclined to go with Adriano's mood.

"I had him, Adriano," Riley growled.

Adriano shrugged. "I don't care."

"No, I wouldn't think you do," Riley spat. "Why should you?"

Adriano smirked but said nothing.

"And do you know what he demanded when he brought her to my doorstep?" Riley asked.

"No, but I'm sure you'll tell me," Adriano replied.

"A marriage! Between you two!"

"I'm game for that," Adriano said, giving Alessa a wink.

How was he so blasé in the face of his father's rage?

"Have you never heard of a condom?" Riley asked.

Adriano chuckled. "It's done, Dad. Drop it."

Riley didn't. His anger exploded in a violent shout of words.

"I had him! I had Joel by the fucking throat and just like that … just like that, Adriano, you fucking ruined it. Your recklessness ruined everything."

"For you," Adriano murmured, turning to face his father. "It ruined things for you. But for me, Dad? I got everything I fucking wanted."

"You little bast—"

Adriano held up a single hand, stopping his father. Then, he dropped it and offered that hand to Alessa. She took it without question.

"Are you ready?" Adriano asked her.

"For what?"

Adriano flashed her with a sensual smile. "To go home with me."

God, *yes.*

She was so ready for that.

"Yeah," Alessa whispered.

She got it.

Right then, with Adriano's hand in hers holding tight and promising to take her home, Alessa got why her sister did what she did. Riley would hate them, surely. The Outfit would again be upset as Riley was forced to make amends for his son's mistakes and choices with Alessa.

That didn't matter a bit to Alessa or Adriano.

They got what they wanted.

All was perfect.

Thank you, Ella, Alessa thought.

She never would have been able to tell Joel on her own. Abriella forced Alessa into it whether she wanted to or not.

"Let's go home," Adriano said.

"Home," she echoed.

The angelic tone of the choir filled the church with its melody. Alessa settled into the pew beside Adriano, comfortable and content. His hand rested on her eighteen week swell.

Like he usually did, Adriano kept one eye on the people around them, and one on what was most important to him. He never hid his affections for Alessa or the pregnancy no matter where they were. She figured they had spent so much time hiding one another that now that they didn't have to, they didn't even try.

Alessa loved Adriano all the more for it.

She couldn't help but glance around the church at the guests. When they first arrived earlier, people had stared and whispered. It wasn't uncommon, after all, her and Adriano had created quite a scandal together. Especially with the whole baby thing, now.

Evelina sat at Alessa's other side, smiling but faking it. Alessa knew the truth. Her soon-to-be sister-in-law was pissed about the groom and bride.

Alessa wished she could somehow help Evelina. It had to be horrible to see her father moving on already after her mother's death. But really, Evelina had been a big help and support to Alessa and Adriano over the last couple of months. When Alessa had been alienated from her family because of her choices with Adriano, Evelina was there. When Adriano worked late, Evelina was there to keep Alessa company.

She appreciated Evelina a great deal.

Alessa reached over and held Evelina's hand silently. Evelina squeezed back.

"Another month, babe," Adriano said quietly.

Alessa smiled. "And this will be us."

"I can't fucking wait, Lissa."

She knew that, too.

Alessa and Adriano's conversation quieted as the ending of the ceremony was performed at the front. Riley Conti's young bride looked incredibly beautiful in her ball gown style dress standing next to her new husband.

Young.

It was worth repeating.

Courtney was only three years older than Alessa.

It seemed like the wedding had practically come out of thin air. Not a man in the Outfit or the families around them seemed bothered by the fact that Riley Conti was marrying a new, young woman just months after his wife's death.

The boss needs a wife, Adriano had explained weeks ago.

Alessa thought it was all a little sad.

"Did your father talk to you last night?" Alessa asked.

They had gone to a dinner at the Conti home to celebrate the night before the wedding. Things between Adriano and his father were incredibly tense and had been ever since news of their pregnancy was announced. Riley practically turned his son away at every chance he could.

Adriano didn't act like he cared.

"No," Adriano said.

The couple's marriage was announced by the priest and a thunder of clapping and hollers answered the first kiss. Alessa waited at Adriano's side as the bride and groom made their way back down the aisle. Then the guests started to flood out as well.

Joel passed by Alessa with Abriella at his side. Her sister gave her a smile and a wave, but Joel kept his eyes forward and never gave Alessa a second thought. She wasn't important to him anymore. He got what he wanted, in a way.

Joel had mysteriously become Riley's underboss. According to Adriano, Tommas Rossi was the new front boss for the Outfit. But there was a lot of love lost between the three men and issues always had a way of creeping back in before anyone knew what happened.

Alessa and Adriano filtered out of the church with the rest of the people. Outside, she couldn't help but notice how the people spread out into their usual groups. It gave her the chance to see everyone who had showed up to the wedding. It had been a large event with a rather big guest list. One group was missing: the DeLucas.

"Where is Theo?" Alessa asked.

Adriano visibly tensed. "Somewhere."

His vagueness only made Alessa worried.

"Did something happen?"

Adriano chuckled. "Shit, something has been happening for a while."

"Like what?"

"I don't want you worrying about the Outfit's nonsense," he said.

"Too late," she replied softly.

Adriano drew Alessa in to his side. "It started out quiet."

"What did?"

"Theo's moves. Quiet violence, little things. A man down here with no explanation and a shootout there with no witnesses. Bad shit, Lissa."

Alessa shivered. "Theo did that?"

"Is doing it," Adriano corrected. "It's happening more and more every day."

"What does that mean?"

Adriano sighed. "It means he wants to go to the mattresses again."

War.

When was this going to end?

How many more people had to die?

"We're good," Adriano said, drawing Alessa from her thoughts.

"Are we?" she asked.

"Very." Nodding at his father standing with his new bride at the bottom of the church steps, Adriano added, "But Riley, he needs to be careful."

Alessa swallowed hard. "Careful?"

"Yes. And he can have fun doing it alone." Adriano smiled coldly. "I gave him everything he wanted and he did nothing for me. My father can protect his own ass. I have nothing left there to save."

"Don't you?"

Adriano shook his head and held her tighter. "Nope. I got everything

I wanted, Alessa. And I'm holding it."

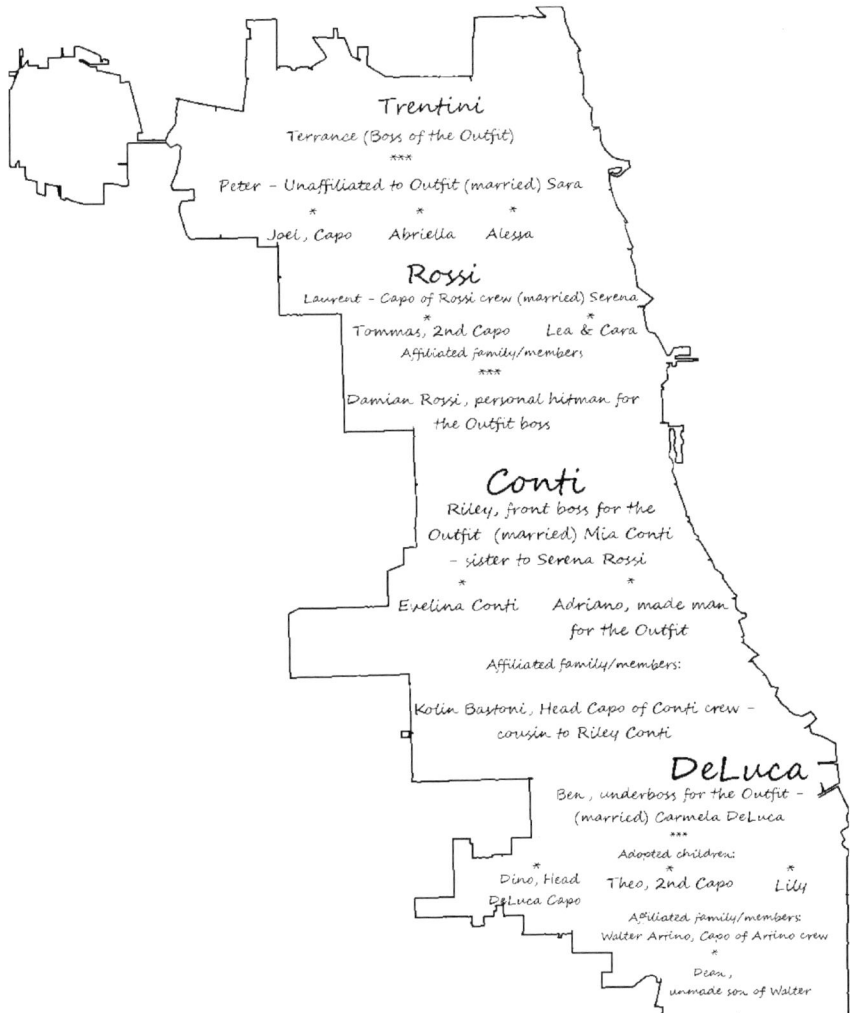

Trentini

Terrance (Boss of the Outfit)

***

Peter – Unaffiliated to Outfit (married) Sara

*   *
Joel, Capo   Abriella   Alessa

Rossi

Laurent – Capo of Rossi crew (married) Serena

*   *
Tommas, 2nd Capo   Lea & Cara

Affiliated family/members

***

Damian Rossi, personal hitman for
the Outfit boss

Conti

Riley, front boss for the
Outfit (married) Mia Conti
– sister to Serena Rossi

*   *
Evelina Conti   Adriano, made man
for the Outfit

Affiliated family/members:

Kolin Bastoni, Head Capo of Conti crew –
cousin to Riley Conti

DeLuca

Ben, underboss for the Outfit –
(married) Carmela DeLuca

***

Adopted children:

*   *   *
Dino, Head   Theo, 2nd Capo   Lily
DeLuca Capo

Affiliated family/members:
Walter Arrino, Capo of Arrino crew

*
Dean,
unmade son of Walter

ABOUT THE AUTHOR

Bethany-Kris is a Canadian author, lover of much, and mother to three very young sons, one cat, and two dogs. A small town in Eastern Canada where she was born and raised is where she has always called home. With her boys under her feet, a snuggling cat, barking dogs, and a spouse calling over his shoulder, she is nearly always writing something ... when she can find the time.

Find Bethany-Kris at:
Her website www.bethanykris.com,
or on Facebook at www.facebook.com/bethanykriswrites,
on her blog at www.bethanykris.blogspot.ca,
or on Twitter - @BethanyKris.

Sign up to Bethany-Kris's New Release Newsletter here:
http://eepurl.com/bf9lzD

49664568R00147

Made in the USA
Charleston, SC
02 December 2015